Shabbeer Ahmed MS is a qualified engineer and a professional MC. He quit the rat race of engineering to follow his passion—entertaining people with the magic of words. He went on to become a renowned host of events and has shared a stage with eminent personalities such as Bill Gates and Steve Ballmer as well as various Bollywood actors and sportspersons.

Having hosted the ICC Cricket World Cup in 2011 for the Bangalore matches, Shabbeer is also a well-known team-building professional, with two game-design patents to his name. He has hosted international music shows as a radio jockey on 101.3 FM and entertained music lovers as a video jockey with the erstwhile SS Music. He is also a TEDx speaker.

This novel marks Shabbeer's foray into the world of fiction writing. He currently lives in Bangalore, India.

AF516657

Djinns & Kings

The Curse of Zoa

Shabbeer Ahmed MS

Om Books International

First published in 2024 by

Om Books International

Corporate and Editorial Office
A-12, Sector 64, Noida 201 301
Uttar Pradesh, India
Phone: +91 120 477 4100
Email: editorial@ombooks.com
Website: www.ombooksinternational.com

Sales Office
107, Ansari Road, Darya Ganj,
New Delhi 110 002, India
Phone: +91 11 4000 9000
Email: sales@ombooks.com
Website: www.ombooks.com

Text copyright © Shabbeer Ahmed MS 2024

ALL RIGHTS RESERVED. This is a work of fiction. Any names or characters, businesses or places, events or incidents, are fictitious. Any resemblance to actual persons, living or dead, or actual events is purely coincidental. The opinions expressed in the book are those of the fictitious characters in the story and should not be deemed to be that of the author's. No part of this book may be reproduced or transmitted in any form by any means, electronic or mechanical, including photocopying and recording, or by any information storage and retrieval system, except as may be expressly permitted in writing by the publisher.

ISBN: 978-81-19750-11-5

Printed in India

10 9 8 7 6 5 4 3 2 1

This book is dedicated to all the readers of fantasy fiction who seek stories about mythical beings and beasts from select lores of the Eastern Hemisphere of the world. This book is also dedicated to those who have tried hard to hold on to their loved ones and to those who seek greatness against overwhelming odds. As a person who delights in taking long walks by the beachside and collecting shells of various shapes and colours, I wish that you may find what you are looking for as you sift through this book.

Contents

Epigraph	ix
A Note on Djinns	xi
Prologue	xiii
Regional Map	xx
1. Fake Djinns and Lost Love	1
2. The Whale, the Sorcerer and the Sea Serpent	22
3. The Ruins of Afra-Zun	63
4. The Sins of Rhuzbeh	86
5. The Dead Man and the Monkfly	119
6. The Firstborn Son	154
7. The Floating Fortress	171
8. The Terror of Ungaal	200
9. The Twice-Dead King	220

10. The Missing Sanaa 250
11. Symphony of the Frogs 264
Acknowledgements 290

My bull no longer crouches in its cow pen;
its herdsman is gone.
My sheep no longer crouch in their fold;
their herdsman is gone.
In the river of my city, the dust has gathered,
and the holes of foxes have been dug there.
In its midst, no flowing water is carried;
its tax collector is gone.
In the fields of my city, there is no grain;
their farmer is gone.

–The Lament for the City of Ur*

---

*Translated from the original by the ETCSL Project, Faculty of Oriental Studies, University of Oxford

A Note on Djinns

At the very beginning of the world, there were great mountains and oceans, and there were beings formed and unformed. The djinns were created in those aforementioned times.

The word 'djinn' means 'the unseen'. The fact that djinns have the ability to remain unseen is their most formidable weapon. The human imagination makes djinns a lot more potent than they really are.

Although djinns are invisible to most humans, they dwell amidst us and occasionally reveal themselves in their natural or even human or animal form. Like humans, they have families, cities and kings.

There are various types of djinns, and, as the author of this book, I have taken artistic liberty to tweak their characteristics and even add a few fictional ones. In this book, the djinns and their nature are thus:

The gargantuan *marids* that dwell in oceans as giant fish (the Bahamut or the behemoth is alleged to be a marid).

The *janns*, which are the ruling class, are allied with the *silat*, the wise ones. They are traditionally pitted against *ghouls*, *nas nas* (which appear as hybrid creatures), *pilaf* (a djinn that slobbers red saliva), and *phisas* (a favourite in haunted houses).

The *ifrit* (one of them was imprisoned in Aladdin's lamp) is a powerful class of djinn that can swing over to any side. There are other types of smaller djinn like the *shiq* that are diminutive and *hinn* that move around mostly in dog-form.

Like humans, djinns are complex and can't be generalised. A djinn can be classified as good and bad based on its individual nature and not kind—and, of course, by one's own definition of good and bad.

Prologue

Bathed in beauty, soaked in the seasons and favoured by the zephyr passing thus, lay the storied fallen city of the djinns —Afra-Zun, a name accompanied by a sigh.

Legend has it that in antiquity, the djinns constructed a majestic city called Afra-Zun—a city steeped in harmonious tradition—that would bring different factions of djinns together. Before Afra-Zun came into being, all djinns, including the jann, silat, ifrit, ghoul, nas nas, shiq, pilaf, et al., lived on their own lands, amongst their kind, and often clashed with one another. The djinn world was afflicted by strife and factionalism until, one day, King Ammuna, the great djinn king of yore, decided to construct a city where djinns of all hues would come together, celebrate their differences and live in harmony. The idea was that when same type of beings live together, they tend to view beings not living amongst them or interacting with them as others. This makes it easy to vilify and fester hate against the others. Afra-Zun was the string that would weave the different kinds of djinns together. The city would belong to all djinns; here, they could coexist and thrive in each other's company. Afra-Zun would melt differences and create bonds that would bridge divisions and heal scars. Since the djinns were enraptured by trees, the city was covered in trees, which were varied and wondrous and so large that a single tree covered an entire garden. The trees were covered in translucent flowers that dropped down like thick hangings. Their colours switched with sunrise and sunset, and their fragrance varied with the journey of the sun. Rubbing stems, if not shoulders, with their superior cousins were the petite shrubs and flowering plants that jealously filled the place with a riot of ridiculous colour. The naked earth was carpeted with grass, moss and multi-coloured mushrooms. Although the djinns obsessed over flowering trees, the city was also abundant in fruit-bearing trees, which resonated with the ballads of the songbirds. The gurgling of water was music to the djinns, and Afra-Zun was dotted with beautiful lakes, streams and fountains. King Ammuna invited djinns from all over to live in Afra-Zun and represent their kind. The discerning silat built houses out of pellucid tree amber that shone with various shades of gold, copper, red and pale pink. They were shielded from the sun by large canopies of trees. The proud janns boasted of grand palace-like structures with crystalline walls. The fearsome ghouls dwelt in foreboding structures made of hard-baked red clay. The walls were surrounded by dense trees, making them unnoticeable—the only tell-tale signs being the horde of crows that perched on the roofs.

The unpredictable blue ifrits either lived under a pebble or built large palaces according to their whims. Cedar-lined cottages were home to the red saliva-dribbling pilaf, and the attention-grabbing shiq inhabited stone structures. The nas nas, hinn, phisas and their ilk made homes in the foliage and rocks of the wooded Afra-Zun.

The bazaars and meeting places were abuzz as various kinds of djinns traded and interacted with each other. Afra-Zun was the melting pot of the djinn world. The city was a living pact that as long as it stood, the djinns would always be at peace with one another.

Ammuna built a mighty moat that surrounded the city on all four sides, with one end of the moat providing access to the sea. It was as broad as a river and had the depth of ten full-grown oaks. Large gates controlled the flow of seawater to the moat so that if the water level in the moat dropped, seawater could be let into the moat.

The djinns were fascinated by water. For them, water was the symbol of life. Water was also an invitation for the sea-dwelling marids. Although the mighty marids could never forsake their ocean dwellings, they would take solace in the fact that the environs that surrounded Afra-Zun were familiar.

The moat was filled with creatures beautiful and rare, such as a polygamous merman with a hairy chest and a curly beard who lived with a bevy of comely longhaired mermaids, swarms of red-coloured fish that spouted water synchronously like moving fountains, and bejewelled fish that leapt above the water, their bodies sparkling like coloured diamonds in the sun. Aristocratic pink and white swans glided across the waters, along with snakes, seahorses and turtles that moved so lazily it felt like they could rewind time itself.

All they needed was Zoa—the last remnant of an ancient creature that was a perfect mixture of allure and enigma. It had the head of a human girl with a chiselled face framed by aquamarine hair and the body of a shining emerald-green butterfly. Fins—twice as long as its body—sprouted two on each side. The purple-patched emerald fins looked almost like wings so that when Zoa swam in the water, it resembled a bird in the sky. The creature sang a lilting song that filled people with hope and dispelled despair—a song that could only be heard in the listener's mind.

When Zoa swam across the water, it momentarily streaked it with colours reflecting its mood. It turned the water pink when happy, pale sappy green and blue when serene, purple when melancholic, and when it sensed danger, it streaked the water black and yellow.

However, Zoa was not an easy creature to catch. In fact, it could never be captured against its will. When forced, it would streak the water with such colours that entire water bodies would turn rancid, all life in that water would die and Zoa's songs would become so sad that the minds of men and djinns alike would never be the same again.

However, Ammuna was insistent that he would have Zoa in Afra-Zun, and so he came up with a solution. 'Get me three rare pearls of the purest white harvested from the ocean's depths,' he commanded the djinns. The marids from oceans around the world collected three of the rarest pearls, each the size of a peach. Then, to the ifrits, he said, 'Take the pearls to the dying volcano of Freasea and heat it in the last of its dying fires until they turn a fiery crimson.' To the ghouls, he said, 'Take these reddened pearls to the labyrinth of Xigar the Ancient and ask him to soak the pearls in a vial filled with a dragon's blood until it shines like the crimson evening sun.' 'Part with your soul!' he commanded an obliging shiq. And to the wise silat, he said, 'Infuse the parted soul into the pearls until they dance and look life-like.'

Thus were made three of the most beautiful gems, the likes of which would never be made again, available nowhere, neither land nor sea, capable of enticing any being. Ammuna named those pearls—*sanaa*.

Ammuna knew how to use the sanaa to trap the Zoa. He hung the sanaa tantalisingly over a ship's hull and dipped it into the water so that Zoa could see it. As sanaa was from the ocean, its appeal to aquatic creatures was irresistible.

When Zoa first saw the sanaa, it instantly fell in love—it was the deepest love, the sort that sears the soul. The ship slowly sailed towards Afra-Zun, and Zoa, unable to resist the temptation, followed like a lamb. When they reached Afra-Zun, the three sanaa were placed inside three strong metal cages and sealed in the floor at three points inside the moat, thereby making Zoa a willing prisoner, restricting it to the confines of the space between the three pearls inside the moat.

Finally, Ammuna had in his possession the three sanaa, and adorning the moat was the chief ornament of Afra-Zun, the pride of the djinn folk—Zoa. This was the pinnacle of Ammuna's achievement. Djinns, far and wide, travelled to see Zoa, and Afra-Zun soon became the symbol of djinn power.

However, over time, differences arose in Afra-Zun. Although all djinns had worked together to create the sanaa and all the djinns owned Afra-Zun, the jann king, Ammuna, started dominating and lording over the djinns. The ghouls, in particular, were given a bad deal and were discriminated against.

The ghoul chieftain, Xakoof the Terrible, rallied the djinns around him. Surprisingly, quite a few jann, silat, and ifrits also supported him. They felt that Ammuna was turning autocratic, which was disrupting the peace at Afra-Zun; they wanted to bring Ammuna down a notch or two.

For the first time since the construction of Afra-Zun, the djinns were headed for a possible skirmish. But, just as the rebellion began to gain steam, news streamed in that Zoa had been murdered—someone had thrown a spear at the Zoa and killed it.

There were various theories as to why Zoa was killed. Ammuna claimed that ghouls and their supporters killed the creature because it symbolised Ammuna's success. The ghouls, on the other hand, claimed that janns deliberately killed Zoa and were blaming it on ghouls so that the entire djinn world would rally against them; others contended that the silat had murdered Zoa to stop the war. Nevertheless, the undeniable reality was that Zoa had been murdered.

As it was dying, it had cursed the city loudly enough for every djinn to hear and feel the impact of its words. It said:

Fall Afra-Zun
To dust, to ruins, houses crumble
Wither you trees, no bird's warble
No bustling feet, no lovers dine
Engulf the city in creepers and vine
Fall Afra-Zun
No redemption, no recourse
Not through your wickedness or force
The fiery ones cannot sprout the city
Their hands are soiled with blood and pity
Fall Afra-Zun
From clay will my beloved return to these lands
Till then, swing swords and wring your tainted hands
Flee the home, flee the hearth and flee the fertile field
Flee with the wretched weapons you ungainly wield
Fall Afra-Zun

The moat waters immediately went rancid, killing all the creatures in it. A week after the passing of Zoa, the trees of Afra-Zun died. The birds flew away, and the houses started collapsing. The alarmed denizens started vacating the cursed city. Creepers and vines quickly covered its ruins. Mysteriously, the sanaa also went missing. Some claimed that it was washed away into the ocean. The symphony of concordant notes was disrupted and replaced by a cacophony—Afra-Zun fell into ruins.

The wise amongst the djinns tried to interpret the curse in an attempt to break it.

The 'fiery ones' addressed in the curse were understood to be the djinns since they were said to have been created from a smokeless fire. As per the curse, they would lose Afra-Zun due to the murder of Zoa.

The 'beloved' of Zoa was, of course, the sanaa, which had to be returned by 'clay'. The elder djinns reasoned that this referred to humans, since they were said to have been created from clay.

The sanaa had to be returned by the humans alone, of their own accord, because the djinns were guilty of killing Zoa. And until then, the djinns would know no peace till Afra-Zun lay in ruins.

Regional Map

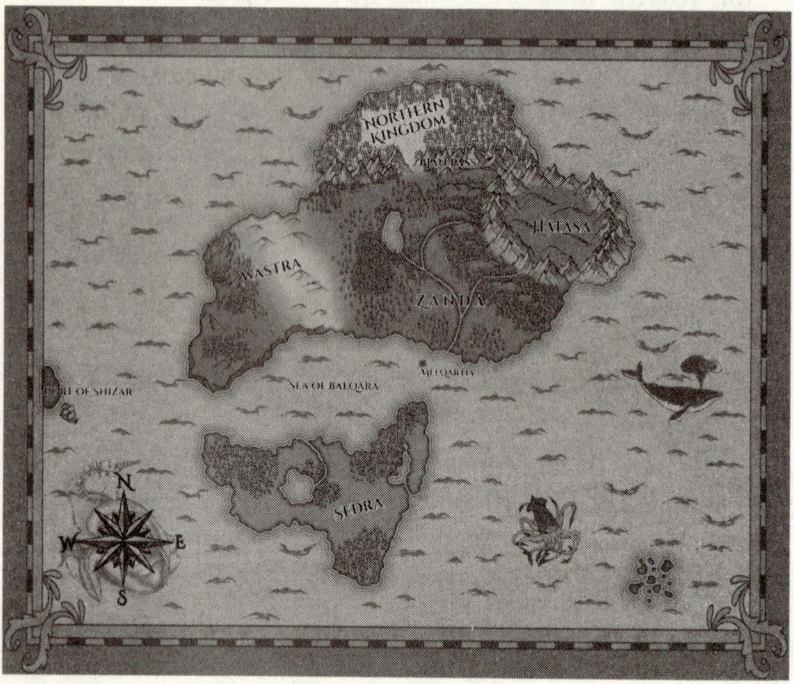

CHAPTER 1

Fake Djinns and Lost Love

All great journeys begin from a house.

The house was desolate, its windows creaked with age, and the place smelled of mould and misery. The fears of the villagers lent credence to the place as a djinns' haunt, a typical human trait of giving unto others what one doesn't desire.

In a corner, a maiden sat, anticipating the advances of her lover. He did not disappoint. She heard his footsteps, brisk and enthusiastic, as they approached the door. The footsteps did not pause; in one smooth motion, the door was flung open with uncouth violence, and the man strutted towards her. Anticipating his touch, the maiden quivered ever so slightly. In the dim light, he could not see her. She was fully covered, her back towards him, her face to the wall and her gaze to the floor.

'Playing coy, are we?' he sneered. 'It's strange that we have never spoken to each other.'

Until then, communication between the two had been confined to amorous letters. Hearing no response from her, he continued, 'You are bold, huh! To come to a place like this after what happened here in the recent past. I admit I would never have come here on my own. But then I thought, if she can muster the courage, I must too. It's a good thing; it really is! No villager will dare come here and witness our escapade nor hear their headman's daughter's moans. Djinns, murderers, bah! Nothing can keep me away from you. I will not disappoint you tonight.'

He chuckled, licking his lips in anticipation as he began to run his fingers down her back.

The maiden responded to his touch and stirred. She turned slowly to look at him for the first time, a sweet smile playing on her lips. The man froze out of shock, the *maiden* turned out to be a man he knew well, dressed differently only to deceive him. In one smooth motion, the cross-dressed murderer swung a blade and cleanly sliced open the over enthusiastic lover's throat. Blood started gushing from his neck faster than his libido could subside. The murderer then proceeded to chop off his victim's head and dragged the decapitated body to the designated place in the house—this was his second murder.

Rhuzbeh, the short and fat village orphan, with his muddied past and unclear future, sat by the muddy, unclear lake. He watched the early morning sun emerge, lighting the lake-side scene that, apart from lonesome rocks and stoic herons, included a red-wattled lapwing with its loud and alarming "ti-ti-to-it" calls. The bird's calls sounded accusatory: "Did-he-do-it?" The accusations grew in volume and urgency as if demanding an answer. He threw a stone at his accuser, who flew away screaming angry accusations: "Did-he-do-it?"

He thought it ironic that the accusations were not flying at him but away from him.

His mind dwelled on the circumstances that had made him an orphan. He was just ten years old when they had discovered the bloody, mangled remains of his parents. The villagers said they were attacked and killed by a manticore, a creature half man-half lion. Nobody, admittedly, had ever seen such a being. Whenever the villagers could not explain someone's death or disappearance, they attributed it to a manticore. It was simply another way of saying, 'We don't know how they died.' Attributing the death to manticores made the villagers sound less ignorant and the deaths a lot more exciting.

These stories fuelled his nightmares. He had recurring dreams of his parents being attacked by the strange creature, its body glowing red like burning coals, and its tail swishing high in the air. He would wake up in a panic, only to be reassured by the familiar barren, mud-plastered hovel, whose only decoration was a rough drawing of two snakes devouring each other's tails in a perfect circle.

A tragedy often does one of the two things—it either breaks a person down or it numbs them. In this case, the tragedy of losing his parents in such a violent manner had made Rhuzbeh wholly numb and fearless. He was now considered the village's collective property. The villagers gave him food, odd chores and taunts.

He stood up, brushed away the dust and worries and started walking back to the village. On the way, an irksome gossipy woman accosted him. 'What is that bruise on your eye, Rhuzbeh?' asked the gossipy woman, more out of curiosity than concern.

'The wolves pounced on the sheep, eh?' she quizzed.

She was joined by a tragedy-loving fidgety woman, who added, 'Those louts are pounding up the poor boy like *taftoon* dough. But the boy does not complain or even cry out loud, prompting those dogs to try and soften up this dough.'

Fidgety thought the reference clever, and both of them tittered. 'The boy does look like the flatbread dough,' said *Gossipy*, 'a puffy, black and blue dough.'

'Rhuzbeh might look round, but he is not soft. Barely fifteen-and-three-quarters but all that hard labour of chopping trees, drawing water and running after sheep has made him tough; you might break your teeth if you ever try to sink them into him,' added Fidgety.

'Now, now, no one is sinking their teeth anywhere, although I admit I am ravenous,' Gossipy laughed.

Rhuzbeh was embarrassed. He lowered his head and pretended to be interested in the wriggling earthworm that had half-popped up from the ground as a result of fervent digging by his big toe.

Fidgety sobered down and added gravely, 'Who are these villainous bullies? They seemed to have crawled up suddenly in the village like chickenpox and inflicted themselves on this poor orphan.'

With gusto, Gossipy replied, 'A thousand curses on these rats! My husband tells me that the well-armed and able-bodied rascals are dacoits everyone is afraid of. As long as they don't bother us, we won't bother them. Unfortunately, this poor wretch is an orphan and fodder for the bullies. Someone has to take a stand.'

Gossipy nodded and, after absently rubbing Rhuzbeh's hard and rounded shoulders, added, 'Yes! It's a good thing that one of them died last month. Good thing, indeed! Tried to steal from djinns, he did. The greedy bully had heard someone mention that the djinns had buried their treasure there, and the unthinking oaf had gone there alone. Can you imagine, alone, in the dead of night digging for djinn treasure? What greed does to a man! The angry djinns chopped his head and left it there as a warning to others. What else did he expect? Stealing from djinns, I tell you!'

Fidgety clucked and looked even more fidgety than her usual self.

'Tch! It is really not a bright idea to steal from djinns, possessive about their gold, they are,' she added.

On that sobering note, the three of them walked back together, with Gossipy berating the blacksmith's daughter on her virtues or the lack thereof.

At noon the next day, the second bully's decapitated body was found in the same haunted house where the first one had perished. A chill ran through the village.

Gossipy told everyone who cared to listen, 'Just yesterday, we discussed djinns with Rhuzbeh. There are djinns in that mansion just like there is a treasure there too. Would you steal your neighbour's daughter's virtue just because she is pretty, eh? Won't your neighbour kill you? Why mess with the djinns and their treasure?' And Fidgety fidgeted with her numerous amulets to ward off the fiendish djinns. The village scene was now dominated by turmeric claws on door frames as fear clawed through them.

Of course, no one felt the fear more intensely than the last surviving bully. It was clearly not a coincidence that both his accomplices died violently at that same place. Although scared of djinns, he suspected foul play. For the first time in his life, he felt like a hunted animal, curling up in his cottage and seeking foetal comfort. Seeing his lonely state, Rhuzbeh started visiting him at night.

'I don't want the villagers to spot me in your unflattering company,' stated Rhuzbeh as his reasoning for the nightly visits. 'They would think I am the new ring member. Not ready to be ostracised yet, I am not.'

The bully was surprised by the food and company Rhuzbeh offered him. He had least expected help from someone he had so tormented. But, within the four walls of his cottage, he still felt brave and refused to show gratitude to the orphan. He was a typical bully, and being his usual cruel self, made him feel good.

'This is all you could muster?' he asked with contempt, 'These are scraps for rats. Next time, make sure you bring food that is fit for people and not for a louse like you.'

Rhuzbeh nodded meekly. Every day he brought the bully leftover food and regaled him with stories of the village, for which he was amply rewarded with burps, barbs and blows.

'The blacksmith's daughter is getting prettier by the day,' Rhuzbeh said one day.

'Does she even look at you? Why would anyone look at a fat lump like you?' asked the bully, his voice laden with sarcasm.

Unperturbed, Rhuzbeh continued, 'Just the other day, she looked at me and even smiled.'

The bully slapped him hard. 'Don't you even look at her; she is mine,' he admonished.

The gravest of fears melt away in the face of ill-tasting food. A month later, tired of eating leftovers and aching for the thrill of the hunt, the bully felt brave enough to finally step out on his own.

'Let us go out after sunset,' suggested Rhuzbeh. 'I spotted some plump rabbits at a patch last week, and they come out only during the dark.'

The bully agreed and the duo set out after sunset to hunt rabbits. 'Ah, to be free and feel the fresh air again,' he said. 'Finally, away from your filthy leftovers and to experience the taste of a fresh game.'

Eventually, they spotted the rabbits and the bully managed to kill a couple of them. 'Skin them, you useless swine,' he ordered, kicking Rhuzbeh gently on the rump as a sign of fondness.

Rhuzbeh passed him a bag filled with fruits and said cheerily, 'Two plump, delicious rabbits coming up. Till then, help yourself to these fruits.'

As the bully gladly put his hand inside the bag to pick fruit, a poisonous snake bit him. The shocked bully immediately withdrew his hands in pain and collapsed to the ground, 'Aaaah!' he cried. 'There is a poisonous snake inside the bag and it bit me. Help me!'

Rhuzbeh sat a little distance away, ignoring the plea for help and continued sharpening the knife. 'You bastard!' cried the bully in utter shock and distress. 'You deliberately put the snake in the bag to kill me, didn't you?!'

And in those dying moments, the curtain lifted off his eyes and he began to think more clearly than he had in days.

'It was you! It was you all along,' he cried. 'It was you who killed the other two by tricking them as you have tricked me. I thought you were a worm but you turned out to be a snake. I now know why you met me only at night; you did not want the villagers to suspect you of murdering me. Ah! I will kill you before I die,' he screamed, trying to get up. But the venom was spreading fast through his system now and he fell back writhing in pain. Rhuzbeh calmly continued to sharpen his knife. The bully was in pain, passing in and out of consciousness.

Rhuzbeh quietly stood up, hauled the bully's bulky frame to the same place inside the haunted house, and placed more snakes on the almost-dead man. The bully succumbed to snake venom shortly. In the morning, when the villagers discovered his bloated blue body covered in snakebites, they presumed this too to be the handiwork of djinns as the latter were known to assume the form of snakes.

Although Rhuzbeh had worked hard to keep his role in eliminating the bullies a secret, he now began to feel that he needed some credit. Middling, bottom rung evil has to be hidden from people as it is easily classified as wrong. But anything classified as great—even as great evil—remains great.

Rhuzbeh did not want greatness to pass him by, and so he paid a small boy to let slip the rumour to Gossipy that he himself had killed the bullies. Gossipy promptly cooed it to anyone with ears that the orphan boy had murdered the bullies—a charge that Rhuzbeh continued to deny with a mysterious air.

The villagers were suspicious but did not press home the charges. There were three reasons why the villagers decided to let the whole matter go: One, the bullies had been a scourge and nobody missed them. Two, as an orphan, Rhuzbeh was severely abused by the bullies; so if he did seek revenge, it was well-deserved. Finally—and this was the most important reason—the villagers did not want to antagonise the djinns. Indeed, even mentioning their name would draw their attention and the investigation was thus discarded as a bad idea.

Now there was newfound respect for Rhuzbeh. Men respected him and women desired him. And while some people continued to believe that it was the djinns that had caused the deaths, others simply believed Rhuzbeh to be the murderer.

When Rhuzbeh turned seventeen, the headman called on him and smilingly said, 'I have been following your progress. That's quite a following of boys you have. You have the qualities of a leader. Planning to take up my position, are we?' Rhuzbeh smiled back and shook his head from side to side.

'I am afraid you can't stay here anymore,' said the headman with a tinge of sadness. 'I keep hearing rumours about you. Violent men can't be kept in civil society as they are a bad influence on the youth. Why don't you join the King's army as a soldier? I am sure you will excel there.'

King Kashan, the ruler of Zanda, was a popular king with a formidable army and Rhuzbeh joined him as a foot soldier and fought under the 'coiled serpent' banner of King Kashan's forces. He had to go through rigorous training, and after three years of practice, he was an expert with a blade and handy with an axe.

Although still short and stout, the lad was built like a bull. Whenever the army set up camp, he was made to chop trees and build the camp wall. It was here that he made an impression. It was indeed a sight to watch, no matter how strong the tree, all it took was ten mighty blows for Rhuzbeh to bring it down.

Kashan led the troops from the front. Whenever there was a lull, the king organised duels and wrestling matches. It helped increase morale, provide entertainment and also spot talent. Soldiers would bet on the winners, and it was good fun all around. During one of the fights, his fellow soldiers dared him to participate in a duel and Rhuzbeh agreed.

At the sight of the stout Rhuzbeh, Kashan laughed and said, 'Is this what my army has come to? Why do we have someone resembling a sloth bear? Don't we have noble knights and graceful warriors?'

Nevertheless, the king did not want to disappoint a foot soldier. The opponent stood tall and Rhuzbeh did not measure up to him, literally. As the former was a well-known swordsman, famous for his technique and willingness to use it, this was slated to be a short fight.

The duel began. To Kashan and the soldiers' surprise, Rhuzbeh removed his armour and tossed it away. He then flung away his shield and addressed his opponent loudly. 'To the fear that creeps up on me, hear me loud: I am Rhuzbeh, the Fearless! What I have is not worth keeping, including my armour and my shield. No name to soil, no fame to lose; I shall take everything that is yours and add to mine!' he said and ran straight at the swordsman. As the latter thrust his blade forward to return the attack, Rhuzbeh swiftly stepped aside with surprising agility for one so bulky and using the hilt of his sword, he rendered a great blow to the opponent's shield. The swordsman staggered and Rhuzbeh dealt another mighty blow. This time the impact was so brutal that it dented the shield and the swordsman fell down. Although shaken up, the opponent stood up and charged at Rhuzbeh, who parried the blow with his left hand blocking the swordsman's forearm.

With his sword-wielding right hand, Rhuzbeh again struck the shield hard and knocked it off the swordsman's hand. He followed it up with a hard kick on the chest, leading his tall opponent to lose balance and fall down. Rhuzbeh stood tall in his stead, placing the tip of his sword at the opponent's neck. It was all over—Rhuzbeh had won.

The king and his soldiers rose in unison and applauded. Throughout the lull period, Rhuzbeh battled numerous opponents and remained undefeated. So impressed was Kashan that he declared, 'I appoint you as one of the officers of my vanguard and I confer upon you the title Rhuzbeh the Fearless!'

King Kashan, the ruler of Zanda, was on an expansion spree. Kashan's banner of the coiled serpent was ready to strike down any kingdom that opposed it. Zanda was a beautiful and fertile kingdom that had known peace for centuries until Kashan had the desire to expand his empire. He wanted to be known as the 'King of kings' and so he started a war campaign, trained his troops vigorously, constructed siege machines, hired mages and trained animals to assist him.

The concept of war was simple. If your king won, he had fame, accolades and bounty heaped on him and if he lost, his subjects were pillaged, burnt and tortured. So, it was understandable that the citizens of Zanda were not happy to have war imposed on them, but Kashan would not stop until he was made the King of kings. Kashan's army was massive, and he laid waste to any kingdom that stood in his way.

He began his campaign by invading the Northern kingdom, which had never been conquered by any outside force and was considered invulnerable to any attack. After two months of marching through the Zandian range, Kashan's army reached the narrow Bjan Pass—the only route to the Northern kingdom. The latter boasted of formidable warriors and crafty mages. The Northern mages could cast spells and befuddle the opponents. Although challenging, Kashan did not fear the Northern mages for he had at his disposal one of the greatest mages in the known world, Metishin.

Both armies faced each other, ready to spill blood. The Northern army rallied under the twin-headed eagle banner. In order to avoid bloodshed and the loss of thousands of lives, King Nahal, the young Northern king, called for a duel, with the winner taking over the other's kingdom. Kashan accepted the challenge. The eagle and the snake would fight for the throne.

Nahal sent a giant of a man, who was mounted on an armoured black horse and was carrying two mean-looking swords, one in each hand. The Northern king's mage poured some liquid and set the man's swords and armour on fire such that the blaze would not hurt the rider but only the enemy. He also cast a spell on the horse, causing it to appear half leopard and half horse—indeed, a fearsome sight.

Kashan sent Rhuzbeh to battle the challenger. Rhuzbeh knew that the real enemy was fear. When you display fear, you feed magic. When you are fearless, neither spirits nor humans have an advantage over you. Rhuzbeh walked to the middle with a great battle-axe. The enemy started jeering and making fun of the portly soldier on foot, armed with nothing but an axe, who dared to face their fearsome champion.

Rhuzbeh threw down his shield; the enemy began to rejoice, believing that Rhuzbeh was already surrendering. He removed his chainmail and threw it on the ground as well. Then he forsook all his weapons, except the battle-axe, and declared aloud, 'To the fear that creeps up on me, hear me loud: I am Rhuzbeh, the Fearless. Beat me hard and hear my sound: I am empty. Be bigger, my yearn, my want! Fill out the breast of men with fear, be a foe worth slaying! I am now but a stone: your death will make me a hill!'

The two competitors charged towards each other and were about to collide head-on when Rhuzbeh bent and stepped aside, deftly avoiding the rider's fiery sword that sliced through the air, missing his head and singeing his hair instead. He then swung his axe to cut down the leopard-horse's neck. The beast fell with a mighty thud, trapping the rider under its weight. Rhuzbeh walked up to his fallen opponent and, with one swing of his axe, decapitated him. With the fall of his champion, Nahal surrendered. His eagle banner lay trampled. The defeated king accepted Kashan's suzerainty and became a vassal.

After subjugating the Northern kingdom, King Kashan crossed the sea of Balqara to the south and vanquished the prosperous kingdom of Sedra. He then moved east, conquering the smaller lands ruled by the local chiefs until he reached the powerful kingdom of Hatasa. The domains of Hatasa and Zanda had been together once but a dispute between two successors had split the empire apart. They had been separate kingdoms for hundreds of years now. Kashan wanted to be the unifier in an attempt to portray himself as the legitimate king of the joint kingdoms of Zanda and Hatasa.

Hatasa was a mountainous kingdom with battle-hardened warriors. The king of Hatasa, King Hitkar, had no reason to be fearful of Kashan. His kingdom was surrounded by a ring of mountains that acted like steep walls offering protection from all sides. The southern side of Hatasa sloped to the sea. The jagged rocks and treacherous currents could smash any ship to smithereens.

Wide cobblestone roads led directly to the entrance of the mountain ring. The mountain ring was lined by a high wall which boasted ramparts, parapets and a running platform where the archers and lookouts were stationed. A heavy iron door blocked the entrance to the Kingdom of Hatasa. On either side of the metal door were carved two formidable-looking serpents, which appeared to be guarding the place. The fort wall was impregnable, and no siege machine could break it. Flying high on the fort wall was a Hatasan flag with an ibex crest on it, representing the wild goats with long curved horns that were native to the surrounding mountains.

As the war began, Kashan's siege engines pounded the walls to no avail. The Zandian mages tried to set the door on fire but the Hatasan soldiers easily doused it with water. Kashan's army had no option but to stand and watch helplessly as the Hatasans simply refused to come out to battle. After a month of waiting, the Hatasans finally obliged. The sudden attack by the Hatasans caught the Zandian army unawares, scattering them all over the battlefield. On the back foot now, Kashan rallied his forces bravely. Thus, encouraged by their king, the formidable Zandian army regrouped and counter-attacked in full force, driving back the enemy.

The Hatasans retreated methodically to the fort and reorganised themselves for the next attack. King Hitkar surprisingly lined up only the light cavalry mounted on male ibexes, which were the size of small horses. His held his heavy cavalry, infantry and archers on the reserve within the safety of the fort walls.

Although nonplussed at seeing only the light cavalry, Kashan did not pause to think. To him this looked like a chance to finally engage the Hatasans in a frontal attack. He had arranged the Zandian cavalry on both flanks and infantry in the middle. His heavy cavalry would mow down the ibex-mounted soldiers like grass. He gathered his troops, shifting them from the flanks to the centre. He would make an all-out cavalry charge. He would slaughter them like the sheep they were. He laughed at the thought.

Kashan, the canny tactician, made sure that his infantry took up defensive positions with long spears to deter any surprise attacks by the Hatasan heavy cavalry stationed inside the fort. The Zandian cavalry was heavily armoured and was more than a match for the lightly-armoured ibex cavalry at the fort's entrance. As Kashan's horsemen charged, fearing a massacre, the heavily out-numbered Hatasan ibex-mounted cavalry did an about-turn and started racing towards the mountains, clinging close to the fort walls. Sensing glory, the entire Zandian cavalry chased after them. What the Zandians had not accounted for was how adept the hardy Hatasan ibex was at climbing up the steep mountain sides. As Hatasan ibex-mounted cavalry quickly gained the upper ground, the Zandian cavalry, which was in hot pursuit, found themselves stuck in the middle of the mountain with nowhere to go. Since they were heavily armoured, the Zandians could not climb up or go down on the mountain slopes swiftly and were rendered sitting ducks. They had walked into a perfect trap.

As per King Hitkar's orders, the ibex cavalry had stayed close to the fort walls, enabling the numerous Hatasan archers on the ramparts to quickly pick off the Zandian horses and riders. To make things worse, the Hatasan ibex-mounted cavalry turned around and attacked their pursuers with renewed force. Since they were on higher ground, they had momentum on their side. On the mountains, they outran and out-manoeuvred the Zandians.

The Zandian cavalry scattered and was annihilated under the two-pronged attack. It was over all too quickly. King Hitkar was on the platform of the ramparts, personally directing each foray. He blew the horn for the fort gates to swing open and the Hatasan horse-mounted cavalry charged, massacring the demoralised Zandian infantry.

The Hatasan soldiers surrounded Kashan on all sides. During the fierce attack that followed, Rhuzbeh stood bravely before his king and fought like a lion until a mace blow struck him down, knocking him out senseless. Eventually, Kashan was taken prisoner by the Hatasans.

After a while, Rhuzbeh, who was lying knocked down, woke up to an eagle trying to peck at his arm. He thought it strange since vultures rather than eagles sought carrion.

The eagle looked at him in the eye unblinkingly and flew away. Rhuzbeh gained his composure and looked around. Only dead bodies of enemy soldiers were visible as far as the eye could see. Thinking quickly, he removed the attire of a dead Hatasan soldier and put it on himself. He noticed that all the injured Zandians had been killed and their belongings looted. Rhuzbeh joined in the loot and managed to collect a few gold coins from the dead soldiers. He then proceeded to join the Hatasan army in the celebration.

Hitkar and his victorious army entered Hatasa with Kashan in chains. Rhuzbeh slipped into the city, marching with the victorious soldiers and blending in easily in the commotion of the revelry and festivity. Kashan was now a prisoner and placed under the palace guard's charge to serve as a warning to others. Hitkar was not keen on conquering Zanda, since his armies would be stretched. The Hatasans were formidable in mountain fighting, but on the plains of Zanda, they would be useless. So, he left Zanda to its own fate.

With the fall of King Kashan, the Northern and Southern kingdoms declared themselves free from Zandian rule. Meanwhile, Rhuzbeh bought a merchant's dress, and with the looted gold, he purchased some spices to pass off as a travelling spice merchant.

In the bazaars of Hatasa, he learned all about the spices, their origin and usage. He also learned how to assess their quality and price. Also, it was in these bazaars that Rhuzbeh met the love of his life. As he was plying his trade, his eyes fell on a maiden. She had red hair with green eyes; an exquisitely beautiful creature. He was smitten. She lifted her eyebrows like a limp wave upon seeing him. The thing about limp waves is that they can grow and crash on someone's shore—crash it did!

She smiled and asked him, 'Do you have musk?'

Before he could answer, she got distracted and moved on. Rhuzbeh was twenty-five years old, and for the first time, he experienced a pain such as he had never felt before.

The next day, as she passed him by, he felt an ardent desire to embrace her in his arms but traded that yearning for a meek query. 'You were asking me about musk?'

'Yes,' she said. Rhuzbeh handed her a small vial to smell. 'Where is this musk from?' she asked as she sniffed deeply. 'This musk,' he said, 'is from the eastern lands that lie far beyond the ocean.' Her eyes lit up as she asked, 'Have you ever been to the farthest east?' 'Yes!' he lied and her emerald eyes lit up like tiny flecks dancing in the sunlight. She looked at him from head to toe with newfound respect and said, 'Tell me all about the East!' But before he could respond, she spotted her father turning the corner towards her and quickly hurried away, whispering, 'I will come back tomorrow.' 'What is your name?' he blurted out.

Her feet halted a moment as she looked at him coyly and smilingly said, 'Ceba,' before she ran away without glancing back.

Rhuzbeh was grateful for that timely disruption in their conversation, since he did not know much about the world beyond Hatasa. However, for Ceba's sake, he was determined to try and began making enquiries around town. He was informed about an old man who was known to have travelled to the farthest east and beyond. The imaginative amongst the townspeople even claimed that the old man had seen the serpent that guarded the ends of the earth.

Rhuzbeh excitedly went over to meet the old man who looked threescore and ten with rivulets-like wrinkles carved deep into his face.

'Salutations!' said Rhuzbeh.

The old man had seen his share of fat and eager young men and concluded that this particular young man's salutation did not warrant a reply either. Rhuzbeh sat next to him uninvited and said, 'I have heard of people talking about your fascinating adventures in the east. Will you share your tales with me?'

The old man coughed in his face and said, 'Begone! I don't tell my story to every fat otter that ambles my way.'

Rhuzbeh was not discouraged. He persisted, 'I know that you have not seen the serpents that guard the ends of the earth—for that is but a figment of imagination. But I do know that you have seen wondrous marvels, and it is said that only the intrepid are rewarded with such sights.' He added with utmost politeness, 'It would be such an honour if you would break bread and suspense. Come, share a cup.'

Something about Rhuzbeh's persistence had the old man giving in. 'Is it difficult to cross the ocean?' asked Rhuzbeh after plying him with food and drinks.

The old man smiled and said, 'I see that you are truly keen to know about my adventures, and so I shall share my tales with you.'

Thus began the fascinating tales of the old man's travels. Every night, the old man would regale Rhuzbeh with stories about fantastic birds, beasts, djinns, kings and queens. He spoke about incredible cities, markets and open seas that never seemed to end. For twenty-one days, the old man shared his adventures, and for twenty-one days, Rhuzbeh entertained Ceba with his stories. Those were the most magical moments of his life until then. The couple would sit in a nearby meadow by a flowing brook. Ceba would bring bread, meat and fruits, and Rhuzbeh would narrate the stories that the old man had told him, passing them off as his own and enjoying the food and attention.

She loved musk and implored him, 'Tell me more about musk.'

Praised openly by merchants, traded by its weight in gold and sought by royalty and commoners alike, indeed, Rhuzbeh had heard a lot about musk.

He smiled and said, 'A fragrance interpreted variously as the emotions of a bride behind a veil, a fragrance like the riddle of philosophers, a fragrance that permeates the halls of great kings, a fragrance that is so divine as to transcend its earthy origins and become the mortar of paradise—musk. It embodies all things that seem ordinary from the outside while being extraordinary on the inside. The element that implores you to explore further before you decide its worth. Enlightened men often talk about musk as the ultimate transmutation of imperfections to perfection, and how the symbols of transience like blood, sweat and fluids can be transformed into something as divine.'

He pulled out a vial of musk and said, 'Musk is what you deserve for musk is what you are. When I first met you, I thought you were beautiful. And when I probed further, I realised that your green eyes conceal your true beauty just like the cardamoms from the bazaars of Hatasa, whose inner fragrance is hidden by the green pods. Your essence ascends your physical being and it seeps into my very soul, filling me like water in an empty earthen jar.'

She listened to him with awe, and when he finished speaking, she blushingly said, 'Your eyes see beautifully! Ahem, do my eyes really conceal my true beauty?'

He smiled and said, 'You are now hunting for compliments.'

They both began chuckling. Rhuzbeh then handed her the bottle of musk and said, 'Adorn yourself with this musk, and please allow me to take a whiff of you, so that henceforth, every time I smell musk, I smell you!'

She politely declined his offer three times, as was the custom, and upon his insistence, she finally accepted the gift with great joy. They spent many such happy days together. One day, she asked him to narrate one of his older adventures again. However, since these tales were not his own, he faltered, unable to remember all the details.

She looked him in the eye and asked, 'Is your love for me true?'

He said, 'Yes, my love! May my unworthy life be laid at your feet for my love for you is true.' She then asked him, 'Are your stories true?'

He hesitated until she asked again firmly, 'Are your stories true?' He mumbled, 'No.' She looked at him, hurt brimming her eyes. 'You have lied to me ever since we met. The reason we spoke to each other itself is a lie. Everything about us is a lie.' She started berating herself for being so naïve. He held her hand and said, 'My love for you is purer than the morning dew. The flowing brook is a witness that I did not intend to deceive you. They say sometimes a thousand lies are acceptable to win one true love. I wanted to win you over and prove myself worthy of your love. That is the only reason why I passed those stories as my own. I would die if you were not by my side for the rest of my life.' He tried to take her in his arms but she pushed him away and said, 'Don't touch me. You have ruined everything. You cannot win someone's love with lies and deceit for a thousand lies cannot turn night into day.' Ceba ran away sobbing, leaving Rhuzbeh feeling ashamed of himself. He wanted to pursue her but held himself back because he knew she would not be convinced. Desperate to prove himself to her, he decided to go to the east. He would travel across the ocean for his love, experience foreign places, see fantastic creatures and come back triumphant to claim his beloved's affection.

With this thought, Rhuzbeh set off towards the east. After crossing the immediate eastern lands, he arrived at the vast ocean. There were no vessels large enough or men brave enough to cross the fiery ocean, which was called so because the rising sun made the sea appear to be ablaze.

Chapter 2

The Whale, the Sorcerer and the Sea Serpent

When nights decide to wash and clean up, we call it morning.

It was a misty morning, pregnant with promise—the sort that eventually delivers but not before a cup of tea. While Rhuzbeh waited to be served at the local inn, he heard a loud slurp followed by a satisfying click. He looked at the grizzly, gap-toothed man next to him enjoying his morning cup with a wide grin. Rhuzbeh smiled back. 'The thing about tea is,' began the gap-toothed man, 'that it unlocks its flavours only when one opens the mouth; suppress it and it fails to impress.' And thus followed two more clicks.

'What brings you here?' he asked.

'I am looking to join a ship sailing for the unknown East. Would you happen to know any vessel headed there?' Rhuzbeh inquired in response.

The gap-toothed smile widened. 'You are in luck,' he said, adding, 'We are sailing to the far unknown east in a week. You can join us if you like.'

Fortune was smiling on him. Rhuzbeh was overjoyed and gladly joined the chorus of slurps.

A week later, he was on board a magnificent ship, huge enough to house sixty sailors, horses, livestock and rations that would last for at least five months. With a song in his heart and prayer on his lips, he set out. Nauzar, as Rhuzbeh now discovered the gap-toothed man to be known as, was good company, but after a few weeks, all they had left to talk about was stagnant fish jokes.

'Look,' said Nauzar, 'swarms of suicidal flying fish. I suspect they had a bad marriage, due to which they've been landing on the ship and eventually in our soup.'

'Yes!' smiled Rhuzbeh, saying, 'A bad marriage does land one in soup.' And they both laughed.

But not all days are the same. After five months, they encountered a storm—the likes of which they had never seen before. The clouds went inky black, the sea turned rough and most of the crew were relentlessly throwing up until nothing but their guts remained inside. The storm raged for a week, tossing and killing livestock, people and morale. When the storm subsided, the crew did not know where they were, for their compasses had stopped working. They were now privy to a sight that bordered on the absurd: giant water lilies. And just to reinforce that they were water lilies, they were coloured water-lily pink, blooming right in the middle of the ocean, complete with lily pad et al.

'Pinch me!' said Nauzar.

'I won't poke you with a rake, let alone pinch you in your current state,' said Rhuzbeh, wrinkling his nose. 'And yes! Incredibly, those are water lilies right in the middle of the ocean. But I thought lily pads and lilies only bloom in freshwater,' Rhuzbeh said, adding, 'Look at those lilies. They're almost the size of a mule!'

Throwing caution to the wind, Rhuzbeh jumped into the sea and climbed onto the nearest lily pad. Excitedly prancing around, he began singing a happy song. 'Sing ang li-li-li-li-li-ly, watch me sing ang gooo.'

The whole scene was so unreal that the crew burst out laughing. Suddenly, Nauzar screamed in horror, 'Look! A giant frog!'

Rhuzbeh turned just in time to see a giant yellow and black coloured frog appear behind the lilies and shoot out its tongue. He instinctively drew out his sword and swung it, cleanly chopping off the long rope-like tongue. The tongueless yellow and black wart-wielder seemed indifferent to its loss and showed no signs of pain. It blinked its eyes rapidly and sat statuesque, wondering how to swallow its erstwhile dancing prey. Luckily, its dilemma was resolved when the crew harpooned it, dragged it back to the ship and skinned it. A good bath and a bad song later, Rhuzbeh examined his booty.

'Look at this frog's tongue!' said Rhuzbeh, tying up Nauzar with it to the mast to test its strength. 'Stronger than any rope! And this magnificent yellow and black skin will keep me dry during the rains.'

'And what do I get?' asked Nauzar, still tied to the mast.

'You, my friend, get a healthy dose of slaps,' responded a laughing Rhuzbeh.

And the entire crew indulged in playfully slapping him, much to the chagrin of a hapless Nauzar. On that foggy night, the entire crew feasted on the amphibian's meat and the sailors swore that they had never eaten a lump of flesh more delicious.

Since their compasses were unreliable, they decided to sail straight ahead but their journey began to take an even stranger turn.

'This is an eerie place,' said Nauzar. The air hung heavy, and the ocean stood very still.

The uneasy silence was suddenly shattered as a large whale rose up the water surface, with a loud splash accompanied by a long, low, haunting shriek. Rhuzbeh cried, 'Look!' He need not have said it. It was too large to be missed—twice the size of an average whale. Its entire back, from head to tail, was coloured in a brilliant bronze shade, and its belly was bright silver and mottled with green spots.

'What a gigantic creature! I have never seen anything like this before!' murmured Rhuzbeh. Awe-struck, Nauzar and the entire crew could only stare at it mutely.

'By my dead grandfather's bones, I will be damned if that is not a *gus* whale,' whispered Nauzar.

'I have never heard of a gus whale before,' said Rhuzbeh.

'It is actually not a whale,' said Nauzar, his eyes wide open as if they had seen a ghost. 'It is a djinn. Some sort of a marid perhaps. I always thought the gus whale to be a legend, not real, and I never thought I would see one in my lifetime.' As they continued looking, the gus whale let out a loud cry that seemed to resonate with the howling wind and slapped its tail in the ocean, splashing water all over the ship.

Nauzar continued, 'There are men who spend their entire lives looking for this marid since the gus whale is the source of one of the most precious objects on earth, the gus ambergris.'

'What is a marid?' asked Rhuzbeh.

'Marids are ocean-dwelling djinns which traverse the great depths of oceans in the form of giant fish or sea serpents. They come in varying shapes and sizes. Some are so gigantic that it is said that the earth itself is balanced on one such fish and that if the seas of the world were placed in one of the fish's nostrils, they would be like mustard seeds laid in the desert.'

Rhuzbeh was in a trance and found himself being strongly drawn towards it. He realised that he was experiencing an inexplicable urge to follow it and not let it out of his sight. Unable to resist this pull any longer, Rhuzbeh finally burst out, 'The gus whale is calling out to me. I must go.'

'Have you lost your senses?' rebuked Nauzar. 'It is a djinn!'

But Rhuzbeh was a man possessed. He quietly packed a boat with supplies, including the frog's skin and the belt made using its tongue, and proceeded to lower the small vessel into the sea. 'Wait!' cried Nauzar, 'If you must go, then allow us to come with you. Perhaps a little later, we might be able to talk you out of this madness.' And so Nauzar, along with another sailor, accompanied Rhuzbeh on the boat.

They followed the gus whale which always kept its distance, never allowing them to get too close. It blew great fountains of water, taller than the tallest of junipers, and with its great mouth wide open, it ascended in the middle of the night, swallowing phosphorescent krill in their multitudes with great relish. The giant whale thrashed its great tail in the water, making the boat rise to towering heights with the waves. The sailors aboard thought that their boat would smash to smithereens, but miraculously, the boat held.

The ocean was a flurry. Reptilian creatures of prodigious proportions glided against the whale—enormous turtles, mermaids and creatures strange and bizarre, all wanted to be in the vicinity of this beast. The sky and water turned to various hues in this mesmerising world.

'Nauzar, what is this that we are witnessing? Are these whales, serpents, frogs, and lilies real?' asked Rhuzbeh.

'They are real—as real as you and me,' replied Nauzar. 'Certain places and animals exist, but we cannot see or locate them. Here we are able to see them only because the djinn has chosen to lead us to them. It is said that some places exist which compasses can't point towards. What I can't understand is why the gus whale is calling out to you in particular.'

Rhuzbeh shrugged and moaned, 'I am hungry, sick and out of my mind. Our skin has turned sallow like that of corpses. I wonder how long we have to subsist on this diet of fish and rainwater.'

After three days of sailing and following the whale, they were set upon by magnetic storms. The sea was vicious and littered with flotsam. 'This is a graveyard for ships,' said Nauzar. 'This is where we say goodbye to each other. I will see you in the afterlife.'

'Don't say that; we may yet survive,' said Rhuzbeh.

'Do you think there is life after the afterlife?' asked Nauzar.

Rhuzbeh's answer was drowned in the storm as their boat was tossed around like a twig.

Had it been a ship with a mast and sails, it would have been smashed into nothingness; sometimes being small has its benefits. A day later, the storm subsided, and after another two days of sailing, they sighted an island.

'Land!' said Nauzar. 'I would have exchanged my eyes for just a glimpse of this dry land. The very air seems delicious.'

With the whale still frolicking around them, they decided to visit the land and stock up on supplies. It was a large island inhabited by beautiful people: tall and proportionate. The islanders offered the three weary sailors food and lodgings, which were gladly accepted. The rigours of the ocean had been forbidding, and as the luxuries of the warm sands engulfed them, days turned into weeks. The sailors were enjoined by the natives to participate in their daily routines on the island, where the three began to work on farms from early morning till late noon, have lunch with the farmers and participate in dinner revelries before finally going off to sleep. The island was beautiful and its food was delicious.

As the sailors explored more of the island, they discovered drawings of sea serpents, tridents and some strange devices that had Rhuzbeh asking the island chief, 'What are these?'

'These are the memories of the past. It is said that some serpentine beings rose from the water and bestowed our ancestors with know-how and wisdom. In antiquity, our civilization was buried under a giant ocean wave. We are the remnants of that lost civilization, whose accumulated knowledge is lost, buried under the ocean,' replied the chief.

On this island, Rhuzbeh met Tasia, a beauty with brown eyes, shapely brown eyebrows and long brown lashes that fluttered like a sparrow's wings. Although he was intimidated, he was not browbeaten; he tried to draw her attention by winning friendly wrestling matches with the island youth who swarmed around her like bees around honey. These duels were nothing more than cockfights with a semblance of civility. Rhuzbeh knew he did not paint a pretty picture physically. He was stout, with matted hair and the burnt skin of a seafarer. The only thing that could drive Tasia towards him was curiosity and the fact that the great gus whale had allowed him to follow it. So when Tasia and Rhuzbeh finally spoke, they spent a whole day talking about the latter's adventures. Soon, they were like oysters and pearls. 'What's with the gus whale? Why does everyone go quiet when I mention the gus whale?' he asked her one day.

She took a deep breath, 'There is no love for gus whales on this island. They are believed to be the kin of the ocean-dwelling djinns called marids. Their kind has been around since antiquity.' She continued in a hushed tone, 'The legend goes that a large landmass existed here in the ancient past, which was much bigger than the present island. Its inhabitants, our forefathers, had made massive progress in construction and technology. They built a great city, had kings and queens, and were the marvel of the ancient world. So arrogant were they in their achievements that they decided to hunt a gus whale and slit its throat to possess the fabled gus ambergris.'

'What exactly is ambergris?' he asked, interrupting her.

'Ambergris is also called ocean gold,' she replied. 'When the gus whale's excreta is cured by the sun and saltwater, it turns into a sweet-smelling waxy white lump called ambergris. It is high priced and much sought after as an additive in perfumes, medicine and magic.'

'Bah!' he belched. 'All that fuss for whale poo? I can't imagine applying it on the body. What does it smell like anyway?'

She laughed, sounding like a sparrow's chirrup. 'The odour of ambergris is difficult to define. You belittle it by dismissing it so easily. It is defined as musty and reminiscent of the sea; it is sometimes called the 'mother of all fragrances'. Ambergris is like a mother, although incredible by herself, she delights in her offspring's qualities. As an additive, ambergris brings out the best in perfumes and makes a fragrance linger. A house without a mother is insubstantial; so it is that perfumes and certain medicines just do not hold together without ambergris.'

'Is gus ambergris simply whale poo or is it extracted in a specific manner? And what miracle does this fabled gus ambergris perform that makes it so special?' Rhuzbeh asked.

'Gus ambergris, unlike normal ambergris, is excreted through the gus whale's mouth as a ball—peach-coloured and waxy,' she replied. 'Gus ambergris has some remarkable properties. It is an exaltant and enhances a person's dominant trait. If a person has leadership abilities, it makes the person a great leader. If a person has sparks of wisdom, gus ambergris makes him the wisest. In an evil person, it brings out his worst traits and can wreak havoc, but when ingested by a good person, it amplifies his good qualities. When it is ingested with rose water, it strengthens the blood and fortifies the spirit. It attracts power, and usually, a person who has consumed gus ambergris is destined for kingship. Since it is a product associated with the djinns, they bond with anyone in whose veins gus ambergris flows. A person who drinks this concoction can converse with any djinn, and most importantly, the power of the djinn does not affect them. No gus whale in the history of mankind has ever given out gus ambergris willingly. Legend says that the person to whom gus ambergris is given voluntarily by the gus whale will have his destiny tied to the djinns and will immortalise his name amongst djinns as well as humans. Gus ambergris also increases longevity. People who are known to consume it live extraordinarily long lives under normal conditions.'

'That's amazing! Does the gus ambergris make one immortal?' he asked.

'Of course not!' Tasia replied. 'Any soul that is born must die. Immortality is reserved for God.'

'Did your ancestors actually hunt down a gus whale?' asked Rhuzbeh.

'Unfortunately, yes,' she replied and took a deep breath to narrate the account at length.

Tasia began, 'The power of green crystals made our forefathers arrogant. The now lost art of making green crystals was apparently handed over to us by the serpents who emerged from the waters and taught a select few various secrets. The wise amongst us were afraid of incurring the wrath of the gus whale and the disapproval of the serpents. But, against the oracles' and temple priests' advice, some of the islanders decided to hunt the great gus whale. When the island chief refused to heed the warnings of the oracles, four large groups of forefathers, fearing catastrophe, left the city sailing in four unknown directions.

Meanwhile, the whale hunters assembled a fleet of fifty ships with three hundred men. It was the most extensive whale hunt ever. No one in centuries had seen or hunted a gus whale; nobody even knew what gus ambergris looked like. When a gus whale was finally spotted for the first time in centuries, it matched the description—twice the size of an average whale, shiny bronze with a silver and mottled green belly.

The hunt began. The gus whale let out a long shriek that shook the whole island. The hunters surrounded the whale and were ready to harpoon it when they were attacked by swarms of seagulls that tore the canvas masts apart with their beaks. The islanders threw explosive green powder in the air to scare away the gulls. Just then, strange creatures appeared in the sea. Giant sea crabs crawled up the ships, decapitating the sailors and destroying the ships. The sailors attacked the creatures with green crystal-tipped explosive arrows, sending them back into the water, and threw great spears tipped with green crystals at the gus whale. The whale attacked in return, sinking fifteen of the ships, but the sailors were relentless.

A giant turtle suddenly appeared, lifting a ship and upturning it. It was also met by explosive arrows and chased away. The ocean churned with these massive beasts thrashing about. Driven by bloodlust, the men did not stop. They finally managed to thrust large, crystal-tipped harpoons into the gus whale's body and hauled it close to the mothership. The colossal creature screamed in agony as twelve men jumped on the whale and drove lances deep into the thrashing giant's head. Blood gushed out from the wounds like fountains. In the throes of pain, the gus whale let out painful shrieks that could be heard for miles. The ocean turned rubescent with blood and the whale slumped over, dead. The sea creatures slunk back, birds flew away and there was an ominous calm.

The sailors dragged the carcass to the beach, slit the throat and took out the fabled peach and waxy gus ambergris ball. They declared three days of festivities, after which gus ambergris would be distributed. The entire city joined in on the celebrations. They mounted the gus whale on a massive structure and put it up in the city centre for all to marvel at. They had reached a pinnacle, for even the noblest of creatures, the largest and most venerated, was no match for their prowess. They went mad with celebrations and it was then that the rains began. There was continuous downpour for two days and nights. On the third day, a massive earthquake occurred, followed by a giant wave that swallowed the entire landmass, leaving no trace of land.'

'Did the gus whale cause it?' asked a wide-eyed Rhuzbeh.

'No one knows for sure,' said Tasia. 'Some attribute it to the sin of slaying the gus whale, while others theorise that the gargantuan marids caused the cataclysmic wave to avenge their kin. And some just call it a coincidence—a giant wave which coincided with the killing. Either way, the entire landmass went underwater along with the inhabitants' achievements, advances and the gus ambergris.'

'That is tragic,' said Rhuzbeh. 'What happened to the populace?'

'Some remnants of the population were scattered across four directions. We are one such group. Did the city resurface after some time? Were more people saved? No one knows for sure.'

'That was a hair-raising tale. No wonder nobody wants to talk about it,' said Rhuzbeh. Tasia shook her head ruefully.

As they lay under the night sky, she shared with him her surprisingly vast knowledge of stars, which she claimed was passed down from generation to generation. She taught him the intricacies of determining true north and unravelling various other astronomical secrets. He taught her swordsmanship and was surprised at how quickly she mastered the art. He was settling down with her and it was the first time that he experienced domesticity and its joys. She smelt the same as the fresh ocean breeze. Her hair was the brown quilt that sheltered his eyes from the early morning sun as he slept peacefully. He enveloped her in his wide arms as they slept under the open skies. In the mornings, they would both catch unsuspecting fish and delight in each other's catch. Nauzar and the other sailor also found women who presumed the men were a good catch and absorbed themselves in domesticity.

Then one day, the gus whale made an appearance close to the shore, much to the trepidation of the islanders. As he watched the gus whale, something stirred in Rhuzbeh, and he had a deep yearning to follow it again. He informed Nauzar, 'I have to follow it.'

'Do you have to?' asked Nauzar. 'Why can't we stay here for the rest of our lives?'

'I can't,' replied Rhuzbeh, 'I will know no peace until I follow it.'

The other shipmate flatly refused to follow him. The gus whale frolicked around for two days and two nights, frequently beckoning Rhuzbeh. He decided to leave and told Nauzar,

'I have been thinking that domesticity is one of the biggest enemies of greatness, Nauzar. If I stay back and sire children, I will lead a normal and comfortable life, but I will be stuck here forever. It is a trap! And not all traps look dangerous. Some look beautiful and comfortable, and before you realise it, they take away your youth and leave you relegated to nothing but emotional and familial bonds. Come Nauzar! Let us brush away these bonds and follow destiny.'

So they forsook the newly-bonded relationships, and on the following night, when Tasia was asleep, Rhuzbeh, with Nauzar in tow, jumped into the boat and followed his calling—the gus whale.

'Do you know where we are headed to this time?' asked a grumpy Nauzar.

'Haven't you heard,' replied Rhuzbeh, 'that where there is a whale, there is a way.'

After four days of sailing, they witnessed something that they would never forget for the rest of their lives. The ocean parted and a monstrous black and pink squid, with a terrifying beak and multiple tentacles, rose from the sea. The squid measured up to the whale and more. A spectacularly epic battle ensued.

The squid grabbed the whale with its tentacles and tried to swallow it whole. The whale thrashed about and wiggled out, but the squid lunged and swallowed the whale in one giant gulp.

Rhuzbeh, who witnessed this event in horror, could not bear to see this vile creature from the darkness devour something as august as the gus whale. He threw a spear aimed directly at its dinner-plate-sized eye. The spear pierced its pupil and the squid let out a loud squeal. Upon belching out the whale whole, it descended to the ocean floor. The gus whale blew great columns of water to show its gratitude and moved on ahead. The sailors followed the whale, still shaking in absolute fear. So much was their fear that they both fell sick and passed out.

The next day, they woke up startled; someone was hosing them down with water. Rhuzbeh too woke up with a start and saw a fantastic scene. They were surrounded by elephants in the ocean, which were spraying water on them with their trunks. He asked, 'Nauzar, have I lost my mind or do you see elephants in the ocean as well?'

'No! You are sane; or we have both gone insane,' replied Nauzar. The elephants swam around them, comfortably paddling with their legs and keeping their trunks above the water's surface to breathe.

Then the elephants gently nudged the boat towards an island. As soon as the sailors reached the elephant isle, they hopped down and tied up the boat. The elephants appeared to be larger than usual, with long fleshy ears which they apparently used as oars.

'These elephants are curious, sniffing and feeling us with their trunks and bringing leaves and fruits,' observed Nauzar. 'I wonder why they brought us to this island?'

'I know why,' said Rhuzbeh as he pointed to an old tusker lying on the grassy floor. 'The tusker looks larger and darker than the others. It looks so withered and wrinkled that it must be an ancient creature. I think it is on the verge of dying,' said Nauzar. 'Possibly, they thought we could help?' he added.

'Sadly, there is no wall that can stop death,' said Rhuzbeh. 'You can't play hide and seek with death for long. When death comes calling, even the mightiest must answer. May his memory remain green! Come Nauzar, let's move to the nether part of the island and away from this tragic scene.'

As the elephants were tending to the stricken animal, Rhuzbeh and Nauzar started exploring the island and found large rocks shaped like abstract elephant parts. Someone had carved large stones into elephantine shapes. There was a steep hill, and at its peak was an abstract elephant head. The elephant head peak was formed with several uneven and precariously balanced rocks.

'I wonder who carved these huge rocks on this remote island?' asked Rhuzbeh.

'It must have been the djinns,' whispered Nauzar, looking around fearfully.

As if in confirmation, the two heard eerie sounds in the descending darkness that sent shivers down their spines. They huddled close to each other and spent the night under a tree. The next day they took a walk around the island again in the comfort of daylight. The elephant isle was really big and had a pool of clear water. The hills surrounded the island in a circular ring, as if balancing the island and preventing the landmass from drifting away.

'How do you think the elephants came to be on this remote island?' asked Nauzar.

'Perhaps they were ancient animals that had already been on the island before it was torn away from the mainland, or they could have been stranded here due to a shipwreck,' guessed Rhuzbeh. 'Either way, the elephants seem to have been here for generations because they have clearly adapted to the water. They are at ease swimming in oceans and eating ocean kelp.'

'They seem to have grown large since their bodies are immersed in water most of the time,' added Nauzar.

Four days passed in peace as they explored more parts of the island, with the elephants mostly leaving them alone. Then suddenly one day, Rhuzbeh was nonplussed with the elephants getting agitated and trying to attack and chase them away. It was then that he and Nauzar noticed the sick tusker. The mighty beast was dead, and as the rotting flesh was parting, they noticed a small stone shining in the moonlight. It looked like a sparrow's egg and had a dull glow. The elephants were also looking at it in wonder.

'What is that stone gleaming in the dead elephant's skull?' asked Rhuzbeh.

'*Gajmuk*!' Nauzar whispered, with eyes and mouth wide open as if he could not believe what he saw.

'What is a gajmuk?' asked Rhuzbeh.

'Gajmuk is the fabled elephant pearl,' answered Nauzar. 'A rare precious stone present in the head of certain elephants, which occasionally drives them mad.'

'Is gajmuk ornamental or does it have any other properties too?' asked Rhuzbeh.

'Gajmuk is the treasure of kings,' said Nauzar. 'It protects its bearer against curses of men. Poisoned food turns green when touched by a gajmuk, and poison has no effect on the man who possesses a gajmuk. Indeed, a person bearing a gajmuk can drink poison like wine is drunk from a chalice. Magic and spells bounce back harmlessly like sun rays off a mirror.'

'Now I know why the gus whale brought us here,' said Rhuzbeh. 'It wants to reward us for saving its life from that evil squid-like creature's attack. It wants us to have the gajmuk... Anyway, what use is the gajmuk to a dead elephant? Let's steal it and leave the island to the elephants.'

'It is not going to be easy. Look! The matriarch is getting restless and agitated,' said Nauzar.

Young elephants are born without any instincts. As the oldest mother, the matriarch is instrumental in teaching her daughters how to care for their young. It was the first matriarch who took the baby elephants to the sea, with the young babies holding on to their mother's tail with their little trunks and paddling around in shallow waters. As soon as they entered the ocean, the lumbering land giants turned into ocean-faring beasts. When they swam in the deep sea, the matriarch always led them. In the middle were the daughters and aunts, with the males always bringing up the rear or guarding the flanks. When fatigued, the very young calves climbed on top of their mothers and lay sprawled as the mothers paddled around. The matriarch sought out kelp from the shallow parts of the ocean since it was a high source of nutrition. Such a diet and swimming had made these elephants larger than regular elephants.

The current matriarch was as large as a mammoth and wise as a grandmother. The herd always rallied around her. After the death of the mysterious beast, the herd stuck very closely to her. She seemed to have a calming effect on them. It was she who had decided to bring the humans to the island. Now she seemed keen to get rid of them. It was as if the matriarch could sense their intentions.

Rhuzbeh came up with a plan to steal the gajmuk. He told Nauzar, 'Soak yourself in thick wet clay and mud so that the elephants won't be able to smell you and wait hidden near the dead elephant until I give you a signal.' Nauzar nodded. Rhuzbeh headed towards the elephant hillock. On the way, he saw the bones and tusks of a dead elephant. He picked up one of the ivory tusks and cut off its sharp end, turning it into a horn. He tucked the ivory horn into his belt.

There was a small elephant calf gambolling around. Rhuzbeh caught the calf and tied it to a rock at the base of the hill using his frog belt. He then collected ants from the hill and put them on the calf, who trumpeted loudly in fear, drawing all the elephants to itself. The matriarch had seen Rhuzbeh put ants on the baby from a distance. She was infuriated and charged towards him. As if on cue, the other elephants charged as well. The earth shook beneath them. Now he quickly untied the baby, retrieved his frog belt and climbed the steep rocks. The elephants rapidly reached the calf. The matriarch blew air from her trumpet to blow off the ants and soothe the calf. Once the baby had calmed, the elephants looked at Rhuzbeh with baleful eyes. A war had been declared.

Rhuzbeh had a good lead on them and the elephants' flat feet and ponderous weight was not ideal for climbing. He quickly reached the top and, with one mighty heave, pushed down the stones that made up the elephant head formation. Although large, they were precariously balanced and thus easily undone. As the rocks came tumbling down, the elephants scattered helter-skelter, skidding down and rolling out of the way to avoid getting harmed.

Meanwhile, as Rhuzbeh kept the elephants distracted, Nauzar quickly grabbed the gajmuk from the dead tusker. But then greed overtook him. He used an axe to chop off one of the large tusks, losing valuable time in the process. With the gajmuk and the ivory tusk now secured, Nauzar ran towards the beach to make a getaway. However, the sound of the axe chopping down the tusk had not escaped the matriarch. She rushed towards the dead elephant and quickly spotted Nauzar running towards the beach. He reached the water and started swimming towards the boat. She gave chase, and in the water, she was faster. She grabbed Nauzar by the trunk, brought him back to shore and trampled him to death. She then picked up the gajmuk and walked back to the hill.

Nauzar was the only friend Rhuzbeh had ever had, and watching him being trampled right in front of his eyes shook him deeply. Nauzar's entrails were squished out, and his innards lay scattered on the sand. In just a few moments, seagulls descended in angry droves to feed off his body. The matriarch looked up at Rhuzbeh vengefully and trumpeted loudly, as if to say, 'You are next.'

The elephants surrounded the hill Rhuzbeh was on and did not move for a day and a night. They also did not climb the hill out of fear that Rhuzbeh might push down rocks again. The matriarch, leading from the front, looked at him with malevolent eyes, constantly trumpeting at him as if challenging him to a fight with her. He knew he was no match for her might, but it was the second day, and he had not had food or water; his strength was failing him. He was getting desperate and could think of only two choices: He could either die of hunger or thirst on the hillock or die fighting her.

Rhuzbeh chose the latter. He stood up, took out the ivory horn and blew it three times to announce his challenge. The matriarch trumpeted back. He slowly descended the hill, continually blowing the horn.

The other elephants backed away almost in unison. The entire population watched as the matriarch stood her ground. He was the challenger; the winner would take over the herd. The matriarch was carrying the gajmuk, which she placed to the side, and both man and beast faced each other. He was no match for the matriarch. While she was a behemoth, he was but a fraction of her weight. She was two and a half times his height, yet he stood tall and announced:

'To the fear that creeps up on me, hear me loud,
I am Rhuzbeh, the Fearless!
I have none to witness my death,
And none with cause to hide my shame.
I don't fear you because if I die,

I die battling a colossal beast.
Fear me, for an ignoble death awaits
At the hands of a scurrying thief.
Kill you, I will!
I shall rise above me,
I shall soar in my own eyes.
From a thief, I shall ascend
To a warrior who won the prize!'

The matriarch trumpeted loudly and charged head-on. When they were about to collide, Rhuzbeh dropped down, rolled to the side and tried to slice her leg with his dagger, but she caught his hand by her trunk and flung him away like a ragdoll. Rhuzbeh crashed with a thud, the wind knocked out of him. He knew he could not attack her with his body, for she was built like a rock. He quickly stood up and tucked in his dagger. He picked up a large stone and flung it at her head, targeting the area between the eyes with all his might. The stone made a flat noise and harmlessly bounced off her. He turned and quickly ran towards a strong tree and climbed up furiously. She waited as if enjoying his attempts at survival. When he had climbed high, she uprooted the tree and sent him crashing down. Rhuzbeh got up and saw the matriarch ambling towards him, entirely unhurried. In the calmness of her gait, he knew that his fate was sealed. He looked around and up ahead, where he found a huge rock almost fourteen feet high, with a tree growing between its cracks. The tree was tenacious. It had split the rock open and sprouted from it as if to say the hardest and toughest can be torn asunder if the will is strong. Rhuzbeh stood up and ran towards that tree. He flung the frog tongue belt at the tree. Using the tree for support, he climbed on top of the rock. He stood on the edge and waited for her to charge.

The rock was the same height as the matriarch. As she charged, lowering her great head to knock down Rhuzbeh with a head butt, he took a step back at the very last minute and, flinging the belt around her neck, jumped onto her back. He then blew the elephant horn right into her ear. The matriarch went mad. She could not think clearly. She crashed against rocks and trees in an attempt to shake him off. He clung on for dear life, all the while blowing the horn into her ear. Finally, she could take it no more. Since she could not use her tusks or legs against him, she sat down and lifted her posterior to topple him. He quickly wrapped his belt tighter against her neck to strangle her.

Man and beast struggled for a long time. She thrashed and swayed, but the doughty strangler held on. It was an epic battle witnessed by the assembled elephants. Slowly but surely, Rhuzbeh managed to choke the matriarch until she passed out. While she was still breathing, Rhuzbeh quickly loosened up the stranglehold. He blew his trumpet three times as the elephants watched in a daze. He then picked up the gajmuk and walked towards the water. He swam to the boat, and once he reached, he lifted up the gajmuk and blew his horn again. He had won it fairly in a duel and did not steal it like a petty thief. As he blew his horn, the matriarch rose up and other elephants surrounded her to offer support and consolation.

All of a sudden, half a dozen elephants charged into the water as if to give chase. Rhuzbeh felt a chill run down his spine; he knew that the elephants could swim faster than he could row. He dropped the horn on the boat and waited for death to approach him.

Just when Rhuzbeh had given up, there was a loud cry like a banshee's scream, and the elephants froze. It was the gus whale. Blowing a great fountain of water, it floated in like a protective mountain between Rhuzbeh and the elephants. The elephants turned tail and retreated to the island, trumpeting aloud. The gus whale kept blowing out huge spouts of water till all the elephants had retreated. Then it calmly turned around, allowing Rhuzbeh to follow it to the sea. His voyage continued.

Rhuzbeh sat on the boat, drinking the water and eating the little food that they had stored in the small vessel. Suddenly, his eyes fell on Nauzar's belongings, and the full weight of his companion's loss hit him. He was engulfed by grief and wept for a person whom he had never formally called a friend and yet had become closer than a brother. Fatigue and grief took over and he passed out on the boat.

He passed in and out of sleep. Soon it started raining, and Rhuzbeh was soaked. He realised that he still had the frog's skin and covered himself with it, finding it surprisingly warm. Two days later, he reached the coast, where a giant bird—rather like a large cormorant—sat atop a big rock. It stared at him and its expansive, outstretched black and brown wings looked like they were demanding a hug. The bird had clear green eyes, a yellow gular pouch and white cheeks. With a wingspan of at least twelve feet, it looked foreboding. Suffice it to say that the hugs were not forthcoming.

Rhuzbeh tied his boat down and walked to the rocky coast to look at this massive bird. As he approached closer, he saw a leather band around its neck. The coastal people use cormorants for fishing. They tie a loose band or string around their necks, preventing the birds from swallowing the larger fish that are held in their throats. The fishermen then take those fish for themselves. Sure enough, there was a metal clamp with a small lock and chain on its leg. The chain was tethered to the rock—the bird was a prisoner.

'Which human could have been powerful enough to enslave this giant cormorant?' Rhuzbeh wondered aloud.

He then realised that the gus whale had brought him here to free the cormorant from captivity. He walked cautiously towards the bird, which looked back with a steady eye. As soon as he got close enough, in one fell swoop, the bird picked him up in its beak. His head and shoulder almost reached the bird's throat, his face brushing against its rough pink tongue. The cormorant struggled unsuccessfully for quite some time to swallow him and then gave up. Finally, when Rhuzbeh could claim his head as his own, he wondered why the bird had tried to swallow him. He then realised that he was still dressed in the frog's skin and the bird had mistaken him for a giant frog. He quickly removed the frog's skin and dipped himself in the ocean. After cleansing himself, he lay thinking as to how he could remove the band and chain.

He began to walk around the coast looking for some clues as to who had imprisoned the bird. He saw no sign of settlements till after a day's travel when he came across a small colony of huts. The entire colony was abandoned. He found pottery, food grains, clothes, wells and livestock, but the people were missing. He was puzzled because whoever the inhabitants were, they had left abruptly. Rhuzbeh decided that this was a good place for a day's halt. For the first time in many days, he relaxed. He had a freshwater bath, changed into fresh clothes, caught a live chicken and roasted it and made porridge out of grains. He felt strength returning to him. He slept a relaxed sleep for a whole day and night. When the floor below doesn't rock and you have a warm blanket, a sense of security pervades your entire being. After a sound sleep, Rhuzbeh gathered his belongings, packed some food and resumed his journey. Later that day, he finally arrived at what looked like an inhabited village. On getting closer though, he noticed that the inhabitants looked edgy. He tried to make enquiries about the small settlement and why it had been abandoned but most townsfolk just gave him sullen or nervous looks and hurried away. Unable to get any answers, he sat down on a rough stone bench at a street corner, with his head resting in his hands. Unexpectedly, he caught the scent of freshly baked bread and followed it to find an old woman baking *sangak*—a type of bread with sesame and poppy toppings—on a bed of small river stones for sale.

He approached her and asked, 'Can I help you in baking?'

She replied, 'Yes! By all means. But I have no money to pay you.'

He agreed and was soon baking the sangak on the pebbles, watching the speckling, hearing the popping and taking in the smells of the whole wheat leavened flatbread.

When they were done, she invited him to join her for a meal. Between bites he asked her, 'Why is the settlement by the ocean empty? It looks like it has been abruptly abandoned. What happened to it?'

She replied, 'There is a powerful sorcerer who has imprisoned a giant bird. Word has it that the bird is a djinn—a nas nas who has assumed bird form—and until the chain and clamps remain on its legs, it will not be able to transform into anything else. The sorcerer used spells to chain the bird and now takes it in his boat to catch fish or dive for precious gems. The cormorant usually brings him a good catch of fish from the ocean. However, the sorcerer is after something that is much more precious than fish. One day a brave lad from the settlement took pity on the bird and tried to break the chain with his axe. The sorcerer was so angry at seeing him attempting to free the bird that he killed the youth. Afraid of the sorcerer's wrath, the other members soon abandoned the settlement and moved away.'

'Thank you for confiding in me. Can you show me the way to the sorcerer's dwelling?' asked Rhuzbeh.

She was alarmed, 'No! Please don't go there. He will kill you as surely as my pomegranate bud turns to fruit.'

He smiled and said, 'Don't worry. I know how to handle sorcerers.'

Reluctantly, she pointed in the direction of the sorcerer's home and bid him farewell. While Rhuzbeh was leaving, she sprinkled clear water from a small container behind him for his safe return as per the local custom. Rhuzbeh carried the gajmuk in the folds of his belt and clutched it tightly. He knew that as long as he held the gajmuk, he was as safe from sorcery and poison as a baby is in its mother's womb.

Rhuzbeh walked up the hill and reached the sorcerer's stone cottage which was bolstered by a large wooden door. After persistent knocking, the door was opened by a simple-looking man with a glowing face, a black beard and a pointed nose. Rhuzbeh presumed the man to be the sorcerer. The man stared incredulously at Rhuzbeh. No one had dared to knock on his door in a long, long time...

He asked tersely, 'What do you want?'

Rhuzbeh replied, 'I am a sailor. My ship crashed and I was washed ashore. The villagers wouldn't help me as they are scared of strangers. I saw this stone mansion and thought that you might help me. Can you please spare a meal and a bed for me? I will be gone tomorrow.'

The sorcerer looked at him for a moment and said, 'It is not often that I, Dahel, get willing guests. Come in.'

The sorcerer gave him food and drinks and indulged him with small talk. 'So where do you come from, and what do you do?' he asked.

'I was born in a small town near Zanda, and I ply my trade as a spice trader in the bazaars of Hatasa,' replied Rhuzbeh.

The sorcerer was intrigued and asked, 'Do you have star anise or aniseed, as it is called?'

Luckily, Rhuzbeh had aniseed and handed it over to him.

'How much does it cost?' asked Dahel.

'Oh! It's nothing and it's not worthy of you,' said Rhuzbeh gracefully. Dahel warmed up to him, and they had a lengthy discussion on herbs and spices.

'Do you live alone?' asked Rhuzbeh, changing the subject.

'No, I live with my wife but she is away,' replied the sorcerer. 'The villagers fear my company as I am a sorcerer,' he said, watching for Rhuzbeh's reaction.

'I have met sorcerers and, in fact, consulted with some of them to increase my profits from trade, woo fair winds and return home safely,' said Rhuzbeh.

The sorcerer got visibly angry and said, 'Do not compare me with petty fortune-tellers who dabble their hands in colourful, bubbly liquids. I'm Dahel the Bearclaw.'

'Oh! You are Dahel the Bearclaw?' asked Rhuzbeh. 'I have heard of you. Your fame travels far and wide. Forgive my ignorance, for I am an imbecile with knowledge lesser than water in the driest of deserts.'

Dahel was flattered that the spice merchant from faraway lands had heard of him. 'So what have you heard of me?' he asked.

'Great things!' said Rhuzbeh. 'Across the seas and in every corner, sorcerers abound but none with your magical prowess. You have no equal in power and skill. You are a sorcerer to be respected and feared. Surely sorcery runs in your blood. You must be from a lineage of great sorcerers, mustn't you?' asked Rhuzbeh.

'Yes! I am,' replied the sorcerer. 'But my parents were not the nurturing kind, and as they were busy with their own sorcery and travel, they abandoned me to one of the most powerful sorcerers of the time, Isvil.'

'So you learnt your craft from Isvil? Was he a great teacher?' asked Rhuzbeh.

Dahel uttered with a sneer, 'Isvil was a great sorcerer. He taught me everything I know—all my magic is his.' He broke into an evil chuckle with a mad glint in his eyes.

'Was he fond of you?' asked Rhuzbeh.

Dahel smiled sarcastically and said, 'Yes, he was fond of me. But that did not stop him from continually abusing me. He wanted my fingers, for some of his concoctions needed human parts. He could not cut them for nothing, so he came up with some tasks, failing which, he would have an excuse for doing so. My first task was to collect *aspand* from the sacred gardens and hand it over to Isvil.'

'Oh, aspand!' exclaimed Rhuzbeh. 'The seeds and dried fruits of the garden rue! What did Isvil want apsand for?'

'The dried fruit has many tiny blackish brown seeds that have magical and medicinal usages,' said Dahel, adding, 'Burning of aspand seeds wards off evil, but the substance also has uses in other types of magic.'

Dahel smiled benignly, reminiscing those peaceful days as if he could still see those gardens and robed priests.

'If the sect of the holy men who cultivated the sacred aspand gardens knew that it would be used for dark magic, they would not part with it,' he said. 'So Isvil sent me, a mere boy in rags, to get it from them. I approached them and offered to work in return for food and shelter. I looked dirty and starved; the priests took pity on me and took me in. They gave me a warm bath, fresh white robes and a hot meal. My job was to help the others harvest and peel the aspand. I participated in religious rituals that helped cleanse my soul. The townsfolk visited the priests and paid them money to conduct aspand-burning rituals to ward off the evil eye. When the priests burnt aspand, they chanted a prayer:

Thirty-three seeds to ward off the eyes
Eyes of means, eyes of none
Eyes of enemies, eyes of the jealous one
Eyes of relatives, eyes of friends
Eyes in the skies, eyes on earth ends
Burn in this crackling fire

This simple but powerful incantation chanted by the holy priests warded off the bad spirits, protecting the townsfolk from the malice and mischief of the evil eye.'

'What happened next?' said Rhuzbeh impatiently. 'Did you manage to get the aspand?'

'I did,' said Isvil. 'I was adopted by the priests at the sacred aspand gardens. After spending many days with them, I had won their confidence. One night, when everybody was sleeping, I stole some aspand and ran away. With a smug smile, I handed Isvil the aspand and narrated my exploits. I looked at him with pride, expecting praise for my bravery.'

'Well, did he offer it?' asked Rhuzbeh.

'He was delighted to receive the aspand, but then he tied me to a stout pillar, and with great ceremony, he chopped off my thumb as a punishment for participating in religious rituals of the priests. He then threw my thumb into a bubbling cauldron. I watched as the skin on my severed thumb peeled away and my bone floated in that cauldron even as blood oozed from my hand,' Dahel winced while recollecting the incident and went quiet momentarily.

'So what was the next task?' asked Rhuzbeh.

'When my wound had healed, Isvil sent me on my second task, which was to fetch ticks that feed off aurochs.'

'Aurochs?' asked Rhuzbeh.

'Aurochs is a variety of large wild cattle. Just to give you some perspective, an aurochs is more than ten times the weight of the scrawny self that I was. It has formidable horns and a very mean temper. Taming an aurochs is a task for heroes. Aurochs is more feared and revered than lions.'

Rhuzbeh gasped and asked, 'Did you battle an aurochs?'

'Ha! ha!' laughed Dahel, explaining, 'I said I was scrawny, not dumb. I tried to sneak up on an aurochs and pick ticks, only to be charged at by the beast. I ran and hid behind a tree. But the angry aurochs hit the tree with such force that I was flung to the ground. Quickly, I came up with an idea. I had once watched Isvil tame a peacock by giving it a potion he had concocted—one that worked only on birds—and then coercing it to do his biddings. I stole the concoction from him. If I couldn't get close to the aurochs, then the idea was to find someone who could. I could only think of one such creature that the aurochs tolerated—egrets. So I trapped a few cattle egrets—white birds that sit on top of the cattle and pick off ticks and other insects.

It is a symbiotic relationship. The egrets get to eat ticks, and the aurochs get rid of the troublesome parasites. Egrets also hitch a ride on the aurochs if they feel fancy.

Anyway, I fed the potion to the egrets and instructed the birds to drop the ticks they picked from the aurochs' body into a small container that I had. Once the container was full of ticks, I returned to Isvil. This time I knew that he had no reason to punish me.'

'And did he?' asked Rhuzbeh.

'Oh yes!' replied Dahel. 'He asked me how I managed to get the ticks, and when I told him, he cornered me by asking how I had managed to make the egrets do my bidding. I had no answer and Isvil immediately knew that I had stolen his potion. So he tied me to the pillar once again and chopped off one more finger.'

Dahel sighed, sadness writ large on his face.

'What a cruel and heartless man!' remarked Rhuzbeh, who then asked, 'What was your third task?'

'I had just turned seventeen when Isvil assigned me my third task—getting a strand of hair from a virgin's head. My search took me to a nearby village, but I did not know what to do next. If I went around asking girls if they were virgins, I was sure to get lynched. I sat down in the village square, watching people go about their daily chores. That is when I spotted a simple village girl, frail and vulnerable-looking. As she passed by, she looked at me and smiled and my heart lurched. Nobody had ever looked at me like that. Till I figured out my next move, I decided to pass my time there as a labourer doing odd chores in exchange for food and small pay. Every day she would pass by and smile at me.'

He continued, 'One day, as she walked by carrying a pail of water, the girl stopped and offered me some. We got talking and over the next few days, she gradually grew fond of me. I learnt that she was an orphan. Soon she began to secretly get bread and meat from the orphanage for me. Slowly, we fell in love with each other. She was slightly younger than me and the only soul who ever really loved me. I felt safe confiding in her, telling her everything about myself, except that I was on a quest for a strand of a virgin's hair.'

'Did you tell her that you were a sorcerer? Was she shocked?' asked Rhuzbeh.

'Yes, I told her I was a sorcerer,' said Dahel. 'And no, she was not shocked. As a matter of fact, she was delighted when I revealed that I was a sorcerer. Her life was mundane and dull and the thought of being with a sorcerer excited her. One day, while we were sitting behind a large stone in a deserted place, I held her hand and asked if she had ever made love to a man. Her cheeks turned red, she blushed and shook her head. Taking that as a cue, I plucked out a strand of her hair and tucked it in my pouch. She was puzzled and looked at me quizzically.'

'I told her that I wanted something personal to remember her by. She was delighted and hugged me, and then we made love. I went back to Isvil and gave him the strand of hair. Isvil was quick to pounce on me and asked how I was sure that it had belonged to a virgin. I was forced to tell him the whole story. Isvil immediately got upset and said that I had ruined the source now and how we could have gotten more strands from her in the future. And with that as an excuse, he cut off another of my fingers,' he further stated.

'That was a lovely story, and it is a pity that it had to end like that,' said Rhuzbeh.

'But my love story did not end there,' said Dahel mysteriously. 'Rather, that was only its beginning. I was not a boy anymore; I had been with a girl. I felt like a man now. Something in me snapped. I couldn't take it anymore. In my anger, I told Isvil, "You keep sending me on errands just to find faults and chop off my fingers. If fingers are all you want, then take them." Upon saying that, I myself chopped off the remaining fingers from my left hand. When Isvil recovered from his shock, he said, "As a reward, your hand will not look mutilated. I shall fix long bear claws in place of fingers, and henceforth, you shall be addressed as Dahel the Bearclaw".'

Saying this, Dahel swiped across the table with his hand, knocking everything down, and revealed a grotesque bear's claw. Rhuzbeh stepped back in fear.

'And how did you become a greater sorcerer than Isvil?' asked Rhuzbeh.

'I had to go through what Isvil never had to,' answered Dahel. 'I was not moved by what Isvil had done, and as soon as he granted me these bear claws, I struck him and knocked him out. I then proceeded to pick up a knife and cut his head off and hung it on a pike inside the house. When a sorcerer dies, his powers inhabit another living person. But if a sorcerer is murdered, the powers do not inhabit the murderer. Isvil's powers left the body and swished around like a tornado, seeking release. I shut the doors and windows to prevent the powers from escaping. Since I could not harness Isvil's power, I went back to the village and brought the peasant girl back to his house. As the only living person in the room apart from me, Isvil's powers inhabited her. I renamed her Daheli and married her.

My fame spread far and wide. I had killed one of the greatest sorcerers ever known. I was a capable sorcerer with a respectable knowledge of spells, but I was no match for Daheli. She painstakingly and lovingly taught me everything she knew instinctively from Isvil's powers. After I had learnt the finer details of sorcery from Daheli, I travelled around the world, learning and practising some of the most dreaded dark magic under the tutelage of various masters. I learnt secret dark spells and even indulged in acts of sorcery like trapping a djinn to make it do my biddings.'

Dahel's narrative was in full flow now, and he bragged, 'Even if I come across a more powerful sorcerer, he can't kill me. I am invincible!'

'And why is that?' asked Rhuzbeh.

Dahel looked at him with shifty eyes and replied, 'I would not normally tell anyone else, but you—my harmless, stout spice merchant—I shall.' He laughed and continued, 'I cannot be killed because I have stored my magical powers in this black cat.' Dahel pointed to a small black cat with evil green eyes. 'If someone wanted to kill me, they would have to kill that cat first. Without the cat, I would have no powers and would then become easy to kill,' he said.

'Where is Daheli, the powerful dark sorceress?' asked Rhuzbeh.

'Daheli, although one of the greatest dark sorcerers of our times, is currently travelling to different kingdoms to seek and acquire more power, as all sorcerers normally do,' Dahel replied.

Suddenly, Rhuzbeh saw white lambs walk into the room, 'What are these lambs doing inside the house?' he asked.

'They are not lambs,' replied Dahel. 'They are actually maidens. Do you want to see how I changed maidens into lambs?' Dahel asked.

'Yes, I would like to see that,' replied Rhuzbeh.

'Let me show you, you fat villager! I shall make you a fat sheep to be roasted on a spit!' The sorcerer sneered and cast a spell on Rhuzbeh, who clenched the gajmuk tightly, leading the spell to immediately bounce back.

Rhuzbeh stood up and declared, 'To the fear that creeps up on me, hear me loud—I am Rhuzbeh, the Fearless. Like the dew that slides off the grass blades, your sorcery cannot impact my personage, for I bear the gajmuk, the sorcerer's bane!' Saying this, he took out his frog belt and flung it around Dahel's neck. The sorcerer almost choked.

Having captured Dahel, Rhuzbeh went around his cottage releasing the djinns he had imprisoned in lamps and bottles. He forced Dahel to overturn spells and converted the lambs back into maidens. However, despite everything Rhuzbeh did, Dahel refused to part with the knowledge of where the key to the cormorant was hidden. Left with no other option, Rhuzbeh walked to the cat and wrung its neck, killing it instantly. Dahel went limp, no longer a powerful sorcerer. He meekly handed over the key to Rhuzbeh. Now that Dahel was harmless, Rhuzbeh spared his life and left him to wallow in his misery.

With the key in his hand, Rhuzbeh walked to where the cormorant was, unlocked the clamp and cut off the leather band in one swift motion. Now that the bird was free, it immediately dived into water, transformed into a small fish and swam away. The gus whale, which was watching this entire incident, blew out great spurts of water in gratitude, once again calling out to Rhuzbeh to follow it on his boat. The whale nudged the boat a little further into the ocean and slowly and ceremoniously circled the little vessel seven times. Then it approached Rhuzbeh, opened up its huge mouth and produced a peach-coloured waxy ball. It was the fabled gus ambergris! The whale dropped the ball into Rhuzbeh's outstretched hands, leaving him overwhelmed. No human in known history had received the gus ambergris directly from a gus whale.

Rhuzbeh thought to himself that he was an ordinary man—a lonely orphan at that—but once he ingested gus ambergris, he would be destined for power and glory. With this knowledge, he rowed back to the town, proceeded to the town square and announced that he, Rhuzbeh, had rendered the sorcerer powerless. The townsfolk were grateful to him for releasing the maidens and gathered money to pay him. They ceremoniously presented the prize money to him for ridding the town of the evil sorcerer.

'This money is unworthy of a hero like you, but this is all we have. Please do accept it,' said a village elder as he presented the generous sum of money to Rhuzbeh.

'Ridding the town of the sorcerer is a reward in itself,' said Rhuzbeh politely.

'May your breath be warm!' blessed the village elder. 'You would honour us by accepting this money.'

Rhuzbeh politely refused thrice, and in response to the fourth request, he graciously accepted the reward. He also asked for a cup of rosewater. He added a small portion of gus ambergris into the rosewater and drank. He consumed a little every day until he finished the last drop—gus ambergris would run in his blood and that of his progeny.

He spent a fortnight in the town, but the gus whale splashed around as if it still wanted him to follow. With the money he had won, he bought a sturdy boat with masts, packed food and water and sailed back to the sea. The gus whale led him back to the middle of the ocean and disappeared. He was flummoxed. He sailed on for three days, not knowing where he was heading. On the third night, there was a hurricane accompanied by thunder and lightning. Between flashes of light he saw a form slithering in the water towards his boat. To his horror he realised that it was a giant sea serpent. The serpent crept up to the boat and coiled up to the mast. Rhuzbeh was petrified, he shrank to one corner of the boat, closed his eyes and prayed fervently. There was nothing he could do, if he jumped into the water the sea would kill him, if he remained on board the sea serpent would. The creature, however, remained coiled around the mast, as if protecting the boat against the storm, with its hissing matching that of the winds. Rhuzbeh kept his eyes shut tightly and did not realise when he drifted into a deep sleep. The next day, when the winds subsided and the sun rose, he woke up and hoped that it was all a nightmare. A chill ran up his spine when he saw the serpent coiled up against the boat and soaking up the sun. Something about its demeanour made Rhuzbeh calm down. He looked at the creature closely for the first time. Its body was covered in green and blue scales, and it had sharp tooth-like ridges running the entire length of its back. However it was its face and eyes that gave away its age. It looked ancient and almost benign. As he ran his gaze across its body, he noticed the spear stuck behind its neck. The serpent looked at Rhuzbeh with imploring eyes as if it wanted Rhuzbeh to remove that bothersome spear. With great trepidation, Rhuzbeh climbed up the mast of the boat and extended his hand towards the great beast. As if on cue, the serpent moved its neck closer. Its muscles rippled, and its armour-like scales glistened in the sunshine. He wondered what spear could pierce through the skin of the mighty beast. There was a large wound, and pus had formed near the spear tip. Rhuzbeh reached out and held the embedded spear with both hands. He gently placed a leg on its body for balance and, with a mighty heave, pulled out the spear. Blood gushed from the serpent's body as Rhuzbeh triumphantly held up the spear with a green crystal tip to examine it. The creature immediately grabbed the spear with its mouth, snapped it in two and threw the pieces in the water.

The Ajda shook and trembled as it said, 'Stay with me for some time.'

'Sure! But...I can understand you,' said Rhuzbeh, surprised.

'Yes, you can,' said the Ajda, adding, 'Gus ambergris runs in your veins, so you can understand me.'

'I have never seen or heard of a creature such as you. Are you a snake?' asked Rhuzbeh.

'I am the Ajda or the Ajdaha. I am related to the marids and I hark back to the time of the jann lord, Ammuna,' said the ancient creature. 'When I was small, I was caught by a sorcerer who experimented with me. He took me out of the ocean and, using his dark magic and potions, bound me to him. He would conduct strange rituals on me. He made me mate with vile, evil creatures who bit me and injected me with their venom. I was filled with hatred and longed to bite other creatures. Wherever I went, I left a trail of death. Birds, animals, any living thing that crossed my path, I would kill it. The sorcerer was working with assassins; he would direct me to kill other men. My first victim was a merchant. One night, when he was sleeping, I slithered under his door, crept up the bed and slithered up his chest. When he woke up and saw me, he was terrified. I struck and killed him. The second time the sorcerer sent me to kill a person, I did the same, except I also killed his entire family including his wife, toddler and dog. I was growing larger and stronger. My next victim was a powerful chieftain. By now, I was so strong that I broke open a wooden door by coiling around the door lock. I raised my body to the same height as the man's. I stood in front of him at eye level and bit him so hard that his skull broke open. When I went back to the sorcerer, he was alarmed at my ferocity. He wanted to cage me but I was having none of that. I was so consumed by my fury that I tore his body apart. Even as I grew stronger and larger, I was a creature of water and living on land was taking its toll on me. I had a burning sensation in me, as though my body was on fire. I could not take it anymore and attempted to kill myself many times. I would bite myself and pass out, or I would tear off chunks of my own body. Fortuitously, one day I met a ghoul in snake form and attacked her. But the djinn managed to fend me off and calm me down. She took pity on me and brought me to the djinn city of Afra-Zun. There, amidst all the splendour, the djinn led me to the moat of Afra-Zun and left me in the water. I had never experienced living in water before. The water's cooling effect immediately relaxed me. The next few days, I would lazily swim around, sit on the rocks and bask in the sunshine.

There were other water snakes there in the moat and I would coil around them and feel safe. During a particularly bad episode of shaking and trembling, Zoa came up to me and sang melodiously. I stared admiringly at the bewitching creature as it crooned a song that was so soothing that my body started to heal.'

'What is Zoa?' asked Rhuzbeh.

'Zoa was the most beautiful jewel of Afra-Zun,' Ajda replied. 'A creature of the sea so beautiful that the king of djinns created three beautiful gems, called sanaa, to entice it. Zoa was lured using these irresistible gems from the ocean to the moat of Afra-Zun. The three sanaa were sealed in three corners of the moat, and since Zoa was irresistibly drawn to them, it remained a willing inmate of the moat, thus enhancing the beauty of Afra-Zun.'

'What happened next?' asked a wide-eyed Rhuzbeh.

Ajda continued, 'Moving in water was easier and kept my body cool. Being in my natural element I started growing large. But since I was growing larger than the moat, I made a secret opening in it that led to the sea. I would venture into the open sea to catch fish and quite soon, I became adept at it. One day, a war broke out amongst the various factions of the djinns, and to my utter horror, someone killed Zoa. While dying in agony, Zoa cursed the city of Afra-Zun, due to which it started to crumble. The moat waters became black and poisoned. I was afraid that the city's ruins might fall and bury the moat.

I owed the djinns a debt of gratitude, and so I wanted to restore the sanaa to them. I broke open the three underwater cages that contained the sanaa, put the gems safely in my mouth and headed for the open sea. The death of Zoa had poisoned the water and almost all the creatures in the moat were dying. By the time I escaped and reached the open sea, I had passed out. When I woke up, I realised that I had dropped the two sanaa somewhere in the ocean and there was only one left in my mouth. I searched for the other two but in vain. I have been searching for many years for the right human who could pass on the sanaa to the djinns and break the curse. I am old—almost ancient—and feared that I would never find someone to carry forth the sanaa. Then you came along with gus ambergris cruising through your veins. To make things more certain, a great gus whale itself led me to you. Can you do me a favour? Can you pass the sanaa on to the djinns?'

Saying this, Ajda opened its mouth wide, revealing a sanaa gem stuck to one side. Rhuzbeh summoned all his courage and put his head inside the serpent's mouth. He avoided its perilous yellow fangs and plucked out the sanaa with all his strength. Ajda gave out a sigh of relief upon being relieved of its burden. Rhuzbeh then proceeded to examine the ruby-red dancing pearl and immediately fell in love with it.

The serpent, who knew the power of the sanaa, warned him, 'Do not look at it for you will fall in love and will not be able to part with it. I stuck it at the side of my mouth so as to avoid ever having to look at it.'

Rhuzbeh quickly put it in a pouch and tied it to his frog belt. Ajda bade him goodbye and slunk back into the ocean.

After sailing uneventfully for a while, Rhuzbeh reached a small town. He decided to halt his sea journey and stay in the town for some time. It was a frontier town, with forests on the fringes. After resting and regaining his strength, Rhuzbeh did not know what to do next and began to get restless. He woke up every day, went hunting in the forests, prepared a meal and took a nap at noon. His evenings were spent chit-chatting with the locals. Having no aim in life, he felt irrelevant and started losing his self-worth.

And isn't that the problem with heroes? Without an adversary to fight and hapless people to protect, heroes feel irrelevant, pointless even. Heroes are defined by their opponents—the more formidable the opponents, the more potent are the heroes. So rather than defining the hero by his own merit, heroism is relative. If a man killed a small poisonous snake, he would be applauded for a minute. If he slew a lion, he would be spoken of for years. If he slew a dragon, generations would talk about him.

The other thing about being a hero is that every spectator has a different sense of what is right. A hero in the eyes of one could be a murderer in the eyes of another. By that logic, one man's hero may not be another man's hero. A mongoose is a hero when it is fighting against a cobra, and when there is no cobra, it is just a rodent—a pest.

A snake is poisonous and can kill. A lion is dangerous and can tear you apart. And a dragon is fearsome and can burn you to ashes. And a hero that kills them becomes part of the folklore.

But has someone asked the snake's mate, the lion's cub, or the dragon's worshippers what they think of this hero?

More importantly, has someone asked a person living with a hero constantly? Imagine being reverential every time you see or talk to them forever. It is impossible! Once the awe fades, you see a hero as an average person. Peace and normalcy relegates a hero to the crowds of commoners going about their daily chores.

Rhuzbeh stayed on for a month. Slowly as the hero was getting familiar, his neighbours asked him to join them in their daily chores. Rhuzbeh decided to leave the town and continue his journey. He was told that beyond the forests were unknown lands with unknown people, and even further were the forbidden lands of the centaurs, simorghs, djinns and other magical creatures.

CHAPTER 3

The Ruins of Afra-Zun

Dark and light,
With meek and might;
Clad and naked,
With raw and baked;
Peace and violence,
With song and silence.
– *Ode to Afra-Zun, a name accompanied by a sigh.*

The confounded cuckoo's love poems are guilty of murdering innumerable noon slumbers. Rhuzbeh was a victim. One warm, sultry noon, as Rhuzbeh lay under a cypress tree, he was woken up by the perpetual calls of the cuckoo. The handsome fellow, with a pale grey beak and inquisitive crimson eyes, was covered in glossy blue-black feathers.

Rhuzbeh was irritated with the cuckoo bird's song, which increasingly became repetitive and urgent. He tried to shoo away the bird, but it remained firm in its resolve. It turned its back to Rhuzbeh with a contemptuous, sly glance and continued to coo in increasing tones of desperation—its lovelorn calls went unrequited.

This continued for two more days until Rhuzbeh could not take it anymore and he let fly an arrow. The arrow missed the bird; and the feathered scoundrel, unfazed, took flight and settled down on another tree.

Rhuzbeh went after the cuckoo in murderous rage—it was man versus a male bird in heat. Before he could let fly another arrow, the feathered creature flew away.

Rhuzbeh came back to the town and slept in relief. However, the very next day the cuckoo made another appearance. It was as if the bird was mocking him. He could take it no more. He resolved to kill the bird. This was the opportunity he was looking for—the perfect excuse Rhuzbeh needed to get back on the road.

It is not uncommon that the gravity of an impending task pins a person down, and then, all it takes to get one back on track are cuckoo calls. He packed his things, procured a horse, wore his gajmuk-mounted wristband, tied the pouch containing the sanaa to his frog belt, slung his bow and arrow, and left for the jungle.

'The cuckoo's days are numbered,' mumbled Rhuzbeh to himself. But it was easier said than done. The crafty deceiver of crows always seemed to be a step ahead of its pursuer. As the days passed, the jungle grew dense and foreboding. Rhuzbeh lost track of the cuckoo, but he decided to continue his quest.

On and on he went until he could see djinns—mostly in the form of snakes and wild dogs. They left him alone as is the wont of djinns—they never disturbed you if you didn't disturb them. With gus ambergris running in his blood, he felt safe.

Finally, the jungle started thinning out and gave way to a barren and windy desert called the Forbidden Desert. Rhuzbeh stepped into the vast nothingness.

One does not merely enter the desert. The truth is that the desert swallows him, and if it could not digest him in its sands, it spits him out—Rhuzbeh had just been swallowed. No rustle of animals, no chirping of birds and no complaints of crickets. The only sound that could be heard was the howl of the desert winds.

With all sounds of other beings having ceased, Rhuzbeh suddenly felt alone. He needed to feel a warm being to dispel his solitude. He tightened the horse's reins and rubbed it for comfort; the horse responded with an understanding neigh. They suffered the day and huddled through the night. He felt trapped between the vast expanses of the sky and the sand. Sleep came in fits, and the morning sun brought back light and new worries.

To his horror, he realised that his waterskin had burst and that he had significantly less water left for himself and his horse. They journeyed through the day with the hot, dry wind blowing hard and the unforgiving sun radiating intense heat. At midnoon, they stopped to conserve their strength. Rhuzbeh drank the last drops of water and poured a few drops into the horse's mouth. The animal whinnied in protest. Rhuzbeh knew the water was little—he had heard it from the horse's mouth, if you will—unfortunately he could not help it. So he lay down, closed his eyes, covered his face from the noon sun and tried to sleep.

He wondered why there was no water in the desert. Did deserts miss the rain? It dawned on him that deserts did not miss the rain and that deserts did not want water. The desert valued itself and jealously guarded its identity. If it rained regularly and if there was water, it would not remain a desert.

That evening, the horse and the man continued their travel until both collapsed from thirst and fatigue.

Rhuzbeh rose the next day with the first rays of sun hitting the sand, lighting up the grains.

He noticed the sand grains for the first time. He picked one up and marvelled at it. He felt like he himself was a grain amidst a sea of sand. What if he was ignored and left to perish? Every grain of sand has its own journey and story which deserves to be told. He brushed the sand away and woke his tired and protesting horse. He mounted it and rode away. The hot sun was unbearable, and without food and water, the horse was greatly weakened. Just before noon, the horse gave up and collapsed. Rhuzbeh had to abandon it and keep moving or else he would be dead as well. By evening, he too collapsed out of thirst and hunger. To make the situation worse, it started getting darker, hot gusts of wind assailed him and he was enveloped in dust. The winds grew stronger, carrying voluminous mounds of sand with them and covered him like a sandy grave. Rhuzbeh thought, 'This is the end.'

Suddenly out of nowhere, a tall, handsome man appeared, donning a white cloak and grey hair. He seemed cheerful.

'Quite a howler, this storm,' he said, smiling at Rhuzbeh. The half-buried Rhuzbeh looked up with bewilderment and relief.

'Let's get you out of the sand,' said the cloaked stranger, dragging him out. He brushed the sand off and covered him with his cloak.

Rhuzbeh said, 'Thank you! If you hadn't come on time, I would have met with a sandy death.'

'Don't thank me. Thank the one who directs every grain of sand on and off you. I am but an instrument,' the stranger said with a low bow and offered a relieved Rhuzbeh food and water.

'The sandstorm does tend to be beautiful,' said the stranger with delighted eyes.

'Are you a djinn?' asked Rhuzbeh.

'Yes, I am a jann,' said the stranger. Rhuzbeh had heard about the janns, a type of djinn that helps humans in distress.

'Who are you and what madness beckons you to attempt crossing this barren sea of sand?' asked the stranger.

'I am Rhuzbeh, an orphan from Zanda. I have nothing! No mother whose tears to wipe dry, no wife to make love to, no son to raise and no daughter to indulge. I have nothing on me except responsibility. I have an object so transcendent that I care not about the sandy bowels of the desert. I must hand it over to the djinns, for it belongs to them and unto them must it be returned,' replied Rhuzbeh.

The jann smiled and said, 'Then head to the djinn city of Alainis, meet the great king of the janns, Amirast, and hand it over to him. Beware! It is not easy for a human to walk to the land of djinns: the path is fraught with danger. The lands of the centaurs and simorghs lie before the djinn lands.'

The jann stayed by Rhuzbeh's side till morning. Rhuzbeh was curious and asked the jann, 'Before I go to Alainis, tell me more about the djinns.'

'The word djinn means the unseen. Although most djinns look like humans, they can assume any form they like,' replied the jann. 'The ifrits project large and powerful bodies, the ghouls assume fearful bodies, the marids traverse the ocean as sea creatures, the janns and the silats look like tall humans. Most djinns choose the snake form to travel across forests as our great kin of yore did. Snakes and djinns are alike in many ways; both blend with the surroundings, and although dangerous, both are extremely secretive and prefer to live by themselves, seldom bothering anyone unless they bother them.

The hinns travel in dog form. Early dogs were not nocturnal; they would hunt during the day and sleep at night. Ever since the hinn started assuming the canine form, the canines started behaving like them. It was not a one-way process; the hinns increasingly started taking canine forms until it became their second nature.'

The jann then told Rhuzbeh all about the djinn cities such as Alainis, Tamiir, Qar, Afvasp and Vigildar. He spoke about various djinns that often clashed with each other. He spoke highly of the janns who clashed with the ghouls; other djinns like the marids, ifrits, silats, shiqs, nas nas and pilafs allied with any of the sides or remained neutral.

Rhuzbeh listened to stories about the djinn-folk till early morning and, when the sun rose, bid his companion goodbye. 'Walk straight ahead,' said the jann, adding, 'and by early evening, you will reach the ravines.'

'I can't thank you enough,' said Rhuzbeh.

The jann smiled and said, 'You walk in my eyes, travel safe!'

Rhuzbeh travelled on, and the desert soon gave way to grassy lands. Further on, he arrived at the ravines. Here he was met with an astounding sight—centaurs. Half-horse, half-human, they were burdened with human ambitions but free as animals. Centaurs actualise what every human dreams of—wild enough to gallop across the meadows and wise enough to construe the stars.

He could not believe his eyes. He saw several herds running amok. He inched closer carefully, as horses generally tend to be skittish. He need not have worried though as these centaurs were distracted. Two herds were at loggerheads, and currently, the lead centaurs were embroiled in a duel. A chestnut centaur with brown hair was facing off a black centaur with curly black hair. Rhuzbeh watched as if hypnotised as the centaurs pandered to their animal self. They lunged at each other: an amalgamation of skin and hide, a confluence of muscle. They reared up on their hind legs and attacked one another with their deadly hooves. Their loud grunts and shouts rent the air as they threw tree trunks and rocks at each other.

Rhuzbeh watched the fight with fascination. After it ended, he settled under a tree. To his surprise, he was approached by a centuaride. He saw her trotting towards him and was struck by the vision of loveliness. She was a mare with a glossy black coat that glistened in the setting sun. Above the mare's legs and abdomen, she was all girl: pale as a peach, with thick black tresses that rode the wind. Her cheeks, like roses, were flushed pink. To Rhuzbeh, she looked like a shower of petals blowing toward him.

She circled him haughtily with the arrogance of beauty before the ordinary. She raised her eyebrow imperiously and asked him, 'What are you doing here, human?'

Rhuzbeh smiled and replied, 'I am here just to behold your beauty before I die.'

She blushed and said, 'Continue talking like this, and you will surely die.'

'I am on a mission,' said Rhuzbeh. 'I have something that belongs to the djinns, and I must return it to them.' She looked at him from head to toe for the first time, taking an interest in him.

'We could do with some company tonight,' she said. 'My name is Farmin. Join us for dinner and tell us more about yourself.'

Rhuzbeh accepted the offer and sat down with the centaurs. They were good listeners. He noticed both the chestnut and the black centaur sitting peacefully in different circles, tending to their wounds. The centaurs loved to talk. Turning to Farmin, he asked her, 'Has the fight ended? Who is the winner?'

'A centaur duel lasts for nearly a week,' replied Farmin. 'The contenders start their fight at twilight and when the sun sets fully, they stop fighting. The winning alpha takes over the loser's herd and impregnates all the centaurides that do not have a partner. But most fights are largely inconclusive, and these fights are also an excuse for the alphas to let off steam and impress potential centaurides.'

Every evening after the fight, they would gather and share stories. Centaurs were surprisingly intelligent and highly knowledgeable about astrology and astronomy. Thanks to Tasia, he had acquired limited knowledge about the stars. As soon as he thought of Tasia, he felt a twinge of guilt for he had deserted her, a woman who truly loved him. Regardless, he impressed the centaurs with his knowledge and shared his adventures with them; he spoke of his travels, strange islands and magical creatures. He spoke about how the gus whale had guided him to the sea and the sea serpent that had given him a sanaa pearl to hand over to the djinns. There was an uneasy silence.

There was no love lost between the centaurs and the djinns. In fact, both the groups had clashed numerous times in the past, with the djinns getting the better of the centaurs.

The centaurs were great at metallurgy; they had a fine metal called zer. The metal was lustrous like gold and as tough as steel. Despite being prodigious with metalwork, the centaurs would never use weapons against a fellow centaur. It was considered a mark of cowardice to use weapons against each other. After a week of fighting, the centaur duel ended in a draw. As Rhuzbeh began to bid them goodbye, he asked them to spend more time in the pursuit of knowledge.

At this, the chestnut alpha, whose name was Farda, took offence. He snorted and said, 'A human hectoring us about our way of life... This is us and this is what we are!'

'I apologise,' said Rhuzbeh. 'I meant no offence.'

'I'd challenge you to a one-on-one duel, but since that would not be fair as centaurs are much stronger than humans, I propose a game.'

'A game?' asked Rhuzbeh. 'What sort of a game do you propose?'

Farda explained, 'The game is about retrieving two ribbons, one placed anywhere by your choice and one by my choice. Both of us would have a common starting point. The one who retrieves both the ribbons first is the winner.'

Rhuzbeh went quiet.

'Sounds fair,' said the black centaur, who was within earshot. 'Although violent, there would be no bloodshed in the game.'

'This is not fair!' Rhuzbeh said. 'I can never be as fast as him.'

Farda was offended and said, 'Let it not be said that I, Farda, was unfair! This is what I propose: instead of two ribbons, let there be three ribbons placed anywhere, two ribbons located as per this human's choice and only one as per mine. If I retrieve all three ribbons, I win and if this human retrieves even one ribbon, he wins. I am faster, so I will even allow him to mount any centaur he deems fast enough. You see, I am more than fair! I have but one condition. If I lose, I shall give away my ancestral *zer* sword. If you lose, you shall give me the sanaa gem you carry.'

There was a hushed silence. Rhuzbeh said, 'The sanaa is not mine to give—I cannot accept the bet.'

His answer angered Farda, who reared up and said, 'I put myself at a disadvantage, I offered that you could ride any centaur you choose, I bet one of the finest swords ever made—an ancient family heirloom—and yet, you declined the offer! You are not Rhuzbeh the Fearless. You shall be known as Rhuzbeh the Coward, turning tail at the slightest sign of a challenge. Begone coward! Take your false tales of bravery and valour with you!'

Saying this, Farda spat on the ground. All the other centaurs looked at Rhuzbeh with disdain for they valued bravery and looked down on cowards. Farda's offer was more than fair; it was heavily tilted in his opponent's favour. Rhuzbeh felt like a braggart who had spun fanciful tales about his adventures and was backing out of a challenge.

He gave in and said, 'I accept your terms!'

A smile appeared on Farda's face.

Farda said, 'So be it! We shall play the game tomorrow before sundown.'

Rhuzbeh approached Farmin and said, 'I don't know any centaurs here, and I can't trust anyone. With your permission, can I mount you?' he asked.

She blushed and replied, 'Yes! You can.'

Rhuzbeh mounted her, and they were off like the wind. Farmin did not stop until she was far away from the ravines. They spent the night under the blanket of twinkling stars. When they returned fresh in the morning, they were one.

As the sun simmered down, the centaurs gathered around to witness this historic game. Both Farda and Rhuzbeh, sitting astride Farmin, reported to the field. As the game began, Rhuzbeh gracefully said, 'I would like you to place the first ribbon at a location of your choice.'

Farda accepted and tied the ribbon to a bough of an oak tree standing straight ahead at approximately three hundred gallops. Both the contenders had a common starting point. The horn sounded, signalling the start. The centaur and centauride lunged ahead. Farda pulled alongside and gave a mighty heave crashing into Farmin with a sickening crunch.

But Farmin, with Rhuzbeh sitting astride, could not be pushed aside because of their combined weight.

They were now riding side by side. Rhuzbeh said, 'Farmin, part away. Since we are heavier, let us give him a taste of his own medicine.'

Farmin parted to create momentum and, with one mighty heave, bumped into Farda, sending him crashing. Rhuzbeh let out whoops of joy while Farmin strutted towards the ribbon. It was all too easy. Just before they could grab it, Farda galloped at full speed, leapt in the air and plucked the ribbon from the tree like a hawk that snatches its prey. He was simply too fast; Farmin, burdened by the stout Rhuzbeh, was no match for him.

Rhuzbeh was crestfallen. Farmin tried her best to cheer him up by saying, 'It's okay. We might yet win; there are two more chances. Remember, all you have to do is win once!'

'We can't win against him,' said Rhuzbeh. 'He is simply too fast.'

'That's true,' said Farmin. 'If you can't outrace him, then outfight him!'

So they came up with a new strategy for the next day's dash.

On the second morning, Farda said, 'Go on, place your ribbon.'

Rhuzbeh said, 'Thank you! Since this race is turning violent, can we both arm ourselves with wooden clubs?'

Farda agreed, and both the contenders, armed with heavy wooden clubs, assembled at a common starting point. As soon as the horn blew, Rhuzbeh turned Farmin and blocked Farda's way. A mighty tussle ensued, with both contenders matching blow for blow. Finally, Rhuzbeh used the same manoeuvre that had brought the mighty elephant down. He used his frog tongue belt to latch onto Farda's torso and jumped onto the centaur's back. In his zeal to execute the idea, he was oblivious to the fact that the centaur had a human torso with hands; Farda simply turned, picked Rhuzbeh with both hands and dropped him to the ground. He would have trampled Rhuzbeh had not Farmin interfered and heroically saved him. Meanwhile, Farda galloped away and, in one mighty leap, picked the ribbon.

By now, beating Farda looked impossible. Rhuzbeh was crestfallen. He told Farmin, 'This was a big mistake! I cannot give away the sanaa! It is not mine to give away—I would be letting the gus whale and Ajda down. I am worried and nervous.'

'Don't give up!' Farmin said. 'There is one more race. If you win, you not only save the sanaa but also win the zer sword of Farda.'

In order to win, one should be a winner in one's own eyes. It is in the mind that the first battle is fought, and most fights are lost in the mind before they even begin on the ground. Rhuzbeh had already lost the race in his mind.

It was day three. Farda bowed low to Rhuzbeh and gloatingly said, 'Mighty Rhuzbeh, place your ribbon anywhere you please!'

Rhuzbeh chose to tie his ribbon to the branches of a pomegranate tree two hundred gallops away. By now, Farda was aware of Rhuzbeh's strategy. Rhuzbeh could not outrace him, so he would try to block and battle him. Both contenders took positions at the starting point. As soon as the horn sounded, instead of charging ahead, Farda peeled away to the left in a sharp turn and started galloping swiftly. He cleverly approached the ribbon in a roundabout direction. Rhuzbeh charged straight ahead; he now had a lead on Farda. But once again, the faster Farda pipped Rhuzbeh and surged ahead to grab the ribbon in front of his outstretched hands—it was all over.

Farda was victorious. With great guilt and sorrow, Rhuzbeh handed over the sanaa to the centaurs. And so it was that for the second time in history, a sanaa gem was held by the centaurs. Farda was now a hero amongst the centaurs; he had managed to whisk one of the fabled sanaa gems away from the djinns. His name would be spoken in the same breath as that of his illustrious ancestor, Farsang. This raised his stature amongst the centaurs, and he gloated about it to the other alphas.

The black centaur was highly resentful and said, 'Had Rhuzbeh chosen me, you would have never won.'

Farda haughtily replied, 'You can never outrace me. Watch out—your centuarides are going to be mine.'

Meanwhile, it was time for Rhuzbeh to leave. 'My eyes will miss the sight of you,' said Farmin. 'It pains me to see you sad—I wish I could do more.'

He hugged her and said, 'You did your best, Farmin! It was I who fell short.'

She wished him a teary farewell and said, 'Take the circuitous route to the djinn lands of Alainis and Tamiir. A word of caution, avoid the foggy mountains, as it is the domain of the simorghs.'

Rhuzbeh thanked her and left. That evening on the ravines, he lost two things: the sanaa and his honour.

Despite his disappointment, he was keen to see the legendary djinn cities. When he reached the fabled city of Alainis, he was met with a rich tapestry of sights and smells. Alainis was a jann city. The city was like a newly-wed bride, decked up and full of enthusiasm. It woke up with the eagerness of the young and let the sun drape its pathways, domes and towers with a golden hue. A city befitting the mightiest of djinns—the janns.

The janns moved around in human shape, slightly taller and draped in white robes. Their soldiers were dressed in white and gold and had a very strong sense of self-righteousness. The great jann king, Amirast, ruled over Alainis. Under his benevolent rule, the janns had prospered and were at their zenith. Amirast had heard about Rhuzbeh, a human with gus ambergris running in his veins and gajmuk on his personage. Amirast welcomed him warmly to the royal palace and made him sit in the royal hall of the kings.

'Great king, I thank you for this honour, but I am afraid I am not worthy of it!' Rhuzbeh said, his head hanging low.

'And why is that?' asked Amirast.

Rhuzbeh narrated his adventures of the gus whale and how Ajda had entrusted him with the sanaa. He informed them about the ill-fated contest and the loss of the sanaa to Farda, the centaur. The djinns listened in awe, and once he had completed his narration, Amirast said, 'I am highly impressed by you. You did your best. Thank you for coming back and letting us know, and do not worry; even if the issue is as daunting as a mountain, Ghanazaqi will move that mountain.'

Then he turned over to the greatest of djinn heroes, Ghanazaqi the Wise, and asked, 'Should we talk to the centaurs about the sanaa?' Ghanazaqi was not a jann—he was a silat. As a matter of fact, he was the Hakif of Silat.

Ghanazaqi looked at Amirast broodingly and said, 'No! They will never surrender the sanaa. They are proud and stubborn. Our ancestors have taught us that the centaurs' stubbornness leads to unnecessary bloodshed. We should instead find a better way to get the sanaa back through Rhuzbeh because the prophecy says that all three sanaa would have to be returned by humans and that only then will the city of Afra-Zun rise from its ruins. It is most remarkable that the gus whale chose

Rhuzbeh. Maybe it is through Rhuzbeh that we will retrieve the sanaa; his destiny is bound to ours.'

Amirast nodded and said, 'I leave this matter to your judgement. You are the wisest amongst us and I am confident that you will bring back the sanaa.'

Amirast invited Rhuzbeh to stay at his palace for a few days to recuperate from his travels. 'Be our guest, enjoy the hospitality of the janns of Alainis and the comforts of the palace. Relax and recuperate. Ghanazaqi will meet you soon and discuss how to get back the sanaa from the centaurs.'

Rhuzbeh thanked Amirast and Ghanzaqi and retired to his chambers. After a full night of rest, he rose up refreshed. He felt his aches, pains and disappointments wash away. He was surprised as to how well Amirast had taken the loss of the sanaa. He wondered who Ghanazaqi was and why Amirast had so much confidence in his abilities.

His curiosity got the better of him. He asked a palace help about Ghanazaqi. She smiled and said, 'Ghanazaqi the Wise, the Hakif of Tamiir and the Tamer of Xamaroof the Red, is perhaps one of the greatest heroes of the djinn world. He and his friend, Irash the Ifrit, are legends. Their tales are sung in the streets of djinn cities like Alainis, Tamiir, Qar, Afvasp and Vigildar.'

'Tell me more about Ghanazaqi,' implored Rhuzbeh.

'Ghanzaqi is a silat from the city of Tamiir and the silat are the wisest amongst the djinns. As a child, Ghanzaqi adopted Irash, a blue-coloured abandoned ifrit. Since Irash had no one, he looked up to Ghanazaqi as an elder brother and fondly called him Dadash. Although massive and powerful, ifrits are susceptible to being enslaved by humans. They are often trapped in lamps, rings and books by humans, where they spend a lifetime doing their biddings. Ghanazaqi is very protective of Irash. They grew up together as children, from competing in cockfights to running successful businesses together. Today, they supply the armour that the janns wear. They have partnered with Arborz, the legendary half-djinn armourer, to mass-produce the gold-like armour of the janns, which is actually made of a metal called *sheshamp*. They also control the hornhoney trade. Hornhoney is the staple food of the pilaf. The pilafs are greedy, hornhoney-loving djinns, who constantly slobber red saliva, thereby giving the impression that they drip blood. They have partnered with Pofis the Pilaf and own vast hornhoney farms. As Irash says, their fortune was built on the painful hornhoney bee stings inflicted on him in the early days.'

The help burst out laughing and said, 'The hornhoney bees have a painful sting, and Irash has developed a mortal fear after being bitten constantly at the start of their hornhoney business. There is no djinn city where the Ghanazaqi-Irash duo does not have any business interest. Ghanazaqi rose in stature when he converted Tamiir into a knowledge centre, recorded the history of djinns and created a repository of knowledge and know-how that all djinns could access. He famously stood against the elders who opposed the idea and declared, "If any being seeks knowledge and makes seeking knowledge his mission, let him blow like the dandelion seeds, let him glide unfettered without a goal, let him fly with the winds, let him plant in any place the wind takes and let him absorb from that soil. Let him inhale the wind, let him soak in the sun, let him germinate, let him grow so much that he develops the papus, or the proverbial white beard, and once again, like the fluffy dandelion seeds in multitudes, let him take to the winds." In recognition of his services, the silat of the city of Tamiir elevated Ghanazaqi to the role of Hakif—

which loosely translates as a guide or a quasi-ruler—much to the chagrin of Amirast.'

'But you also called Ghanazaqi the Tamer of Xamaroof the Red. Who is Xamaroof?' asked Rhuzbeh.

'Xamaroof the Red is a ghoul,' she said, adding, 'For generations, the ghouls and the janns have clashed with each other, and the clash between them is considered the classic good versus bad kind. However, it is much deeper than that. Xamaroof has earned the begrudging respect of his enemies for his old-world mannerism and chivalry. He shows mercy to the weak and defenceless, while he is ruthless with the oppressors. Although Xamaroof tries to keep to himself, Amirast considers him a rival. Ghanazaqi fell in love with Xamaroof's daughter, Xilana, a wicked ghoulan who spurned him. She treacherously tried to kill her own father, Xamaroof, with tacit support from Amirast. Ghanazaqi helped Xamaroof overthrow Xilana and earned the wrath of Amirast.

Ghanazaqi, the master tactician, knew well that Amirast was the overlord of the djinn world and quickly visited him in Alainis. He won Amirast over with his silver tongue and pledged to be his vassal. He also presented magical, impenetrable golden armour, made by Arborz, to Amirast, thereby winning his favour. Amirast accepted him as a vassal and recognized him as the Hakif of Tamiir. Amirast has grown to respect his counsel and considers him highly for his wisdom and intellect. Since he is trusted by both Amirast and Xamaroof, he helps to keep up the fragile peace in the djinn world.'

Rhuzbeh thanked the palace help and looked forward to meeting Ghanazaqi. The next day when he met him and Irash, he was overwhelmed. They spent a lot of time discussing Rhuzbeh's adventures.

Ghanazaqi rested his hands on Rhuzbeh's shoulders and said, 'We had lost all hope of getting back the sanaa. Surprisingly, we have never heard of a gus whale passing on the ambergris to a human willingly. Your destiny is bound to ours.'

Rhuzbeh said, 'Thank you, O Hakif of the Silat! I am but an orphan from a small village. I owe my name to the djinns, and if my destiny is tied to the rise of Afra-Zun, then I shall be honoured. I shall do all I can to retrieve the sanaa. Advise me, O wise Ghanazaqi! How can I beat Farda, the chestnut centaur?'

Ghanazaqi told Rhuzbeh to rest. Ghanazaqi thought about the contest the whole day and night and came up with a plan. When they met the next day, he said, 'Go back to Farda and challenge him one more time. Place your gajmuk as a bet; he will be tempted and will accept the contest. Once he accepts, let us execute our plan and win back the sanaa.'

Rhuzbeh protested and said, 'I don't want to lose the gajmuk as well. Farda is too fast. He will beat me this time as well.'

Ghanazaqi smiled mysteriously and said, 'If you do the same things, you will get the same result. Do not think from the same perspective. Change your perspective. Why should you go towards the ribbon? Why can't the ribbon come to you?'

Saying this, Ghanazaqi whispered the plan to Rhuzbeh. Feeling confident, Rhuzbeh went back to the centaurs and challenged Farda. He said, 'Farda! I challenge you to a race once again! If I lose, I shall give away my gajmuk, and in case you lose, I shall take back the sanaa.'

Farda was wary and refused to race against Rhuzbeh. 'You were beaten three times, and yet you are back, pledging another legendary stone. What are you up to?' he asked.

'I was entrusted with the sanaa,' said Rhuzbeh. 'And I must try and restore it to its true owners. Just give me one chance. We will race only one round; the winner takes what the other has. Unless you are a coward and want to back out.'

Farda reared up and said haughtily, 'If you want to lose your gajmuk, so be it! I shall happily take it off your hands. As a matter of fact, I shall even let you tie the ribbon wherever you want.'

That was exactly what Rhuzbeh wanted to hear. Meanwhile, Farmin was joyous to be reunited with Rhuzbeh. He mounted her, took the ribbon and, to everyone's surprise, tied the ribbon to the black centaur's hand. The black centaur held a grudge against Farda. He was Farda's rival and felt delighted to contribute to his defeat.

'You can't do this,' said Farda indignantly. 'This is not fair.'

Rhuzbeh reminded him of the rules of the game. '*The participant can tie the ribbon wherever he wants*—that is the rule of the game. Unless, of course, you are afraid! Then you can hand over the sanaa without a race.'

Farda muttered something grudgingly and arrived at the starting point. The horn sounded and the contest began. Once again, Farda peeled away to the left and started racing towards the black centaur. To his surprise and shock, as he reached out his hand to grab the ribbon from the black centaur, the latter galloped away. Farda followed in full pursuit. The black centaur went around a rock, closely followed by his chaser. Farmin was galloping hard to meet the black centaur in the middle. Farda had a sling with metal balls at both ends, which he rotated and flung at the black centaur's leg. The sling tangled around its legs, and the black centaur toppled and fell hard. But just before he hit the ground, he threw the ribbon in the air. Farda was close behind. Both Farmin and Farda jumped up in the air, facing each other to catch the ribbon. Farmin was burdened by the weight of Rhuzbeh, and hence the lighter Farda managed to leap higher. Farda was about to grasp the ribbon when Rhuzbeh whipped out his frog belt in the air and caught the ribbon. It was all over—Rhuzbeh and Farmin had won.

A disgruntled Farda handed over the sanaa back to Rhuzbeh. Rhuzbeh dismounted Farmin, and they hugged each other. Time seemed to stop. Farmin looked at him with imploring eyes and said, 'Now that your task is done, why don't you stay with us?'

Rhuzbeh wanted to move on. He said, 'Even if I so desire, I couldn't—my place is not amongst the centaurs.'

Farmin understood, for she too could not stay in the world of humans. With a heavy heart, she bade him goodbye. As he was leaving, she gifted him with a very rare zer sword—a blade mightier than even Farda's. 'I want you to hold on to something of mine,' she said. 'I wanted to see you win. Now you have won both the sanaa and this zer sword!'

He thanked her. 'The most precious thing I won in this ravine is your affection,' he continued. 'Alas! I have to leave it back here.'

After that emotional parting, Rhuzbeh returned to Alainis, and in front of the whole court, he ceremoniously handed over the sanaa to Amirast. So it was that Ghanazaqi the wise had guided Rhuzbeh to retrieve the first sanaa.

Amirast, the great jann king, was at his peak. He had suzerainty over all djinns and human kings who were aware of the djinns' existence. He wanted to create a legacy as the greatest djinn king ever by breaking the curse of Afra-Zun. Ghanazaqi, however, did not desire power; he merely wanted to see the djinns get back their legendary lost city.

Meanwhile, Amirast was also involved in a power struggle with his younger brother, Amstrap. Amirast doted on Amstrap.

As children, they had played together. Amstrap was a poetic diviner who advocated syncretic interactions among djinns and creatures of all hues. He was more inclined towards philosophy and mysticism rather than power and ruling a kingdom.

However, Amstrap had fallen in love with a beautiful jann called Awa, who belonged to a royal bloodline from the far north. She was extremely ambitious. She had wanted to marry Amirast, but since Amirast was already taken, she had married Amstrap. She goaded Amstrap to usurp power and depose Amirast. Amstrap loved his wife dearly, and so he reluctantly acquiesced to his wife's demand and rebelled against his brother.

Amirast called a council of war to discuss this problem. At one end, he had Xamaroof the Red, the ghoul chieftain, challenging his sovereignty and at the other end, he had Amstrap threatening his throne. Xamaroof the Red had refused to ally with Amstrap. The fight between janns did not bother him, and he just wanted to be left alone.

Amirast did not want any bloodshed, and he also loved his brother. Left to himself, Amstrap would never go to war against Amirast—it was Awa who was fomenting trouble. The djinns generally did not like violence, preferring to sort things out by reason, tact and, at worst, deceit.

Amirast once again turned to his friend and the wisest of djinns, Ghanazaqi, to sort out the issue. The latter devised a plan; he wanted to send Rhuzbeh into Amstrap's camp.

Amirast asked Ghanazaqi, 'Why send a human? Why not send one of our own?'

'An unidentified djinn walking into a war camp would look suspicious and might even be recognized as belonging to the enemy, whereas a human could unwittingly wander into the camp. Fortuitously, we have just the kind of human we need,' replied Ghanazaqi.

Ghanazaqi knew Amstrap's tastes and thus trained Rhuzbeh on various philosophical concepts before asking him to visit Amstrap's camp and engage with him. So Rhuzbeh visited Amstrap's camp as a wandering philosopher who was lost. The guards produced him before Amstrap. Rhuzbeh delighted Amstrap with his stories and philosophical knowledge. Amstrap, who had never had a human companion, much less someone who could discuss philosophy, spent so much time with Rhuzbeh that he forgot about the war. He would not even share his bed with Awa. He did not visit her tent, and he made Rhuzbeh share his tent.

Awa called the commanders and asked them, 'Why is there a delay in attacking the enemy?'

'Amstrap is busy with his philosophical indulgences, and we cannot attack without his permission,' they replied.

'Prepare for war! I will end this nonsense tomorrow!' thundered a visibly irritated Awa.

Ghanazaqi's spies warned him that Awa might try to kill Rhuzbeh. Ghanazaqi sent a message instructing Rhuzbeh to swap places with Amstrap that night. Awa soon realised that her power waned when she came close to Rhuzbeh, and so she could not kill him when he was awake. She could not murder him in the tent as he slept either, for that would make Amstrap angry. So, she came up with a plan—she would wrap him in his blanket as he slept and toss him in the river. He would drown, and his body would not be found. That way, Amstrap would presume that Rhuzbeh had slipped out at night and gone away.

Meanwhile, Rhuzbeh persuaded Amstrap to exchange his bed with him as a philosophical experiment. Amstrap indulged him. Awa wanted to kill Rhuzbeh personally. So that night, she placed the guards loyal to her as sentries. At midnight, she sent off the sentries and entered the royal tent. She saw a royal bed and an ordinary bed. She went to the ordinary bed, wrapped the person in his blanket and threw him into the river.

Rhuzbeh followed her with a company of jann soldiers, quickly rescued Amstrap and caught her red-handed in the attempt to kill Amstrap. The latter could not kill Awa as he loved her; so he banished her instead. When king Amirast heard the news, he visited his brother to console him and brought him back to Alainis. And so it was that Ghanazaqi, the wisest of the djinns, had helped Amirast secure his throne the djinn way. It was clever. There was deceit involved but there was no bloodshed.

Amirast was highly grateful to Ghanazaqi and promised him the hand of his daughter, Princess Ameira, if he succeeded in guiding Rhuzbeh to retrieve the second sanaa. As a gesture of gratitude and with Ghanazaqi's permission, he handed over his golden body-armour that was made by Arborz to Rhuzbeh and said, 'Take this. No ordinary weapon can pierce through this armour. Only a weapon made from powerful magic can penetrate this armour, making the wearer almost invincible in battle. This armour is for you and your descendants as an acknowledgement of your great service to Amirast—the king of janns.' He also handed Rhuzbeh gold and silver pieces as a reward.

It was time for Rhuzbeh to leave, and he departed with a promise to do his best to retrieve the remaining sanaa.

Many years later, when Rhuzbeh's fame would've spread far and wide, and he'd have become a legend among the djinns, he would be called upon as a witness during the swearing-in ceremony of the djinn book of laws, *Za Habab Za Ha*.

Chapter 4

The Sins of Rhuzbeh

Humans are like dust. After swirling around, they eventually settle down.

Rhuzbeh, now rich and famous, returned to Zanda to settle down. He had the gus ambergris flowing in his veins, and owing to his travels, he had secured the fabled gajmuk from the ocean-faring elephants, the zer sword from the centaurs and the golden armour from Amirast. He also wore his frog-tongue belt over his attire.

Meanwhile, King Kashan, who had been taken prisoner by the Hatasans after his failed attempt at overpowering their mountain city, died in a Hatasan prison. Since the Hatasans did not annex Zanda, a Zandian general called Zogdu went on to murder a loyal minister who was the king regent and usurped the throne.

Kashan's son, the rightful heir, was held captive and confined to his chambers under the watchful eyes of Zogdu's guards.

Zogdu was not a Zandian. He was born in the Northern kingdom. He had enrolled in the services of Kashan and risen to the rank of a general.

Fame travels faster than a pony, and Rhuzbeh's fame preceded his arrival. The wealth and magical objects on his person only confirmed his rumoured exploits. The people of Zanda were overjoyed when they heard about the return of their hero and thronged to see him. But all Rhuzbeh wanted to do was eat and sleep like a bear. After nearly three months of rest, Rhuzbeh felt that the tiredness had wrung away from his body like water from a cloth.

Meanwhile, the ordinary citizens clamoured to remove Zogdu and replace him with their rightful king—the young son of King Kashan. Zogdu sought legitimacy, and he decided that getting endorsed by a hero would elevate his position amongst his subjects. He called on Rhuzbeh to swear fealty to him publicly. Rhuzbeh, although powerful, could not take on the entire Zandian army that was at Zogdu's disposal. He had no choice but to oblige.

When Rhuzbeh arrived at the court to pay his respects and swear fealty to the tyrant, Zogdu was sitting on a throne, and placed behind him was the crest of an eagle with outspread wings that was accompanied by a serpent in its talons. In the presence of the Zandian citizenry, Zogdu ordered Rhuzbeh, saying, 'Kneel before me and swear fealty to me.' Rhuzbeh kneeled in front of Zogdu, kissed his ring finger and said, 'I am at your service, Regent of Zanda.'

Zogdu said, 'Rise and be my general, and as you served King Kashan with loyalty and bravery, so shall you serve me!' So it was that Rhuzbeh once again joined the Zandian army, this time as a general. The ceremony was a rousing victory for Zogdu as the Zandians looked on Rhuzbeh as a liberator.

Their hero had kneeled and sworn fealty to a tyrant. The citizens walked away, dejected.

Zogdu revelled at this meek capitulation of a renowned hero and took particular delight in tormenting Rhuzbeh. He mocked him by saying, 'Rhuzbeh the Fearless, through whose veins the gus ambergris flows, fetch me my wine.' Rhuzbeh seethed but had no choice but to oblige. Zogdu sent Rhuzbeh to collect taxes, and when a hamlet refused to pay their dues, he had Rhuzbeh torch it; the cries of the villagers would torment Rhuzbeh for a long time to come. Rhuzbeh was a hero, but he was also just a mortal. He could not fight an entire army. For the first time, he felt impotent. The Zandian court was seething at these insults being heaped upon their local hero. Zogdu was not a Zandian, and they looked upon his regency as an occupation. The renowned court mage, Metishin, who had served King Kashan as a mage, physician and counsel, called on Rhuzbeh and said, 'Bide your time. As the cycle of sun goes by, the tyrant shall fall.' One day, Zogdu called on Rhuzbeh and said, 'Ah! The brave Rhuzbeh—the conqueror of the centaurs and the beloved of the djinns—I have a task for you.'

'What can I do for the Regent of Zanda?' asked Rhuzbeh.

'The task I have for you is rather delicate and personal,' he replied. 'I want you to go and meet King Nahal from the Northern kingdom and ask for his daughter Naheira's hand for me. King Nahal is a Northerner like me, and any alliance between us would strengthen both of us.'

'Why me?' asked Rhuzbeh.

'Oh! I want to impress my future father-in-law,' replied a grinning Zogdu. 'Along with rich gifts, if a legendary hero were to propose the alliance, it would add weightage.'

Rhuzbeh had no choice but to oblige. So, he headed a huge caravan laden with rich gifts of gold, carnelian, lapis lazuli, silks and spices and headed to the Northern kingdom. When Rhuzbeh landed in the Northern kingdom laden with gifts, the citizens thronged to see him. Rhuzbeh saw the twin-headed eagle insignia everywhere.

When he reached King Nahal's court, the courtiers applauded Rhuzbeh.

'Welcome to the Northern kingdom,' said King Nahal. 'We have heard much about your exploits and are delighted to see you in person. Come, tell us with your lips. Our ears long to hear and affirm what we already know is true in our hearts.'

Rhuzbeh regaled Nahal and his court with his heroic tales. When Rhuzbeh had finished, Nahal had a surprise for him. He laughingly said, 'Rhuzbeh, you might be a hero, but I stand like a stone wall between you and your destiny. I am the hero's bane.'

'What are you talking about?' asked a nonplussed Rhuzbeh.

Nahal gave a mysterious smile and took out a shiny red gem from the folds of his robes and held it up. It was round and brilliant red and danced in the palace lights. Nahal held up the second sanaa.

'I had to pluck the first sanaa from the mouth of a serpent and battle a centaur and yet I find the second sanaa in the robes of a friendly king,' said Rhuzbeh with a big grin.

Nahal looked at him and said, 'Yes! I have what you seek, but I cannot just give it to you. It was given to my ancestors by the great eagle and it shall remain in the Northern mountains.' Although disappointed, Rhuzbeh bowed and said, 'I understand. We all play our part and let the hand of destiny guide us. Let us proceed with the matter at hand. The regent of Zanda, Zogdu, would be delighted by your approval. I shall convey your sanction to him.'

'Before you do your duty as a carrier pigeon, bearing the news of the alliance, I must confide in you that I do not like that man,' said Nahal. 'As much as I hate giving my daughter to Zogdu, the fact is that he is from the North and that the alliance would make our kingdoms stronger. You must stay a little longer. My daughter, the beloved Princess Naheira, would like to hear about your adventures.' Rhuzbeh thanked the King and spent time with Princess Naheira, delighting her with his tales. Heroes and princesses make for a volatile combination, and Naheira soon flung caution to the wind and herself into her hero's willing arms. Rhuzbeh delighted in his royal conquest, and when he returned with glad tidings, he was given a conqueror's welcome by Zogdu. A few months later, Zogdu's marriage was conducted with all the pomp and ceremony as befits a king. All the nobles from near and far presented the royal couple with gifts. Rhuzbeh, too, presented Zogdu with gold but the regent refused, saying, 'Give me a gift worthy of a king; do not insult me with trifles.'

Rhuzbeh asked, 'What gift can I give you?' Zogdu replied, 'I want the gajmuk.' Rhuzbeh said, 'I can't give away the gajmuk. It is a gift that I have earned—it is for me and my descendants.' This enraged Zogdu, who retorted, 'How dare you refuse your master? Give it now or I will have you hanged from the fort walls.' Rhuzbeh reluctantly obliged, but he was furious and swore revenge. With the gajmuk in his possession, Zogdu grew more arrogant. He became crueller and more aggressive and gave himself the title 'The Bearer of the Gajmuk'.

A dejected Rhuzbeh decided to take a break and visit Hatasa. The bazaars were still vibrant with vegetables, fruits and all manners of birds and animals. The fragrances of myrrh, frankincense and musk drifted in the air. His heart longed to see Ceba, the woman he truly loved. Her red hair and green eyes singed his heart. He made discreet enquiries and discovered her house. Once there, he knocked on the door and waited with bated breath. Ceba opened it and was shocked to see him at the door.

Rhuzbeh burst out, 'My musk! My beloved! I have come back.' She turned ashen and said, 'Hush!' After throwing a quick glance behind her, she said, 'Meet me in the bazaar after an hour.' And she shut the door in his face.

When they met again, there were tears in her eyes. She asked, 'Why did you go away?'

He replied, 'It is quite a story.' They went to the gurgling brook by the meadow that they used to visit often in the past and he explained, 'After you called me a liar, I went off to the east to find my own adventures.' As he narrated his adventures, she listened with wonder and amazement. Finally, he took her face in his hands and said, 'Whatever I did, I did for you. When I followed the gus whale, I knew it would make me worthy of you, and when I was sailing the stormy seas without food and water, your thoughts kept me going. The distance and time have not melted my love but made it stronger! After years of wilderness, I have come back to my garden to gather my flower—will you marry me?' She started crying and said, 'When you left abruptly, I sought you out. Of course I was angry, but I loved you. You did not have to go halfway around the world, slaying mythical beasts and acquiring magical stones to prove anything to me, for I truly loved you. All you had to do was meet me again and say sorry and I would have come back to you.' She looked at him, her green eyes laced with hurt, and said, 'Why have you come back now? Go away!' Rhuzbeh said, 'Hush! I am here now. Let's celebrate and make babies.' Her voice rose sharply. 'You are too late!' she cried, 'I am a married woman now, and I have a daughter. You left me heartbroken. A year later, I met a merchant. He is a kind and sincere man and he loves me and our daughter. You are late. Just go away!' She ran away sobbing.

Rhuzbeh was shattered. In one day, he had lost the gajmuk and the love of his life, Ceba. He was incensed; he stood up and screamed:

'To the fear that creeps up on me, hear me loud
I'm Rhuzbeh, and I shall be resolute!
And from my nothing shall come my everything!'

He returned to Zanda and planned Zogdu's downfall for snatching away his gajmuk and insulting him. In the Zandian court, there was a powerful general called Beresh who was as handsome as he was gallant. Rhuzbeh walked up to Zogdu and said, 'My lord! I am sorry to say that there are rumours regarding Princess Naheira.' Zogdu looked at Rhuzbeh quizzically. 'Apparently,' said Rhuzbeh lowering his eyes, 'the Princess is having an affair with Beresh.' Zogdu was incensed and said, 'How dare you say such a thing? I shall have you skinned alive for this affront!' 'My lord! I have your best interest at heart. You must question the Princess and Beresh,' said Rhuzbeh.

Zogdu was afraid to take action without proof. If he killed Beresh, his army might rebel, and if he killed Naheira without proof, then Nahal might invade to exact revenge. He needed proof. He asked Rhuzbeh to support his claims. 'You bark like a dog at moving shadows! Do you have any proof to substantiate your accusation against my wife?' Rhuzbeh said, 'My king! If the Princess possesses musk in her chambers, discreetly clear it and forbid her from wearing musk.' Zogdu thought it strange but agreed and said, 'I always oblige a dying man's wishes.' Six days later, Rhuzbeh sent a perfume merchant to Beresh with a vial of rare strong-smelling musk from the land of two rivers. The merchant met Beresh and said, 'I have heard about your bravery and gallantry. I would be honoured if you accepted a humble gift from a lowly merchant.' Beresh was pleasantly surprised and obliged.

The merchant said, 'Let me dab some on you right away.' He proceeded to apply musk generously on him. A delighted Beresh insisted on paying, but the merchant politely refused and said, 'It is a gift and I shall be hurt if you tried to pay me with a coin.' Meanwhile, Rhuzbeh met Naheira discreetly and made love to her. He had liberally applied musk to his body. When Rhuzbeh left, Naheira's body smelled heavily of musk. Rhuzbeh, on the other hand, hastily took a bath and rushed to Zogdu. He told Zogdu, 'My Lord! I have the proof that you wanted. Visit Princess Naheira and embrace her, your nose will tell you the truth.'

An irate Zogdu marched into the queen's chamber, pulled her close to him and sniffed suspiciously—she smelled of musk. He called on Beresh and he of course reeked of musk as well. He accused them of adultery and had them both beheaded. When Nahal heard the news, he was heartbroken and in great sorrow, he lamented:

'They tarnished my daughter, the flower of the North, with vile accusations. My child! My delicate bud! Flogged by whips, dragged by her hair and beheaded on a wooden slab. The light of my eyes, the nightingale who sang to my ears. My little dove who slept in my lap. Her every wail I calmed, her every wish I fulfilled. They stilled my baby's hand, which played with my beard. No sleep will ever bring me peace, and no food shall ever nourish me until I have my revenge. I swear by everything holy, I shall behead the perpetrator, scatter his flesh and let the crows and vultures feast on his corpse.'

Nahal was mad with grief; he sought vengeance and declared war on Zogdu. Zogdu was expecting this, and he elevated Rhuzbeh to lead the army. An army commanded by the mighty Rhuzbeh could not fail, he thought. This was the opportunity that Zogdu was waiting for. He would personally oversee the battle, and once Nahal was defeated, he would occupy the Northern kingdom and crown himself as the king of both the realms. The Zandian army crossed the Bjan pass and reached a flat plain. They found the Northern army entrenched. Being more powerful, the Zandians decided to make the first move. Rhuzbeh himself headed the vanguard of the Zandian army; the vanguard was a collection of the mightiest warriors and was flanked on both sides with two divisions. Each division was composed of infantry and cavalry units. Zogdu stood on a platform behind the lines and directed the attacks. The Northern Army was amassed in one giant cluster with cavalry in the middle that was headed by King Nahal. Zogdu laughed as he imagined his next steps. He would send his cavalry around and surround them from behind. The infantry would attack from the sides, and the vanguard would be the battering ram from the front. The Northern army would be encircled and crushed. Breaking into these thoughts, Rhuzbeh sounded his ivory horn, and the battle began. The two divisions of the Zandian cavalry, in a flanking movement, surrounded the Northern army and took up their position at the rear, and the infantry on both flanks charged to the sides. Surprisingly, the Northern army did not move. As the Zandian army, now positioned at the flanks and rear, closed in, they realised that the Northern army had dug a deep circular trench with an opening only in the front. The Zandian cavalry and infantry stranded in the rear and sides were thus rendered useless. Meanwhile, the

Northern cavalry charged through the gap in the middle and moved straight towards the vanguard as the flanks watched helplessly. Rhuzbeh waited until the Northern cavalry was almost upon them, and then at a pre-decided signal, he blew his horn. At his command, the vanguard turned and left the battlefield and just like that, Rhuzbeh had traitorously deserted Zogdu. Zogdu tried to flee, but Rhuzbeh shot an arrow at his horse, killing it instantly. Zogdu realised that he had been deceived by Rhuzbeh, who had allied with the Northern king. Nahal rode to Zogdu and, in one swift swing of his sword, beheaded him. With Zogdu dead, the Zandians stopped fighting. Rhuzbeh rallied the entire Zandian army under his banner and declared the battle over. Nahal had his soldiers chop Zogdu's body into small pieces and spread it around the battlefield. He had avenged his daughter by killing her murderer and scattering his flesh to the scavengers. Nahal was grateful to Rhuzbeh for collaborating with him and deserting Zogdu. Nahal appointed Rhuzbeh as the king regent of Zanda. He also returned to Rhuzbeh the gajmuk, which he had retrieved from the dead Zogdu.

Taking the opportunity, Rhuzbeh asked for the second sanaa as well, but Nahal firmly refused. Rhuzbeh decided to bide his time and was soon immersed in administering the large kingdom of Zanda.

He ruled Zanda as a regent for a year. In a couple of months, the young prince, the scion of King Kashan, would come of age, and Rhuzbeh would have to abdicate his position, which he was unwilling to do. He planned to murder the prince. Figuratively, a man is made as an onion. There are many layers. Once a layer is removed, it can't be restored. When a person indulges in sin, thinking that he has already done it before, it is like peeling one more layer of an onion because he has already peeled a layer. With each layer that is removed, the peeling becomes increasingly nonchalant, repetitive and brazen until he is naked with no sense of worth or self-esteem. In Rhuzbeh's case, he peeled away rapidly. He had King Kashan's son poisoned and himself crowned the King of Zanda.

He was already a traitor, and his treachery had led to the slaughter of many Zandian soldiers. He had committed adultery, for which he had a princess and an innocent general murdered. Now he had poisoned the rightful heir to the throne and got himself crowned the king. And he justified all this with one excuse—this is what all kings do; they eliminate the competition. The weak sometimes have to die for the greater good, he told himself. In a herd, the weak get eaten so that the strong can survive, ensuring that the progeny is strong and the herd remains healthy, he reasoned. Thus, he managed to silence the niggling voices inside him. He, Rhuzbeh, would build a great empire, and his descendants would carry forward his name. He shook off his little remorse and assumed the role of the King of Zanda. Although the citizens of Zanda were shocked and repulsed by the murder of the rightful heir, the reasoning that an errant hero was better than a tyrant placated them. The kingdom of Zanda had a new king, Rhuzbeh the Fearless—the wielder of the zer sword, the proud bearer of the gajmuk and the one in whose blood ran the gus ambergris! A noble king admired by both men and djinns! He adopted Zogdu's crest, the eagle with outspread wings and snake in its talons, as his own.

As fate would have it, when Ceba's husband—the merchant—was out on a journey to sell his merchandise, hungry bears attacked him. They mauled him, tore his body apart and ate some of it. Ceba was disconsolate. Rhuzbeh spent a lot of time consoling Ceba and her young daughter,

Darya, who was barely four years old. After six months of mourning, Rhuzbeh approached her for marriage , and she accepted his proposal. Rhuzbeh and Ceba became the King and Queen of Zanda. Metishin, the powerful court mage, advisor and healer, had his own network. Although aware of court intrigues, he did not interfere. In the forests of Zanda, when the wolf hunted, nobody stopped it. That was the way of nature and nature always finds a way to balance things out. But he warned Rhuzbeh against his misdeeds. 'Murder, adultery and regicide—is that your legacy, sire? You are the hero that humans and djinns look up to. Are you going to let the darkness creep up on you?' asked Metishin.

Rhuzbeh said, 'Do not ask your king to account for himself. Kings are made by bloodshed. Had I been servile to Zogdu, he would have taken everything I had. Indeed, he would have even robbed my grave after killing me.' Metishin said, 'Yes! But to kill him, you indulged in an illicit relation with Naheira, accused an innocent man of adultery and had them both executed. Hundreds of soldiers from both sides perished in the subsequent war. Then you went ahead and committed two more murders that cannot be spoken about.' Rhuzbeh stood stoically and said, 'People have to make sacrifices for I am your king and you are my subjects.' Metishin bowed low and said, 'As you command, sire. I have a request though—would you let me train your stepdaughter, Darya, as a mage? I am getting old and you need someone you can trust to guard and guide you. I feel a strong force in her. Allow me to train her.' Rhuzbeh agreed.

So it was that at a young age, Darya prepared to become a mage under Metishin's tutelage. Meanwhile, the Zandians gradually accepted Rhuzbeh as their king. He was a good and wise ruler, who brought in tax reforms, protected the weak and punished the oppressors. Under his able administration, Zanda prospered. Rhuzbeh and Ceba had a son and named him Axer. Rhuzbeh had never been so much in love with any living being. He was obsessed with his son—a fact that would prove to be his undoing. It was the third year of his reign and Rhuzbeh was getting used to his kingly duties. He was a doting father and loving husband. He had nothing to fear except his guilty conscience. Every time he heard his courtiers or his subjects whisper, all he heard was *usurper*. He did not want Axer to be known as the son of a murderer or usurper.

Rhuzbeh craved for the one thing he lacked—legitimacy. He even made the royal scribes rewrite history by portraying that the young prince was not poisoned but died of sickness as he had been neglected by Zogdu. But the whispers only kept growing louder in his mind. The kingdom of Hatasa had once been a part of greater Zanda. Rhuzbeh now decided to attack Hatasa. By annexing Hatasa, he would be seen avenging Kashan, the erstwhile famous ruler of Zanda, and present himself as the rightful ruler and not a murderer who usurped the throne. Rhuzbeh ordered the invasion of Hatasa. King Hitkar, the king of Hatasa, appealed to Rhuzbeh. 'It was Kashan who invaded us. We were merely defending our kingdom. You are the son-in-law of Hatasa and Queen Ceba is a Hatasan. Please don't invade and destroy us!' But Rhuzbeh did not agree and said, 'I am a Zandian King. You had my predecessor imprisoned and left him to perish in your wretched dungeons. We will avenge the death of King Kashan.' Rhuzbeh did not heed the advice of Ceba, who implored him not to go to war. He did not listen to his mage Metishin's counsel either. He brushed them aside, rallied a massive army and reached the gates of Hatasa. Hitkar and the Hatasan army could not be taken lightly.

Rhuzbeh remembered how Hitkar's bravery and tact had decisively beaten Kashan's Zandian army.

Hitkar called his ministers and generals and sought counsel. He asked, 'How do we beat Rhuzbeh? He is one of the greatest warriors ever known. How do we combat a foe as formidable as him?'

Hitkar's son and heir, Hitsar, said, 'Father, our army beat them back once and we can do it again. We should face them and teach that usurper a lesson.' But the Hatasan mage said, 'No! Do not underestimate Rhuzbeh and engage him in a frontal attack. A ring of mountains surrounds our kingdom. The mountains act like steep walls, covering the kingdom on all sides. Their army, heavy with weapons and equipment, cannot climb our steep mountains. Our fort walls are strong, and the Iron Gate at the mountainous ring entrance is the only way into Hatasa. If we can defend the central fort wall and the gate, we can hold off the Zandians for as long as possible. Rhuzbeh will spend all his energy trying to breach our walls, and once his army is tired and spent, we will counterattack.' The attack began. The Hatasans manned the ramparts of the wall, and their archers held the Zandian infantry at bay. Rhuzbeh tried bombing the Hatasan walls with artillery but the walls held. Seeing his attempts go futile, Rhuzbeh asked for one-on-one combat with Prince Hitsar, with the winner taking the other's kingdom. Hitsar said, 'Father, let me battle him and take him down.' Prince Hitsar had just been married to a beautiful princess, who was expecting a baby. Hitkar forbade his son and said, 'This is not a fair contest. Rhuzbeh would slaughter you and make us his slaves.' They denied the combat offer, but Rhuzbeh tried to goad them into the combat. He said, 'Do the Hatasans have a coward for a prince? Will the prince not defend the honour of his people? If he doesn't accept the offer, I shall take Hatasa by force and make Hitsar's sister, Princess Hitti, my slave. I shall not marry her but keep her in my quarters as a slave to do with her as I please.' Princess Hitti was barely seventeen; the Hatasans were shaken but resolved to stand against the oppressor. After the initial skirmishes, Rhuzbeh sounded the battle horn and the siege of Hatasa began in earnest. The Zandian army pounded the Hatasan gate, but the metal door, guarded by the metal-plumed serpents, held its resolve. The Zandians put up ladders against the fort walls and started climbing, but they were beaten back. They tried to batter the fort wall with a giant battering ram, but the Hatasans poured oil and set it on fire. Three months of siege and there was no result in sight.

Just as the Zandians were getting weary, Rhuzbeh came up with an idea. He rounded up the ibexes in the nearby forests and slaughtered them. He chose a bunch of his elite warriors and dressed them up in ibex skin and horns. During the night, the camouflaged Zandian soldiers started climbing the mountain adjoining the fort walls. From afar, at night, they looked like ibexes, so the Hatasans did not suspect anything. After three nights, the warriors reached the mountaintop, which connected to the fort walls and ramparts. Once they reached the ramparts, they killed the sleeping soldiers. With the fort walls secure, they clambered down into the fort and opened the main gate. The Zandian Army poured in and captured Hatasa—Rhuzbeh's eagle flew high on the ramparts of Hatasa.

King Hitkar, Prince Hitsar and the Hatasan mages were publicly beheaded. Princess Hitti was taken to Rhuzbeh's quarters, where Rhuzbeh raped her. Thus was conquered Hatasa.

Rhuzbeh was now the king of both Zanda and Hatasa. He had managed to avenge King Kashan's death and reunite the two kingdoms. He returned to Zanda to a hero's welcome. The conquest of Hatasa lent him the legitimacy he so desired. He scooped up his beloved son, Axer, who would now be the heir to the joint kingdoms of Zanda and Hatasa.

Hitkar's daughter Hitti was sent to the inner quarters of the royal palace. The inner quarters were where Rhuzbeh's family lived: his wife, Queen Ceba; his step daughter, Princess Darya; and his son, Prince Axer. Darya and Axer received their education there as well. The inner quarters also housed numerous female slaves from different kingdoms. The female slaves were not meant solely for sex and indeed Rhuzbeh never had sex with them. As a rule, if he ever had physical relations with any slave, they were moved to the family quarters. The slaves indulged the king with singing, dancing and good conversations. Rhuzbeh had some of the finest teachers of mathematics, astronomy, politics and arts brought in for the slaves. Some of the slaves were brought in young and from far-flung corners of the known world. There was a lot of power concentrated with these slaves, for they had the king's ears. They had the potential to influence the king, who sometimes awarded them with wealth and lands. They were also married off to his subjects who pleased him or given away as gifts to other kings as they were beautiful, highly educated and trained in royal manners. Into this world was brought the young Princess Hitti, the daughter of the Hatasan king, Hitkar. Rhuzbeh had raped her symbolically as an insult to her father. Although she was shifted to the royal chambers, Rhuzbeh never visited her once. She cried day and night, mourning the loss of her father, her brother and her own dignity. And to make matters worse, she discovered that she was pregnant with Rhuzbeh's child. This turned her disconsolate. Rhuzbeh heard of the news and immediately ordered Hitti to visit him in his chambers. 'Come in and sit next to me on the bed,' he said. She shook like a leaf but obliged.

'Are you pregnant with my child?' he asked her. She shook with anger and said, 'As you ravaged our lands, so did you my body and soul.' She cried inconsolably and continued, 'What am I to do with this? I hate this baby and I want to kill it.'

She reached out for the fruit knife, but Rhuzbeh apprehended her and took the knife away. He apologetically said, 'I am sorry for what I did. I am truly ashamed. I was consumed by anger and hatred. That baby is innocent and of royal blood. Please do not hate it or kill it.' 'Babies should be born of love. What will I do with something that was given to me as a mark of humiliation and hatred? Let me kill it myself,' she said, sobbing. Rhuzbeh consoled her and kept her company through the night. That day onwards, he would spend time with her every night. He brought in entertainers to humour her and showered her with gifts. He was slowly falling in love. This made Ceba jealous and she admonished Rhuzbeh by saying, 'Remember, she is but a slave. You are not married to her and the child that she is carrying is illegitimate. Come, your family needs you. I need my husband and the children need their father.' And so it was that Rhuzbeh divided his time between the two. Nine months later, Hitti delivered a baby boy, and he was named Hittash. Immediately the palace intrigue began.

The courtiers were placing bets as to who would be the king's successor: Prince Axer, the first-born legitimate heir from a commoner, or Prince Hittash, the second-born illegitimate child from a royal. Rhuzbeh's love for Axer was absolute—it almost bordered on weakness—but Ceba was suddenly insecure. She was well aware that she was not of noble blood. She was an ordinary widow from the streets of Hatasa that Rhuzbeh had picked up and made the queen. Hitti, on the other hand, might be a slave now but was a princess of noble birth. 'I do not want my son, Hittash, to be called a bastard,' complained Hitti bitterly and in order to lend legitimacy to his son's name, Rhuzbeh married Hitti, much to the chagrin of Ceba. Although partial to Ceba, Rhuzbeh tried to balance his attention between both the queens.

The queens were free to spend money and land on whomsoever they chose. Hitti, being of noble birth, was a patron of fine arts. She filled the palace with exquisite things and artists from far-flung lands thronged the kingdom of Zanda. She invited painters and sculptors who brought in their beautiful creations. The palace was soon dotted with intricate carvings of cedar and mahogany. She adorned the palace walls with paintings so bewitching that they were almost magical.

However, Hitti's true love was music; she was particularly fond of singers and musicians. The palace resounded with music from instruments like the harp, balag, oud, ub, neyanban and dotar. On one occasion, the court was graced with the presence of a legendary singer and musician, Butosh. It was said that when Butosh sang, flowers blossomed even during the harshest of winters. For years, farmers had been paying Butosh to sing in their orchards, for his melodious voice was thought to sweeten fruits. In the past, there was a big ancient walnut tree that was rotting and dying. Butosh had sung to it and it had healed. Butosh had a strange ritual though. Before he started his performance, he would ask forgiveness from the king and all the noblemen in the court for what he was about to do. He would ask for an earthen spittoon and in front of the royal court, he would spit into it and hold his earlobes with the thumb and index fingers of both hands. It was a symbolic gesture, which implied that the glory of the great court and its riches paled in front of the greatest of all art—music.

Legend had it that when Butosh was little, he did not cry—he sang. He sang like a bird. So convincing were the songs that birds like nightingales and bulbuls would try and feed him, mistaking him for a bird. He would sing happy songs of the thrush, the melancholic calling of the loon and even the long calls of the peacock in the monsoons. His neighbours thought that he was a demon. They asked his father to abandon the child in the forest, threatening to torch the house otherwise. Since leaving the child in the forest was out of the question, the father travelled with the baby to the Vale of Music. The Vale of Music was a very small settlement in a valley where masters dedicated to music passed on their art. It was a place where young students were left in the care of these masters, completely cut off from the outside world. Butosh's father left him there because he knew his baby would be safe in a place where they practised music. With tears in his eyes and a heavy heart, he left his child and returned to his village. The inmates cared for the baby, and when he was eight years old, the age at which musical training starts formally, the masters refrained from teaching him. They would train the other pupils to sing and play musical instruments, but each time Butosh approached them, he was told that he did not need any training as he was a master himself. He did not know how to play musical instruments. He often broke down thinking that the masters were taunting him and depriving him of knowledge. The other students regularly made fun of him. He stopped trying to sing and started doing manual chores for the community. For years, he served the masters and students. The masters treated him with respect but the students treated him like a slave. At eighteen, most of the students, who were now proficient and had a reputation of being skilled musicians, left the valley to spread the art of music and seek their place under the sun. Butosh, however, had resigned himself to being a helper. Now that his contemporaries weren't around to taunt him, he was finally at peace. He would wake up early in the morning, go out to pick roots and fruits, prepare breakfast, cook lunch, take an afternoon nap, go for an early evening walk and prepare dinner at night.

One morning, as he was walking by a small river, he noticed water passing between two narrow rocks. He stopped and listened. It was slow at first, but soon he could hear the music. There was music being created by water when it passed between the rocks. When he tried hard to listen, there was no music. But when he relaxed, emptied his mind and listened to the gurgle, slowly, the music emerged. At first, it was faint but with time, it became progressively louder until music pervaded the river. He could hear it everywhere—music, when the river flowed between the rocks. Music, when the river flowed fast. Music, when the river flowed slowly. Music, when the river splashed on the banks. Every drop of water had its own music, blending harmoniously into the sounds of the river. Slowly, week after week, Butosh began to feel the music in the winds as though passing through the trees, the rustle of dry leaves, the splatter of fruits, the peeling of vegetables and the sounds of cooking. Soon, he could see music and taste music and was one with music. From the age of eight, Butosh never sang; all he did was soak up the music. And it was only when he turned forty years old that he was requested by one of the masters to sing. He protested, 'I cannot sing. Indeed, I have never ever sung in my entire adult life.' 'Then it is time you sang,' said the master and assembled all the students around.

For the first time in forty years, Butosh sang. And the music was surreal. The trees around blossomed, grass sprouted from dry ground and the eggs of the birds hatched—it was like all of the spring season packed into one song. Everyone was awed. Butosh was astonished himself. He would never be able to sing with this intensity again—for this was forty years of music bottled into one song. It is said that seven peacocks stood in front of him and spread their tails in unison to acknowledge him. The masters and students cried out of ecstasy, their bodies shaking; never would they hear something like that ever again. The masters immediately asked Butosh to leave, as no student would ever attempt to sing after hearing what they had all just heard. How can you hold up a bronze coin when you have seen a mountain full of gold? Butosh left and set out to travel with no clear destination in mind. In his journeys, he sang and performed miracles and his singing helped heal people who were sick. He was rumoured to have made a whole desert green, and farmers sought his help during famines and locust infestations. But slowly, Butosh's music lost some of its prowess because he was now performing for people who were paying him. These days, his music was not as potent as that first time, but it was still magnificent. Meanwhile, Queen Hitti was mentally disturbed. The trauma that she had suffered made her gaunt. She could not sleep and was withering. When Hitti heard of Butosh, she sent for him. His music filled her with love and healed her; she blossomed and became visibly happy and beautiful. When Rhuzbeh heard of this miraculous singer, he invited him to perform in his court. When the court heard Butosh sing for the first time, they were awestruck. Never had they heard music like that. Many of the courtiers wept openly. Hitti, as Butosh's patron, guarded him jealously as her find and possession. Rhuzbeh would plead with her to have Butosh sing and every time Butosh enthralled the court with his music, he lavished gifts on Hitti for such a find. This enraged Ceba. She publicly accused Hitti of trying to bewitch the king by using the musician. She called it a conspiracy and demanded a trial.

The king called Butosh and Hitti to clear the allegation. He knew it was untrue but thought it best to put the accusations to rest. During the trial, Ceba accused Hitti of trying to bewitch the king using magic—a charge that Hitti angrily denied. Hitti turned to Rhuzbeh and cried, 'My lord! If I were trying to influence you, I would ask for something. Have I ever asked you anything? Or has Butosh ever asked for anything?'

It was true that both Hitti and Butosh had never asked for anything. Indeed, Butosh's music had refreshed Rhuzbeh, made him forget his ugly deeds and exhorted him to be a better person. Rhuzbeh replied, 'No, my Queen! You and your musician have never asked me for anything. What I have given is out of my own free will and accord. I will not hear any more accusations against my queen and the mother of my son.' Ceba realised that to speak any further against Hitti would be unwise and so she said, 'My Lord! Maybe Queen Hitti is innocent but this man means to influence you and harm you. He bears nothing but malice. He looks down on you and the glory of this court.' 'Can you prove it?' asked Hitti, her voice loaded with scorn.

'Yes!' said Ceba, 'My King! This scoundrel publicly spits on your royal personage and defiles the glory of this great court by spitting in full view. I ask him to sing after kissing your feet, implying that the glory of the king and his court supersedes that of his art.' Rhuzbeh and his court watched in silence as Ceba ordered Butosh to do her bidding. He stood in front of Rhuzbeh and said, 'As the walnut tree is my witness, I hatched no conspiracy, great King. But I cannot kiss your feet before I sing because with that gesture, I will have acknowledged universal music to be inferior to a man and then I shall lose my ability to sing.' Ceba indignantly said, 'This man would rather spit on your royal personage than submit to your authority. He has no respect for the sanctity of this court. He wants to enslave you and this court with his music so that he can have his way. Cut off this tongue and throw this scoundrel back to where he came from.'

Hitti intervened and said, 'O King! Please spare him. I assure you he means no harm.'

Rhuzbeh raised his hands and said, 'I know he means no harm, but the man defies my authority. If he refuses to obey his king, then others would follow and I would not be a king anymore. But to cut his tongue would be too harsh a punishment. He has brought me great joy with his music and hence I want his punishment to be light. Cut off his thumb and banish him from my kingdom. And let it be known to all my subjects that I will not tolerate defiance or disrespect.' So it was that Butosh was caught in the court intrigue and lost his thumb. Hitti was furious and vowed vengeance against Ceba. Ceba did not share Hitti's taste in music and arts. She was from the streets of Hatasa and preferred more materialistic things. She liked exotic food and spices; saffron was her favourite spice for it added fragrance to her food. The crimson saffron matched her hair and the king would naughtily call her 'the saffron that laces my dessert'. She would go to great lengths to get the best saffron available. She had it as an aphrodisiac. She sometimes slept naked on a bed of saffron with Rhuzbeh. It calmed her down and made her skin glow. She even dyed her clothes with saffron. However, Ceba's true passion was carpets; it was the closest she had come to appreciating art. She had picked up the love of carpets from the bazaars of Hatasa. She covered the inner chambers and her quarters with the finest quality carpet, interwoven with silk and wool. She was obsessed with these hand-woven masterpieces. In her search for the greatest carpet, she came across Ardahast. He was the fabled grandmaster of weaving—a living legend. She lavished him with gifts and became his greatest buyer. She even had towns named after him. The Ardahast carpet was the most expensive and sought-after carpet in the known world. It was said that it was Ardahast who introduced the popular tulip pattern woven into carpets. Ardahast was born into a wealthy family which had always been into carpet trade. The young man had mastered the art of making fine carpets, but he despised mediocrity and wanted to make the finest carpets in the known world. His father always said, 'The answer to a practical problem is always the obvious.' He started with the most basic material needed for making a carpet—wool. Usually, the wool of sheep, goat and camel was used to make carpet, but Ardahast decided that he would work exclusively with sheep wool. Not only did he want the finest of wools, but he also wanted it to be unique and extremely rare. He received information that on the Hills of Kark, there was a variety of sheep called the karkzeb that was unique to these mountains. These sheep were short and had thick wool with a silken quality. The wool around their neck was highly prized.

Ardahast journeyed to those faraway Hills of Kark in search of the karkzeb sheep. When he reached the mountains, he saw flocks of this precious animal. However, there was trouble on the hills. In the last few years, eagles had invaded the hills. These were not regular eagles. These birds were so large and powerful that they were able to pick these sheep in their talons and fly away. Once they had flown to an appropriate height, they would drop the sheep down, smashing them on the stones and killing them. The eagles would then feast on the dead sheep. Of late, the eagles were getting increasingly emboldened. An eagle had attempted to carry away a child. However, an alert villager had thrown a heavy stone that made the eagle drop the child. The angry eagle had turned around and mauled the villager before flying away. When Ardahast reached the Hills of Kark, he offered gold for a hundred of the Karkzeb, but the villagers agreed to sell the animals only if he helped them get rid of the birds. There were close to twenty of these big birds, and Ardahast came up with a series of ideas to help rid the villagers of these eagles. He designed sharp metal spikes that could be tied to the sheep's bodies so that when the eagles tried to pick up the sheep, their talons got impaled. Some of the eagles bled to death. Ardahast's next idea was to have hounds covered in sheep wool. When the eagle would pick up a hound mistaking it for sheep, the hounds would turn around and bite the eagle. His masterstroke, however, was to train a large group of crows to combat the eagles. Generally, when an eagle was attacked by a murder of crows, it flew away. If ever an eagle attacked a crow, the other crows rallied around and fought it off. Even at a later date, the crows remembered the particular eagle which had attacked one of them, and tried to attack it whenever they saw it. It was in their nature—a crow never forgives. Ardahast urged the villagers to catch crows from nearby regions and to feed and reward them every time they chased away an eagle. Finally, his efforts yielded results as the eagles were driven away. After successfully getting rid of the eagles, the villagers sold a hundred of the prized karkzeb to Ardahast.

He brought them back to a farm on a hill and crossbred them with a variety of sheep called lian, creating the Ardahast sheep. The Ardahast sheep was bigger than the karkzeb, with a rich quality of wool, especially near the neck, from where the finest wool was harnessed. He mastered the art of weaving and knotting. He travelled extensively searching for the most nimble-fingered craftsmen, and he settled them in his hometown. His carpets were populated by the highest number of knots, lovingly made over many months. But it was in the dyeing process that he truly excelled. It was his fabled art of dyeing that made the Ardahast carpet legendary.

He did not reveal his secrets to anyone at all and mixed the dyes personally. He travelled to the ocean regions and learnt to use crushed snail shells, seashells and certain fish by-products to create the bright dyes. From the far-off forestlands, he learnt how to use beetles, insects and animal by-products to make dyes. From master artisans, he learnt how to make plant dyes from indigo, pomegranate rinds and berries. For the richest of colours, he employed lapis lazuli, emeralds, pearls and rubies and mixed them with plant or animal products to create dyes of such brilliance as were never seen before. He dyed with a limited batch of colours, and when he remade the same dye, there were small colour variations. These variations in the colour made the carpet even more beautiful, giving it depth and character. 'Carpets should not be evenly dyed,' said Ardahast famously. 'Carpets are like humans and their beauty lies in their imperfections.' When a buyer asked, 'Shouldn't a carpet be perfect?' He said, 'Carpets should be beautiful; perfection is reserved for God.' The knowledge of the art of dyeing was scattered around the world; Ardahast had managed to collect it all and invent some new methods as well. He was the pride of the carpeting world and his carpets were so famous that they were used as diplomatic gifts. These carpets were termed magical—they were not the work of humans but djinns, people proclaimed. Indeed, they were not only appreciated by humans but by djinns as well.

Unknown to Ardahast, djinns owned quite a few carpets made by him. The jann king, Amirast, was gifted a few Ardahast carpets by Ghanazaqi. The djinns, in the guise of humans, visited him and bought from him. During one of his travels in the search of the requisite ingredients, he came across an old man who was selling some dyes. The old man did not have the dyes that he was looking for, but Ardahast decided to indulge him and started talking. They spent a whole day discussing carpets. The old man was impressed with Ardahast's dedication and revealed that in the distant past, his ancestors had made flying carpets. Normally, other people would scoff at such claims but not Ardahast—he had heard legends of flying carpets before and took the old man's claims seriously.

Ardahast's heart was thudding against his chest but with a semblance of calm, he asked, 'I have heard the stories and always thought them to be just that—stories. Are the stories true?' 'The ancients indeed made flying carpets,' said the old man in a matter-of-fact tone.

'Then why was it discontinued?' asked Ardahast. He replied, 'A very few craftsmen knew the art of making flying carpets, and they guarded it jealously.' He continued, 'Contrary to myths, these carpets did not always fly at high speeds or cover great distances. That depended on the carpet's construction. It is said that there was a period of great lament—a time when civilizations nearly perished. Volcanoes erupted, the earth shook and the great sea engulfed the land. Clouds and ash blocked the sun and days turned into never-ending nights. It was a catastrophe—plants and animals died. Swarms of violent people landed from the sea, burnt down and wiped out entire cities. When the natives recovered from the disaster, they no longer possessed the fine quality of materials and dyes required to make such a carpet—their master craftsmen were dead and their skill levels were mediocre. The carpets produced by half-skilled craftsmen, using inferior materials, could barely fly. These carpets were unreliable and would simply drop down, injuring the riders. As time went by, only thieves used these mediocre flying carpets and thus, the latter began to be looked down upon. The menace of the thieves was growing so bad that the kings ordered that anybody who ever made a flying carpet would be put to death. Gradually, due to threats and the lack of demand, all knowledge was lost.

'But what makes a carpet fly?' asked Ardahast. The old man smiled, beckoned him closer and whispered the secret in his ears. Ardahast heard him out and absorbed the secret like a parched earth absorbs water from the sky. When he was done, Ardahast held the old man's hand and thanked him profusely.

The old man acknowledged and added, 'Be sure to use only the volcanic ash of Antza in the right quantities, along with the correct mixture of dyes, of which Tyrian purple is an important component. Also, add the resins along with mercury.

Ardahast thanked the old man and left. He was obsessed with making a flying carpet and made it his life's mission. After three years of hard work and numerous failed attempts, he finally managed to make two carpets. He hid one carpet and planned to gift the other to his greatest patron—Queen Ceba. When the court was in full assembly, Ardahast presented to Rhuzbeh three of the most beautiful carpets ever seen. The courtiers were awed. To Queen Ceba, he presented only one carpet that he called "my finest creation." Ceba looked at the carpet. No doubt it was beautiful, but there was nothing extraordinary about it. Ardahast laid it down and sat on the carpet, and that is when the miracle happened—it rose in the air. The carpet was flying! The courtiers gasped. Ardahast had achieved the impossible—he had created a flying carpet!

The queen was delighted with the gift and wanted to try it immediately. But the court mage, Metishin, wanted to ascertain if the carpet was possessed or had any spells on it. After a thorough check, he declared the carpet safe. Nevertheless, he asked Ardahast to fly around the palace frequently for two days to ascertain its safety. On the second day of the trials, as Ardahast was flying around late in the evening, Hitti, who was on one of the upper floors, happened to see him through her window. She beckoned him to come closer. Ardahast obliged and drew close to the window. A visibly delighted Hitti invited Ardahast to come in, and he floated in through the window. As soon as Ardahast was inside the room, she closed the window, stepped on the carpet, removed her robes and started screaming for help. Ardahast was confused. The soldiers stationed outside her door rushed in, and Hitti screamed, 'Arrest this man! He tried to molest me!'

Ardahast was bound in iron chains and thrown in the dungeons. During the trial, Hitti cried and falsely claimed that Ardahast had peeped into her window while she was dressing. Seeing her naked, Ardahast had flown in through the window and tried to force himself on her after shutting the windows, she claimed. Rhuzbeh was furious and ordered Ardahast to be beheaded. However, Ceba intervened and begged for forgiveness on behalf of a defiant and unapologetic Ardahast. Rhuzbeh relented and agreed to spare Ardahast's life, but he ordered his hands to be cut off, saying, 'He tried to outrage the modesty of my queen and for this affront, I shall chop his hands off as a warning. Besides, his pride lies in his craft.'

Hitti was not content with the verdict and demanded that Rhuzbeh either kill Ardahast or burn the carpet. So, Rhuzbeh agreed to cut off his hands and burn the carpet, and with that, the art of making flying carpets was seemingly lost once again. The hatred between the queens had taken a toll on one more illustrious legend of that age. Rhuzbeh had been a party to the decapitation and mutilation of great men just to pacify his wives. Meanwhile, although the queens were at each other's throats, Princess Darya, daughter of Ceba, completely adored Prince Hittash, the son of Hitti. She was six years old when she had first set her eyes on baby Hittash. She loved his dark hair and dark eyes and fussed over him like a mother. Surprisingly, siblings Darya and Axer were not very close, although both looked like their mother with red hair and green eyes. Axer was the son of Rhuzbeh, a born prince, whereas Darya was the daughter of a merchant. This was the period in which Ghanazaqi invited Rhuzbeh to Alainis as a human witness to the book of laws, *Za Habab Za Haa*. The book had a clause that stated that the djinn folk would not shed any blood in war amongst themselves. There was also a clause that djinns would not participate in human wars, they could ally with humans on a quest or help each other, but they would not shed human blood. After the book was legitimised, Ghanazaqi and Amirast had a conversation with Rhuzbeh. 'We have received a message regarding the second sanaa. We know that King Nahal has it in his possession,' said Ghanazaqi.

'I was but a commoner without an army then,' said Rhuzbeh. 'I now command the armies of Zanda and Hatasa. If you permit me, I will go to war against Nahal and regain the second sanaa.'

'No!' said Ghanazaqi. 'Do not wage war! Not on our account! Let us wait. If the circumstances are right, the sanaa will find a way to come back to us.'

'I trust your wisdom and fine judgement, O Ghanazaqi!' said Rhuzbeh. 'Also,' began Ghanazaqi in a hesitant tone, 'we have been getting news about you. Disturbing news. We have been made aware that you have been indulging in murder, treachery and forcing yourself on women. This is not the noble Rhuzbeh we know.' Rhuzbeh said, 'They forced my hand, and in the human world, the weak and meek are not respected.' Ghanazaqi said, 'You are our friend and almost our kin. Gus ambergris runs in your veins. King Amirast owes his crown to you. You are a witness to our book of laws. Be a just king—be the king that humans and djinns look up to.' Rhuzbeh bowed his head and said, 'I shall try and live up to your expectations.'

After parting from their company, Rhuzbeh returned to Zanda. Twenty-six years of peaceful administration of Zanda was now making him restless. He had the urge to seek conquest and glory.

But he wanted to start with an easier goal. Thus, he embarked on a war to capture kingdoms beyond the western desert. They were easier targets than the Northern kingdom even though the desert was arid and it took a twenty-day march to cross. This would be a good test for his children. Both Axer and Hittash were accomplished warriors and leaders. Hittash had returned from his misadventures from Hatasa. Darya, who was just back from her travels, also accompanied them. Metishin had declared that Darya was the greatest mage in the known world, even stronger than him. The water and food supply were laden on camels, horses and oxen. The heat was relentless. Many soldiers died in the first ten days of the march. On the twelfth day, there was a sandstorm, and the pack animals bolted. When the storm subsided, the army realised that they had food and water enough to last only one more day. The army's morale broke and they refused to march further. They were beset by another raging, howling sandstorm.

In the midst of the storm, Rhuzbeh stood up straight and declared, 'To the fear that creeps up on me, hear me loud—I am Rhuzbeh, the bearer of the gajmuk and the wielder of the zer sword. Gus ambergris runs in my veins, and I am the human witness at Alainis. If any jann is around, I seek help—guide us out of this storm and to an oasis.' Suddenly, a man appeared, clad in white and gold, and greeted Rhuzbeh. He guided the army away from the storm and took them to an oasis; Rhuzbeh and his army were overjoyed. They drank and refilled at the oasis. By the next day, the strange man had rounded up the pack of animals and brought them back. Buoyed by this incident and goaded by the presence of the princes, the armies proceeded to fight valiantly. The princes had proved themselves in the battles that ensued. They had each individually led armies and captured various kingdoms. Meanwhile, Darya was gaining a reputation for her fearsome skills as a mage. The very mention of Darya demoralised the opposition. Metishin stayed by the king's side to counsel and protect him while Darya accompanied Hittash. Her spells and combat skills had saved a disturbed Hittash numerous times. Once, during one of his reckless charges, Hittash was ahead of his lines and was completely surrounded by the enemy. Darya conjured up a black panther and unleashed it on the enemy. This caused the encirclement to be broken, and like an avenging typhoon, she laid waste to the enemies, snatching Hittash from the jaws of death. The king was pleased with his sons, but Darya's prowess overshadowed Hittash's victories. Ceba gloated that had it not been for Darya, Hittash would have been killed in battle. Hittash, who was perturbed by a murder accusation, resented Darya for protecting him; he did not want her to babysit him. Through this campaign, Rhuzbeh had captured four large and rich kingdoms beyond the western desert. The kingdoms were collectively known as Wastra. Now, Rhuzbeh was the king of the entire belt from Hatasa to Wastra. The kingdoms beyond the Western desert were his, and it was just a matter of time before Rhuzbeh would turn north or south. The Northern and Southern kingdoms were getting jittery. Nahal, the Northern king, knew that once Rhuzbeh felt powerful enough, he would seek an excuse to launch an attack and take away sanaa. He started preparing for war. Rhuzbeh had achieved a great victory, and once they returned to Zanda, he organised a grand banquet to celebrate the success. He was pleased that his favourite son had proven himself in war, both as a warrior and a leader. Feeling magnanimous, he presented Axer with the golden jann armour of Amirast, much to the dismay of Hittash.

Chapter 5

The Dead Man and the Monkfly

The roar of a lion cannot rouse a man if the buzz of a housefly fails to wake him up.

A week after the successful campaign of Wastra, the palace witnessed an incident that did not happen every day. Indeed, it had never happened before.

Lying motionless on the floor of the inner palace chambers was a man who was stiff as a prude and immune to prods. The intruder held in his hands a wooden figurine in the shape of a woman. The man could not be coaxed to speak—after all, the dead do not speak.

Rhuzbeh called his advisors and commanders for answers. 'Who was this man? How did he infiltrate the palace? Did he plan to kill someone? Who killed him and why?'

Metishin replied, 'O King! We do not know who he is, but he was holding a wooden figurine in his hands. We have retrieved it and are trying to ascertain its significance.'

Rhuzbeh nodded and said, 'Make an announcement that anybody who has information or can solve the mystery of the dead man with the figurine will be rewarded.'

Ten days later, a tall and handsome man from the south came to Rhuzbeh's court and asked for an audience with the king. When Rhuzbeh granted him the request, he said, 'Mighty King! May I have an opportunity to look at the figurine?'

By now, several people had tried and failed, so Rhuzbeh did not even bother asking his name. He instructed Metishin to hand it over to him. To everyone's surprise, the stranger took out a small monkey from a bag. The monkey had transparent wings like a dragonfly, and it started hovering around. The stranger asked for a banana, and once the flying monkey was fed, he handed the wooden figurine over to the creature. The monkey gave three gentle taps at the right places on the figurine and a secret cabinet popped open. Inside the cabinet was a small note which was rolled tight. The man handed over the note to Metishin. When Metishin unrolled the paper, he found a word and a symbol scribbled on it: Pashem I=. 'Pashem means wool. What does that symbol mean?' asked Metishin aloud.

Rhuzbeh asked the stranger, 'Do you know its meaning?'

The stranger shook his head and said, 'I am afraid not.'

'Thank you for retrieving the note. What is your name, and where are you from?' Rhuzbeh asked.

'My Lord, my name is Tiran, and I am from the Southern kingdom,' he replied.

'I am delighted with your services, Tiran,' said Rhuzbeh, 'You shall be rewarded well. But I have a question. How did you come upon a flying monkey?'

'This is not a monkey. It is a monkfly,' replied Tiran. 'I bought it from a wandering merchant. I have trained it to become quite adept at many things, including opening locks. Great king, I have a request. I do not desire any reward; all I ask is an opportunity to serve you. I am a warrior, and it would be an honour to fight for you. Please accept my services,' pleaded Tiran.

Rhuzbeh agreed, and Tiran was drafted into the king's service. The stranger seemed highly polished and had an air of a nobleman about him. There was something mysterious about Tiran. After dismissing the court, Rhuzbeh called on Metishin and Darya and asked, 'Who is this man? There is something strange about him. I clutched the gajmuk tight; I did not feel it change. Yet I have a feeling that I know this man and that he is not who he says he is. Is he a djinn, a sorcerer or a spy? How come he walks out of nowhere with a monkfly—no merchant ever sold me a monkfly! Who is he? Does he mean harm? Metishin, find out more about this man!'

Metishin nodded. He also had reservations about Tiran. Metishin passed on the task to Darya. She met Tiran and initiated conversations with him. She was also surprised by his gentle manners and vast knowledge. He was handsome, and indeed there was a mysterious air about him. Soon, she found herself flirting with this stranger. Although equally fascinated, Tiran kept her at an arm's length.

Darya invited him over to her chambers where she kept an earthen vessel to burn a substance composed of aspand, frankincense, aloes, resins and other herbs. Darya put a spell on this incense such that if Tiran were an evil spirit or a djinn, the smell would change. Tiran walked in, sat down and started chatting with Darya.

The fragrances added to the mood. She indulged him in light-hearted banter, and they chatted about his childhood and life down south. Unable to resist herself, she reached across, ruffled his hair and asked, 'Do all people down south have such lovely hair?'

He instinctively drew back and asked, 'Have you ever been to the south?'

'No,' she replied truthfully and continued, 'You seem knowledgeable and have the condescending attitude of educated people, the street smartness of a city-dweller and the mannerisms of a courtly person. What an intrigue you are!'

He laughed and said, 'You are a beautiful princess with green eyes and flaming red hair. You are the daughter of Queen Ceba, the ward of King Rhuzbeh and a mage who Metishin himself calls 'the greatest in the known world'! And yet! You are calling me an intrigue?!'

Her cheeks flushed—he had called her beautiful. She composed herself and began to sniff but the air was redolent with the unchanging sweet smell of aloes. It was confirmed that he was not a djinn or an evil spirit.

She bit her lips and flushed red. An idea struck her. She asked him to join her for a drink. She intended to spike his drink with a love potion that had a temporary effect. If he were a sorcerer, he would recognise the love potion from its smell and taste. But the unsuspecting Tiran drank it all. As soon as he had gulped down the potion, he looked dazed. Darya drew closer and kissed him. She placed his head against her chest and looked down deeply into his soft brown eyes before kissing them. She held his hand and sat with him quietly for a long time. Then she sighed, stood up and gave him a potion that broke the spell. Tiran looked like he had woken up from a deep sleep as he wiped his lips. He suddenly looked scared and perplexed, for he did not know what had happened. He stood up hastily, bid goodbye and walked out. As he left her chamber, he clutched his pockets to check if he still had his red ruby on himself. The rounded ruby felt hard and reassuring through his robes.

Darya reported her findings back to Rhuzbeh and Metishin. 'That person is not a djinn, an evil spirit or a sorcerer. He is a warrior from the south. He seems knowledgeable and has noble manners. Is he a good man? Does he mean harm?' She shrugged, stating, 'I don't know!'

'We must be on our guard,' said Metishin. Both Rhuzbeh and Darya nodded.

Darya came back to her chambers, upset with herself. She had never cast a love charm on anyone, and indeed it was considered the skill of a dark sorcerer. What had she done? Just because he had not responded to her advances, she had cast a spell and kissed him!

She cringed at her actions. Childhood memories came flooding back to her mind. She was the daughter of an ordinary merchant from the streets of Hatasa. He was not a king, but she was his princess. She could still see his loving face and kind eyes. How she would squeal with delight on seeing him. How he would smother her with kisses, buy her toys and sing funny songs. He was her life, and that life was rudely and abruptly ended when he was torn apart by beasts. She had cried until her heart burst and refused to eat for two days. Her mother, Ceba, had feared that she would die too. It had taken Ceba all her love and willpower to make Darya eat again.

In those times, a stranger would come and console them. She never liked him much and would shirk away if he tried to pat her. Six months later, her mother married him. That day, she had cried even more.

Her mother was now the queen and she was a princess. But Darya hated the attention. Dressing up, learning courtly manners and staying in the inner palace chambers stifled her. All she ever wanted to do was run free in the bazaars of Hatasa with her father. Metishin had spotted the lonely and distraught girl. He had seen a spark in her and took her under his wings. He was a wise and kind old man, and she immediately took to him. He had taught her the art of being a mage. Metishin's crest was a winged dragon—a symbol, he said, that stood for timeless wisdom.

Darya's thirst for knowledge was unquenchable, and she embarked on a long journey to learn from the hallowed mages and wizards who were scattered around in far-flung places. She mastered the art of conjuring great creatures to duel against other mages. Darya could now create her own spells, which was what differentiated mages and wizards magic-wise. She mastered the art of fighting magical beasts and wielding their by-products. She also learnt how to battle the unseen forces of djinns and other spirits. But what she really cherished to know was the intricacies of alchemy and the secret knowledge of the great serpents.

Unfortunately, she could learn but very little about both. When Darya was finally an accomplished mage, she acquired a staff with a serpent that seemed to stir sometimes. She wielded a wooden staff that had a snake carving. The snake was so life-like that it seemed to stir.

But with knowledge comes temptation. She became curious about the darker side of magic. For knowledge does not make you wise—wisdom is the offspring of experience. A large number of mages sought and dabbled in the dark arts, but they would not teach anyone because they were not proud of it. Only sorcerers would teach dark magic and Darya wanted to learn only from the best. And so it was that her search took her to Dahel the Bearclaw.

She vividly remembered her stint with Dahel, as if she could relive it through her mind's eye any moment. After Rhuzbeh had defeated Dahel the Sorcerer and killed the black cat, his adversary had lost all his powers. How, then, had Dahel become the most formidable black sorcerer again?

When she met him, Darya was traversing the volcanic mountains of the northwest in the search of the dark sorcerer. She knocked on Dahel's door, and he opened it. She said, 'Greetings, Dahel the Bearclaw. I, Darya, a mage and ward of King Rhuzbeh, seek an audience with you.'

Dahel was delighted. He had been planning revenge against Rhuzbeh, and now Rhuzbeh's step-daughter had just voluntarily walked into his lair. Dahel let her in.

'I thought you lost your power. How did you become the all-powerful black sorcerer again?' asked Darya.

'Indeed, that encounter with Rhuzbeh rendered me as powerless as a peasant. I wanted my powers back. If Daheli, my wife and the greatest sorcerer in the land, had found out that I was no longer a sorcerer, she would have abandoned me. So I started plotting my return.'

'What did you do?' asked Darya.

'I remembered the evil sorcerer Isvil. I had killed him, and since his power could not inhabit his killer's body, it was trapped in his room and was bouncing around. His magical powers then inhabited Daheli, making her a great sorcerer. What I planned to do was truly evil—I planned to kill the love of my life and harness her powers. I hired a mercenary and hid him behind the door. As soon as a travel-weary Daheli returned and knocked on the door, I knew it was her. I locked all the windows and hid the assassin. When she stepped inside the house, I shut the door and hugged her. Daheli was glad to return to the arms of the man she loved. I lovingly said,

'Daheli, I missed you so much. I love you forever and ever.' That was the cue for the assassin to stab her in the back, and he did not disappoint. Daheli did not immediately understand what happened, but before dying, she cast a powerful spell on the assassin. He was burnt to ashes at the exact spot where he was standing.'

'And her power inhabited your body?' asked Darya.

'Yes,' said Dahel, 'With Daheli dead, her magical powers, seeking release, swished around the house and, upon finding no way out, inhabited me. And I, Dahel the Bearclaw, became an all-powerful sorcerer again!'

'Hmm,' mumbled Darya.

'So, what does the stepdaughter of Rhuzbeh want from me?' asked Dahel.

'I want to learn the dark arts,' she replied.

'Go away! You have too much goodness in you. Your power comes from natural elements, so I cannot teach you,' said Dahel.

She pleaded with him, but he pushed her out and shut the door on her. She simply sat outside, refusing to move. Every day hence, he would throw garbage, filth, blood and faeces at her. He would call her names and physically abuse her until she lost all sense of self-respect. After two months of Darya wallowing in her own filth, Dahel acquiesced. He began his teachings by first filling her heart with hatred by telling her about the sins of Rhuzbeh.

'Do you know his biggest sin?' he asked her.

'No, master,' she replied.

'Let me tell you a story,' started Dahel, 'There was a king who was in love with a merchant's wife. While the merchant was crossing a forest, he caught him and threw him in a cage with two hungry bears. The hungry bears mauled the merchant to death and even ate a part of him. His half-eaten body was thrown into the forest, and the bears were released. After six months, he married the merchant's wife. Do you know who that merchant was?'

She listened in shock, for she knew the answer. 'That man was your father,' said Dahel.

Darya broke down and sobbed inconsolably. It was a gut-wrenching pain. Deep down, she had known it all along, and now it was confirmed. Dark thoughts of revenge and hatred filled her heart, and she wanted to kill Rhuzbeh. She was now ready for the dark arts. With her soul soiled with hate, she learnt the dark arts for two years from the most potent dark sorcerer, Dahel the Bearclaw. The animal that she conjured during any battle, such as a black panther with a sharp metal tail, was actually the black cat of Dahel.

When she finally returned to Zanda, she confronted Metishin regarding her father's murder. Metishin confirmed it but implored her not to tell her mother. 'One day, Prince Axer will be crowned king, and she will be the queen-mother. If she knew the secret, the future of the kingdom would be at stake. I am sure Axer will be a just king and bring in peace and prosperity,' said Metishin and added, 'By the way, who told you about Rhuzbeh's misdeed?'

Darya opened up to Metishin and told him about her brush with the dark arts. They had a long conversation about light and dark.

'In order to thwart darkness, one has to know darkness intimately. It is a mage's choice to seek magic through the elements in the universe or from the dark side. Indeed, some of the finest mages have dabbled in both. Sometimes, the good overpowers the dark in a person and other times, the dark overpowers the good. And sometimes, like a snake coiled around a rosebush, they coexist with each other. It is not the magic but the mage—that is, the soul of a mage—that decides which way to swing. Do you feel like exacting revenge?' asked Metishin.

'No,' replied Darya. 'As I was sufficiently trained, Dahel wanted to use me. He implored me to kill Rhuzbeh and avenge us both. But I resisted. I did not want to be used as a tool. I told myself that my hatred does not define me. Dahel, in a fit of anger, tried to kill me but I fended him off. I realised what a huge threat the dark forces were and resolved to stop it. But since Dahel had taught me, out of respect, I did not want to kill him at his place. So I left him with a warning that if he ever tried to fight against Zanda or Hatasa, I shall step in and do my duty.'

'Go, my child and discover what you are made of,' said Metishin. He had a great fondness for her but decided to keep a keen eye on her. He knew that once a person was touched by black magic, the dark forces would relentlessly try to overpower them. Darya was headed for trouble.

Meanwhile, Rhuzbeh was warming up to Tiran and enjoyed his company. They would often go hunting, discuss politics and dine together. Rhuzbeh loved him like a son, and young Tiran was gaining an undue influence over the king.

Once during a hunting expedition, Tiran asked, 'I have heard of the sanaa gem that you returned to the djinns. What does it look like?'

'Although it looks like a brilliant round ruby, the sanaa is actually a red pearl that is as large as a peach and shines so spectacularly that it looks like it's almost dancing in the light.'

Tiran was speechless for a few minutes and eventually said, 'I have seen something like that before,' and bit his tongue instinctively. 'Of course, I could be wrong,' he added hesitantly

'Where have you seen it?' asked Rhuzbeh eagerly.

'Oh! I have seen many rubies like that in the Sedran court,' said Tiran evasively, 'Although not the size of a peach, they are almost cherry-sized. I am sure I am mistaken; it must not be sanaa.'

Rhuzbeh's excitement gave way to a frown.

'Oh!' exclaimed Rhuzbeh, unable to hide his disappointment.

Tiran touched his robes and felt his gemstone's presence.

A month later, there was a report that the royal armoury was raided. Weapons and other equipment were upturned and ten distinctively fine swords had gone missing. The palace guards also found a note with the same inscrutable "Pashem I=" scribbled across it. Whoever raided the palace was not discreet. It was as if they wanted the people to know. This was not just a raid; it was a taunt.

More significantly, this was a challenge to the king. Since the word 'pashem' meant 'wool', Rhuzbeh ordered all the woollen shops to be raided and the wool merchants to be questioned but the whole exercise turned out to be futile. The conspirators could not be traced. The missing swords were a cause of concern as they could be used in an armed conspiracy.

Rhuzbeh called his court and announced, 'I know there is a conspiracy being hatched. I don't know what it is but know this: I am Rhuzbeh the indomitable, and I have no reason to fear these louts. Just to show my contempt for these idle threats, I declare five days of games and entertainment. The finest warriors of the realm will participate, along with my sons.'

Rhuzbeh formed the King's League and populated it with six warriors—himself, Axer, Hittash, Darya and two other warriors. Rhuzbeh threw an open challenge to anyone who wished to take on the King's League.

Rhuzbeh called on Tiran and ominously said, 'I have figured out how I am going to get the second sanaa.'

Tiran looked at Rhuzbeh with terror-struck eyes.

'Do you know how I am going to get it?' asked Rhuzbeh.

'I don't know,' replied Tiran.

'You shall know soon,' said Rhuzbeh with a meaningful look aimed at Tiran.

Tiran took leave of the king and hastily removed the sanaa from his robes. He stared at it for a long time before hiding it in a secure location.

Meanwhile, Rhuzbeh procured dancers, jugglers, exotic beasts and the strongest warriors to participate in the games. While the idea was not to kill each other, some injuries and accidental deaths were indeed unavoidable. Regardless, these games were a show of strength, and all the kings from neighbouring kingdoms were invited to attend. They came with great pomp and ceremony along with precious gifts.

Rhuzbeh made sure his two great rivals attended the games. King Shaha from Sedra, who arrived with a vast retinue under his sea-serpent banner, and King Nahal from the Northern kingdom, who attended the games wearing the sanaa just to rub it in.

The herald announced the king's arrival: 'Behold! King Rhuzbeh the Fearless: the undisputed king from the east to the west; the bearer of the gajmuk; the wielder of the zer sword, the ally of the djinns, the tamer of elephants, the champion of centaurs and the lord of all that he surveys.' There were loud cheers and fanfare as the assembled kings and commoners cheered Rhuzbeh.

To everyone's surprise, a king from Wastra stood up and loudly announced, 'I do not believe that Rhuzbeh has it in him anymore. I think he is old and undeserving of these accolades.' The crowd gasped at the insult to their king.

The commanders drew their swords, but Rhuzbeh stayed their hand. The western king continued his taunt and said, 'The kingdoms from the far west have brought a khavees, a true giant that is the last of its species. Does Rhuzbeh have it in him to battle the khavees?' His banner of twin snakes facing each other fluttered in the wind.

Meanwhile, the khavees was let inside the empty stadium. He was two and a half times the size of Rhuzbeh and nearly five times his weight. The khavees held a massive wooden mace in his hand. When the crowd booed, the towering giant let out a loud bellow that cowed the crowd into silence. The sheer size of the giant was unnerving.

Rhuzbeh went quiet when he saw the giant.

The western king laughed and said, 'Rhuzbeh the Fearless is diminished by his fear. Look! Your king is old and a quivering wreck.'

As if on cue, the khavees bellowed. All the assembled kings laughed.

'Why,' continued the western king, 'if that is not incentive enough, then king Nahal will himself bet his sanaa. If you win, you win the sanaa, and if you lose, you die!'

Axer, Hittash and Tiran intervened, saying, 'The king need not fight personally. He has brave warriors at his service; choose any one of us.'

King Nahal sensed an opportunity to rid himself of Rhuzbeh forever. He quickly said, 'I agree, sanaa is destined to be returned to the djinns through Rhuzbeh. But it was gifted to my ancestors by the great Simorgh. If Rhuzbeh can beat the khavees, he can have sanaa.'

Rhuzbeh rose and said, 'I accept.'

The crowd roared. They could not believe that Rhuzbeh would stake his life against such overwhelming odds to win sanaa.

Metishin tried to dissuade Rhuzbeh. 'My King! The khavees is a dangerous opponent. One blow and he could squash you like an insect. No armour can protect you from an impact like that. Besides, you are not as young as you once were. Let some other warrior face the khavees.'

Rhuzbeh brushed aside Metishin's concerns. He was not intimidated by the spectre of belligerence looming ahead.

Axer also pleaded with Rhuzbeh and said, 'Let me fight the giant.' But Rhuzbeh took his son's hand and said with a smirk, 'Son, watch and learn as your father brings the khavees to its knees.' He ruffled Axer's hair and prepared to fight.

Rhuzbeh asked for a horse and clad himself in full-body armour with the frog belt around his waist. He also carried a mighty hammer with him and wore his zer sword by his side.

He entered the stadium and blew his ivory horn, which was the signal to commence the fight. The crowd rose to their feet and cheered for their hero, Rhuzbeh.

The khavees stood in the middle, slowly swinging the wooden club. Rhuzbeh charged toward the khavees, who swung the club at the oncoming rider. Rhuzbeh ducked, and as the mace swished harmlessly above his head, he rode past the giant landing a mighty blow on his fleshy lower back using his hammer. The giant howled, and the delighted spectators cheered. This happened a few times.

And then, the unthinkable happened.

As Rhuzbeh rode towards him, the khavees dropped the mace and quickly grabbed the horse's leg. Using his great strength, the giant flung the horse, which dropped with a thud. Meanwhile, Rhuzbeh had slipped and fallen from the horse just as it was being grabbed and so he was not seriously injured. The horse—even with four horseshoes nailed to its legs—was not so lucky. The crowd gasped and were now on their feet. The giant charged and tried to grasp Rhuzbeh in a tight grip. Rhuzbeh dodged the giant's hand and ran between its legs and swung the hammer between them. The blow made the giant collapse, marking the end of the duel. The crowd rose to acknowledge their champion, and a thunderous applause filled the stadium.

A speechless and visibly disappointed Nahal handed over the second sanaa to the victor, Rhuzbeh. This entire episode had been an elaborate ruse concocted by Ghanazaqi, the wily djinn. When Ghanazaqi learnt that Nahal would be visiting Zanda wearing the sanaa, he laid out the plan and Rhuzbeh had put it into action. The western king was planted to provoke Nahal to bet the sanaa.

It was a great start to the games but the fall had injured Rhuzbeh's shoulder. After taking a bow to acknowledge his doting subjects, Rhuzbeh headed to Metishin's tent for treatment. More fights, dancers, jugglers and all other manners of entertainment followed his act. It was a spectacular start to the games, and the citizens hurried back to their homes in the evening, for they had great stories to share with their families and neighbours.

At night, there was a fire in a section of the marketplace, and all the woollen shops were set ablaze. The soldiers rushed to the market to ascertain the cause of the fire and discovered that the shops had been doused with oil—it was arson. Again, there was that accursed sign "Pashem I=". The king's advisors asked him to call off the games, citing a threat to his life.

Rhuzbeh thundered, 'Let them come. I offer myself as bait to lure out the rats.'

It was the second day of the fight. Two warriors from the King's League were to fight two lions simultaneously. The lions were truly magnificent. They had great shaggy manes, which extended over the shoulder and under the belly to the elbows. Their muscles rippled as they moved fluidly in the arena, and their roars put fear in every spectator. Never before had they seen such animals in captivity.

Rhuzbeh signalled for the game to begin. To everyone's horror, the two lions fell upon one of the warriors. As one of the lions knocked down the warrior, the other pounced on him and separated his head from the body. It was so swift that the other warrior did not have time to react. The lone warrior lost his nerve and tried to run, but he was chased down and his flesh torn from his bones. It was a ghastly sight. The crowd screamed in horror, and a few spectators retched at the grisly sight.

Two of his finest warriors were slain in front of his eyes and Rhuzbeh could do nothing about it. The neighbouring kings were secretly happy. King Nahal, sensing an opportunity, rose up and declared, 'What happened was abominable. I am sure the king or the princes would avenge the slain warriors.'

The gauntlet had been thrown; everyone was still. The princes or the king would have to accept the challenge. Tiran bravely rose up and said, 'I am willing to lay down my life for my king, who I dearly love as a father. I shall fight the lions and, if possible, avenge the slain warriors of the King's League.'

It was a fine gesture, but it would make Rhuzbeh and his sons look like cowards, so Axer rose up and said, 'Thank you, Tiran, for your loyalty to the king, but my brother, Prince Hittash, and I will battle these beasts and avenge our warriors. On the last day of the games, we shall battle these beasts and reclaim our glory.'

The crowd cheered for their princes. The neighbouring kings were gladdened with the outcome of the fight. There was a fleeting chance that both princes might be killed, which would reduce the threat to their kingdoms. Meanwhile, by nominating himself to single-handedly fight the lions, Tiran had won the respect of Rhuzbeh. Later that evening, Rhuzbeh called in his courtiers and said, 'I want to acknowledge Tiran's loyalty and bravery. He single-handedly volunteered to fight the lions to defend my honour. Tiran! Today you have won my respect and trust.'

'It would be my life's honour to die for you, my king,' said Tiran.

Rhuzbeh nodded and said, 'I made enquiries and found out that these lions are not ordinary lions. They are Wrey lions from the peaks of Idurar; they are very rare and extremely ferocious. I am told that they were transported first to the Northern kingdom, from where they were sent later to Zanda. I sense a conspiracy. We must be on our guard.'

The advisors nodded in agreement. Rhuzbeh was proud of his son Axer. What a warrior he was turning out to be—a prince that would make any king proud. He was his father's son every inch and was utterly loyal to him. If Rhuzbeh had anything spotless and pure, it was his son. He was protective of and obsessed with Axer.

Rhuzbeh dismissed his advisors and addressed Axer.

He said, 'Son, I am proud of you. You have proved yourself to be brave and valiant. Please be careful when you fight the lions, for you will be the king someday.'

Axer nodded and said, 'Thank you, father! I shall try to be worthy of being called the son of Rhuzbeh the Fearless.'

He took leave of his father, went back to his own tent and sat thinking. He had to prove his bravery in the field and show that he was stronger than Hittash and a worthy heir. He also had to make Anitsa proud. The thought of the lovely Anitsa put a smile on his lips.

Sometime ago, during the campaigns in the west, Axer was riding with two of his soldiers. He came across a hut, knocked on the door and asked for water. The door opened slightly and a hand with a cup of water was extended. Axer drank the water and was curious about the person inside the hut. 'Come out. I would like to see the face of the person whose hands extended the water,' commanded Axer.

To his surprise, a maiden of surreal beauty stepped out with downcast eyes. She was wearing tattered clothes, and her hair was unkempt, and yet she looked so exquisite. 'Who are you?' asked Axer.

'My name is Anitsa,' she said, 'My father died of prolonged illness, and my mother passed away last week. I am an orphan with no one to care for me.' She started to sob.

Axer saw this vulnerable beauty and fell in love. He secretly smuggled her into Zanda and placed her in a small mansion. After his successful campaign at Wastra, he spent a lot of time with her. He was a man in love and proposed marriage.

But Anitsa was horrified and said, 'I am but a poor orphan. The king would prefer that you marry a princess and make stronger alliances. I am afraid that the king would have me killed for this affront. I fear for my life. Promise me that until you become the king, you will not take me before Rhuzbeh.'

Axer protested, but upon seeing her distraught, he agreed. Slowly, Axer opened up to her. He narrated how he was fond of Darya and how she ignored him.

Axer was born a prince and had the gus ambergris running through his veins. His mother, Ceba, doted on him and he looked so much like her. However, it was his father that he truly loved and looked up to. He would spend his waking hours at Rhuzbeh's side, learning the nuances of warfare from his illustrious father. He had a bizarre relationship with Darya, his elder sister. She had a striking physical resemblance to his mother and him but she was always cold and distant. Since both his parents loved him, he wanted to be loved by his step-sister, but she always avoided him and refused to play with him. During their training sessions, whenever they fought each other, she always won. She was older and used spells to knock him down. She was also handy with a sword. Axer tried his best to win her approval, but she simply ignored him. It was not as if she hated him; it was just that she was not particularly fond of him. After completing her education at Metishin's hands, Darya left him and went to distant lands to learn magic. He missed her but never told her about it.

Anitsa said, 'My grandfather was a sorcerer. Sorcery runs in my blood. Since Darya won't stay by your side, I would like to formally learn sorcery to protect you.'

Although he had reservations about sorcery, he truly loved her and wanted her to pursue her interests. 'I love you and I want you to be happy,' he said.

He made arrangements for her to learn sorcery. Unknown to Axer, the king's spies told Rhuzbeh all about the maiden. The king took it light-heartedly as the dalliance of a young man and laughed it off. In less than a year, Anitsa picked up sorcery very quickly and became surprisingly adept at it.

Axer was wary of Hittash, who was tall, dark and powerfully built. Although born not of mutual consent, Hittash had the blood of his father and that of a princess mother as well as gus ambergris running through his veins. Even as children, Axer and Hittash had always been rivals. Hittash was better at academics, and Axer was slightly better at swordsmanship.

On the final day of the games, he not only had to survive but also show the king that he was better than Hittash. The fight against the Wrey lions would have far-reaching repercussions, as the winner would make a lasting impression on the populace as a worthy potential candidate for the throne of the joint kingdoms.

On the third day of the games, it was Princess Darya's turn to fight a powerful and well-known mage. She carried her snake staff in one hand and a sword in the other. The other mage held only his staff. They started by casting light spells on each other, trying to assess each other's strength. The mage cast a spell that conjured up a giant snake. The crowd screamed in horror. Darya conjured up an eagle that caught the snake in its talons and devoured it. The mage then conjured up a mean-looking magical spear and threw it at her. Darya tried to sidestep but the spear followed her. She tried to deflect it with her staff, but it grazed her hand and left her bleeding.

Darya was livid. Suddenly, it looked like she had grown larger. She turned glowing red as if she was on fire. She smote the ground with her staff. The other mage's staff started burning and turned to ash. Darya strode towards him and struck him down with her staff and he collapsed to the ground. The awed crowd rose to their feet. It was not for nothing that Metishin called her 'the greatest mage in the known world'.

That night, three noblemen who were favourable to Ceba were murdered, and again there was the mark, "Pashem I=". One of the stolen swords was found lying on the ground next to the dead bodies. Rhuzbeh asked Tiran to head the investigation and put a task force under him for tracking the conspirators. He wanted to be focused on the games as his heart was in a lurch at the thought of his sons' impending fight against the Wrey lions.

Rhuzbeh thought of Hittash. He was a loyal and worthy son. But unfortunately, he did not feel the same love and affection for him that he felt towards Axer. He sent for Hittash, which was quite rare as the young man was a constant reminder of his misdeed towards his mother. Rhuzbeh hardly spoke to him, but he was his own flesh and blood. Gus ambergris ran in his veins, and although Hittash was suspected of having committed a murder, it was not proven. Still, he was a prince of Zanda, and under unforeseen circumstances, he could be a king someday.

Rhuzbeh said, 'Hittash, your brother has nominated you as his companion during the fight. Take care of yourself and protect your brother.'

'Yes, my king,' replied Hittash. They did not have much to say to each other after that and there was an awkward silence. Hittash quickly excused himself when he realised that Rhuzbeh had nothing more to add. He had an expressionless face, and nobody could tell what he felt or thought. He came back to his chambers and sat thinking.

In reality, Hittash hated Rhuzbeh. He wanted to kill him. He was a constant reminder of his grandfather's murder and his mother's shame. As a child, he was very reclusive and had only Darya for company. Possibly, Darya was the only one who saw the pain in his eyes. She did not have a father, and Hittash did not want to have a father.

Ever since he was five years old, Darya had protected him against other children who whispered behind his back and picked on him. She even beat back Axer when he tried to bully Hittash. Although Hittash loved her as his own sister, he did not want her to protect him. When he was fourteen years old, he left Zanda for Hatasa. After all, he was the grandson of King Hitkar, and the Hatasans looked upon him as the rightful king. In Hatasa, he spent his finest years. He was now a master horseman, and he could also ride an ibex. He quickly acquired a reputation as an able warrior.

When he was twenty years old, he fell in love with a girl called Zera, one of the daughters of a small hill chieftain.

Zera and Hittash were both madly in love. However, when he expressed a desire to marry Zera, her father, the chieftain, said, 'I cannot give my daughter to you as I have promised to give her hand to the Descendant of Edal, and I cannot back out.'

'Who is Edal?' asked Hittash.

'Edal was an illustrious warrior of yore. His exploits were legendary. He had a magical bow, which is said to have passed down from generation to generation. The bow is made from the bones of a simorgh. The arrows are made of simorgh bone as well, and the tip of the arrows are made of hardened ashsilver, a metal that is hard as stone and shines like silver. No armour can stop an arrow fired from the bow of Edal.'

The Descendant of Edal was a young man who ruled a small fleck of a kingdom on the Hatasan border. Although highly respected, the kingdom was not rich and did not have a standing army. Hittash rode up to that kingdom with a division of the Hatasan army. Any attack on the impoverished realm would have been carnage. Hittash decided against bloodshed, challenged the young king to one-to-one combat and laid down the condition that the winner would take what he desired. The descendent was young but proud and he came out to combat. The duel was hard, but the young king fought well and almost killed Hittash. Hittash used all his skills and eventually disarmed him and made him a prisoner.

Hittash was curious about one thing though. 'Aren't you the bearer of the Bow of Edal?'

'Yes!' said the king.

'Then why did you not use it on me?' Hittash asked.

'That would be unfair. Only a coward would use a magical weapon on someone not magically armed,' said the young king.

Hittash realised then that he had been reckless. He could have been killed had the young king used the Bow of Edal. Hittash released him and said, 'You have won me over with your noble gesture. Please accept my apologies and friendship.'

'Please don't apologise,' said the young king. 'You won in a fair fight. Yet, you chivalrously apologise to the one you vanquished.'

There was mutual admiration, and a bond was struck. Hittash spent three days as a royal guest of the young king, and he spoke about his love for the chieftain's daughter. The young king acknowledged Hittash's love for Zera and convinced the chieftain to marry his daughter off to Hittash. And so it was that Hittash was betrothed to Zera.

When Rhuzbeh heard about the assault, he was upset that his vassal had been attacked. He summoned Hittash to Zanda and sought an explanation. When Hittash narrated the story, Rhuzbeh calmed down. A royal wedding took place, and Hittash and Zera were married. Two months after the marriage though, the Descendant of Edal was found murdered and the Bow of Edal went missing. A Hatasan gold coin was found near his dead body, and all blame fell on Hittash.

The needle of suspicion swung towards Hittash for a particular reason. Axer owned Amirast's impenetrable golden armour that only an arrow shot from the Bow of Edal could pierce through. If ever there was a battle for succession, Hittash would have the wherewithal to take on

Axer with the bow's help. And hence people assumed that Hittash murdered and stole the Bow of Edal. The fact that a Hatasan gold coin was found near the dead body only confirmed the suspicion.

As the Descendant of Edal fell, Hittash, in turn, fell in everyone's eyes. Before his guilt was proven, the populace assumed the role of couch-mounted quasi-judges and announced him guilty to their families. Hittash was devastated. Not only had he lost his friend, he was also being blamed for his murder. Rhuzbeh called the council and Hittash was put on trial. Hitti personally intervened and confronted the king and his court.

'How dare anyone accuse the prince without any proof,' she thundered. 'Is there a witness to attest that Prince Hittash committed a murder? Can anyone show proof that he conspired to kill the Descendant of Edal? Does Hittash have the Bow of Edal in possession? Indeed, has anyone ever found the Bow of Edal? Do you have nothing but suspicion and hearsay to blame my son and your prince? How dare you try and tarnish his reputation? I, Hitti, will not even allow a trial without proof,' she admonished.

Rhuzbeh nodded. What she said was true. Nobody knew where the Bow was. It was a legendary weapon, and if it had ever surfaced, someone would definitely have noticed. For the lack of proof, the council could not even put Hittash on trial, let alone convict him. Rhuzbeh let go with a warning that if ever proof was found, Hittash would be prosecuted.

So it was that a tainted Hittash joined Rhuzbeh's campaign against the western kingdoms and fought even more recklessly. He did not care whether he lived or died anymore.

The thing about innocent people stigmatised by an unproven accusation is that they cannot afford to be either quiet or raise their voices. If they remain silent, they are pronounced guilty, for if they were not guilty, why would they stay quiet? And if they raise their voice and do small acts of kindness to quell doubts, they are presumed to be trying to cover and wash their sins.

If one is accused by people they don't care about, the accusers become like the water of the lake, and like a proverbial duck, one can shake off the waters easily from its feathers. But when the accusers are those one cares about, they become like lamp oil, for the accusations are not shaken away so easily.

Hittash did not seek advice from people who believed in him. He did not ask Metishin or Darya or even his own mother, Hitti, who had interceded on his behalf. He stopped talking to everyone except his wife; he could not look anyone in the eye. His small acts of generosity and kindness were mocked, and his intelligence and strategy were considered proof of a devious mind that planned a dastardly murder. So, during the war, he looked for ways to redeem himself. He waded into the enemy ranks just to prove that he was not a cowardly murderer. He became so reckless that at one time, he charged head-on at full speed and found himself to be way ahead of his army and almost alone. The enemy surrounded him and he would have been killed that day had Darya not charged in and used her magic to cast her black panther. She defended him until the army caught up with them. He hated her for defending him though. He did not want anyone to protect him. If he died, so be it!

Darya knew Hittash was innocent, and wanted to make sure that he did not throw away his life in battle. She gifted him a magical metal bear-glove with claws. The claws could tear through anything and even block a sword, arrow or spear. The claws had the ability to magically grow longer if the wearer wished. Darya had used a considerable amount of magic to make it. Spells are temporary but magical objects are rare and take a toll on the maker. Darya had used all her knowledge—both elemental magic and black magic—to make the bear-glove. The bear-glove itself was inspired by Dahel the Bearclaw. He still had considerable influence on her mind, and she simply could not shake off that little bit of darkness in her. Hittash did not want the glove, but he thought it would be too rude to refuse such a gift. Besides, it would keep Darya from babysitting him, and so he accepted the gift.

Hittash had fought well in the Western campaign, but his father did not heap accolades because of his taint. Now he had returned to Zanda, and the games were on. His impending fight against the lions was a chance to redeem himself. He struggled to sleep, and when he finally fell asleep, it was fitful.

That night, Tiran had a breakthrough. He managed to catch a thief who was trying to poison a minister and carried a note on his person, along with a stolen sword. Tiran, being in charge of the investigation, arrested the man and detained him in the dungeons for interrogation.

On the fourth day, two warriors walked in to challenge the Zandians. One was light-skinned, and the other was swarthy and dark-skinned. They were chained to each other, and they used the heavy chain as a weapon. These powerful warriors had trained with each other as children and had one thing in common—ruthlessness. They were killers, and their assaults were aimed to kill.

What started as an exhibition match turned bloody very fast. The duo mercilessly killed the two opponents who fought against them by wrapping the chain around them. Once their opponents were knocked down, they smashed their skulls into the ground, spilling the brains of the fallen on the floor of the arena. Rhuzbeh was outraged at this display of barbarity.

He sent two heavily armoured horsemen to challenge them, but they brought them down as well by using their chain. They then proceeded to decapitate the riders and the horses.

As the crowd watched in revulsion, they threw an open challenge to Rhuzbeh. The princes and Darya rose up to volunteer, but Rhuzbeh made them sit down. He wanted to see if any other warriors could take up the challenge. Tiran rose and said, 'I can beat them.'

Tiran had volunteered against the lions but had not been given the opportunity. This time, Rhuzbeh nodded his assent. Tiran put on his armour and entered the arena for the battle. He carried a sword, a lead-tipped spear and a small flying monkey. The duo laughed when they saw the lead-tipped spear and monkey. Indeed, thought Rhuzbeh, Tiran could have carried a better spear. The horn was sounded and the fight began.

The duo spread out, tightening the chain, and rushed towards Tiran. The heavy chain hit his body with force, pushing him down with a thud. It looked like Tiran was knocked out and would not be able to get up. The duo walked to the nearby wall of the arena, turning their rump towards Tiran to mock him. With their hands raised up in the air, they bent backwards, spreading out the chain taut against the wall. Before they could turn and throw themselves at him, however, Tiran recovered and, in a flash, threw his spear on the chain, breaking the metal chain into two parts. The crowd gasped. How was it possible to cut a metal chain with a lead spear? The duo was cut off from each other. Before they could recover from the shock, Tiran instantly threw a dagger at one of the fighters and killed him. The other was enraged and shocked. After the chain got cut, he was confused like a baby cut apart from the umbilical cord, but the death of his partner made him snap back.

He thirsted for vengeance. Tiran threw a dagger at him as well, but by then, he had recovered from the shock and easily dodged it. He regained some of his confidence, and even without his partner, he was formidable and quick. Tiran was armed with a sword in his right hand and the lead-tipped spear in his left.

As his attacker leapt mid-air towards Tiran with swords in both hands, Tiran's roguish monkfly shoved a twig in the man's ear. Instinctively, the man drew one of his sword hands to protect his ear. Just then, Tiran blocked the other sword using his own sword and, with the lead-tipped spear in the other hand, skewered him. Tiran had won against the murderous duo. It was a great victory, and the crowd stood on their feet and applauded.

That night, the prisoner who was being interrogated died of poisoning, and again there was the sign, "Pashem I=".

On the fifth and last day, it was the princes' turn to tackle the Wrey lions. When the princes made their entry, the stadium was packed, and there were huge crowds outside the stadium as well. The kingdom would be bereft of its heirs if the lions killed the princes, and if either of the princes got killed, the other would become the heir apparent. This was going to be a deciding fight.

Rhuzbeh blew his ivory horn, and Metishin announced the princes' arrival. 'Behold!' he said, 'The mighty Princes Axer and Hittash.'

The crowd let out a deafening cheer. The princes looked resplendent. Axer was clad in the golden armour of janns, and Hittash bore metallic bear-gloves gifted by Darya. Suddenly, all went still. Slowly the gates were drawn up. The stadium was so quiet that everybody could hear the squeak of the gates. The Wrey lions slowly entered the arena. They walked together in unison as if choreographed. They looked up at the crowds and roared. So terrifying was the roar that a petrified teenager urinated in his clothes.

The princes stood close to each other because they had realised that the lions isolated their prey like they did while hunting in forests. Metishin had given them oversized rectangular shields, which were burnished and highly polished. They were so smooth that they almost looked like mirrors. When the lions approached the shield wall, they could see themselves. To the lions, it looked as if two other lions were approaching them. When they roared at the reflection, the sound reflected back, and it seemed that the other lions were roaring as well. The lions did not know what to think of it. To them, it might have seemed like two humans and two lions were attacking them.

The lions started circling the two princes. The princes turned and stood back-to-back with the shields in front of them. There were no weak, exposed areas for the lions to attack.

Suddenly, while circling, one of the lions attacked. It swiped a powerful paw at Axer's shield. The shield went tumbling, and the crowd let out a collective gasp.

Quickly, Hittash turned around and swung his axe, making a cut in the lion's body. The lion roared in anger and attacked Hittash. Now both lions were attacking Hittash. Axer ran and grabbed his shield and threw his spear at one of the lions. Although the lion was injured, the spear could not pierce through its thick mane. In anger, the injured lion turned to Axer. The two princes were now battling two different lions. Meanwhile, the other lion attacked Hittash by leaping on his shield. Hittash swung his axe, injuring the lion, but in two swift swipes of his paw, the lion knocked out both the axe and the shield. Hittash drew his sword and faced the lion.

Sensing victory, the latter began closing in on him. Meanwhile, Axer had his shield knocked out again; his spear lay on the ground where he had earlier thrown it.

Both the princes were almost defenceless, with just a sword in their hands. Rhuzbeh was wringing his hands, and the other kings looked secretly delighted. Some women in the crowd had already started wailing. Darya was about to cast a spell, but Metishin said, 'No! Let the princes prove themselves. They knew what they were getting into when they volunteered to fight the lions.'

The princes faced off the lions. One of the lions swiped at Axer's armour-clad body. The jann armour was almost impenetrable, but the impact sent Axer reeling. The lion pounced on Axer and bit him in the head. The crowd screamed in horror, but luckily, his helmet prevented him from any serious injury. Using the sword hilt, Axer gave a mighty blow to the lion's head. The lion was dazed and reeled back. Seizing the opportunity, Axer recovered and pulled himself up. Meanwhile, the other lion leapt and swung his mighty paw at Hittash ripping away his body armour and knocking out the sword in his hands.

Hittash was now completely unarmed and bleeding heavily. In an act of bravado, Hittash leapt onto the lion's back and, with his bear-gloves claws, ripped out the lion's throat.

The crowd cheered lustily. One prince had overcome a lion.

The other lion attacked Axer again and its mighty paw swiped at him, ripping out his armour and knocking him to the ground. Axer hit the ground hard and lost his grip on the sword due to the impact. Fortunately, the lion paused and looked up in anger to see its fellow lion's throat ripped open by Hittash. The angry lion ignored Axer and prepared to rush towards Hittash.

This was the opportunity that Axer was looking for; he stood up and ran. The lion noticed Axer running and started chasing him. It gave a mighty leap and landed on Axer. For what seemed like an eternity, nobody moved. The crowd went still. Everyone thought Axer was dead. But suddenly, Axer pushed off the body of the lion and emerged from under the dead body to the deafening cheer of the crowds. When the lion had leapt on him, he had reached the spot where the spear had fallen and managed to hold it up just in time, effectively skewering the pouncing lion. Although injured, both the princes had killed off the lions, and Rhuzbeh was proud of them.

The crowd was on their feet, cheering and whistling. After acknowledging the cheers, the princes bowed low to a proud Rhuzbeh.

Just as they were exiting the arena, a fire broke out in the stadium. In the panic, someone shot an arrow that narrowly missed Rhuzbeh. The arrow had the words "Pashem I=" on it. The king was whisked away to safety, the crowd was disbanded, and the other kings were escorted safely back to their kingdoms. The panic caused a stampede, taking a few lives. Although most of the people escaped unscathed, the fire raged throughout the night and burnt the wooden stadium to ashes.

Rhuzbeh was livid and immediately sent for Tiran. He demanded to know the result of the investigation. Tiran said, 'My Lord! When I was investigating, we had arrested a man. He did not confess even under torture. But he kept looking at a woollen thread with seven knots tied to his wrist. Further investigations revealed that the wool comes from the Sarjein sheep from the north. It is my theory that some noblemen had conspired with Nahal to spread anarchy and kill you, thus paving the way for a Northern invasion.'

The king looked up and said, 'Well done. Don't reveal this to anyone. Find out if anyone in my court wears the woollen thread with seven knots.'

'Yes, my king,' said Tiran.

'Let me congratulate you once again! You are a great warrior and a loyal servant,' said Rhuzbeh. 'When all this is over, I shall suitably reward you.'

'Thank you, my lord,' Tiran said and walked away.

Meanwhile, Queen Ceba called Darya to her side. It had been some time since Ceba had spoken to Darya as she had been busy obsessing over Axer. She remembered the simple times when she was just a merchant's wife, and they were happy and content. Ceba had spent a lot of time with Darya then—she played with her, combed her hair and fed her. Darya looked just like Ceba. When she carried Darya on her hips, it looked like she was carrying a miniature version of herself. All that had changed since her husband's death.

Rhuzbeh had rekindled their relationship and married her. He was the love of her life and she was besotted with him. She had married the merchant only because she thought Rhuzbeh would never come back. After her marriage to Rhuzbeh, she spent less time with Darya, and when Axer was born, she almost completely ignored her. When Darya started training as a mage, nobody had any objections as Rhuzbeh looked upon his stepdaughter without any fondness. Although Ceba loved Darya, her love for Axer far overshadowed her love for Darya.

After completing her training with Metishin, Darya had travelled to distant lands to learn various arts, and she had come back a woman. Ceba could see the pain in her eyes. She had seen much suffering and lost her soft innocence. She looked like a battle-hardened veteran who had seen it all.

Ceba had then cried out, 'My daughter! My beautiful daughter! You have come back after ages; how was your journey?'

'It was good, mother,' was all Darya had to say.

She would not speak to Ceba of her own volition. After trying for months, Ceba had given up. Now, Ceba sent for Darya to discuss a matter of utmost importance.

'Mother, you sent for me?' asked Darya.

'Yes,' said Ceba, 'the nobles in our favour are getting killed. There is a threat to the king's life. I fear Hitti may be behind this.'

'Do you have any proof?' Darya asked.

'No,' said Ceba, 'but who else can plan the death of nobles who favour me. She wants Hittash on the throne, and she is plotting a conspiracy against Rhuzbeh and me.'

Darya got upset and said, 'It is not she who is planning a conspiracy, and I will not investigate just to indulge your fanciful theories.'

Ceba fumed and said, 'Whose side are you on? Would you rather side with a concubine-turned-wife and her illegitimate son than your own mother, your own flesh, and against your father, the king?'

'He is not my father. My father was murdered by the king to marry you,' Darya blurted out in anger.

Ceba was shocked. Her jaw dropped and she demanded, 'Who told you that?'

Darya narrated what Dahel had told her and how Metishin had corroborated the story as well.

Darya asked Ceba, 'What I really wanted to ask you is, did you know?'

Ceba broke down. 'I promise you I did not know this.' She continued, 'That question was always on my mind but I never wanted to ask Rhuzbeh as I was afraid of the answer.'

And they both broke down in each other's arms. Ceba's feeling for Rhuzbeh changed after this revelation. She harboured a deep resentment towards him. He had treated her like an object. When she "belonged" to another man, he killed him and snatched her away.

Meanwhile, Tiran captured three noblemen who confessed to conspiring with Nahal. He personally executed them and presented their decapitated hands with a woollen thread, which had the same seven knots, as proof. Now, Rhuzbeh had enough proof. He declared war against the Northern kingdom.

Before he left to attack the Northern kingdom, Rhuzbeh headed for Tamiir with the second sanaa.

Ghanazaqi and Irash welcomed him with open arms, and Rhuzbeh asked, 'When is your wedding with Ameira slated?'

Ghanazaqi smiled and replied, 'When I hand over the second sanaa to Amirast.'

'Here is my wedding gift in advance,' said Rhuzbeh with a broad grin and handed over the second sanaa that he had won from King Nahal.

The trio left for Alainis, where a delighted Amirast organised a great royal wedding with all the appropriate pomp.

So it was that Rhuzbeh brought back the second sanaa and ensured the marriage between Ghanazaqi and Ameira.

The hunt for the third sanaa was on.

After a brief stay at Alainis, Rhuzbeh was preparing to leave for Zanda when Ghanazaqi and Amirast met him and said, 'Thank you once again for the second sanaa. We hear that the third is in close vicinity. I have a feeling that the time has come for the return of the third sanaa and the revival of Afra-Zun.'

'I am glad to be of any service to you, O King!' said Rhuzbeh and continued, 'I shall spare no effort to retrieve the third sanaa and help revive the legendary city of Afra-Zun.'

However, Ghanazaqi had a word with him before parting. 'Rhuzbeh, be the king that djinns and men look up to. Be kind and just. The eyes of both djinns and men are on you.'

Rhuzbeh nodded and said, 'I will try but an attempt has treacherously been made to rob me of my life. If I don't retaliate, I will be seen as a coward. After this campaign, I shall focus on being a just and righteous king.'

Ghanazaqi and Amirast bid him a fond farewell and Rhuzbeh returned to Zanda and prepared for war.

Chapter 6

The Firstborn Son

Foibles are like alphabets; they collate and cascade into a prose of follies.

Rhuzbeh was intent on seeking revenge and displaying his might. He marched with the combined armies of all his captured kingdoms. A thousand horsemen rode along with heavy siege machines to break through any defences. He planned to unleash the combined might of Zanda, Hatasa, Wastra and all his vassals. He himself was the greatest warrior in the known world. Accompanying him were his sons, who were lion killers and tested warriors. He also had at his command two of the greatest mages in the known world, Metishin and Darya. The combined army looked formidable, and Rhuzbeh was confident that they would reduce the Northern kingdom to rubble in days and that on their fields, he would sow salt.

The mighty army entered the Bjan pass, which was the only way to access the Northern kingdom. They found the pass to be blocked—the Northern army had pushed large boulders from the mountaintops, effectively sealing the route.

There was no way of clearing the pass. The only option was to climb over the wall of rocks but if they did that, then they would have to leave behind all their horses, heavy weapons, food and supplies, which would allow any army with cavalry to massacre them in a battle.

Rhuzbeh's army was stuck in a narrow pass between high, steep mountains. They were sitting ducks and the archers who had been placed on the mountaintops already began to pick them off easily. The pass was narrow and easy to defend. The numbers and strength of Rhuzbeh's army were useless when stuck in that narrow pass. So Rhuzbeh decided to withdraw to the mouth of the pass—it was a stalemate. Rhuzbeh did not know what to do next.

On one such night, there came persistent calls from the mountaintop: 'Rhuzbeh! Rhuzbeh! Where are you?'

There were shrill bone-chilling calls mixed with sweet sounds of the songbirds. The soldiers looked up at the mountain and saw a small fire. In that light, they spotted a bearded face peeping beside a rock. It looked like that person was making the noises. Rhuzbeh, along with his sons, came out to see the face as well. Slowly, the face moved in front of the rock. Attached to the face was a blood-red body of a lion; it was a manticore. It was a sight to behold. The Zandians and Hatasans had heard of manticores but had never seen them.

The manticore walked in full view and started devouring the body of a Zandian soldier it had killed earlier. It had multiple rows of teeth, and it ate the captured Zandian soldier with relish, without sparing even the bones and clothes. Rhuzbeh and his soldiers watched in horror as it let out a terrible roar and, then immediately after, sang a sweet song in a feminine voice. It sent a chill down everyone's spine.

Darya thought it was only a spell cast by the Northern mages. She cast a spell of her own to dispel the vision but it had no effect. The creature was real. Manticores are magical beasts and spells do not affect them. She knew that although invulnerable to magic, a manticore is still a mortal and could be killed. Consequently, she advised Rhuzbeh to have his archers shoot arrows at it. However, it was impossible to shoot at that height and when they did attempt, the manticore shot spikes from its tails, killing four of the archers. Once again, the manticore sang a shrill song in a female voice and swiftly disappeared.

Rhuzbeh's soldiers had seen a manticore for the first time and it was a creature right out of their nightmares. Its fear was ingrained in them as they had grown up on stories about manticores. Every mother in that part of the world threatened her children with tall tales of how a manticore would devour them if they misbehaved or did not eat and sleep on time. Teenagers were asked not to venture out at night, alone or with friends, using the same threat. Growing up, the soldiers had laughed at those stories. But now that they had seen a manticore for real, they were shaken.

There were many theories about manticores. Some thought it was the offspring of a lion who had mated with a human, which in turn had mated with a scorpion. Others whispered that they were creatures that slipped out from the dark side to torment the human soul. Nobody categorically knew about the origin of the manticores. More importantly, how had a manticore turned up at the Bjan pass just then? Were they in league with the Northern king? Were there many more of them? Would they be attacked by a pride of manticores? These questions kept everybody on tenterhooks.

It was a bizarre turn of events, and the soldiers were heavily demoralised. On the battlefront, it was an impasse. Every night the manticore terrorised them. It would raid the camp several times a night, shoot spikes from his tail, kill soldiers, and leave behind half-eaten bodies. Sometimes, it would even steal a wounded soldier and eat him on the mountaintop. The king and his soldiers had to stay alert the entire time. No one could sleep.

The manticore kept singing and making birdcalls. It was nerve-racking. And the sleep-deprived soldiers were panic-stricken. Both princes volunteered to take out the manticore but Rhuzbeh decided to deal with the manticore himself.

Rhuzbeh devised an elaborate plan to kill the manticore. He placed bait at the edge of the camp—two soldiers smoking by a campfire and singing loudly. As soon as the manticore appeared, it was trapped in an iron net. Before it could chew through the iron net, Rhuzbeh appeared wearing his golden armour. The manticore shot its spikes, but they bounced off the jann armour. Rhuzbeh was just about to swing his zer sword when the manticore emerged from the nets and swiped its paw, knocking Rhuzbeh down. His zer sword was knocked out of his hands. Seeing a defenceless Rhuzbeh, the manticore pounced on him and pinned him down. Just when it raised its scorpion-like tail to kill Rhuzbeh, Darya rushed to Rhuzbeh's aid, picked up the fallen zer sword and swung it, slicing away the tail. The manticore howled in pain, turned and gave Darya a long, baleful look before fleeing back to the mountain. The manticore would hold a grudge against Darya for a long time.

The next night the tail-less manticore appeared on the mountaintop making feminine sounds again. It would sing songs, chirp like birds and call out random names. Although the manticore did not come down the mountain for some days, its cries continued to have a nasty effect on the soldier's morale. They started crying aloud and tearing out their hair. Some soldiers even ate their own fingers out of fear and stress.

Even without the tail, a manticore was formidable—its hide was thick and its powerful lion's paws had claws that were capable of ripping open a person with ease. Slowly, the manticore started coming down and killing the sleeping soldiers once again. The manticore was stealthy and difficult to track. If ever a hunt was launched, it crept inside the blankets and spoke like a human. The Zandian soldiers turned on one another out of suspicion and began to use this situation as an excuse to settle personal scores. There was anarchy in Rhuzbeh's camp.

If the Northern army attacked now, the Zandian army would be effortlessly routed. However, Rhuzbeh refused to acknowledge this. He was arrogant and did not want to lose a military campaign after all the pain and loss they had faced. Rhuzbeh made his decision. He ordered his sleep-deprived, bedraggled army that was now extremely low on strength and morale to abandon heavy equipment and horses and climb over the rocks blocking the pass.

Although not happy, the soldiers obeyed their king. They grabbed their shields and used them as a metal umbrella against the rain of arrows. Despite the shields, hundreds were killed or badly injured while crossing the pass. Finally, the army were over the rocks, and after two days of marching with dwindling food and water supplies, the combined army was face to face against a well-rested enemy cavalry. Rhuzbeh's worn-out foot soldiers were no match for the heavy Northern cavalry, and they were mowed down like ripe barley. Rhuzbeh grabbed a horse from one of the Northern soldiers and was in the thick of battle. Indeed, he was heroic.

The mages, Darya, with her spell of black panther, and Metishin, with his falcon spell, were awe-inspiring. The princes were rallying the soldiers and fighting valiantly. But the tired, sleep-deprived foot soldiers were no match for a heavily armed cavalry. Suddenly, an arrow shot from the Zandian lines struck Rhuzbeh in the back. Rhuzbeh the Fearless, in whose veins the gus ambergris flowed and who was the bearer of gajmuk, the wielder of the zer sword and the ruler of the East and West, fell. The battle stopped. As Rhuzbeh fell, both armies stopped fighting as a mark of respect for the king.

Metishin stepped forward to Nahal and said, 'O Nahal! Our king is mortally wounded. We have no king to rally around. Let us stop further bloodshed.'

Nahal said, 'Wise Metishin! Take back your king and your armies; it is over.'

'Give us food, water and medicines, O King! For we are starving,' asked Metishin.

Nahal was graceful in his victory. He had defeated the renowned Rhuzbeh, and so he acquiesced. But he knew that the arrow that knocked out Rhuzbeh from behind did not come from his army—Rhuzbeh had been betrayed.

The combined army went back unmolested through the Bjan pass all the way to Zanda. Rhuzbeh, although mortally wounded, still held on and was passing in and out of consciousness. Metishin pulled out the arrow and made a salve that he applied to the wound. The blood flow had stopped. Rhuzbeh was alive but he had slipped into a coma.

Now the real question arose—who shot the arrow? Who among the ranks tried to kill the king? Rhuzbeh's wound looked mortal. The kingdom was in disarray and it needed a king. Seizing the opportunity, the Eastern and Western kingdoms declared independence.

Metishin abandoned Rhuzbeh to his fate as he knew that the king's time had come. But after attending court for a day, the panicked Metishin rushed back to Rhuzbeh and spent all his time and energy trying to revive him. He knew only Rhuzbeh could deal with this unforeseen problem. Meanwhile, Ceba declared her son Axer as the king, which triggered a war of succession. Hitti and Hittash escaped to Hatasa and declared Hittash as the king of the joint kingdom. Darya marched into Axer's court and announced, 'I, Darya, am leaving Zanda for Hatasa to support Hittash's claim to the throne.' Such was her stature that the courtiers did not muster the courage to even look her in the eye. Axer, although stung, was too egoistic to stop her, and he merely nodded. Darya spun around and walked out of the palace.

Axer was formally crowned the King of Zanda and adopted the crest of his father, the eagle with outspread wings and serpent in its talons.

Since Hittash was the grandson of King Hitkar, the entire Hatasan army considered him to be the king. The kingdom was formally split into two, with each ruler claiming the whole kingdom. The other vassals remained neutral, and many declared their independence. The kingdom that Rhuzbeh had painstakingly built was fragmented.

Surprisingly, there rose a third claimant—Tiran.

Tiran approached Metishin and said, 'O wise Mage, I, Tiran, claim the throne of the joint kingdom of Zanda and Hatasa.'

'And on what basis do you make that claim?' asked a perplexed Metishin.

'I claim the throne as the firstborn son of King Rhuzbeh,' replied Tiran.

Metishin was stunned and waited for Tiran to explain. 'Rhuzbeh, during his travels, met my mother, Tasia,' said Tiran.

'My mother loved him and hoped to grow old with him. But what did he do? When he had had his fill, he abandoned her. He used her like a piece of cloth to protect himself from the sun, and when he no longer needed her care and was bored, he discarded her and walked away towards more exciting things. My poor mother wept when she thought about him and those happy times that they had spent together laughing, running and sleeping under trees on the sand. A month later, she realised she was with child—Rhuzbeh's child. She named the boy Tiran.'

Metishin looked at Tiran carefully and knew that he was telling the truth. No wonder he had spent so much time with Rhuzbeh, as if trying to make up for his father's absence during his childhood. 'Did you come to avenge your mother?' asked Metishin

'Yes,' said Tiran, 'Rhuzbeh abandoned my mother when she was pregnant. There were times when my mother thought she could not do this without Rhuzbeh but slowly, she resigned herself to the task. Even after all these years, she spends her entire time pining for him. I resolved to avenge my mother. I trained hard and knew that I had to turn my body into steel if I were to face the legendary Rhuzbeh and win against him. The island chieftain was like a father figure to me, and he taught me the intricacies of fighting and the knowledge cultivated by our people.' 'When I was finally ready to leave, my mother, Tasia, implored me to not go but I promised her that I would gloriously challenge my father, defeat him, drag him back to her to seek forgiveness. I asked her the way to Zanda and following the stars, I set out on my own. 'Before I could leave, I met the chief, who warned me about the possible challenges ahead. "No one amongst us has left this island for centuries for fear of the gus whale and storms. Our race is cursed. Do you still want to risk it for someone who abandoned you and your mother?" 'I replied, "Yes! I do. I don't care whether I survive or not. I have no identity, and my mother cries all the time. I must find the man who did this and punish him."

'The chief then gave me a spear with the ancient green crystal and said, "This is the last ancient weapon of our ancestors. The crystal is powerful; it can cut across any man or metal, and it is the bane of the gus whale. I shall lend you this spear called the whale-killer. Keep it safe and return it once your quest is completed." I gratefully accepted the gift, stocked a large boat with food and supplies and set off on my journey across the sea. I decided to avoid the stormy ocean, which was also the domain of the gus whale. As the bearer of the whale-killer, I was afraid that I might upset the gus whale, which might attack and kill me. So, I decided to travel south and then cut across the sea until I reached Sedra. After forty days of sailing and fishing, I got sick and forlorn. I was tired of the sea, the great gusts of winds and the unknown creatures. I thought that the vast ocean would swallow me. I scratched out my face with my nails out of fear and panic. I missed the island, especially its warm food and happy people.

'I heard voices in the winds, and I saw creatures in the waters that I had never seen before. Suddenly, I had an urge to jump in the water and end it all when a voice deep inside me said, "Just be." I sat down and started breathing. I concentrated on the air flowing in, like a nourishing river and emptying out through my mouth. I watched with fascination as if someone else was breathing that warm air. I did not want to shut my eyes to escape. I did not want to fight. I did not want to resist. So, I sat with the sun rays filtering through the green crystal; I wanted nothing. I was just there. I was the wave that gently lifted and danced in the sunlight. I was the sunlight that decided the colour blue was mundane and tinted the ocean with golden flecks in the morning and fiery red in the evening, as if upset at being replaced by the darkness. I was the darkness that fell like a blanket across the sea, as if the ocean and its creatures needed to be tucked in so that they could wake up and face the next day's tribulations. I was the next day that washed away yesterday's disappointments and brought with it infectious warmth and hope in the air.

All through these trying times, the crystal spear was my constant companion. It lit in the night, giving me light. I used it as a harpoon to impale fish, and it even turned fiery when I needed heat. I don't know what I would have done without the spear.'

'But where did you get the monkfly?' asked an intrigued Metishin.

'Oh! I found him on a small island on my way to Sedra,' said Tiran. 'After forty-seven days of travel, I reached a small island. The island was a patch of rocks and dense trees. I got down on the island to discover that just half a dozen monkeys inhabited the island. Surprisingly, the monkeys were tiny and had wings. I called them monkflies. The monkflies had frail transparent wings. They swung around and climbed trees like monkeys, and when they wanted to hover, they'd flutter around like butterflies. They couldn't fly but just flutter for a short distance. I wanted to stay on land for some time. I walked around and discovered a pool of fresh water and fruits. After I had my fill, I relaxed under a tree. The warm, firm earth was inviting, and I slipped into a long dreamless sleep. I did not know how long I slept, but when I woke up, I felt fresh and ready to travel again. As I was packing up to leave, I realised that my spear was missing. I looked around and saw that one of the monkflies had taken my spear and climbed a tree. I climbed up to the monkfly, who patiently waited until I reached him and threw the spear to another monkfly, who caught it and flew away. There was much delight and hooting. I came up with an idea. I picked some fruit and threw it to the monkfly who was holding the spear. Instinctively, the monkfly tried to catch the fruit and, in the process, dropped the spear. I dashed, picked up the spear, loaded up food and water on the boat and sailed away. After a couple of hours of sailing, I heard hooting—it was a stowaway monkfly. It was too late for me to turn the boat, so I continued with the journey. I now had a companion as I sailed across the ocean. The monkfly was half the length of my hand, but it was surprisingly strong and could hover around. I realised that the monkfly was a female. I taught her to catch small fish with bare hands and rewarded her with my stock of food. I became very fond of the monkfly, and together, we sailed towards our destination.'

'So, you gave the gus whale the slip and reached Sedra?' asked a smiling Metishin.

'It was not that easy,' said Tiran. 'On the way, the sky turned dark, and suddenly, with a great scream like the rush of the wind, the gus whale appeared. Until then, I was feeling smug that I had avoided the cursed whale because I didn't expect it this far down south. I stood on the boat with the whale-killer in my hand. The dreaded gus whale half rose from the water and seemed twice the size of an average whale, its brilliant bronze and silver body shining against the inky sky. The green crystal lit up bright. This was the creature that purportedly caused the annihilation of an entire race and scattered them to the four winds. I accosted the gus whale with the spear that had killed one of its ancestors. I could sense that the gus whale was about to unleash its fury on me.

'I stood up erect and screamed in the wind, declaring, "I am Tiran, the son of Rhuzbeh, and in my veins, the gus ambergris flows! I seek my father and I mean no harm to you." My voice was drowned by the heavy wind as if I had never said it. Suddenly, the ocean calmed down, sunlight streaked in and the great gus whale blew water in the air a few times and slunk back into the sea.' 'The gus whale knew you were Rhuzbeh's son, and hence it spared you,' said Metishin. Tiran nodded in agreement.

'As I sailed further,' continued Tiran, 'I came across treacherous waters—the water was shallow in some places with rocks jutting out, making the sea impassable. My boat crashed on one of the rocks. I held a plank and paddled with the monkfly on my shoulders until I reached a rocky island with a mountain.

'I was apprehended by a savage tribe, which inhabited the mountainous island, and was held captive by it. The savages worshipped an idol, on whose head they had stuck a brilliant ruby-like stone that almost danced. Every night, the savages participated in singing and dancing rituals. They imprisoned me and used the monkfly for plucking fruits from the trees. After a month of beatings and semi-starvation, I was chained by them as a slave inside a hut.

'The hut belonged to their leader, who was a bulky hulk of a woman. Every night, she abused me and took pleasure in punching and making small cuts on my body using a knife. She also snatched away the crystal spear, adding it to her collection as the latest acquisition.

'One night, the monkfly managed to escape and flew in through the window of the hut where I was held captive. The monkfly had also managed to steal the crystal spear and handed it back to me. Using the green crystal, I cut myself free. My tormentor heard the sounds of the chain being cut and woke up with a growl. She tried to reach out for her sword, but I thrust the crystal spear into her, killing her instantly. I rushed out, plucked out the red dancing ruby from the idol's head and, after stealing a boat, sailed away to Sedra.'

Metishin asked, 'Can I see the ruby?' Reluctantly, Tiran handed over the gem to Metishin.

A stunned Metishin took the ruby in his hand and watched with mesmerised eyes. He shook like a leaf and handed the dancing ruby back to Tiran and asked, 'How did the savages come upon this ruby?' Tiran shrugged. 'I guess it might have been washed ashore from the sea.'

'Do you know what this ruby is?' asked Metishin. 'Yes, it is a sanaa,' replied Tiran.

Metishin was now convinced that Tiran was indeed Rhuzbeh's son, for his illustrious father had managed to retrieve two sanaa. Maybe, the sanaa chose Tiran and not the other way around, thought Metishin. He did not say anything else to Tiran. He knew destiny would find a way.

'Please continue your story,' said Metishin

'As soon as I reached Sedra, my unusual height, the crystal spear and the flying monkey drew undue attention. The king of the Sedra, Shaha, heard of my arrival and called me to his court. King Shaha was fascinated by anyone who was tall. He had a contingent of tall soldiers and would force tall farmers to draft as soldiers. Even the neighbouring kings would gift him tall soldiers to be drafted into his army. He was quite taken with my height and, knowing that I was a trained warrior, recruited me as an officer.

'I had to reach Zanda, but I was afraid of rejecting the offer, lest King Shaha take umbrage and arrest me. I had to bide my time and wait for the right opportunity to come by.

'Meanwhile, Shaha took a liking to me and taught me battle strategies and the nuances of commanding armies. After the death of Kashan, Shaha declared independence and built a strong and formidable navy. I volunteered as a naval officer in the Sedran navy, and when we were sailing near the Straits of Balqara, I abandoned my ship, sailed on a boat and reached Zanda. Meanwhile, the crew, sensing that their commander had defected, left without me.'

'Hmm,' said Metishin, 'that makes you one of the prime contenders for the throne of the joint kingdom.'

'Yes, indeed,' said Tiran. 'That is why I must flee for now. It is dangerous to stay here. Axer is already crowned as the king, and he might have me arrested if I challenge his kingship. I must flee and seek help as I don't have an army to back my claim.'

Tiran handed over a formal letter stating his claim, and bid Metishin goodbye before leaving for Sedra. Metishin recognised his claim and made a formal announcement to the court.

Meanwhile, Tiran reached Sedra, where Shaha gave him a warm welcome. After a lavish dinner, Shaha heaped praises on Tiran.

'Congrats, Tiran,' said Shaha. 'You far exceeded my expectations.'

'Thank you!' said Tiran with a bow. 'I couldn't have done it without your help.' 'So, tell me all about it all and do not spare any details,' said Shaha, rubbing his hand and warming up for the imminent story.

'You were apprehensive that like his predecessor, Kashan, the ambitious Rhuzbeh would eventually cross the sea of Balqara and invade Sedra, and you promised to help me ascend the throne if I helped pull off this plan,' began Tiran.

'Yes,' said Shaha impatiently.

'I made my disappearance look like a defection. I coated my crystal spear with lead as you had advised and left for

Zanda. I hatched the "Pashem I=" conspiracy. The plan was to frame the Northern kingdom and make Rhuzbeh go to war with Nahal. After the war, when Rhuzbeh was weakened, you would invade Zanda and place me on the Zandian throne,' said Tiran.

And I, in turn, would rule Zanda by proxy, thought Shaha silently. 'The conspiracy turned out better than I expected,' said a backslapping Shaha.

'Yes, the assassin that you sent dressed as a Zandian palace guard managed to sneak into the inner chambers. The assassin, who was on a heavy dose of hashish, loyally committed suicide by consuming poison. The killer held the wooden doll as he was instructed to do. The doll's mechanism, as you know, was devised by one of your master craftsmen. I repetitively trained the monkfly to tap the doll in the right sequence, and every time the monkfly did it correctly, I rewarded her. When I, with the help of the monkfly, successfully retrieved the note from the assassin's doll, I managed to impress everybody, including Rhuzbeh. But Rhuzbeh was cautious. I had to be careful, so I deliberately wrote the notes with "Pashem I=" in a different hand each time. But the real danger was Darya. When she was convinced that I was a human, she fell in love with me and even kissed me after lacing my drink with a love potion. I was highly attracted to her. Her red hair and green eyes haunted me, and I could smell the aloes every time I thought of her. I cut myself gently on the forearm. Every time I thought of her, I would squeeze the cut, and the pain would bring me back to reality.' Saying this, Tiran trailed off as if reliving the moment.

'Ahem,' said Shaha clearing his throat, 'the conspiracy?'

'Oh yes,' said Tiran, snapping out of his reverie. 'When I gained Rhuzbeh's confidence, I put my plans into action. I sent the monkfly into the armoury, scattering weapons, stealing ten fine swords with distinctive markings and leaving the sign "Pashem I=". Stealing weapons would signal that there was an armed conspiracy and that someone was stealing weapons for a violent attack. Rhuzbeh reacted to the conspiracy threat with bravado and declared a five-day games festival.

'After the first day's fight, I slipped away in the dark, set the woollen shops on fire and left the note "Pashem I=" there to mislead the king and his ministers. I volunteered to fight the Wrey lions that you sent through a Northern merchant to sell to Rhuzbeh for the games.'

'Why did you risk your life? What if Rhuzbeh had granted you the permission to fight them?' asked a concerned Shaha.

'I know Axer well,' said Tiran with a smug smile. 'He wouldn't have missed the opportunity to kill the lions and prove his bravery to Rhuzbeh. I had hoped that at least one of the princes, if not both, might get killed. Unfortunately, both managed to kill the lions, but by volunteering, I gained Rhuzbeh's trust and respect. 'On the third day, after Darya's fight, I went to visit three noblemen. They were Ceba's supporters and they had no cause to be suspicious of me. I dined with them, and in the middle of the dinner session, I nonchalantly took out my dagger and slit the throat of the nobleman on the right. Blood gushed out on the floor as he slumped and fell on his dinner plate and turned the saffron-laced rice red. The others were stunned. I slashed at the nobleman on my left before he could recover from the shock, killing him. The third nobleman reached for his sword and stood up. I pulled out my own and, in the ensuing duel, slew him. I then left the note "Pashem I=" behind. I also left one of the stolen swords from Rhuzbeh's armoury amongst the dead bodies.

'Meanwhile, Rhuzbeh was distracted by his sons' upcoming fight against the Wrey lions and appointed me as the chief investigator. I simply picked up a criminal from the street, claiming that he tried to poison a minister and put a woollen thread with seven knots on his wrist. This thread was made from the Sarjein sheep's wool from the North. I killed him in prison and left the note "Pashem I=" beside his corpse. The next day, after the princes won against the lions, I set fire to a portion of the arena and personally shot an arrow to make it look like an assassination attempt.

'When Rhuzbeh demanded to know the conspirators, I slipped woollen threads with seven knots to three ministers—one through a courtesan, one at a place of worship and one at the bazaar. The unwitting ministers wore them, thinking it would bring them good luck. I arrested the dumbfounded ministers and, without a trial or investigation, killed them. I even produced the stolen swords and claimed that they were recovered from their houses as evidence of their compliance. Since King Nahal was implicated in the conspiracy, I knew Rhuzbeh would declare war on the Northern kingdom.' 'I had already warned Nahal about the impending invasion,' said Shaha gleefully, 'and together we devised a well-laid trap, which Rhuzbeh fell for.'

'Although Nahal won the war, it is you who are the true champion,' said Tiran.

Shaha smiled and said, 'Thank you. One question still troubles me: who shot Rhuzbeh from the back? Was it you?'

Tiran rubbed his chin thoughtfully, ignored the question and said, 'Let us prepare for a Zandian invasion.'

CHAPTER 7

The Floating Fortress

A man is never wrong in three situations—saving a living being from a raging fire; salvaging a drowning body from the sea; and in the presence of his woman.

With an impending war of succession and Rhuzbeh mortally wounded, Axer hastened to marry Anitsa and elevated her as the Queen of Zanda.

Surprisingly, Metishin did not approve of Anitsa. 'I know it is a personal matter, but I must warn you against this wedding. Stay away from this woman,' he said.

Axer got irked and replied, 'How dare you speak against your queen? Should I choose my wife according to your likes? Begone, old man!' A hurt Metishin replied, 'I made a huge mistake; I was hasty in my judgement. Things have changed, and I need to rethink my priorities.'

After that conversation, Metishin confined himself to Rhuzbeh's chambers and stuck to administering medicines to his king. Rhuzbeh was teetering on the brink of death, and he had to be nursed back to health. It could take a year, and chances were that Rhuzbeh might not even survive. Meanwhile, Axer wanted to bring the murderer to task and avenge his father. He spoke to his wife, Anitsa, about the matter. 'My father gave away the golden armour of Amirast to keep me, his beloved son, safe. He rode into battle, void armour, risking his own life.' Tears rolled down his eyes. Anitsa walked over to him and drew him towards her bosom.

'Who would have the motive to do this?' Axer asked. 'There are several suspects in my head,' replied Anitsa. 'Queen Hitti always held a grudge against her husband as he had killed her father and raped her. She could have paid a soldier to shoot the arrow. Prince Hittash himself is an illegitimate son, and Rhuzbeh would have never crowned him king. The killer could very well have been Tiran since he has now come out as a claimant for the throne. He could have shot Rhuzbeh and fled. Your stepsister, Darya, is a suspect as well. She is not related to the king. For her, Rhuzbeh is simply a murderer who killed her father and snatched her mother away.' Axer nodded thoughtfully. Ceba had confided in Axer about Rhuzbeh's misdeed. Anitsa continued, 'Finally, there is Ceba herself. When Ceba got to know that Rhuzbeh had killed her former husband and married her, she must have lost her feelings for him. Although Ceba visits Rhuzbeh, she does not seem to spend a significant amount of time by his bedside.'

'No,' said Axer firmly, 'I do not think my mother tried to murder my father. She loves him too much. I must find out the real murderer and deal with this issue firmly and swiftly. Such an affront cannot go unpunished.'

'Who should we deal with first?' asked Anitsa.

'Tiran,' replied Axer. 'Tiran is a bigger threat than Hittash. He is a great strategist, and now he has the powerful navy of Sedra backing him. It was Tiran who goaded my father on during the Northern misadventure, and I am sure that it is Tiran who shot my father.'

'If you attack Sedra, the Northern armies or the Hatasans might attack and occupy Zanda,' warned Anitsa. 'The idea is fraught with risks.'

Axer nodded thoughtfully and said, 'It is a stalemate scenario. We need to strengthen our army and also build a navy just in case the Sedran navy attacks.'

'Do we have master shipbuilders to build us a navy?' Anitsa asked.

'Unfortunately, no!' replied Axer. 'Zanda is not a maritime nation anymore. The only king who had a navy was King Kashan. After his death, we lost our naval prowess, and the shipbuilders left Zanda for Sedra. I must cross the straits of Balqara and head westwards to the port of Shizar, a place famous for its shipbuilders. I will personally select the shipbuilders and bring them back with me. I will be back in a month with the shipbuilders and in my absence, you shall be the ruler of Zanda by proxy.' Anitsa gave him a small amulet to wear around his arm. 'Wear this. This is inconspicuous, and if ever you miss me, you can rub it'. Meanwhile, Ceba tried to persuade Axer out of his adventure and asked, 'Why do you have to go? The journey is fraught with risks. Why can't you send someone else in your stead?' Axer replied, 'I do not want the Sedran kingdom to get a whiff of our plan. If they figure out that we were attempting to get shipbuilders to form a navy, they might attack us immediately. I want to be discreet. I shall personally go incognito, hire the best builders and sneak back into Zanda before anybody even notices my absence.' The truth was that Axer did not want to live overshadowed by his father's fame. He wanted to make his own mark and pacified Ceba by saying, 'Don't worry mother, I shall be back in a month.' 'But what if they attack us in your absence?' asked Ceba.

'We will announce that the King is at his hunting lodge in the mountains for two weeks and that Queen Anitsa will rule the kingdom in his absence,' replied Axer. 'After two weeks, you may announce that I have extended my stay. Every week, take a letter signed and sealed by me to my ministers so that no one suspects anything.' So Axer wrote four letters, signed them and put his seal on them. He also wrote two extra letters in case he was further delayed. Then, in preparation for his trip, he shaved off his hair and beard, smeared himself with dirt, wore dirty breeches and started out to the coast alone. Relieved of the burden of kingship and the reverential looks of his subjects, Axer felt light and enjoyed the anonymity of the common man.

At sunset, he found an inn and decided to rest during the night there.

The innkeeper looked at him with disdain, and before Axer could say a word, he said, 'If you have coins, you are welcome. If you do not have them, then you can sleep in the street like the dirty beggar that you are.' Axer was taken aback. He was not used to people being rude to him, but then he realised that he was travelling incognito. He replied, 'Yes, I have coins to pay for my food and accommodation.' He was given a room, but his admission of possessing money drew the attention of a bunch of card-playing louts, who invited him to play with them. To Axer's surprise, he won handsomely against the rogues who infested the inn. This enraged the gamblers who beat him black and blue and snatched away his winnings. Axer was powerful enough to fight the villains but restrained himself as he did not want to draw undue attention. He retired to his room groaning in pain and made a mental note to arrest the men and beat them personally when he got back from his adventure. The thought put a smile on his lips, and he slept peacefully that night. He reached the coast the next day where he intended to buy a small fishing boat.

He met a fisherman who wanted to sell his boat. Axer asked him, 'What is the price of your boat?' The fisherman replied, 'I shall take nothing less than ten gold coins.' Axer haggled for less and said, 'My offer is five gold coins.' The fisherman spat on him and said, 'You don't beg for my boat; you buy it.' Axer was not demoralised. He haggled further and said, 'I am not a beggar and I will buy your boat and net for eight gold coins.'

A bargain was struck and Axer was now a proud owner of a fishing boat. He set sail across the Sea of Balqara. In order to avoid suspicion, he cast his net and started fishing. After ten days of fishing and sailing, he reached the Balqara straits, which were teeming with ships. Axer, disguised as a dirty, bedraggled fisherman stinking of fish, hardly aroused any suspicion. He moved on to open seas and, in two days, reached the port of Shizar. He stopped to fish, and as luck would have it, he caught a big sea bass and an assortment of other fish. A small vessel approached him and asked to see his catch. Two men boarded his boat. Axer thought it would be fun to sell his fish. One of them asked Axer to lift the sea bass and show him. As he did so, the other man unexpectedly knocked him out with a club and Axer passed out. He woke up as a prisoner on a pirate ship. Axer was chained to the ship and made to scrub the decks. He sought out the captain and beseeched him, saying, 'I think you have made a mistake. Release me and I shall make you rich.' The pirate captain laughed at him and said, 'You have already made me rich, and you will make me wealthier after you are sold at the slave bazaar.' The captain then personally whipped him and said, 'Let this be a lesson, slave. Next time, do not ever address me directly.' Sea journeys tended to be monotonous, so the pirates either tortured the prisoners or made them fight each other for sport. They segregated the prisoners into slaves who could fetch a high rate and those who would not. They considered the weak, sickly and old as flotsam and made them fight each other to death with weapons. The winner lived on to fight and die the next day. But the slaves worthy of being sold were made to fight barehanded because the pirates did not want to lose their merchandise. The less damaged the stock, the higher the price they fetched in the market. While the prisoners fought, the pirates bet vast sums of money on them. The pirates took these fights rather seriously because, although the crew had disagreements, the pirate code did not allow them to fight each other. And if they did, they could end up being hanged on the mast as an example to the others. It was a rough place with rough people. The captain had to be ruthless to keep discipline. Axer's job was to scrub the deck, and every time the pirates passed him by, they would kick him for fun. The games started with the flotsam as there were too many elderly people. The captain and his first mate, Melqart, had a proxy war going on, and they would constantly bet against one another. One day, during one such fight, Melqart's fighter won and the captain's fighter got killed. The captain got up, drew his sword and killed the winner. Prisoners were killed and raped daily and it was Axer's job, along with a few other prisoners', to wash the blood off the decks by relentlessly scrubbing them and throw the dead bodies off the ship.

As days went by, all the flotsams were cleared, and it was now the turn of the able-bodied men to fight. Axer was invariably made to fight in these competitions. He was trained to fight from childhood and effortlessly beat his competition into submission. His victories soon made him a favourite of Melqart, who by now adored him. The first mate would send for Axer in his cabin to feed him and brag to him about his adventures. The captain, however, seemed to take a special joy in torturing Axer and making him do laborious tasks. He took pleasure in kicking him around and ordered his crew to feed him only liquids. Melqart stealthily sneaked in food for Axer as he wanted him to be strong for the fights. Axer was gaining a reputation as a fighter and the captain decided it was time to put him in his place.

The captain had a personal slave who was a prolific fighter, and he made him fight against any potential winner. These fights were called the Captain's Fight. The Captain's Fight was scheduled after two days. The captain made sure that Axer was deprived of food and water to weaken him before the brawl. There was excitement on the pirate ship, and the night before the fight, the pirates could hardly sleep. This was no ordinary fight. This was a battle between the captain and the first mate. The crew was divided on the possible outcome of this fight as both champions were hitherto unbeaten. The next day, the wait was finally over, and the much-anticipated fight began. The captain's champion walked to raucous cheers from his supporters. He was clad in spiked armour and looked fearsome. During past fights, he had gravely injured his opponents by falling on them and impaling them with spikes.

When the much anticipated fight finally began, the champion immediately charged at the weakened Axer and pounded him with his huge fists, leaving his opponent almost half-dead. Axer collapsed under the onslaught. Seeing Axer on the floor, the champion jumped on his sprawled body with the intent of impaling him. But Axer rolled away just in time, and the champion fell flat on his face. Next, Axer got up and, summoning the last ounce of his strength, lifted the champion over his head. He walked over to the edge of the ship and threw him into the sea. The champion sank like a stone. The captain was livid and rushed at Axer with a sword. But Melqart stopped him and said, 'He would fetch a good rate in the market and killing him will serve us no purpose.' The captain barely managed to control himself and, out of anger, punched Axer, who collapsed.

Melqart was delighted at the outcome of the fight. He had won against the captain and this certainly made him look good. The crew looked at him with newfound respect. The next day, they came across a merchant vessel and raided it. The booty was fantastic, and they managed to get food supplies, clothes, gold and women. There was a beautiful maiden on that ship, and it was love at first sight for Melqart. The captain could see how badly Melqart wanted her, and he deliberately denied him the maiden. When Melqart wanted to buy her from the captain, he took the gold and did not sell the maiden. He said, 'You scum! I'm the master of this ship. What I see, I take!'

He proceeded to openly ravish the maiden on the deck as the pirates cheered their captain on. Melqart was publicly insulted. He indignantly demanded his gold back but the captain refused. The captain was upset about losing his champion and looking bad in front of the crew. He wanted to assert his authority. For the next few days, the captain remained busy with the booty and the fresh stock of slaves. Two months later, the courtiers at Axel's court were asking questions of Anitsa. 'Where is King Axer?' they demanded. Every week she had shown a letter that Axer had purportedly sent from his hunting lodge. After two months, she had no more letters to show.

'The king wanted to be alone and went to his hunting lodge. He shall be back when he feels like it. Till then, I shall rule in his stead,' Anitsa replied, and displayed Axer's letter nominating her as the ruler.

The disgruntled courtiers were not quelled. Two ministers objected and said, 'We suspect foul play. Axer has never left his kingdom to go hunting in the past. If the king is missing, we must call back Hittash and place him on the throne of Zanda.'

Anitsa thundered, 'This is treason! How dare you speak to your queen like that? Guards! Take them to the market square and behead them publicly on charges of treason.'

There was unrest in Zanda, and Anitsa tried to quell it with an iron fist.

Once, an argument broke out in court and a Zandian general questioned her authority. Anitsa grew furious and said, 'Get out before I skin you alive.' The general took umbrage and drew his sword, and in response, the soldiers drew their swords to protect their queen. Anitsa knew that she had to impress them. She raised her hands and ordered her soldiers, saying, 'Put your swords back in the scabbard and stand back!'

She picked up her sword and challenged the general. 'You want to slay your queen? Come, raise your sword.' The court was shocked. The general was a well-built man and a famous battle-hardened veteran. Surely, it would be suicide for the delicate queen to fight him. The commander refused to fight her and said, 'I don't fight women. I was a general in the army of Rhuzbeh the Fearless. Send me your best warrior in your stead, and I shall fight him.' She goaded him on by saying, 'I am the best this court has! Come, don't be a coward. Fight me!' The commander unsheathed his sword and a duel was on. The commander swung his mighty sword but Anitsa blocked him easily with her sword hand and, with the other hand, slapped him. The slap was so hard that the brawny, well-built commander reeled and collapsed. The crowd gasped. The stunned commander stood up, threw down his sword and rushed towards her. She threw down her sword as well, and with her bare hands, she slapped him again. It was a loud splat, and the commander crashed against the wall. When he recovered, Anitsa said, 'Kneel and kiss my hand. Accept fealty! For I am your queen now, and I shall spare your miserable life.' He obliged. Thus, Anitsa was firmly established as the ruler of Zanda—a queen to be feared and respected.

Meanwhile, Axer was toiling away as a slave on the pirate ship. The captain was turning crueller by the day. One day, in a drunken stupor, the captain stabbed a senior pirate following an argument.

Finally, Melqart spoke to the captain about the matter. 'The crew is turning sullen and rebellious. You must placate them or you will have a full-blown mutiny on your hands.' 'Oh! Let them rise in mutiny,' said the captain. 'I shall show them who the captain of this ship is,' he gloated, adding, 'Bring me the friends of the dead man.' Just to set an example and discourage a potential mutiny, he tied two of the deceased man's friends and whipped them. The crew was now simmering.

In another four days, the ship would reach Slave Island, where Axer would be sold. That was also the place where the captain was supposed to share the booty that they had looted from other ships. Axer had to do something fast. He was now quite close to Melqart and he constantly filled his ears against the captain. He also let slip a rumour that the captain would not share the wealth with the crew, and instead, as soon as they reached the Slave Island, he would unload the crew and sail away with a new crew. This led to a mutiny.

Melqart tasked ten of his trusted men, along with Axer, to slip into the captain's cabin in the dead of the night. The captain was protected by two of his trusted guards. The crew killed the guards, took the captain as prisoner and tossed him into the ocean with weights tied to his legs. Melqart was now the captain of the ship, and he appointed Axer as his first mate. Axer, the king of Zanda, was now a first mate on a pirate ship. The ship then headed to Slave Island, where all the prisoners were unloaded and sold as slaves. Melqart and Axer distributed the loot amongst the crew and left.

Axer noted that the pirates raided various seagoing vessels, small fishing boats, merchant vessels and even royal ships. They were the scourge of the ocean. Their ships were fast and light, and many of the pirates were professionals. They were enjoined into piracy from a very young age and knew all there was to know about shipping vessels, ocean currents and islands. There were many pirate islands where the pirates convened to share stories and exchange knowledge of ships and loots. In fact, the pirates themselves built ships at these pirate islands. Most of the royal ships were heavy and huge because they had to accommodate soldiers, horses and heavy catapults. The merchant ships were not built for warfare and had a large cargo hold for goods and cabins for accommodation. On the other hand, the pirate ships were as huge as the royal ships. They were lighter and could go into relatively shallow waters or treacherous rocky waters, where the much heavier royal ships could not pursue them. Their construction focused on being fast and manoeuvrable. They used lighter catapults for close-range firing. Their sails were never let down but simply turned in the direction of the wind. The pirates didn't need a compass. Many of them were born into piracy and, after spending a lifetime at sea, could chart their course by the sea.

Often at the end of their careers, the pirates died in poverty because they did not know where to store the looted wealth. If it remained with them on the ship, it was either stolen by other pirates or gambled away on some bet. Some pirates buried their treasure on some remote island lest they were shipwrecked or taken prisoner. Burying their treasure gave them the option to come back and reclaim it at a later date. The problem, however, was that they were often spotted and the treasure looted. A plan was forming in Axer's mind. He revealed it to Melqart, saying, 'I hear that Zanda does not have a navy. We must cross into the Sea of Balqara and head to Zanda. The coastline of Zanda will offer rich and easy picking.' Melqart loved the idea and crossed over to the coast of Zanda immediately. After three days of plunder, Axer asked an emboldened Melqart to raid inland. On one such raid, Axer gave his amulet and a bag of gold coins to a villager stealthily and asked him to pass on the amulet with a message to Queen Anitsa. On receiving the sign, Anitsa instantly sent soldiers on horseback to Axer's aid. Melqart was surprised that such a large number of soldiers had come for a small pirate band. The soldiers surrounded them and the pirates quietly surrendered. When Axer was taken to the palace as a prisoner and brought before Anitsa, she rushed and embraced him. Melqart was surprised by the sudden turn of events. He asked, 'Are you King Axer?'

'Yes! I am Axer, the son of Rhuzbeh the Fearless, the true king of Zanda.'

Melqart knelt and said, 'Forgive me, O King! I have not treated you the way one should treat a king!' 'Rise!' said Axer. 'We have work to do.'

Axer did not want to waste resources on building a navy and training soldiers to be sailors. He intended to patronise the pirates, who would act as a bulwark against a Sedran naval invasion. He formally appointed Melqart as an admiral and asked him to hire pirates from across the seas. He now had a fleet of pirates ready at his command. The pirates were killers and murderers, but Melqart knew how to handle them. Axer built dry docks in Zanda. He asked Melqart to bring in master shipbuilders from all over the pirating world and, along with the Zandian manpower, they went on to make the unexpected—a floating fortress.

The mammoth, square, multilevel floating fortress was called the Melqartia. This type of fort had existed in ancient lands and was talked about in pirating circles. The Melqartia could hold up to three thousand pirates. The idea was suggested by Melqart himself, who wanted to have a fortress of his own. The floating fortress of Melqartia was a marvel. Axer had put his entire army to work and denuded all the nearby forests of their great trees to build this floating fortress. Each plank was meticulously coated with fireproof material, the details of which the pirates refused to share. Great anchors and chains were fitted to the platform to enable the stability of the fortress. The decks were fitted with catapults and trebuchets made of thick and sturdy bamboo. Large furnaces were built inside the ship to heat metal balls to a high temperature to be thrown at the enemy. The fortress had two floors. On the top deck was a garden to grow fresh vegetables and fruits in. There was even a dairy farm that was complete with cows, livestock and poultry. The Melqartia boasted of multiple kitchens and a thousand odd rooms. Melqart even had a live tiger on board to display his prowess. When it was completed, Melqart put up his flag and called it the Melqartia—his own country. Word spread and pirates from different parts of the known world flocked to the Melqartia. They brought with them wealth, manpower and expertise in exchange for permanent accommodation and some security.

The Melqartia was a dream come true for many pirates. This was a haven protected by the King of Zanda with the liberty to pillage any country they wanted except Zanda. Melqart acted as an admiral, directing his ships to attack the merchant and naval vessels of the Hatasan and Sedran kingdoms. The plan had worked effectively for Axer as he did not have to train and pay a regular standing navy. He got a navy almost for free, and now, no nation would ever attack Zanda from the south. The Zandian court, though, was apprehensive about pirates in their waters becoming so powerful. The ministers advised Axer against them, saying, 'O King! It is a folly to have a powerful pirate army at our doorstep. These pirates are savages, and it is just a matter of time before they start looting us, raping our women and selling our children into slavery.'

Axer acknowledged the risk, and he thus built the famous sea wall of Zanda. He created a high wall at a great cost, building towers across the length of the wall. On these towers, he mounted catapults to throw projectiles far into the sea. The soldiers on the wall were heavily armed. He also built a garrison nearby that could be rushed to the wall. Zanda was safe. The other kingdoms, however, were now getting jittery. Zanda had always had a powerful army. King Kashan and King Rhuzbeh were some of the greatest kings ever known. They had, over two generations, built an army that could take on the strongest of armies. During Axer's absence, the Hatasans had tested the Zandian resolve by sending a small skirmishing party but the Zandians defended well and beat back the attacks. Queen Anitsa had proved to be not only authoritative but also surprisingly diplomatic. She had secured a secret deal with King Nahal of the Northern kingdom. This was surprising because Nahal had always had a deep hatred of the Zandians. The Northern army had been the undoing of two Zandian kings, Zogdu and Rhuzbeh. Until the progeny of Rhuzbeh remained, the north would know no peace. He was committed to the annihilation of Zanda. So, it was surprising that Anitsa had secured an alliance with the north. She had met King Nahal secretly, had a one-on-one discussion and secured an alliance. It was a great diplomatic victory. Axer was proud of his wife. With the threat from the north neutralised and the south protected, Axer started preparing for war with Hatasa with the intention of reconquering the kingdom.

Axer was becoming every bit as great a king as Rhuzbeh had been. Indeed, the bards were already singing the glory of Axer. They were sure that Axer would be a greater king than Rhuzbeh.

Meanwhile, as expected, the pirates were becoming a nuisance. They attacked and pillaged the entire Sedran coast. The pirates were now organised and sailing like an armada into the waters far beyond the Sea of Balqara and into the ocean. The Piracy was having an adverse effect and Zanda was losing its goodwill. Meanwhile, the Sedrans were fed up with the incessant attacks. Tiran advised Shaha, saying, 'Let us attack the pirates and decimate them before they get out of hand.'

Shaha agreed and said, 'I will give you all the resources you need. You shall personally head a navy and eliminate the pirates.'

Tiran laid out a trap. He sent a fisherman to Melqart and told him, 'O Pirate king! I shall give you valuable information regarding treasure ships if you give me ten gold coins.'

Melqart replied, 'Speak! If the information is true, then the gold coins are yours, and if the information turns out to be false, I shall throw you into the waters.'

The fisherman trembled and said, 'What I have to say is true. A large number of treasure ships, to be escorted by the Western navy, would be sailing from the western lands to the far-off kingdoms as a diplomatic gift, and they would be accompanied by merchant ships carrying goods for trading.'

The pirates could not resist this piece of news. Melqart, accompanied by thirty pirate ships, left Melqartia and headed towards the open ocean. As the pirate fleet passed through the narrow Balqara straits, they realised they had walked into a trap. The coastline on either side of the straits was lined with catapults and archers. The Sedrans had allied with the coastal kingdoms of the west and placed catapults and archers armed with fiery arrows.

The catapults sank ten of the pirate ships and killed six hundred pirates in a volley of fire and stone. Melqart recovered quickly from the initial shock. His own catapults and archers fired back, destroying the coastal defences. After crossing the straits, they started chasing the treasure convoy. This was when Shaha made his move. He mobilised an additional five hundred soldiers and moved in heavy catapults and trebuchets at the straits to strengthen the coastline. He placed ten of his warships in the middle of the straits, effectively sealing it. Melqart was cut off. He would not be able to cross into the sea of Balqara without going through the straits. Melqart had no option but to continue chasing the treasure convoy. Surprisingly, the treasure convoy did an about-turn. He had been deceived. The ships were lions in the guise of lambs. But Melqart was a veteran of naval warfare, and he defeated the Sedran navy on merchant vessels. The victory had come at a hefty price though. Except for two ships, his entire fleet was destroyed. With the Balqara straits sealed, he had no other option but to reach Zanda through land.

Meanwhile, the entire Sedran navy and their allies attacked Melqartia. In the absence of Melqart, there was no captain, and hence there was no synchronous and coherent defence. The Melqartia still boasted four thousand well-armed, battle-hardened pirates, and they fired the catapults at will from Melqartia's deck. The catapults on Melqartia had a higher firing range, and the Sedran ships were getting pulverised before they could even get close enough to fire.

Tiran came up with an idea—the advantage that the Melqartia had was its height, and when catapults were mounted on the upper decks, the shooting range was very long and could destroy ships at a great distance. Tiran combined three small ships by tying them together and knocked off the masts and built a flat platform that spanned across the three boats. On top of the platform, he constructed a very high tower. He assembled ten such towers and mounted thick bamboo catapults just like the Melqartia's. The Melqartia was now a sitting duck. Tiran spread the towers in different directions and relentlessly bombed the Melqartia from different sides. And since these towers were narrow, it was difficult for the pirates to hit back at them accurately over a distance. The Melqartia was taking massive losses, and on the third night of the attack, under the cover of heavy catapult firing, Tiran sailed towards the Melqartia on a small boat with a few men. Midway through, they jumped into the water and swam the rest of the distance. They doused the sides of the Melqartia with incendiary substances and poured flammable oil in great quantities into the surrounding waters, turning them black. With their tasks done, they swam back towards their boats and sailed back to their ships. They waited at a safe distance till the next morning, and when the sun rose, Tiran took out his crystal spear and directed the concentrated sun rays to the water. The powerful rays travelled the distance and hit the oil on the water, which burst into flames. Although fireproofed, the wooden fortress could not bear the heat. The men, livestock and equipment caught fire. It was a gruesome sight as all the boats attached to the Melqartia went up in flames. The pirates, unable to bear the heat, jumped into the ocean and were roasted alive. Eventually, there was an explosion. The Melqartia burned for two days and finally sank. Only the floating wooden pieces which littered the sea bore evidence of the floating fortress' existence. With Melqartia destroyed, Tiran pressed home the advantage, turned the tower boats and bombed the coastal walls of Zanda, taking out the catapults and soldiers. Once he reached the coast, he dismantled the towers from the boats and shifted them to the walls. He then scaled the Zandian coastal wall using the towers. The Sedran army had breached the wall. The gates were opened and the Sedran army entered the coastal town leading to Zanda. The Sedrans had taken the wall with minimum effort and absolutely no damage.

Axer heard of his losses and was stunned. He led his massive, well-trained army to the gates of Zanda to meet Tiran. Unfortunately, right before the battle, he could not find the golden armour gifted to him by Rhuzbeh. He was heavily demoralised but, nevertheless, went to war. He was accompanied by his wife Anitsa, who was proving to be a formidable warrior. The Sedrans marched under the banner of Tiran, which was a trident with a snake coiled around it. The Zandian eagle swooped down to battle the snake.

The armies met on the plains of Zanda. The fighting was fierce. No quarter was asked and none given. Anitsa was like a force of nature—a whirlwind that destroyed everything in her path. The Zandians, buoyed by their warrior queen, fought like the seasoned warriors that they were and the Sedran army was pushed back.

As Tiran was trying to rally his frightened soldiers who were now running pell-mell towards the ships, Anitsa charged towards him. Tiran was surprised because he was way behind the battle lines and Anitsa was well ahead of her soldiers, alone. Tiran marvelled at the fact that she was as brave as she was beautiful. He knew he had to take Anitsa out and once she was in close range, both drew their swords. Anitsa swung her sword and when Tiran's sword met hers, such was her power that he was thrown to the ground. As she drew close to finish him off, Tiran threw his crystal spear at her. Anitsa gave a blood-curdling cry and the entire battlefield resonated with the sound. She was severely injured. The spear had pierced her armour and struck her thighs making her bleed profusely. Axer, who was rushing to Anitsa's aid, could not reach in time to protect her. He galloped hard, intent on saving his queen and killing Tiran. Upon seeing Axer, Tiran quickly pulled back his spear, mounted his horse and tried to get away. Axer was fast. He closed in on Tiran, drew his sword and was about to swing it when someone shot an arrow at Axer's horse. The horse tumbled and Axer fell. The fallen Axer was pinned down by the weight of the horse and knocked out unconscious. Tiran and the Sedran soldiers quickly turned around, bound up an unconscious Axer and whisked him away before the Zandian soldiers could close in on them. Axer was now a prisoner of the Sedrans. The Zandians had defended themselves at a high cost. Although they beat back the Sedran soldiers, their queen was injured and their king was a prisoner. The injured Anitsa once again replaced Axer as the ruler of Zanda while he was kept prisoner in Sedra. Though the Sedran troops had failed to secure Zanda, they had captured the king and this was a great victory. They wanted to use Axer as a bargaining chip. Axer had fought without his body armour and endured many injuries in the battle. The fall from the horse had fractured his ribs, and he was recuperating.

Meanwhile, there was news that someone had murdered Ceba. There was no explanation for her death. The whole of Zanda mourned the death of Ceba. Their true king was on his deathbed, with his son a prisoner, and now his queen was dead. This was a massive tragedy. Anitsa was visibly weak and she walked with the help of attendants. Tiran's spear had wounded her badly but that did not stop her from reclaiming the throne. She was steadfast and flogged any of the courtiers who showed the slightest insolence in front of her. Meanwhile, efforts were on to seek Axer's release. Anitsa met up with Tiran to negotiate a deal—the Sedrans wanted gold in exchange for Axer's release, but Anitsa refused. The Zandian court was befuddled and asked, 'Shouldn't we pay the gold? Once our king is back, we can always recover it if need be.' Anitsa refused and said, 'That would make us look weak and even the weakest kingdoms would be emboldened to attack us.' 'But then, how do we secure our king? We can't let him rot in a Sedran prison forever,' they persisted. 'We have to be patient, and when the time comes, we will strike back,' said Anitsa. Meanwhile, Metishin was nursing Rhuzbeh back to health. He had not left Rhuzbeh's bedside and he did not allow anyone, including Anitsa, inside Rhuzbeh's bedchamber. After two years of careful nursing, Rhuzbeh slowly regained his strength. Metishin drugged Rhuzbeh regularly to induce sleep. Rhuzbeh never stepped outside his chambers, giving the impression that he was on his deathbed. When Metishin heard that Axer was taken prisoner, however, he stopped drugging Rhuzbeh and made him stretch out his muscles, and after a month, Rhuzbeh was ready. Metishin apprised Rhuzbeh about the current situation. He informed Rhuzbeh of the true identity of Tiran and Anitsa.

One day, when the court was in session, Metishin walked in with Rhuzbeh. As soon as Rhuzbeh entered, he blew his horn loudly and announced, 'To the fear that creeps up on me, hear me loud—I'm Rhuzbeh, your true king, awoken from the lost! My hand bears the zer sword, and my wrist is embellished with the gajmuk! I am back from the unfrequented—back like the monsoon on the parched earth!' The entire court rose. There was a loud gasp and the courtiers started cheering their true king. As he approached the throne, Anitsa rose as well.

Rhuzbeh walked up to her and asked, 'Who are you?' She said, 'I am the wife of your son and the Queen of Zanda.' 'You are no longer a queen. Step down and make way for the true king,' said Rhuzbeh.

You were once the king! I, Anitsa, now sit on the throne of Zanda as its ruler. Guards! Seize this man,' Anitsa furiously ordered her guards. Rhuzbeh flung his frog tongue belt that wrapped around her neck and pulled her down. She fell at his feet. Rhuzbeh then declared, 'This woman is not who she claims to be. She is Awa, the banished wife of Amstrap, the jann. She tried to incite her husband to rebel against the jann king, Amirast. I played a trick on her and got her banished. She met my son in a forest and seduced him but she never came in front of me because I have gajmuk and I can recognize her.'

Anitsa stood and transformed to her true form. Clad in white and gold, she was now Awa, the former wife of Amstrap, much to the shock of the courtiers. 'Yes!' she thundered, 'You made me lose my position as the wife of Amstrap. He might not be a king, but I loved him. I tried my best to make him a king, and if you had not interfered, I would have been the queen.' Even before the words left her mouth, she swung her sword at him. Although weak from her wounds, she was still a djinn. But the powers of a djinn did not affect Rhuzbeh as he had gus ambergris flowing in his veins. He blocked her sword and knocked her down. He proceeded to secure her with his belt and asked her to confess everything. 'I will tell you everything,' she gloated. 'I knew Axer was campaigning in the west. I extended water for him to drink without showing myself. I had laced the water with a love potion. He fell madly in love with me. I knew I could not do anything to him using my powers as a djinn because he had gus ambergris flowing through his veins, and he was anyway not my target—I wanted to get to you through him. Indeed, I even had a soft corner for him. When you fell wounded, I knew my chance had arrived to occupy the throne. Your foolish son wanted to seek glory and he put me on the throne and left. I was finally a queen. But getting to you was still proving to be tough because Metishin recognized me and cast a spell around you, personally guarding you day and night. Besides, you were sick for so long that I was sure that you would die of your wounds. 'When your son Axer started out, I bribed a pirate captain to capture and kill him. But that greedy pirate wanted more money and tried to sell him as a slave. Your son made a comeback as a hero and I made way for him as you know very well that a djinn always relishes a long and elaborate plan. That incompetent son of yours put murderers and rapists in your backyard.

'When Tiran attacked, I was delighted. I hid that cursed golden armour of Amirast so that Axer would go to war without adequate protection and get killed. When I saw your other son, I thought, let me finish the progeny of Rhuzbeh. He did not have gus ambergris flowing through his veins and he was vulnerable. I knocked him down with my sword but he almost killed me with that crystal spear. 'When my dear husband charged after Tiran, I shot an arrow at his horse. Axer fell and was captured, making me the queen once again. When I came back from battle, I was accosted by your accursed wife, Ceba. She revealed that she had seen me walk out of my tent to bury something under a mulberry tree. She dug it out and discovered it to be her son's golden armour. She confronted me with the armour and wanted to know who I was and why I was trying to harm my own husband. She threatened to expose me in front of the whole court, leaving me no choice. So, I killed her and flung her away.'

Rhuzbeh went ashen. Metishin did not inform him of Ceba's death. He suddenly felt weak in the knees and collapsed to the ground. He let out a loud cry of pain and started sobbing. Although fury filled every part of his body, he was too weak and broken to do anything about it. He ordered Metishin who had rushed to help him, 'Take this djinn out of my sight, she has snatched the love of my life away from me. Bind her using your magic, clad her in iron chains and cast her away in the darkest dungeon until I am strong enough to personally punish her.'

Before going, she mockingly asked, 'Don't you want to know who tried to kill you by shooting an arrow in your back?'

'Keep quiet, you vile creature,' he screamed, 'Your only intent is to create mischief and to mislead me against people that I trust and love. You killed Ceba, my wife and the mother of my child. I shall inflict a punishment so harsh that both men and djinn would tremble at what befell you. Metishin! Drag her away, I shall deal with her later.'

Although Rhuzbeh reclaimed his throne as the King of Zanda, he was a broken man. He had started out on an adventure only to impress Ceba. Her memories haunted him. He vividly remembered bumping into her at the bazaar of Hatasa, the beautiful time they spent by the brook in each other's arms, her disappointment when she realised that he had faked his adventures to impress him. He had set out to cross an unknown ocean and strange lands to win back her love. He was whatever he was because of her. He had even murdered an innocent man to marry her and thought that nothing could keep her away from him. But then even kings have to surrender to death.

Rhuzbeh spent the lonely, sleepless night in agony and the next morning, he received news that Awa had escaped. It was no mean task to imprison a djinn let alone a powerful one like Awa. Despite all the arrangements, Awa managed to give Metishin the slip.

Rhuzbeh did not have time to focus on her. Despite his pain and loss he knew he must immediately march against the Sedran kingdom and reclaim his son and heir, Axer.

It was not going to be an easy task. The Zandians still did not have a navy as the pirate navy was destroyed by Tiran. When he thought about Tiran, his chest swelled with pride. Metishin had told Rhuzbeh all about him. He often thought about Tasia. He could still hear Tasia's laughter ringing in his ears like a splash of water as they ran on the beach barefoot. He could still feel her soft breath on his chest as they lay under the trees on idle sunny afternoons. Rhuzbeh had heard the full story from Metishin and remembered how Tiran had spent a considerable amount of time accompanying him on hunts and discussing warfare. No wonder the two of them bonded easily. He realised why Tiran was passionate about astronomy—he had taken after his mother. He thought about the spear that Tiran was carrying—the green crystal coated with lead. No wonder it was able to cut through the chain that bonded the duo who had fought in the arena. He remembered those green crystals, which were a potent weapon since ancient times, and realised that Tiran had learnt to harness the power of the green crystal. He was truly a formidable warrior, who had even managed to gravely wound Awa. Rhuzbeh felt love towards his firstborn son. He wanted to hold him and address him as his son. But then, his heart belonged to Axer. Axer was his beloved son—born of marriage, born as a prince and the legitimate heir to his throne. He remembered every moment he played and cuddled with him and consoled him when he cried and the pride he felt as Axer grew into this powerful and handsome man he was today. Unlike his father, he was good-natured, thought Rhuzbeh. It was Axer, his beloved son, who would be the king. He would talk Tiran into an alliance with him, resolved Rhuzbeh. After all, he was his son—his own flesh and blood—and he hoped Tiran would serve under him. Rhuzbeh asked for a meeting with Tiran and King Shaha. At the meeting, Rhuzbeh embraced Tiran and said, 'For the first time, I get to look at you and talk to you as a father.' 'You abandoned my mother and me,' said Tiran, his eyes filling with sadness. 'You left us on the island and did not think of us when you became a king. You are not my father. You just used my mother for comfort during your stopover and discarded her like a used rag.'

Rhuzbeh hung his head and said, 'I have nothing to say in my defence.' Seeing him like this, Tiran was further enraged. He asked, 'So, Rhuzbeh the Fearless has come to beg for his son? We will cut your son's head and send it as a gift.' Now it was Rhuzbeh's turn to be enraged, and he declared, 'If you ever touch a hair on his head, we will burn this kingdom and enslave every man, woman and child.'

King Shaha panicked and said, 'We do not want to kill your son. Here are our terms—grant us the coastal cities outside Zanda and empty your coffers of gold.' 'Done,' said Rhuzbeh.

'Also,' continued Shaha, 'we want a hundred young unmarried Zandian women as pleasure slaves.' The terms were humiliating. No self-respecting king would have accepted them. But Rhuzbeh had no choice if he wanted his beloved son back. He surrendered the gold and the coastal Zandian town but the really painful part was surrendering a hundred young unmarried women as slaves. There was much crying and mourning in Zanda as nobody willingly wanted to give their daughters into slavery. Moreover, this final exchange would tarnish Rhuzbeh's reputation permanently.

Metishin expressly forbade Rhuzbeh from accepting this last term. He admonished Rhuzbeh and said, 'Everyone's children are dear to them. You can't snatch young women from their homes and give them as booty to save your own child. Is the life of one person worth a hundred others?' he asked.

Rhuzbeh replied, 'I am the king and everything in this land is mine. And yes! One hundred lambs do not equal one lion. Axer is my son and your future king! As loyal subjects, you must be ready to sacrifice everything for your king.' So began the most shameful episode in the history of Zanda. The king's men went around house-to-house, snatching young girls. And when their parents and relatives resisted, they were flogged and punished. When a minister spoke out against the king, his own daughter was picked up and handed over as a slave. Ultimately, the terms and conditions were met and

Axer returned to Zanda. When Axer saw Rhuzbeh, he was overjoyed and said, 'Father, I always knew you would recover. I am so happy to see you.' Rhuzbeh held his son tightly and said, 'I am happy to see you as well, my son.' Axer had cracked his ribs and the Sedran physicians had looked after him well. Axer heard about his wife Anitsa and was depressed to hear the truth about her. He was ashamed of himself. He truly loved her and he could not believe what he heard. He remembered the time he had first met her, only seeing a thin pale hand emerge from the hut with a cup of water, and how after drinking the water, he had ordered her to show herself. She had emerged from the hut young, beautiful and pale as the moonlight. He wanted to talk to her. 'Give me some more water,' he had commanded.

'I will give if you ask nicely,' the girl had said. 'Careful, girl, do you know the consequences of being rude to your prince?' he had asked.

'I don't care,' she had replied. 'I lost my father yesterday and my mother six months ago, and I don't care what you do to me.' She had started to weep. She had looked so helpless and vulnerable at that moment. She had trembled like a leaf, stirring something in him. He had wanted to hold her close, protect her. He had jumped down from the horse and parted her hair to look at those big round eyes. Her cheeks had become red and warm from crying, compelling him to kiss them to calm her down. They had smelled like freshly-baked bread right out of an oven—warm, wholesome and soft. He hadn't wanted to take his face away from her cheeks, but she had pulled herself back and said, 'I'm sorry. You wanted some more water.' 'I think it is you who needs water,' he had said and offered her some.

She had smiled and replied, 'Thank you!'

He had sat with her the whole day speaking about a variety of things. She had been surprisingly intelligent and he had enjoyed her company. Before leaving, he had placed a soldier to guard her and left her food, rations and warm blankets. Gradually, his visits had been becoming more frequent and one day they had declared their love for each other.

All this time later, Axer remembered that she hated his golden armour. Every time he visited her wearing the golden armour, she would say, 'Please don't try and impress me with that golden armour. And anyway, you are not going to war in your lover's bed.' Now he knew why. The armour belonged to Amirast, the person who had banished her. She had not been able to tolerate any talk of Rhuzbeh either. Every time he spoke of his father, she would say, 'Please don't talk about him.' 'I shall speak to the king. Please meet him so that we can get married,' he had pleaded.

She expressly forbade him by saying, 'The King would want you to marry a princess and not a commoner like me. He would kill me if he knew about us. If you want to kill me, please kill me yourself. It is better that I die by your sword than by your father's.' Only when his father was bedridden had she finally agreed to marry him, realised Axer. He had fallen for an elaborate conspiracy, and he still could not come to terms with the fact that his wife had killed his mother. Tears ran down his cheeks and he lashed out. In one fell swoop, he had lost everything. He had lost his beloved mother who doted on him. Memories of his childhood with her came streaming back, and he broke down.

Wherever Axer went, people looked at him with malevolent eyes. His wife had killed his mother and abandoned him. Moreover, a hundred young women had been exchanged in his stead when he was taken prisoner. He knew that they spat behind him and he was burning in shame. In the meantime, Rhuzbeh recovered his health and started preparing for war in the south. He would bring fire and destruction to the Sedran kingdom, he resolved. With this determination, the greatest king in the known world headed towards Sedra.

CHAPTER 8

The Terror of Ungaal

Inflict the past on him who threatens the future.

'I guess this is it,' said Tiran, breaking the silence. 'Rhuzbeh is sailing towards us but we are more than ready for him. It was a masterstroke getting his nemesis out here. I am sure both your surprises will shock Rhuzbeh.'

Shaha was lost in thoughts and ponderously replied, 'We sure are ready for him but I'm surprised that Nahal is not supporting us against the Zandians. I hear Awa, the djinn, has joined Nahal and is influencing him. I'm sure she has something to do with Nahal not coming to our aid.'

'Yes, by taking advantage of Nahal's hesitation, Rhuzbeh has moved in swiftly and reconquered the coastal cities of Wastra once again. I hear he is using these coastal cities as a launchpad to invade us. Word has it that Rhuzbeh has asked the pirate Melqart to assemble a pirate fleet to ferry his soldiers to our lands,' said Tiran.

'Let them come,' said Shaha, stretching out his hands expansively. 'We will be ready with a welcoming party.'

The Zandian army sailed the sea of Balqara and landed on the Sedran shores unmolested. Rhuzbeh and his soldiers marched towards the walls of Sedra. When they reached the walls though, they were in for a shock.

'Look,' said Metishin, 'centaurs!'

Guarding the walls of Sedra were a hundred centaurs. Rhuzbeh's face went ashen. He spotted the lead centaur—the chestnut, Farda.

'Farda is here to seek revenge and he has brought his centaur warriors along,' said Metishin.

'These centaurs are powerfully built and armed with bows, arrows and swords,' said Axer. 'Our soldiers have never seen a centaur. The horses are scared and the men are losing their nerve. Shaha has tasked the centaurs to defend the city walls, but many of our soldiers consider spilling centaur blood a sin and a harbinger of bad luck. How do we overcome them?' he asked.

'We will charge ahead,' said Rhuzbeh in a steely voice. 'Our soldiers are disciplined, and we vastly outnumber them. I'm sure we can handle this.'

'Wait, do not attack yet!' said Metishin. 'Shaha has more tricks up his sleeve. I was informed about Shaha's moves, and I have asked for a few more people to join us.'

'Look around Metishin,' said an exasperated Rhuzbeh. 'We have five thousand Zandian soldiers with us. What difference can a few more make?'

'My king! Please wait for a couple more days,' said Metishin mysteriously.

Four days later, the surprise arrived and Axer cried out, 'Darya!'

As the Zandians looked in surprise, Darya rode towards them accompanied by five other mages, one of whom was called the Shepherd.

Rhuzbeh could not believe the sight and asked Metishin, 'How is she here? Is she fighting for us? Why is she fighting for us?'

'Because I asked her to,' replied Metishin.

Darya met Metishin and bowed low to him.

She remembered how Metishin had asked her to fight for the Zandians and she had flatly refused, saying, 'No! I will not serve under Rhuzbeh.' But when he had explained the situation to her, she had agreed, much to the chagrin of Hittash. She had promised Hittash that she would be back by his side if Hatasa was ever attacked.

With the arrival of Darya, Rhuzbeh decided to begin the attack. He lined up his horses for a charge. Surprisingly, the centaurs were not at the wall, and the walls of Sedra lay seemingly unprotected. Rhuzbeh looked up towards the city walls and froze. He realised why Metishin had called Darya and the other mages, for on the wall was Dahel the Bearclaw.

'I had killed his black cat and rendered him powerless. How is it that he is standing there looking so potent?' asked Rhuzbeh.

'Dahel had his wife Daheli murdered, and he obtained her powers,' said Metishin. 'With her powers, he is arguably the greatest dark sorcerer and is now called Dahel, the lord of the dark winds. He has managed to assemble ten powerful dark sorcerers from all corners of the known world. That is the reason why I called Darya and the other mages.'

Rhuzbeh nodded. He decided to charge the gates of the wall with battering rams and storm the city.

Flanked by his beloved son, Axer, who was clad in the golden armour, on his right and Metishin on his left, Rhuzbeh raised his sword and delivered a stirring speech to his troops. He said, 'To the fear that creeps up on me, hear me loud—I am Rhuzbeh, the Fearless! I have with me my rightful heir and your future king, Axer! These scums have insulted us, imprisoned your prince and dishonoured your women. It is time to make them pay the price.' He lifted his ivory horn and blew it before crying, 'Charge!'

The walls of Sedra were well defended, with catapults, ballistae and archers manning them.

As the Zandian cavalry charged towards the gates, Metishin suddenly cried, 'Watch out!'

The ten dark sorcerers let fly big arrows from ten large ballistae. The arrows flew in the air with a sinister swish, turned into huge snakes in the air and landed on the ground. The snakes were so big that they raised their hoods to the height of the oncoming horses' eyes, bringing the charging animals to a skidding halt. The horses panicked, threw their riders off, turned and bolted.

A stampede ensued and hundreds of Zandian soldiers were either killed in it or picked off by the archers on the wall. The ten colossal snakes stood their ground, hissing ominously. Darya, Metishin and the other mages cast their spells and conjured ten of their own snakes. After a brief standoff, the snakes of the dark sorcerers dissolved into thin air. But they had served their purpose well. The horses were skittish and refused to charge. The attack had to be called off.

The Zandians waited for two more days to look for solutions before Axer came up with an idea. He said, 'Father, let's blindfold the horses and charge. Once we are near the wall, we shall remove the blindfolds.'

It was an excellent idea. They blindfolded the horses and charged the gates. Tiran, who was watching the manoeuvre from the wall, whispered something to Shaha, and as soon as the Zandians charged, the dark sorcerers released their arrows from the ballistae. The arrows turned into gigantic bat-like creatures which flew near the horses and gave out sharp, blood-curdling shrieks. Again, the horses grew skittish and threw off their riders.

Metishin and Darya cast their own spell and warded off the bats, but the horses had been spooked again and refused to charge. Something had to be done about the ballistae.

Metishin summoned the mage called Shepherd, who blew the flute of the musician Tummaru and called forth an ancient magical creature. The creature was of mythical proportions—almost four times the size of an elephant. It had the head of a poisonous snake, a long, snake-like, thick neck and the long tail of a snake, but its body was that of a leopard. Surprisingly, the leopard's paws ended in eagle-like talons. The creature also had wings that were powerful enough to fly great distances. Its entire body, including the wings, was golden coloured, with leopard-like spots. When the creature was still, its wings were so perfectly camouflaged that even the outlines of the wings were not visible. The creature hissed and roared alternatively, and its noise was so loud that it could be heard clearly above the din of the battle.

The creature flew towards the ballistae, and such was the terror it created that the mages abandoned their ballistae and fled. The creature picked up a ballista with its claws and dropped it from the fort walls to the ground. It was smashed to smithereens. Two dark mages tried to cast a spell on the creature, but its impact merely bounced off it like rainwater. The beast turned and bit them both, killing them instantly. Dahel sent up a huge black eagle to chase the leopard-snake creature. The creature and the bird fought, their screams rent the sky, and finally, the Shepherd called the beast back.

There was an ominous quiet. This massive flying beast had shocked King Shaha. 'What is this creature?' he asked Dahel.

Dahel was quiet for a few moments before speaking again, as if still in a trance.

'And we shall make it,
Four of the legs with claws and wings of a bird,
Not yet a bird.
The body and fur of a leopard,
Not yet a leopard.
The head, neck and tail of a snake,
And not yet a snake.'

'What is this creature?' asked Shaha in exasperation.

'This creature is a serpopard called *Ungaal*,' replied Dahel. 'This magical creature was bred to strike terror into the enemies' hearts. Ungaal has a history of death and destruction, but it will do your bidding when tamed with music.'

'I have never heard of a serpopard or Ungaal. Where did this creature come from? Are there more of them? Shaha asked.

'No,' replied Dahel. 'Only one has ever been created to instil fear and to destroy. Legend has it that once upon a time, in King Astabipal's kingdom, reptilian creatures with huge leathery wings flew in the skies. These winged creatures terrorised his subjects by swooping down and devouring them. King Astabipal wanted to deal with the menace, and so he called on his mages to find a solution. The mages approached the Serpents of the Abyss to create a creature powerful enough to beat the threat. The wise serpents crossbred a serpent, a leopard and an eagle. The resulting animal was a serpopard, and they named it Ungaal or the destroyer. The king raised Ungaal as a baby, and it was rumoured that king Astabipal could talk to the creature. He hand-fed it and put it to sleep to the tunes of musician Tummaru.

Ungaal grew into a massive beast with fearsome jaws. It could open its jaws so wide that it could swallow a small horse in one go. As soon as Ungaal had grown up, the king ordered it to destroy the murderous reptilian creatures crowding the kingdom. Ungaal swooped down on them one by one. It proved to be a mighty hunter. If the leathery creatures were sitting on a tree, it would slowly slither its neck up the branch and strangle them. If they were flying, Ungaal would fly parallel to them and, with its poisonous jaws, bite them mid-air. The creatures would drop down like stone. Sometimes, it would snatch them mid-air with its powerful talons. Ungaal chased them to all corners of the empire and killed them all.

Having completed its task, Ungaal came back to the palace to the grateful cheers of the subjects. King Astabipal adopted Ungaal as his kingdom's mascot. It was on the king's flag, heraldry and the motifs in the palace. There were pottery designs and patterns made after it, and it was venerated as the magical creature which had rid the kingdom of the flying scourge. Ungaal would fly with the king during his hunting trips. It would also accompany the king to war and strike fear in the hearts of the enemies.

Ungaal was bred to terrorise and instil fear, and a great majority of Astabipal's subjects believed that it was only a matter of time before Ungaal turned on them. They approached the king and asked him to get rid of it. However, the king loved Ungaal and had raised it as a baby, so he of course refused to part with it.

'So, what did the subjects do then?' asked Shaha.

'They approached the crown prince who lived under the shadow of the great king, his father. The young prince was keen to make his mark, and since the citizens had appealed to him, he decided to slay Ungaal and become a hero. Once, when the Ungaal was flying low, he threw a great spear at it. But Ungaal caught it with his neck and broke it like a twig, and in a horrifying attempt at retaliation, it came swooping down, bit the prince and tore his body to pieces.

'King Astabipal was furious that Ungaal had killed his only son and ordered his soldiers to hunt the creature. Astabipal ordered each town to erect a tower and mount a ballista to shoot Ungaal down. The creature realised that the soldiers were trying to kill it. It would fly above the clouds and dive in straight against the sun. The soldiers couldn't see Ungaal until it was almost on them. The creature destroyed the heavy ballista and ate the soldiers. It swallowed the soldiers whole and spat out their shoes and helmets.

'Ungaal had to be stopped. Astabipal had the favour of the Serpents of Abyss, and they granted him weapons that could kill Ungaal. Armed with the weapons, Astabipal himself came out to fight. He was seated on a large open chariot being dragged by twenty elephants. In the fight, Astabipal sent up weapons that set the sky on fire, burning Ungaal's feathers and fur. Ungaal barely managed to fly away and hide in the mountains. After his anger had subsided, Astabipal's fondness for Ungaal took over, and he reasoned that the creature had killed his son only in self-defence. He knew that Ungaal must be in great pain, and he decided to send the musician Tummaru to put it to rest.

'Tummaru played a small flat flute to pacify Ungaal. For three days and nights, Tummaru played for Ungaal until he soothed it and led it to a dark forest. In a secluded place below an overhanging cliff, he put Ungaal into a magical sleep, where it has slept ever since.

'Trees and leaves covered its body until it was not visible anymore. That is the legend of Ungaal. I thought it a myth and yet here it is...' Dahel trailed off.

'Hmm,' said Shaha. 'Now that Ungaal has been called away, we must counter-attack.'

Shaha attacked with his army, and the centaurs led his cavalry. The chestnut centaur, Farda, led the charge, and they were like a sickle on a cornfield. The centaurs scythed through any Zandian cavalry that came in their path. Farda's desire for revenge was strong. Rhuzbeh had humiliated him. The centaurs galloped close to one another, and they were creating vast gaps in the enemy lines. The tide of the battle was turning. The Zandian soldiers turned and ran. Nothing could stand in the centaurs' way.

Axer went up to Metishin and said, 'Farda and his centaurs are changing the course of the battle. Should I challenge him to a duel?'

Metishin replied, 'Do not ever make that mistake. No human can ever match up to the strength of a centaur.'

'How do we stop them then? Do they have any weaknesses?'

'Hmm,' said Metishin. 'Their only weakness is wine. They become uncontrollable after having it. The wine takes away all their discipline and they cannot differentiate between friend and foe.'

This gave Axer an idea. At midnight, Zandian spies replaced the centaurs' water rations with wine. By morning all the centaurs in the camp had gone completely wild.

Rhuzbeh's horn sounded the attack and both armies thundered against each other. The centaurs had gone berserk by now and they turned on anyone in the vicinity, slaughtering them. Friend and foe fell alike under their swords and thundering hooves.

King Shaha personally rode to Farda to try and calm him. Farda was in a wildly inebriated state and struck his sword hilt at Shaha. Tiran, who was watching this, threw his crystal spear at Farda's chest, instantly killing him. Everything came to a standstill.

The centaurs sobered up and closed ranks. They were confused and did not know which side to attack any more. The centaurs were in a murderous state, and both Zandian and Sedran armies withdrew in fear.

The battle ended that day with much regret and mourning for the centaurs since Farda was a well-loved centaur from a noble lineage. The lament for Farda rent the air as the centaurs mourned his passing.

As moonbeam strikes the barren land,
No strut, no whinny,
No call from the lover,
No proud trots.
The earth weeps and stars sniff,
Snatched by the hand of cruel fate,
In full gaze of the herd,
Wounded and bloodied, we watch,
With hapless wrath.
Snatched from the bosom of the earth,
The proud centalion,
The hammer of the centaurs,
The light of the race,
The keeper of secrets,
The flag bearer of the ancient blood,
Slain in glorious battle.
Farda! Farda! Mighty Farda!

Farda had had a reason to fight against Rhuzbeh. But now, with Farda dead, the centaurs had no reason to continue. After the funeral, the centaurs departed and left without goodbyes. The departure of the centaurs was a major relief to the Zandians, and after the incident of Farda attacking Shaha, the Sedrans were secretly relieved as well.

The departure of the centaurs was a morale booster for the Zandians. Sensing that the Zandians were getting the upper hand, Shaha decided to go on the offensive. When the battle resumed after the hiatus, the Sedrans, led by Dahel and his mages, charged at Rhuzbeh, intent on killing him and finishing the war.

Metishin stood next to Rhuzbeh, guarding him, and Darya walked in front all alone, a sword and staff in hand. As the Sedrans charged, the Shepherd unleashed Ungaal again. The serpopard wreaked havoc on the Sedrans, stalling their charge.

Dahel stepped up to battle Ungaal, but the Shepherd had had enough of Dahel. He drove Ungaal towards him with the intent to kill. Just then, Tiran quickly figured out a way to stop Ungaal. While everyone was focussed on fighting the creature, in a flash, Tiran shot an arrow at the Shepherd and killed him instead. With the Shepherd dead, Ungaal flew away and the battle stopped.

Both sides collected their dead and calculated their losses. The Sedrans had lost their centaurs and a few of their mages—only Dahel and four others remained. Rhuzbeh had lost Ungaal and all his mages except the most important ones—Darya and Metishin.

The next day, Darya challenged Dahel. It was to be a battle of a sorcerer versus a mage. Both were legendary and considered the greatest ever in their respective fields. Unknown to most though, Darya had an edge—she had mastered everything that Dahel had to teach, but she also possessed knowledge that Dahel was unaware of.

After an exhaustive battle, Darya bound Dahel in a flaming rope and whirled it around until he burst into bits. There were shrieks and screams as his magic sought release. As his power escaped him, all that was left of Dahel was a small black cat that sat on black ashes. It looked up at Darya with yellowish-green eyes and meowed pitifully. Darya picked up her sword, walked over to the black cat and, with one hefty swing, cut off his head. Thus fell Dahel the Bearclaw. Darya stormed the fort gate of the Sedrans, and the great fort was breached. Rhuzbeh and his army stormed in behind her. The Sedrans rushed to drive back the Zandian forces, and in the heat of the fight, Darya was shot down with an arrow from the skies.

Everyone raised their heads to look above. It was Tiran.

He was flying on a carpet made by Ardahast. After Rhuzbeh had cut off his hands, the carpet maker had refused to divulge the secret to anyone. He was a proud man, who did not care about wealth. He had only wanted one thing—to see Rhuzbeh dead. Tiran had heard about Ardahast and visited him. He had met with a frail, half-dying man covered in filth. Tiran had approached him and said, 'O great Ardahast! I want one of your amazing flying carpets.'

'Go away!' Ardahast had said. 'I do not have any flying carpets. That tyrant Rhuzbeh chopped off my hands at the behest of his lying wife. How do you expect a cripple to make flying carpets?'

Tiran had replied, 'I know he chopped your hands off. He also abandoned my mother and left me as a bastard on an island. I seek what you seek—revenge.'

Tiran had then narrated the whole story to Ardahast.

Ardahast had looked at Tiran and narrowed his eyes. 'In that case,' he had said, 'I do have a carpet for you and it flies too! I had initially made two flying carpets. I hid one and gifted the other to Ceba.' Saying this, he had gestured towards a locked trunk.

'The carpet is inside that trunk. You may have it but promise me one thing,' Ardahast had said. 'You will kill that tyrant, Rhuzbeh!'

'I shall try my best to kill him,' Tiran had assured.

'I want you to do one more thing for me,' Ardahast had pleaded with tears in his eyes. 'Kill me! I do not want to live the life of a cripple. I will die gladly, knowing that my carpet will be used to avenge me. Have mercy! Kill this cripple who cannot even kill himself.'

Tiran had tried to dissuade Ardahast but to no avail. He had eventually honoured Ardahast's last wish and killed him. He had then proceeded to take the flying carpet, which he now used as a mount when he attacked Darya.

Tiran had to shoot Darya, the woman he loved, or she would kill everything in her path. But he deliberately shot her on the shoulders, ensuring that although severe, Darya's injury was not fatal. An angry Axer shot an arrow at Tiran, who swiftly dodged it. Tiran was vulnerable to arrows while flying the carpet, so he jumped down on a horse, wound up his carpet and rushed to meet Axer in battle.

As Axer and Tiran clashed, a loud lament rose from the Sedrans. Rhuzbeh had fought King Shaha and killed him in battle. The Sedran King was dead. Tiran paused, and in that instant, Axer swung his sword knocking Tiran down from his horse. A moment's distraction had proved costly for Tiran. Although shocked, he stood up and started running. While still running, he unfolded the carpet, jumped on it and flew away.

The sea-serpent banner lay trampled on the ground as King Shaha was killed and Tiran was driven away. Sedra fell to Rhuzbeh.

A victorious Rhuzbeh headed back home with Axer. He had conquered Wastra and Sedra. Only the Northern kingdom and Hatasa remained to be conquered. Her task accomplished, the injured Darya left for Hatasa to recuperate.

Meanwhile, Axer decided to travel around incognito for a few days again and enjoy the liberating experience of being a nobody. He wanted a few days off palace, off politics and off killings. He conveyed the message to his father to leave him alone for a few weeks and set out to the bazaars of Zanda. There he saw an elderly man sitting at a table alone.

Axer asked, 'Can I sit next to you?'

The man replied, 'Yes, please do!'

They started talking, and the man asked Axer, 'What do you do?'

Axer replied, 'I am a daily wage worker looking for work.'

The elderly man took Axer's hands in his own hands and smilingly looked at them before saying, 'If these are the hands of a daily wage worker, then I am the King of Zanda.'

'Then whose hands are these?' asked a bemused Rhuzbeh.

The elderly man looked at them and said, 'These are the hands of a warrior. Look! You have calluses on the handgrip where you hold a sword and nowhere else. Your broad shoulders and healthy skin suggest good food, and hence, you are definitely no daily wage worker. Who did you murder? And who are you running away from?

Axer gave a weak smile and shrugged.

'Do you want to work for me?' asked the elderly man.

'Yes,' replied Axer and joined him as a daily help to do his chores. The man said, 'Tend to my sheep, take the flock out to the hill, make sure they eat and bring them back safely.' Axer took the large flock of sheep to graze and learnt that it was not an easy task to keep them from straying on the streets. He finally relaxed on the hills while the sheep grazed.

They grazed from morning till evening, and when the sun was about to set, he brought them back safely and put them in the pen. This went on for a week. He would sit patiently under a tree and watch the sheep graze. Eventually though, he grew so bored and lonely that he started talking to the sheep and bleating with them. Nothing eventful ever happened.

Every day, the elderly man met Axer and asked, 'What happened today?' and Axer would reply, 'Nothing.'

Axer was getting frustrated. He grew restless, and when he could take it no more, he said, 'I can't do this monotonous job where nothing ever happens.'

The elderly man laughed and said, 'Most people want something to happen all the time. That is because they are not at peace. A shepherd, on the other hand, although vigilant, must be supremely patient, and he must be at peace with himself. That is why some of the greatest teachers and prophets were shepherds. You are restless because you are not at peace with yourself. A fire is restless. It rages and spreads, burning everything in its path. Eventually, it burns out and dies down as fast as it had started. Be tranquil as a tree. When the wind blows, swing with it; when the birds sing, enjoy the song; watch the sheep eat contently at your feet.'

The elderly man indulged Axer. That night as they ate, he said, 'Tomorrow, we will go to the bazaars to sell some of the sheep.'

Axer was happy to go to the bazaar since it would be a pleasant change from his routine.

The bazaar was a colourful conundrum. It was bustling with people eager for a bargain—prospective buyers grasping the midrib of the sheep to assess the meat, probing the teeth to find out how old the sheep were and haggling over the prices. As the merchants checked for the quality of wool for their rugs and carpets, the local ladies were checking Axer out.

The duo managed to sell the sheep they had brought and decided to stroll in the bazaar to check out the wares. Axer took in the sights and smells of the bazaar. The delightful squeals of children, the incessant clanging of utensils, the unremitting bleating of sheep, the blithesome giggles of young maidens, the melodious calls of the songbirds mixed with the angry clucks of chicken, the vivid bright red and yellow clothing of women, the appetising aromas that wafted in the air, the pleasant smell of aromatic spices—Axer was healing.

Earlier, he was tormented by the burden of being a hero's son and the future king. Here he forgot all about it and began to enjoy a common man's daily life, unburdened by the question of legacy. He felt light and happy as if a great boulder had been lifted off his shoulders, at least for some time. With coins jangling in their pouch, Axer and his employer headed to a tavern and ordered food and drink. Suddenly, they overheard three men indulging in a loud, boisterous conversation. 'Axer is a weakling, cowering under his father's shadow. His father had to sell a hundred young women as slaves to rescue him. I think he will make for a weak king. I prefer Hittash or even Tiran as our future king.'

'Axer is no weakling,' said another. 'He is a proven warrior in his own right, who put his life and liberty at risk to serve Zanda.'

But the accuser persisted and said, 'Even his wife deceived him. What kind of a man gets cheated by his own wife? Bah! I don't think a fool like that deserves to be the king. And he does not even have an heir.'

'Hush!' said the other man. 'That woman is a djinn, so don't talk about her.'

There was an ominous silence in the tavern. The keeper gave a dirty glance to the man who had unnecessarily mentioned djinns at his place, risking drawing their attention.

'I do not trust Axer,' said the third person at the table. 'His father is bloodthirsty. He killed a man and married his wife. He raped a woman and had a baby. Axer is his own seed. If he takes after his father, what kind of a king would he make?'

'A good king!' said the other man. 'He is kind and noble. He has the strength and fearlessness of his father and the nobility of a righteous prince. Axer was born a prince and educated by the great Metishin himself. He will make a great king!'

Everyone around nodded in agreement and even drank to his health.

Axer was relieved. His subjects loved him. They looked up to him and defended his name in taverns and inns. He could not control his happiness and smiled widely. The elderly man was amused and asked, 'You seem suddenly buoyed. What brings such good cheer?'

'The maiden's smile across the table,' he said and pointed to a girl who was looking at them with a wide, inviting smile.

'Well, then I think you must speak to her,' said the elderly man, giving him a wink and a friendly shove.

Axer got up and came back with two young maidens with lovely hair and flushed cheeks. There was laughter and lots of food and drink. This was the happiest he had been in a long time. For most men, the company of plump, healthy, happy women was heart-warming—the pleasant plumpness, denoting plenty and a lack of want, implied that all was well with the world. The lack of self-consciousness and hearty laughter washed away all his worries. Axer headed back home with the women and slept the long, careless sleep of someone who did not have to rise with the sun. He was happy and warm.

He knew he had to get back to his father. The next day, he woke up, hugged the old man and said, 'If you ever feel like talking to me, come to the palace.' Axer placed a gold coin in his hand and rode away, much to the surprise of the elderly man.

Axer reached the palace, and when he came face-to-face with his father, he found him depressed, with the stricken look of a man who had lost all his loved ones. At the sight of Axer, his eyes lit up.

Rhuzbeh said, 'Son, we will avenge you. We will get that djinn Awa, kill that renegade Tiran and punish the Northerners.'

Although weary, Axer knew it had to be done. The Northerners were preparing for battle, and it was just a matter of time before they attacked. Rhuzbeh knew that to attack the North would be foolish. He remembered his misadventure and the botched military campaign. The Bjan pass was well guarded and so was the fort. Rhuzbeh decided to wait because he knew that Awa and Tiran would be impatient and attack him soon.

Nahal also knew the importance of waiting. Up north, in his fort, he was safe. If he ever stepped out, there was a chance that he would lose the war and his life. Nahal possibly had the mightiest force that he could ask for, one whose strength was reinforced by the presence of Awa, the jann. Awa had unlawfully assembled a force of ifrits, janns and ghouls, and she had at her command the secret weapon that terrorised Rhuzbeh and his soldiers.

Tiran had fled to the north after Rhuzbeh had conquered the Southern kingdom, and in Awa, he found a kindred spirit; they bonded instantly. Tiran became so fond of her that he gifted her the gem that he had so carefully hidden from the gaze of Rhuzbeh, and Awa immediately knew what it was. It was one of the much sought-after gems created by the djinns—the sanaa.

The return of the sanaa was the key to the revival of the city of Afra-Zun, and she wanted to make sure that Amirast never got his hands on it. She did not want him to attain greatness.

When Awa, as Anitsa, was crowned the Queen of Zanda, she had sought out Nahal and met with him. During the private meeting, she had said, 'I seek peace with you.'

Nahal had laughed and said, 'You and your kingdom are both under my mercy, and I will ravage you both. My spies inform me that Rhuzbeh is on his deathbed, Axer is out at sea and Zanda is ripe for picking. That accursed Rhuzbeh had the gumption to make an attempt at capturing my kingdom.' He had spat and continued saying, 'I will now show him and his son who the real king is, but I will spare you if you adorn my bed, noble queen.' He followed the statement with a mock bow. She had smiled and asked mischievously, 'Do you want to see me?'

Nahal had smirked and replied, 'Show me.'

Awa had thrown off her cloak and taken on a burning form. She then addressed him in a fiery voice: 'You filth! I am not Anitsa, the wife of Axer. I am Awa! Once the Queen of Amstrap! I am made of fire! Mightier than your mightiest! I am the jann who challenged the great Amirast himself, and you are nothing but a centipede below my boot.' Saying this, she had stepped forward and slapped him.

Nahal had reeled back and fallen. She leaned over Nahal's sprawled form and said, 'You worm! Do you know how the manticore came to Bjan pass? Do you know where it went later? You worthless insect! I can snuff out your miserable life but I need you. Listen carefully: you shall not attack Zanda. In case Rhuzbeh wins the war and marches towards the north, I shall guide you, and with our combined might, we shall take on Rhuzbeh.'

The terrified Nahal had accepted the proposal and refrained from attacking Zanda.

The die was now cast. Since Awa assembled an assortment of djinns to fight, Rhuzbeh sent a message to Amirast seeking help. Amirast immediately dispatched Ghanazaqi with a contingent of janns. Irash the ifrit accompanied Ghanazaqi with a company of fearsome ifrits.

This was a contingency measure. If ever Awa attacked the humans, Amirast would be forced to attack her.

Meanwhile Ghanazaqi had lost all affection for Rhuzbeh since he last met him because of his cruel, murderous ways. He expressly declared that the djinns would not fight humans or beasts, and that they were here only because of the renegade djinns. Awa was dangerous. If the djinns under Awa won, then they would get back to Alainis and challenge Amirast, altering the dynamics of the djinn world. Hence, Awa had to be dealt with an iron hand.

Chapter 9

The Twice-Dead King

The most prudent way to mend is to make amends.

Darya's shoulder was mending fast, and this news set Nahal back on his heel. But the Hatasans hailed the fact that Darya was well because she was an essential part of their war effort.

As soon as she left Zanda for Hatasa, she addressed their army: 'The Hatasans are adept at mountain fighting, but when it comes to fighting on flatlands, we are vulnerable. The Zandian army has heavy cavalry, and their soldiers are heavily armed. We cannot match the Zandians in martial strength. Instead, we must opt for speed.'

Hittash said, 'Yes, I have been thinking about that. We must devise light chariots drawn by a single horse carrying a mobile archer who could fight with a sword at close quarters.'

'Add scythe blades on both sides of the chariot wheels,' suggested Darya, 'and also equip our armies with long lances to stave off any heavy cavalry charge by the Zandians. Let us hire former Zandian soldiers and train our armies in the Zandian warfare tactics and weaponry.'

It took four years of gruelling training but Hittash, with Darya's help, mobilised an army that could take on the best in the known world.

Hittash was relieved to have Darya back safe. She was a symbol of hope for the Hatasans, and it was whispered that until Darya was alive, nobody could defeat him. Hittash decided to wait and watch as he did not want to take sides with Nahal and Awa, but he did not want to side with Rhuzbeh either. He reasoned that after the war, the winning side would be considerably weakened, and he would attack and decimate them.

Meanwhile, war clouds were gathering on the Northern front.

Tiran urged Nahal to attack Rhuzbeh. He said, 'Let us mount an attack on Zanda as we have the upper hand. Darya will not ally with Rhuzbeh, and we have Awa with us. Let us attack and decimate the tyrant once and for all.'

'No,' said Nahal. 'It is stupid to leave the safety of the Northern walls, and the Bjan pass is the killing field where we slaughtered the Zandians. If they want to take the North, let them try and cross the Bjan pass again.'

But Rhuzbeh was wary. He did not want to repeat his mistake, and he waited for Nahal to make the first move—it was a stalemate. After two years of planning and waiting impatiently, when both armies did not attack each other, the wily Tiran plotted the demise of Rhuzbeh. Tiran made his move and Rhuzbeh was killed.

But how did the mighty king die?

A year ago, the council of Tiran, Awa and Nahal had met and discussed the best way to win the war.

At the time, Nahal said, 'Unless Awa and the djinns attack, Ghanazaqi would not attack. The affairs of humans do not concern the djinns, and it is said that Amirast does not have a high opinion of Rhuzbeh anymore. To attack with djinns would mean to provoke Ghanazaqi to retaliate but to leave our impregnable fort and invade Zanda would mean losing strategic advantage. What do we do?'

'Let's assassinate Rhuzbeh,' Tiran suggested. 'Assassination is a great political weapon. We would be rid of a potent enemy, and Axer would be forced to step out of his comfort zone and attack us. Axer is an emotional fool! He would try to avenge his father's death. He would come charging at us like an enraged bull, and then we could cut down the Zandian army like carrots.'

Everyone nodded in agreement.

'It is a great idea but who will kill Rhuzbeh?' Awa asked. 'No djinn can kill Rhuzbeh since gus ambergris runs in his veins and he bears gajmuk. He is also protected by the mage Metishin.'

'Let's use a sorcerer,' suggested Nahal.

'No!' said Tiran, 'There is a good possibility that Metishin or Ghanazaqi will see through them and imprison them before they even manage to reach Rhuzbeh.'

'Then how do we kill that accursed man?' Awa asked.

'Through deceit,' said Tiran. 'I know how to win the king's heart. I did it once and I know how to do it again. Use regular people to approach him because the king is suspicious, and he will make enquiries. Never try too hard. Be normal and win the king's affection.'

'But where will we find a person who would be willing to kill a king?' asked Nahal.

'As a matter of fact, I know two such people,' Tiran replied with a broad grin.

When Tiran had travelled to the western lands as a spy for Nahal, he had mingled around and gone hunting as he considered himself a good hunter. He now recalled those adventures.

During a particular fireside chat with the hunters, Tiran heard about a brother-sister hunting pair. They were called Zay and Zana. He was intrigued by their tales, and so he travelled to a small town on the outskirts of a forest where the twins lived.

The twins were lean and athletic and made a beautiful pair. They could make animal noises, track animals and run as fast as the fastest native animal.

Tiran was struck by Zana's beauty. Her lean and chiselled face was beautifully complemented by a feminine softness in her countenance. She moved with the grace and agility of a cat. Tiran tried to seduce her, but she was immune to his charms. Despite his best efforts, she never reciprocated. Tiran did not give up and challenged the twins. 'Let's go hunting, and whoever bags a deer first wins,' he said.

They tiptoed to the jungle, and as soon as they saw a herd, Tiran stealthily tried to sneak up on them. But the twins did not follow suit. Instead, they made a loud noise like a growl and ran in diverging directions, effectively funnelling the deer between them. They ran with the deer, jumping high and kicking the tree trunks for momentum. Every time the deer ran right, the twin on the right made a noise, forcing the deer to go left. When the twin on the left made noises, the deer turned right. They kept the deer running straight until the deer slowed down out of exhaustion and stopped. Then they caught one with their bare hands and tied its legs and slung it on Zay's back.

Tiran lost the challenge, and the twins laughed at him mockingly. He was flabbergasted. He had never seen anything like that before. The twins could run as fast as deer and even drive them to exhaustion.

Zay said, 'Come, don't be a bad loser. Join us for dinner.'

Tiran obliged and went back to their stone hut. He was surprised to see that they had a small farm, and on the farm, they had a herd of deer, much as one would have of sheep.

'All of them hand-caught,' said Zana, her voice ringing with pride. 'My mother does not like a deer being killed with metal-tipped arrows. By the time you bring back a deer after killing and skinning in the jungle, there are flies all over the meat, and the clothes get dirty with thick blood. This way, it is a lot fresher and better.'

Her parents were indulgent and happy to share their meal with him. He saw other birds and animals in cages as well.

In one of the cages, he saw a bear and asked, 'Did you catch that bear with your bare hands as well?'

They laughed and said, 'We only catch grass-eating animals with our hands. For catching animals like panthers and bears, we use traps.'

After dinner, Tiran happened to mention Rhuzbeh's name, and Zay spat out in anger. 'Rhuzbeh may be a great king, but he is not our king! We are westerners. Yet we pay our tax to the Zandians. The Zandian governors are very unpopular since they force even the poorest of farmers to pay taxes. Why should we pay tax to the Zandians? We are a free people!' he bristled. Zana nodded in agreement.

'Given a chance to hunt Rhuzbeh and free the whole of Wastra, would you accept the challenge?' asked Tiran.

'That would be a great hunt,' said Zana, and her eyes lit brightly at the prospect of the hunt.

Tiran smiled at her and she smiled back.

Suddenly, there was an awkward silence. Tiran plucked up his courage and turned to Zana's father. 'I have something to ask of you.'

'Ask,' he said.

'I am attracted to Zana. My intention towards her is honourable, and I want to marry her with your permission,' he proposed.

Her father smiled and said, 'You need to ask Zana.'

Tiran turned to Zana and asked, 'Zana, I'm smitten with you, and I want to marry you. I want you to bear my children and spend the rest of your life with me. Will you marry me?'

She replied, 'Tiran, you are a good man, but I do not feel the same for you. I can't be tamed. I can't be someone's wife. And I can't bear babies and nurture them. I'm a huntress! Hunting is what I look forward to the most. I'm not wild; I'm the wild! Besides, I'm bonded in spirit with my brother. We are one being, the right and left. I can't cut myself in half. I'm afraid I can't marry you.'

Tiran did not give up. Instead, he did what every spurned man does—he spoke highly of himself. 'I am no ordinary hunter,' he said. 'I'm Tiran, the trusted aide of King Shaha from the south and the firstborn son of Rhuzbeh the Fearless.'

Tiran went on to narrate his adventures, and they listened with awe.

When he finished narrating his stories, Zana said, 'You embark on these exciting adventures and heap yourself with glory. Yet you want me to sit at home and wait for you to come home and mount me. You want me to bear your children and hear their tantrums. You want me to cook food and clean their faeces while you come back and regale me with such stories. I'm Zana! A huntress! I shall have my own stories. And none of them would be about cleaning shit!'

Tiran admired her spirit and said, 'It's time for me to take your leave, but when there is a chance of adventure, and I need company, I shall call you.' With that, he left.

Now, when someone was needed to kill Rhuzbeh, Tiran remembered and sent for the twins.

'What explanation will they offer to be allowed to get close to Rhuzbeh?' asked Nahal.

'I remember when I reached King Rhuzbeh's court with my monkfly, the king was intrigued. He loves strange birds and animals,' said Tiran.

'What animal shall we gift Rhuzbeh?' asked Nahal.

'We shall gift him a bird, not an animal,' suggested Awa and continued, 'Rhuzbeh is lonely now since Hitti lives with Hittash and Ceba is dead. Rhuzbeh has lost his sleep and laughter. We must gift him a tasnif.'

'A tasnif? What is that?' asked Tiran.

'Tasnif is a rare bird found in old, secluded jungles,' replied Awa. 'Its body is scarlet, with a yellow breast and yellow colouration around its eyes. It is crowned with a yellow crest, much like a peafowl. It sings so beautifully that it makes a person forget his worries. Its singing lulls all pain and induces sleep—a perfect gift for a lonely, depressed king.'

'How can we catch a tasnif?' asked Tiran.

'The tasnif bird is impossible to spot except during the full moon of spring when it heads to barberry trees and relishes red barberries. After having barberries, it becomes so happy that it sings its heart out, making it easy to be spotted,' replied Awa.

Tiran added, 'And it is the full moon of spring in a fortnight. Let me trap this songbird then.'

A fortnight later, they headed to the spot where the barberry shrubs abounded. They created a giant cage around the shrubs with an open door and asked Awa to transform into a tasnif bird and sing. The idea was that on hearing Awa, the original bird would fly inside, and Tiran would trap it. But when the bird actually came closer, it sensed the trap and flew away.

Tiran decided that he would have to take things into his own hands, literally. He got rid of the cage and sent back all the others. He collected the barberry bushes around him and sat very still. He held out the choicest barberries in his hands. When the bird approached him, he tossed the berries a little distance away from his feet. The bird hopped to the ground and ate them. He slowly kept tossing berries progressively closer until the bird was eating from his hands. Tiran closed his hand and caught the bird. Sometimes, the least elaborate plans work out best.

The tasnif bird now belonged to Tiran, who transferred it into a cage. When he met the twins, Tiran explained the plan and sent them to Rhuzbeh. The twins presented themselves to the King of Zanda and said, 'Greetings, great king! We come from the west bearing a precious gift.'

'What is it?' asked Rhuzbeh.

The twins explained about the tasnif and presented the bird to Rhuzbeh.

That night, Rhuzbeh fed the tasnif some barberries, and it sang a most beautiful happy song.

The king felt all his worries and guilt wash away, and he slept a very peaceful sleep.

The following day, he called the twins and asked them, 'Where are you from?'

'O King! Like we said earlier, we are your subjects from the west,' replied Zana.

Rhuzbeh was happy and rewarded them with gold coins, but Zana refused politely and said, 'Great King! We do not want gold.'

'Then what is it that you desire?' asked Rhuzbeh.

'We are hunters, and we would like to work with you as royal hunters,' replied Zana.

Rhuzbeh looked at Zay and Zana carefully, and he scrutinised them further, checking their credentials as hunters.

Rhuzbeh finally said, 'Stay with us, enjoy our hospitality, and I will take you with us on our next hunting trip.' As soon as they left, he called Metishin.

'Find out more about them,' he told Metishin.

Metishin invited Zay and Zana to have dinner with him. He could tell by their manners that they were hunters. They regaled Metishin with their hunting stories. He listened to everything they had to say and said nothing.

'Does the great mage Metishin have no questions to ask of us?' asked Zay with a raised brow.

'None at all,' replied Metishin. They spent the remainder of the dinner in loud silence. Metishin made his enquiries, and a week later, he reported back to Rhuzbeh, 'It is true! They are who they say they are. As a matter of fact, the brother-sister pair is well-known in the region and are a legend among the hunters.'

'Something is amiss! Perhaps, you missed out on some details, Metishin,' Rhuzbeh said with a raised eyebrow.

Metishin was taken aback.

'Shall I have them arrested and interrogated?' asked Metishin.

'No,' replied Rhuzbeh. 'Ghanazaqi says let's wait and see what unfolds.'

Rhuzbeh enrolled them as members of his hunting party. During the hunt, the hunting party tried to stealthily sneak up on a deer. The twins, in their own fashion, chased down and caught the deer barehanded.

The king was awed by the speed and agility of the brother-sister pair. Slowly, Rhuzbeh grew fond of them. He particularly spent a lot of time with Zana.

Rhuzbeh felt lonely in the absence of his queens, and the dancing girls did not appeal to him. A beautiful huntress with a feminine charm was irresistible. He held her hand whenever he could and most often drew her close to him. 'The tyrant is making advances, and it's getting difficult to fend him off,' complained Zana.

'Then the time is ripe for killing the king,' said Zay.

Zay and Zana had done their preparations. They had met a hunter named Shulgi. The latter was a famous hunter once, but now he was past his prime. He himself was hunted by disease and haunted by advancing age. But Shulgi, by virtue of his experience, had a certain standing in the hunting community.

'Do you want to earn gold coins?' Zay asked Shulgi, placing ten gold coins on the table.

Shulgi looked at them with suspicious eyes and asked, 'What do I have to do?'

'Teach your fellow hunters how to hunt big game single-handedly. Unlike the king and the royal hunters, they cannot hunt big game like bears and big cats alone. Instruct the hunters to dig deep pits. Ask them to place sharp bamboos at the bottom and cover the pit with thin sticks and leaves. If some big, unsuspecting animal walks over the lightly-covered pit, it would fall in the pit and get killed.'

Shulgi thought it a strange request. His hunter's instinct warned him that something was amiss, but the jangle of gold coins deafened the warning. He was getting gold coins for giving hunting tips.

'Consider it done,' he said, placing his hands over the gold coins.

However, when this exchange was taking place, Rhuzbeh's personal bodyguards were seated at the table behind and had heard everything. They pieced together the puzzle and reported back to Rhuzbeh.

'I will skin them alive for this treachery,' said an enraged Rhuzbeh.

'Wait,' said Ghanazaqi. 'Let us hunt these hunters instead. Maybe we can lure other prey with this bait. Meanwhile, can you ask Metishin to summon Darya? We may need her.'

Rhuzbeh obliged, and Metishin summoned Darya to Zanda.

Meanwhile, Shulgi diligently did what was asked of him. Every day, he would meet some hunters, buy them drinks and implore them to dig large pits. For this effort, he would receive gold coins from the twins. Zay and Zana would regularly search if such a pit had been dug, and they finally found a suitable pit.

One fine day, during the hunt, the twins spotted an antler. They chased it from right and left, in their typical way, until it was running straight. Rhuzbeh, who was pursuing the deer on horseback, was almost within touching distance. Just as he was about to throw a spear, Zay made the deer take a sharp right. Rhuzbeh turned his horse sharply right as well. Both the deer and the horse with the king fell into the pit and were impaled. It was a hunter's trap for large animals and had several sharp bamboo spears fixed at the bottom. King Rhuzbeh died in that pit along with the deer that he was chasing. The pit claimed both the hunter and the hunted.

Thus ended the life of one of the greatest heroes of the known world. He did not fall fighting some legendary creature or a fierce warrior. He did not get a glorious death in battle. Instead, he was killed in what was deemed a hunting accident.

'Is that how you died?' Ghanazaqi asked Rhuzbeh.

Rhuzbeh laughed. 'I don't like it,' he said. 'You could have killed me a little more heroically. But I guess that is the story we will be telling the world.'

Zay and Zana stood in front of them in chains.

'It's time for my *funeral*. Make sure that it is grand,' instructed Rhuzbeh with a grin.

Ghanazaqi had thought that it would be a smart idea to pretend that Zay and Zana were successful in their assassination attempt. That would draw out the conspirators behind the dastardly deed.

A dead body was found. Its face was covered in a golden mask, and the body was wrapped in the eagle banner of Zanda and cremated. The Zandians, unaware of the fake death of their king, went into mourning. Kings far and wide visited or sent regards. Hittash and Hitti were forbidden by Axer to come to the funeral.

'The funeral is over. What happens next?' asked Rhuzbeh.

'Zay and Zana escape suspicion and get away scot-free,' replied Ghanazaqi.

'And why did they get away scot-free?' asked Metishin.

'Because,' said Ghanazaqi, 'a hunter was found, who admitted to digging the pit. He swore by his children that it was an accident. Although he had learnt the art from the hunter Shulgi, nobody had instructed him to dig that particular pit at that spot. But Axer, being emotional, slit the hunter's throat and had him burnt.'

'Hmm! That's a plausible story. It may pass muster,' replied Metishin with satisfaction.

'I like the story that you are spinning,' said Rhuzbeh with a grin. 'So what happens next?' he asked Ghanazaqi.

'Well, it is unfortunate that Darya falls in love with Zay,' continued Ghanazaqi, 'and in a bloodless coup, Darya imprisons Axer and makes Zay the king of Zanda. Nobody, including Metishin, will dare rise against Darya. Therefore, without killing anyone, Zay, and by extension, Zana, will share the throne of Zanda. Darya, soaked in love, will be happy just to be by Zay's side.'

'Soaked in love, is it?' asked Darya contemptuously, looking at Zay. 'But it is quite a plot you are hatching there.'

Everyone laughed.

'What about the people? asked Metishin. 'The Zandians will never accept Zay as their king.'

'Ah yes!' remarked Ghanazaqi. 'The Zandians will be outraged. But you forget that Darya is a formidable mage. No one will dare rise against her. A little later, we will pretend that she had to leave for Hatasa because the news of Zay and Zana on the throne of Zanda enraged Hittash. Darya will pretend to go back to Hatasa and pacify Hittash. Now that Rhuzbeh is *dead,* the other djinns and I will have no purpose staying back. We will pretend to leave as well. Zanda will seem defenceless, and the worms will crawl out of the woodwork.'

'Bravo! It's time to hunt the hunters,' said Rhuzbeh appreciatively and started clapping his hands.

And so it was that Zay and Zana were put on the throne of Zanda as bait. The courtiers and the citizens of Zanda, who were not let in on the story, were distraught. Rhuzbeh deliberately floated this false message, and when the news reached the Northern kingdom, Nahal and Tiran were stunned.

'What just happened?' asked Nahal. 'We had sent the twins to kill Rhuzbeh, and instead, they are now the rulers of Zanda?!'

'This turn of events works to our advantage,' replied Tiran. 'Rhuzbeh is dead. Axer is in prison. Ghanazaqi and the djinns have gone back, and there is nobody of Rhuzbeh's lineage to summon them back. Darya herself is in Hatasa. The time is ripe to attack Zanda.'

Awa did not see any reason to join the fight. She said, 'Rhuzbeh is dead and his son, my former husband, is in prison. This fight does not concern me! I had come for revenge, and my purpose is met.'

Nahal and Tiran pleaded with her and said, 'Do not fight! Just stand there with us and be visible to the enemy. They will panic and surrender.' Awa agreed.

Nahal's army invaded Zanda in full force. They marched out of their mighty fort and crossed the Bjan Pass. Awa led the djinns, who chose to be visible to the humans to strike fear in their hearts. She also brought along eight manticores, who were the bane of the Zandian soldiers. She thought wickedly that she might watch the manticores munch on some Zandian flesh. As they marched confidently towards a leaderless Zanda, they expected Zay and Zana to be loyal and surrender the kingdom to them. When they reached the plains of Zanda, however, they saw, to their shock, Rhuzbeh himself mounted on his horse.

Zay and Zana were paraded in front of the Zandians as prisoners.

'We have been tricked!' exclaimed Awa. 'It is that wily Ghanazaqi! He has played an elaborate trick to draw us from the safety of Bjan pass.'

Rhuzbeh sealed the Bjan pass and placed heavily-armoured soldiers and djinns to cut off the exit.

Nahal was trapped and he could not retreat. The die was cast. The two armies faced each other on the plains of Zanda.

In full view, the Zandians beheaded the twins Zay and Zana. Axer sounded his ivory horn and soldiers from both sides charged at each other, with Tiran and Axer leading the two armies, respectively.

Rhuzbeh noticed that Awa had a sanaa on her. He asked Ghanazaqi, 'Should you not attack her and try to get back the sanaa?'

Ghanazaqi said, 'No! The prophecy is clear. All three sanaa would have to be returned to the djinns by the humans. Patience! Since you have gus ambergris in your blood, the sanaa will find a way to get back to us through you.'

The armies were well matched. Awa held on and did not attack, due to which Ghanazaqi and the accompanying djinns did not attack either. A week into the battle, neither side had made any gains. Then Awa decided to make her move—she let loose her manticores.

The manticores made an appearance in the night, singing in a high-pitched feminine voice and randomly calling out names. The effect on the soldiers was so intense that they started crying in fear. The soldiers tried to block the sinister sound that was driving them insane, but they knew from experience that it was just a matter of time before the man-eaters descended on them and devoured their bodies.

Manticores had been known to inflict death on small, unsuspecting djinns. But when it came to humans, they were a gruesome nightmare come true. Since humans were the manticores' favourite prey, they knew how to play with their minds. They knew how to create fear and then exploit it.

After a week of creating fear, the manticores struck. They descended on them at night. The soldiers froze like deer in front of the manticores. They struck the soldiers dead with their darts, and deliberately left half-eaten mangled bodies in their wake.

This happened every night. They incited fear and terror by entering the camps, calling out names and hiding quickly. There was so much trepidation by now that if any soldier called out to another, he would be killed. The soldiers had given up sleeping at night. They were sleep-deprived and weak. Something had to be done soon.

Rhuzbeh confided to Ghanazaqi, who said, 'The only way to fight fear is with fear. These manticores are well-coordinated, confident and wily. Let us do unto them what they have done to us. Let us strike fear and turn them into quivering, unthinking beasts and make them vulnerable, giving us a chance to take them down.'

'What makes a creature like a manticore afraid?' asked Rhuzbeh.

'Elephants,' answered Ghanazaqi.

'Elephants?' asked Rhuzbeh. 'That sounds odd. Why are manticores afraid of elephants?'

'The story dates back to ancient times when manticores dominated jungles,' said Ghanazaqi. 'Although manticores preferred human meat, they could kill any animal, including lions. All animals avoided manticores, but not elephants. Due to some surprising and inexplicable reasons, manticores' poison darts couldn't pierce the hides of elephants. Manticores had never come across a creature that they could not kill with their darts, and so elephants baffled them. Nevertheless, a powerful manticore alpha, in order to impress his pack, sneaked up on a baby elephant that had strayed away from its group. With its powerful teeth, the manticore chewed into the baby elephant's neck and ate its head, including the trunk. When the herd discovered the half-eaten baby elephant, they went mad with fury and attacked the manticore pack. They trampled them, picked them with their trunks and ruthlessly tossed them against the rocks. A bull elephant was on a murderous spree and killed three manticores before being killed itself. So, it got ingrained in manticores that they must avoid elephants.'

'But we don't have elephants,' said Rhuzbeh.

'Oh! We will have them,' said Ghanazaqi. Unknown to Rhuzbeh, before the battle had started, Ghanazaqi had sent Irash to fetch large war elephants.

It was three months since Irash had left. Two days after this conversation, Irash arrived at the camp with the elephants. Now the Zandians were ready for the manticores. The next night, when they heard the manticores sing and come close, the whole camp woke up and lit bright lights. Rhuzbeh's warriors mounted the war elephants—two warriors back-to-back on each elephant, facing both sides. The elephants had the desired effect. Sensing the presence of the manticores, the elephants trumpeted loudly. The manticores were terror-struck at the sound. They mindlessly attacked man and beast. Two manticores brought down an elephant and chewed its trunk away. They were so busy eating the elephant that they did not see an oncoming tusker, which picked up a manticore and gored it and trampled the other into the ground.

The third manticore went for Rhuzbeh, who battled it heroically. In the fight that ensued, the manticore pounced on Rhuzbeh, who fell to the ground and dropped his zer sword. The manticore went for his neck, but the ever-watchful Axer managed to stun him by a blow from his heavy club. Rhuzbeh took advantage of the momentary lapse, grabbed the fallen zer sword and thrust it into the manticore, which, although dying, still tried to chew him. Axer thrust a shield into its mouth, protecting Rhuzbeh.

Fifty soldiers cornered a manticore. The soldiers were bloodthirsty and crazed. Their hatred kept them going, and they rained arrows and spears relentlessly. The manticore brought down thirty soldiers before succumbing to numerous weapons thrown at it. That night, there was a massive celebration in Rhuzbeh's camp. Manticore heads were mounted on a pole and placed outside the camp. They were then skinned, and their skins given to Rhuzbeh as manticore skin is known to repel magic. The joyous army slept a carefree sleep after weeks.

As the army rested though, the remaining manticores sneaked into the camp along with some Northern soldiers a little before dawn and wreaked havoc on the sleeping soldiers. As the elephants were chained, they were easy targets for the Northern men, who managed to kill all the elephants.

Meanwhile, the manticores went on a spree, killing and maiming hundreds of soldiers. A manticore sneaked into Rhuzbeh's tent and attacked him, tearing a chunk of flesh off his thigh. Rhuzbeh retaliated by cutting a gnash with his zer sword. The manticore quickly slunk away. Suddenly, there was a low sharp whistle and all the manticores melted away as quickly as they had come. There was a hushed silence, and the camp was filled with the moans and cries of injured soldiers. Before leaving, the manticores retrieved all the heads and skins of the fallen manticores, except those of the one that Rhuzbeh wore while sleeping.

The next day, when both the armies met for battle, the remaining manticores were placed on the front lines. Nahal threw some Zandian prisoners in front of the manticores, who devoured them alive, limb-by-limb. The Zandian soldiers lost their nerve at this sight and began deserting the battlefield.

Metishin decided to make his move then. He called back Ungaal.

'How did you manage to do that?' asked a delighted Axer.

'When the shepherd was killed, he had dropped the flat flute of Tummaru. I had picked it up and mastered it. I trained one of the djinns to be the shepherd, and the djinn now controls Ungaal,' said Metishin.

'But why let a djinn control Ungaal? Why not one of us?' Axer asked.

'Because the Northern army would not dare to kill a djinn,' replied Metishin, 'for fear of reprisals from Ghanazaqi and his well-trained jann army.'

As the armies approached each other, the shepherd set Ungaal on the manticores. Swiftly and violently, Ungaal hunted down and killed three of the manticores. The last remaining manticore—a tail-less alpha—ran and hid behind Awa for protection. She had seen enough and was livid that her manticores were decimated. She attacked the djinn shepherd and killed him. With the shepherd dead, Ungaal flew away, being chased by Tiran on his magic carpet.

However, Awa had killed a djinn and that meant new trouble. Ghanazaqi, Irash and the djinns accompanying Rhuzbeh had refused to participate in the war against humans, but with Awa killing one of their own, they were forced to retaliate. Awa knew that there was trouble brewing, and in the eventuality that she got captured or lost her life, she wanted the third sanaa to be out of bounds for Amirast. So, she summoned the last remaining manticore, the one whose tail Darya had sliced. She passed on the pouch and instructed it to safely deliver the sanaa. The manticore took the pouch and dashed away to safety.

When the djinns charged at each other, the humans stopped fighting. Fury was being unleashed on a scale not imaginable to humans. Irash, who was battling Awa, managed to defeat and bound her. But unexpectedly, Tiran rushed to Awa's aid. Riding his flying carpet, he flung the crystal spear at Irash, gravely injuring him.

Both armies gasped. This was a huge mistake because now the djinns on both sides would turn on humans. To divert the djinns' attention, Axer threw a mace and knocked Tiran down from the flying carpet. Three Northern soldiers immediately pounced on Axer and kept him occupied as Tiran recovered from his fall, mounted a horse and rushed towards Axer to finish him off.

Meanwhile, Ghanazaqi dashed towards Irash, pulled out the spear and tended to his injuries. Humans and djinns alike watched as Tiran raced towards Axer before being intercepted by Rhuzbeh riding a swift horse. Rhuzbeh did not wish to see his beloved son Axer killed by Tiran, and he stood like a wall between the two brothers, challenging Tiran to fight him.

Tiran lost his nerve and said, 'No! I cannot fight you! It would be wrong to strike you. I cannot strike my father with my own sword! I did conspire to bring you down, but I cannot kill you, not by my own hands. I did have the opportunity to kill you many times. During the games, I even shot an arrow at you. But I realised that I could not kill my own father. I deliberately missed my target. I wanted to humiliate you like you humiliated my mother and me. Why couldn't you love me like you love Axer? Am I not your firstborn? Am I not your flesh and blood?'

In the heat of the battle, Rhuzbeh was blinded by hatred. The speech did not move him. 'If you were my son, you would be on my side. Instead you are a renegade from an island, trying to avenge a spurned woman. You consorted with my enemies and conspired to kill me. You want to kill my son Axer and grab my throne. You are now trying to manipulate me with words as sweet as date syrup. It is too late. My sword will not be denied your blood. If you are indeed my son, then don't be a coward. Fight me!' goaded Rhuzbeh.

Axer headed towards Tiran as well, but he was surrounded by Zandian soldiers, who were under orders from Rhuzbeh to stop him from fighting Tiran.

Reluctantly, Tiran drew his sword. Rhuzbeh, though powerful, was weakened by the wound inflicted by the manticore. In the fight that followed, Tiran constantly switched between the flying carpet and a horse, jumping from one to another and attacking Rhuzbeh from air and horseback. His horse followed the carpet. Soon, Rhuzbeh grew tired from constantly swinging his zer sword. In one of the attacks, Tiran's monkfly tried to hold Rhuzbeh's hand, only to be shortly slain by it.

This angered Tiran, and he dealt a blow to Rhuzbeh's head, who reeled, letting down his guard. Now was the time for Tiran to swing his sword and kill his father. He lifted his sword and was about to slay him when he realised that he could not do it. He slid off his horse, dropped his sword to the ground, sank on his knees and started crying.

He realised that he loved his father and could not bring himself to slaughter him. Perhaps, all that he wanted was his father to love him back and to recognize him as a son. Rhuzbeh, though, did not hesitate. He swung his zer sword at his kneeling, unarmed son and separated his neck from his body. Tiran's head rolled on the battlefield.

The onlookers on both sides gasped. King Rhuzbeh had killed his own son. The battle stopped, and with great ceremony, Tiran, along with his faithful monkfly, was cremated. Soldiers on both sides mourned his loss. Even Awa had tears in her eyes. He had battled even the fearsome ifrit Irash to defend her. Rhuzbeh knew he had done something gravely wrong—he had killed his son. Rhuzbeh was once fond of Tiran and had spent time with him. Tiran had feelings for his father and had dropped down his sword rather than kill him. His love or regard for his father had cost him his life. Both sides declared a three-day mourning period as a mark of respect for Tiran. The flying carpet was handed to Nahal. Tiran's spear, however, had gone missing after striking Awa.

Rhuzbeh was struck with grief. He did not come out of his tent. The army commanders were nervous. The war was still on, and the enemy was still strong. But Rhuzbeh refused to entertain any of his advisors. Metishin tried his best to gain an audience with Rhuzbeh, who knew full well that the mage would rebuke him. The king did not have the courage to face Metishin or any of his Zandian loyalists. In desperation, Metishin turned to Ghanazaqi. Both spent two days together and found that they had a lot to share with each other.

Metishin asked Ghanazaqi thought-provoking questions: 'How can a man be so unfair as to kill one son in full view because he loves the other? How can he justify such a heinous act with love?'

'Love is not noble. As a matter of fact, love is the most abused word that this world has ever had,' replied Ghanazaqi. He paused for effect and continued, 'More hatred has been spread in the name of love than any other reason or cause. Love is more dangerous than hatred because hatred, in its purest form, is simple to understand. But when someone justifies love as the reason for hatred, it becomes a complicated matter. From time immemorial, love has been the reason for humans compromising on their humanity. People profess love for their faith, with all its arcane rituals, only to hate other people's faith, with all its own arcane rituals. They claim that their love for their land, with all its dirt, soil and water, is the reason why they hate the other's land, which too has its own dirt, soil and water. The other's flaws weigh far more than ours because we love our own. We use this as an excuse to kill the other and justify murder with 'patriotism'.

'Poets equate the word love with acceptance, peace and calm. In its ideal form, love must extend to all beings and all lands even if unrequited, but it is not so! What love does is create insecurity, jealousy or superiority. If you love something, it is worth fighting for. If anybody disagrees with our people, faith or way of life, we lash back with greater hatred and justify this with love...' Ghanazaqi trailed off with sadness in his eyes.

Metishin confided in Ghanazaqi, saying, 'Rhuzbeh is no longer fit to be the king.' He further complained, 'A king must make difficult decisions, but Rhuzbeh has simply turned into a tyrant. When he does not even hesitate to spill his own blood, why would he show mercy on his subjects?'

Ghanazaqi nodded in agreement.

'But you support Rhuzbeh because you need to retrieve the third sanaa,' admonished Metishin.

'No,' replied Ghanazaqi. 'I support him for the same reason as you. I always believed in him. I have cast my lot with him. If you observe your friends and family go astray, you do not abandon them. You stand by them and rectify them. As for the sanaa, it will come back when it is destined to. We both stood by his side and tried to guide him. A guide can, at best, point out the right path. It is up to the traveller to choose and follow it. He has greatness ingrained in him, but not all great men are good. I believe that he can be a good man and a just ruler, but he is blinded by love. His love for his women made him commit those atrocities, and now his love for Axer has blinded him. He will come around. I'm sure of it.'

'Then go!' said Metishin. 'Go and convince Rhuzbeh to return to the battlefield and lead the armies. There is a war on, and the soldiers await their king to lead them. There will be plenty of time for atonement after the war.'

Ghanazaqi nodded and sought an audience with Rhuzbeh, and it was granted.

'What have I done, Ghanazaqi?' wailed Rhuzbeh. 'I have killed my firstborn. I am stricken. I have the blood of my son on my hands. I cannot sleep at night! I can see Tiran's brown eyes looking at me, pleading with me for love and acceptance. He could have killed me, but he did not. He preferred to die rather than kill his father. And what did I do? I looked directly into his eyes and slaughtered him. I separated his head from his body and watched as his head tumbled down. He was on his knees, defenceless. He had surrendered, and yet I separated his head from his body. I do not think that there is any redemption for me.'

'You acted as a warrior and not a father,' replied Ghanazaqi. 'Your love for one son is resulting in the death of the others. Perhaps, you have to let go. Stop trying to steer the stars. They will take their own course.'

'I have failed as a father and a human being. All I do is bring death and misery to my loved ones. Yes, perhaps it is time to go and let go,' replied a crestfallen Rhuzbeh.

'Your time will come, great king!' said Ghanazaqi. 'But there is a war on. Throw away your guilt, for there is an enemy knocking on your door. With the manticores and Awa gone, this war will be over soon.'

Rhuzbeh was inconsolable and could not be persuaded even by Ghanazaqi. 'I have to let go. Axer is capable enough. I do not have the will to set foot in the battlefield,' said Rhuzbeh.

On the third day, there was a huge commotion in the camp. Nahal spread a rumour that Rhuzbeh had lost his nerve. The army was getting demotivated. They needed a figurehead under whom they could rally. Axer volunteered to lead the army, but the generals concurred that had Rhuzbeh fallen and Axer taken over, it would seem orderly. But with Rhuzbeh still at the helm and having lost his nerve, it would be a psychological blow for the Zandians.

Ghanazaqi stepped up and said, 'Hand over the command to Axer. Let the prince lead the army into battle. I will make sure that Rhuzbeh steps out in his battledress and oversees the battle. The sight of Rhuzbeh on horseback is enough to rejuvenate the armies. Axer is a capable leader, and he will lead us to victory. The centaurs have left, Awa is taken prisoner, and Tiran and the manticores are dead. This war is in the last stages, and Axer will lead you to victory.'

The next day, the war resumed. Rhuzbeh stepped out of his tent. He was wearing the manticore skin over his chainmail and was covered from head to toe. And when the generals saw him in manticore skin and the royal helmet, they turned to the forces and cried, 'Behold Rhuzbeh! Your King! Fight for the glory of Zanda and your king!'

This cry was carried forward by all the commanders, and the Zandian army let out a loud cheer. Rhuzbeh raised his hands to acknowledge the cheer. He held back at a higher ground along with a contingent of soldiers and oversaw the battle.

Axer led the charge against Nahal's armies, which were commanded by the general Erishum. Nahal himself was missing from action. It was presumed that since Rhuzbeh was not leading his armies, Nahal was following suit.

Axer was frustrated. He was frustrated and embarrassed by his father, who was always trying to protect him. This undue interference was undermining his reputation as a warrior. He wanted to prove that he could handle any adversary by himself—that he was his own man. He would try to finish the war by himself, he resolved.

Axer committed the entire army to a frontal charge. Erishum did not want to engage Axer in an all-out war. He steadily withdrew and sent in his skirmishers, who indulged in hit-and-run tactics. He wanted Axer to break formation, scatter over the battlefield and offer easy pickings. Like pesky mosquitoes, his skirmishers harassed Axer's infantry and heavy cavalry, but despite taking losses, Axer's formation held. Erishum had no choice but to keep retreating. In the beginning, the retreat was orderly and Erishum maintained a healthy distance. But as the sun started to set, Axer, sensing victory, ordered an all-out charge. Erishum's army scattered in all directions.

Axer's army broke formation as they chased small sections of the enemy in all directions. Meanwhile, Erishum had assembled the core of the army in the middle and formed a defensive unit with shields and long spears. The hitherto 'scattered' remnants of his army began to reassemble in an orderly manner to form flanks on either side. Axer realised that he was walking into a trap. His army was stretched, he was far from his lines and he was sure he would be encircled by the flanks. The wily Erishum had lured him into a trap.

Although it was dark, Nahal sensed an opportunity. He knew that Rhuzbeh had lost his nerve. If he managed to kill Rhuzbeh, the war would possibly be over. He took a contingent of his bravest warriors on horseback and skirted Axer's armies. It was a well-crafted plan. Before Axer could regroup and fall back, Nahal skirted behind Axer and charged straight toward Rhuzbeh. In the dark, Rhuzbeh thought the incoming soldiers were Axer's unit. Rhuzbeh did not realise that it was Nahal's horsemen charging towards him until it was too late. Ready or not, Rhuzbeh and his reserve soldiers had no option but to charge and meet Nahal head-on. As Rhuzbeh galloped towards Nahal, his archers shot flaming arrows at the enemy. The arrows were deadly accurate, and Nahal's horsemen dropped like flies. In the midst of this fiery volley, someone threw a flaming crystal spear from the back.

The flaming spear hit Rhuzbeh, and his body burst into flames. It was a spectacular sight. Soldiers on both sides watched in awe as the King of Zanda burst into flames and still rode all the way to Nahal, sword in hand. Nahal was quivering with fear as thundering hooves, and a fiery king tore upon him. He dropped his sword, closed his eyes and waited for his incoming death. Rhuzbeh's steed was almost upon him when he suddenly crumbled, with his body being reduced to ashes. As Nahal passed Rhuzbeh's horse, he wheeled his own horse and galloped away.

Meanwhile, the greatest warrior in the world was no more. He was shot in the back by one of his own. Metishin, Rhuzbeh's mage who was entrusted with the task of protecting him, had set Tiran's crystal spear on fire and thrown it at Rhuzbeh. The lamp that was entrusted with warding away the darkness had burnt down the house. He was instantly surrounded by Rhuzbeh's soldiers, who bound him in chains and rained blows on him. Metishin did not resist and accepted his fate calmly.

Meanwhile, Axer hastily retreated to his line to avoid being outflanked. When he and the main army reached the spot, he was devastated to find that Rhuzbeh was burnt to ashes. The battle now came to a standstill. Seven days of mourning were announced as both armies paid their respects to one of the most powerful kings who ever lived. Axer wept as he could not even make out his father's body. All he could see was Rhuzbeh's royal helmet and the melted light chainmail. The manticore skin had fallen off during the charge. The crystal spear now lay on the ground, smouldering and intact.

Axer had Metishin arrested but he was no ordinary mage. He was the wisest mage in all the lands, and before Darya came along, the most powerful as well. Metishin had taught Axer and Hittash—he was their teacher and almost a grandfather figure. Axer had turned to Metishin for counsel every time he was in trouble. The mage had also healed him from health-related issues. This was going to be difficult.

He cast Metishin in chains and had him brought before the war council. 'Why Metishin? You of all the people! Why did you kill your king?' demanded Axer. He remembered Metishin teaching, admonishing and exhorting him to be a good man, and now he saw the pain in his old, kind eyes.

Metishin said, 'I am tired of all the killings. I constantly warned Rhuzbeh, but he would not heed. He was sinking lower. I warned him when he exploited a married woman and then had her and three other people killed on false charges. I warned him when he killed the poor merchant to marry Ceba. I warned him when he forced himself on Hitti, who conceived a son from it. I could sense that in his quest for greatness, he was disregarding the life of others. He was becoming a tyrant. His pride during the Northern campaign would have got us all annihilated. Yes, it was I who threw a spear at him in the battle for the north to save the Zandian soldiers. Unfortunately, it did not kill him.

'I saw the djinn Awa try to take over the kingdom by marrying you. I was not strong enough to take on a djinn like her. I tried warning you, but you brushed me off rudely and paid no heed to my advice. Awa was the greater of the two evils, so I nursed Rhuzbeh back to life because I knew only he would stop her. Rhuzbeh recovered, and he chased Awa away, but then his evil was back. When he battled Tiran, I saw the young man drop his sword because he did not want to strike down his own father. But Rhuzbeh did not hesitate to kill his own son—a son from a woman he loved.

'I could not take it anymore. I took Tiran's fallen spear and set it on fire and threw it at Rhuzbeh, killing him instantly. It was poetic justice—for Rhuzbeh to be killed by his son's spear! He was a great king, possibly the greatest ever. But had I not killed him, he would have killed Nahal and become an even greater tyrant and brought much misery and sorrow to everyone around. I had to kill him. You, on the other hand, are young, honourable and noble. You have the gus ambergris flowing in your veins, and you will make a great king.'

Axer was crying and said, 'He loved me, and it was his love for me that made him do such dishonourable deeds. He was my father and the greatest king in the known world—the fearless Lord of the East and the West was a warrior who was respected by both humans and djinns. There is no difference between him and you. Both of you wanted to alter the course of history by killing people. If my father was unworthy of being alive, so are you! You killed my father in a cowardly fashion by throwing a flaming spear from behind! I did not even get to see my father's body. He was reduced to ashes! He deserved better. I must honour my father's memory and condemn you to death.'

Axer had Metishin beheaded. There were seven days of mourning for King Rhuzbeh. Kings far and wide visited or sent regards. Hittash rode down with Hitti and Darya to pay his last respects.

Hitti broke down when she saw Rhuzbeh's burnt corpse. His clothes were given to Hitti and his frog belt and manticore skin to Hittash. Axer inherited the zer sword and, most importantly, gajmuk. Tiran's green crystal spear was sent back with some sailors to the mystical island, with a note to Tasia that Tiran and Rhuzbeh were dead.

The jann king Amirast, along with Ghanazaqi, paid respect to Rhuzbeh, a man who had helped them retrieve two sanaas and secure the throne for Amirast and who was also a witness to their book of laws.

After the funeral, the djinns, along with the injured Irash, left for Alainis, with Awa as their prisoner.

A week after the funeral, Nahal and Axer met each other on the battlefield, and after a gruesome battle, Nahal surrendered. Axer pardoned him and made him the governor of the north. Thus, the north was annexed. Axer was now the king of north, south and west.

CHAPTER 10

The Missing Sanaa

You don't always have to overcome obstacles. Sometimes it is wiser to skirt around them.

Meanwhile, back in Alainis, Awa was produced before Amirast to be sentenced. But before he could say a word, she said mockingly, 'Forget your ambition, Amirast. You will never go down in history as the greatest of djinn kings. I have sent the last sanaa off with a manticore. Even Ghanazaqi, with all his wisdom, will not be able to trace it, let alone a human. I hear that Rhuzbeh is dead. How then will you retrieve the third sanaa?' She burst out in a loud cackle.

'Bound her and throw her in the dungeons,' ordered Amirast.

'Ghanazaqi, what should we do now?' he asked next.

Ghanazaqi gave a blank look, eventually wondering aloud, 'Who would shelter a manticore who has a famous gem that belongs to the djinns and incur their wrath?'

Meanwhile, Awa's manticore had delivered the sanaa to its intended recipient.

The recipient asked, 'Why are you tail-less? Which human dared chop off your tail?'

The manticore answered, 'My lord! The person who chopped off my tail is called Darya. Some say that she is the most powerful mage on earth.'

'Bring her to me,' said the recipient. 'I might just have a task that befits the greatest mage on earth.'

Darya was now at Hatasa. The matter of the next ruler of Zanda was at an impasse with neither brother making a move but both claiming the throne in principle. Darya had become a recluse, and she confined herself to her own chambers. She sat contemplating the various secrets that Ghanazaqi had shared with her during her visit to Zanda. He was impressed with Darya's abilities and had instructed her on esoteric knowledge that humans did not have access to. He had also discussed the sanaa gems' importance with her and implored her to keep a keen eye out for them. A grateful Darya had promised Ghanazaqi that she would help in regaining all three sanaa.

One night, she heard whistling outside the window—that dreaded, high-pitched feminine song. The familiar voice called out to her: 'Darya, Darya, follow mee…'

Darya's hair at the back of her neck stood up, and she sat bolt upright. Unable to bear the tormenting voice, Darya stepped out, staff in hand, and confronted the manticore that Awa had handed over the sanaa to.

Soon after catching sight of the manticore, she repeatedly tried rushing towards it, but the creature always stayed much ahead. No matter how fast she walked, it walked faster, continually calling out to her. 'Darya, Darya…' the manticore was shrieking shrilly inside her head. She could not bear it. She wanted to chase it down and kill it.

She walked for the whole night and reached the outskirts of Hatasa. In the morning, the manticore voices couldn't be heard anymore. She slept the entire day. In the evening, a passer-by gave her some bread and water. And at twilight, the voices began reverberating again.

The pattern continued—she would sleep during the day and follow the manticore at night. She did not know how far she travelled or how many months passed. It was as if she was in a trance. Finally, they reached a forest, where she managed to corner the manticore. Darya raised her sword and was about to kill it when there appeared a huge eagle. The eagle had a leonine head that ended in a powerful beak. It had two muscular legs of a lion which extended as talons of a bird. This creature stood between her and the manticore. The lion-headed eagle was huge, and each of its wings was the size of a full-grown man. Its plumed tail swayed in the wind. When the lion-eagle flapped its great wings, so powerful was the wind generated that Darya fell down. The creature picked up the manticore in its great talons and flew away. The manticore kept calling her: 'Darya, Darya…' Even after it was whisked away, she could hear its shrill calls.

Darya had decided that she had to find it and kill it, so she kept going. Finally, she arrived at a village. Exhausted, she fell and passed out. A kind farmer took her home, fed her and gave her shelter. She slept for two days and the voices in her head finally subsided. She thanked the farmer for his hospitality, and he said, 'You look weak. Stay with me until you feel strong and then continue on with your journey.' She agreed.

The farmer was a simple man with kind eyes. He went farming every day. She began to accompany him. She liked his company—something about this simple man made her feel light and secure.

'Why do you live alone?' asked Darya.

'I was married to my childhood sweetheart. We were both from the same village. We were always together as children, and I was deeply in love with her. Unfortunately, I had nothing. I was very poor. I toiled hard day and night. When I finally earned enough money to buy a parcel of land, I spoke to her father and asked for her hand in marriage, but her father refused. However, his daughter prevailed over him. She managed to convince him about my love, and we were married.'

'That is such a beautiful story, but what happened to your wife?' asked Darya.

'After two years of living together in utter bliss, she died during childbirth. I lost her and our stillborn daughter. The villagers said that she had been cursed. Some even said it was the evil eye of the other village women. Whatever may be the case, I lost them both.'

He fell silent. She held his hand for support.

Darya was healing. She began to cook for them, and then they would both go to the farm, where she helped him in all the odd farming chores. In the evenings, they would walk hand-in-hand near the streams, and he would tell her stories.

'I have such happy memories associated with these streams,' he said. 'Once, when we were walking by a stream, my wife whispered something naughty into my ears and ran away laughing. I chased her and caught up with her. She was squealing and struggling playfully and, in that melee, her nose ring fell into a shallow stream. Although shallow, the stream had fast-moving water. The waters carried the ring, and we ran after it. The stream emptied into a shallow pool of water, and the ring fell into the pool. Just as I was about to grab it, a fish swallowed the ring. We jumped into the shallow pool and caught the fish. That evening, we had fish for dinner and retrieved the nose ring as well.'

He showed her a small nose ring that he always kept with himself. His eyes were moist, and she hugged him.

That night, as they were sleeping together, he asked her, 'You have not told me anything about yourself, Darya. I would like to know more about you. Why do you carry a stick?'

Darya had cast a spell so that her staff looked like an ordinary stick. She could not bring herself to lie to him and said, 'I am a mage and I am on a quest. This stick is my staff.'

The man was shocked. 'What sort of a quest?' he asked.

'I am looking for a manticore who has something valuable with him,' replied Darya.

He went quiet. With the mention of the word 'manticore', the voices in her head were back. She could not sleep, and the voices kept getting louder and louder until she started to scream.

Darya exclaimed, 'I have to go.'

'Where will you go?' asked the farmer.

'I don't know,' she replied. 'The last I know was that the manticore was grabbed by a huge eagle with the head of a lion.'

'It is the 'heavy wind' or the simorgh,' he whispered with awe and reverence. He pointed towards a mountain and said, 'The simorgh lives on that mountain.'

She thanked him and prepared to leave. There was a twinge of sadness in her because he was the only man she had ever loved. He held her and said, 'The simorgh is a great creature. People around the mountains revere it. If you confront a creature as powerful as the simorgh, it will kill you. Do not go!'

She was touched by his concern and said, 'I must do what I must do.'

His eyes turned moist, and he said, 'I want you to have this so that some part of me stays with you.' And he gifted her the small golden nose ring.

She politely refused, but he insisted and said, 'This is not a gift worthy of a great mage, but this is all I have. I love you and I want you to have this.'

The nose ring was thin and small, with tooth-like serration at the circumference. She put it on, said her goodbyes and left.

Darya kept walking until she reached the mountains, and it was after an entire day's climb that she found what she had been seeking—the simorgh. The great leonine bird looked majestic. It looked so splendorous in its plumage and so resplendent in its bearing that it made the vanity of the vainglorious peacock look pedestrian. Besides, it rendered the manticore looking small and docile.

The simorgh looked at Darya and said, 'I have been expecting you. The manticore tells me that you are the greatest mage in the world. What is it that you seek?'

'I want to slay this manticore and take back what it carries,' she replied.

'And what does it carry?' asked the simorgh.

'A precious treasure that belongs to the djinns,' said Darya.

'You mean the sanaa,' stated the simorgh.

'Yes, the sanaa! And I also want to kill the manticore because its voice haunts me, and I will lose my sanity if the voices persist,' replied Darya.

'I cannot let you kill the manticore, for the creature is under my protection. I can, however, command the manticore to stop troubling you immediately. But the sanaa is a precious object! I will exchange the sanaa in lieu of something that I need,' said the simorgh.

'What is it that you seek?' asked Darya.

'Fetch me the clay tablet from the bottom of the dark waters,' demanded the great bird.

Darya was perplexed and asked, 'The clay tablet and the dark waters?'

'Suffice it to know that the clay tablet I seek is the tablet of destiny,' replied the simorgh imperiously. 'The dark waters are a dangerous lake. The clay tablet is protected in the water by foul demon fish. The skies above the lake are patrolled by a demon bird, and the land around the lake is guarded by demon riders. If you bring me the tablet, I shall give you the sanaa and spare your life. If you don't, I shall kill you!'

Darya was enraged. She summoned all her powers until her body was radiating light. She stood erect, the stick in her hand now a staff, the snakes on which were wriggling. She challenged the simorgh to a battle.

After a short, intense fight, the simorgh knocked out her staff and said, 'If you fight with me again, I shall kill you. In case you need the sanaa and if you ever want the manticore voices to vanish, get me my clay tablet.'

'Who are you?' asked Darya, surprised at the ease with which the simorgh had overcome her.

The simorgh opened its wings in all its glory and said, 'I am Abzu. I am Anzu. I am the hoopoe. I am the nightingale. I am the owl. Fetch me what I seek or I shall kill you.'

They stood appraising each other. Darya knew that she could not let the simorgh possess the tablet. She could sense that it did not belong to it. The simorgh was unscrupulous enough to let the manticore possess her. The manticore wanted its revenge and the simorgh would oblige the manticore as soon as its objective was met.

The voices were back, shriller and more tormenting than before. She headed towards the dark lake. On the way, she met a mage. He was the oldest mage that she had ever met, with a frail, bent body and a hoarse, raspy voice. When she told him her story, he said, 'You need a kinorse.'

'What is a kinorse?' asked Darya.

'A kinorse is a creature that is neither a bird nor an animal. The creature can run, fly, and even dive in the water. It is to be found in the clear magical waters.' Darya nodded.

'Be warned, kinorses are very difficult to capture,' he added and pointed the way to the clear magical waters. Darya thanked him and headed to the waters. Once there, she immediately saw such a magnificent creature and cast a spell on it, but the creature just shook off its effect. So, she did the next best thing. She cast a spell on a beautiful fish. The kinorse dived for the fish and swallowed it. Once inside its body, the fish started to swell. It became so large that the kinorse could not move.

Darya captured the kinorse and promised to remove the fish if it helped her recover the clay tablet from the dark waters.

The kinorse agreed, and Darya magically shrunk the fish. But the fish still remained inside the kinorse. Darya led the kinorse to the dark waters. There, it dived into the waters and retrieved the tablet, and before the dark water demons could attack, it was out.

It flew up in the air where it was attacked by the dark demon-bird. The kinorse was no match for the demon-bird, and it flew straight into the thick jungle, where Darya was waiting for it. Just as the dark bird swooped on the kinorse, she sent a bolt of white fire, chasing away the dark bird.

She mounted the kinorse and started galloping when she suddenly realised that she was surrounded by dark creatures on all sides.

She took out the tablet and held it high before loudly saying, 'I am the master of the tablet, and I command you to go back to where you came from.' She smote the ground with her staff, and the dark forces dissipated.

She flew the kinorse to the mountain, and when she reached the simorgh, the great bird stood up and acknowledged Darya.

'So what they said about you is true! You are indeed the greatest mage in the world,' said the simorgh. 'Now, give me the tablet!'

Darya held her ground and said, 'Give me the sanaa.'

'Give me the tablet first,' retorted the simorgh.

'Give with one hand and take with the other,' offered Darya.

The simorgh gave the sanaa, and in return, it received the tablet from Darya. The simorgh looked at the tablet, and its expression turned from pleasure to anger as it realised that Darya had handed over a small clay slab which was not the tablet of destiny. The simorgh had been duped.

Darya held the original tablet high in the air and commanded, 'By the power of this tablet, I command you to kill the manticore.'

The simorgh went ahead and, with one blow, slew the manticore. As soon as the simorgh slew the manticore, she held the tablet aloft and smote the simorgh with the clay tablet. The simorgh lost his power and became weakened.

Then, she smashed the clay tablet against a rock, shattering it. A loud explosion rent the air, and waif-like spirits escaped the tablet screaming out aloud. When the noise and smoke subsided, she collected the pieces, sat on the kinorse and flew away to Hatasa.

On the way, she scattered the fragments of the tablet across forests, hills and water bodies. When she reached Hatasa, she dismounted the kinorse and helped it get rid of the enchanted fish. The relieved kinorse flew away.

She reached Hatasa with the sanaa safely in her possession and collapsed on her bed. The next day, after a sound sleep, she reached the court and was confronted by Hittash. 'How could you leave without my permission?' he asked.

'I can go wherever I want. I don't need your permission, little brother,' replied Darya.

'How dare you talk to me—your King—like that?' asked Hittash angrily.

She laughed and smote her staff to the ground, saying, 'I am Darya, the greatest mage in the known world, and you are but a child who is alive because of me.'

Hittash was burning with shame at being addressed as a child in front of the whole court. 'Guards! Seize her,' he ordered. As Hittash's guards stepped forward to arrest her, she killed them all instantly.

Darya ran outside the palace, and Hittash ordered his commanders to assemble a thousand Hatasan soldiers to capture her. He wanted to teach Darya a lesson. With the sun shining bright, Darya stood alone in front of a thousand warriors as Hittash ordered the army to attack.

Then, all hell broke loose. Darya summoned two hundred manticores to attack the army. She blew a flute and summoned Ungaal, and finally, the simorgh himself appeared to Darya's aid. Darya turned herself into a great black panther with wings, and she joined the attack as well.

Hittash summoned ferocious winged wolves. Then, his mage turned Hittash into a rhino, which charged at the manticores. But the simorgh and Ungaal were just too powerful. They laid waste to the Hatasan army and flattened them to the ground. Darya won.

Hittash, as the rhino-human hybrid creature, rushed back to the palace and sat on the throne. Darya strode to the throne, took out a great big sword and sliced Hittash's rhino head off. He was still sitting on the throne without his head, blood gushing from his body when she proceeded to kick the corpse off the throne and climb and occupy his seat. Darya was now the Queen of Hatasa and the east. Once established thus, she announced her invasion of Zanda.

Darya marched to Zanda with the simorgh leading her army. Axer was ready for her, and he marched out to meet her with a hundred winged wolves, five hundred great elephants with metal spikes on their bodies, a company of centaurs, and numerous flying carpets. It was Ungaal, simorgh and manticores versus centaurs, winged-wolves and elephants.

Darya transformed herself into a bear that was five times the size of Axer. She swatted Axer with her paws, lifted him up, snapped his body into two and chewed his head off. With Axer dead, Darya burnt Zanda to the ground. The great city of Zanda was burning, and the soldiers were killing, raping and pillaging.

Darya stood with Ungaal by her side as they both overlooked the destruction, with the simorgh flying over Zanda and the manticores multiplying by the second until the whole kingdom looked like a wriggling mass of these creatures. 'Darya! Darya…' Someone shook her. She woke up with a start and realised that she was on her bed in Zanda. She had been sick and unconscious for many days.

Hittash came to visit her. He smiled at her, kissed her forehead and left. A week later, when she had recovered, she discovered a nose ring under her pillow—the same ring that the farmer had given her.

What had really happened, wondered Darya. Had she got the sanaa back? How much of what she remembered was real and how much was a dream?

She searched for the sanaa and found it in her pouch!

She could not hear voices in her head, so the manticore must be dead as well. The simorgh had indeed killed the manticore, she concluded. She could eat and sleep well at last. On that happy note, she decided to leave for Tamiir and hand over the sanaa to Ghanazaqi.

Darya set out accompanied by two horsemen. They stopped in the middle of a forest to rest, and she thought about how the djinns would be elated by the arrival of the last sanaa. The thought put a smile on her lips. Suddenly, a strong gust of wind blew, breaking her out of her reverie. She opened her eyes to see the simorgh appear before her. Darya looked into the simorgh's eyes for a second and froze. She realised in that moment that despite her knowledge and power, there were and always would be beings that were more powerful than her! She had taken on the wrong creature. She saw impending death and knew her time had come. She closed her eyes and spread out her arms, as if she were embracing death itself.

It all happened too fast: the simorgh bent, bit her head clean off her body, snatched away the sanaa and flew away. The all-powerful eagle had killed the mighty snake.

Thus passed Darya, the greatest mage in the world—she was killed by one of the most powerful creatures under the great expansive sky. Her remains were taken back to Hatasa. Hittash was heartbroken and sank into grief. Not only was she the mightiest weapon that he wielded, but she was also the one person, apart from Hitti, who truly loved him. She had stood as a bulwark between him and his adversaries ever since he was a baby. Axer joined Ghanazaqi and Amirast in mourning. The whole of Zanda and Hatasa mourned Darya's death.

Meanwhile, both brothers were now well-balanced as the Hatasans did not have the advantage of Darya. Also, the singer Butosh, whose thumb Rhuzbeh had cut off, made a reappearance in the Zandian court. Hitti was overjoyed to have him back and the palace once again rent with the lovely songs of Butosh.

A year later, as luck would have it, Ungaal was sighted on the outskirts of Hatasa. Since the flat flute of Tummaru was lost, there was no way to control it. But Butosh, being the legend that he was, tamed the Ungaal with his songs, and he now had control over the creature. So it was that Hittash had in his power the famed Ungaal.

Meanwhile, Amirast was saddened at the turn of events. 'It's a pity Darya is dead.'

'Yes!' said Ghanazaqi. 'It is a pity. Her thirst for knowledge was extraordinary. No wonder she was one of the greatest mages the world has ever seen. She took on the simorgh, which was a courageous thing to do. Even though diminished, the simorgh's sheer physical prowess is unparalleled, which took her by surprise.'

'Why do you think that Darya could not succeed in bringing back the sanaa?' asked Amirast.

Ghanazaqi was quiet for some moments before answering, 'It's a pity I did not think of this before. Darya could never have done it.' He continued, 'She is not destined to bring back the sanaa, because she is not from the blood of Rhuzbeh. Gus ambergris does not run in her blood. The last sanaa would have to come from Rhuzbeh's blood.'

'Hmm,' said Ghanazaqi, 'I get a feeling that after everything that has happened, the brothers would not be keen to spill one another's blood. Why don't we propose a bloodless contest? The person who retrieves the last sanaa becomes the joint king of Zanda and Hatasa, and the djinns would personally recognize such a claim to kingship.'

Both the brothers were relieved that they would not have to go through the kind of warfare that their father had done. So, they gladly agreed.

The problem was that the sanaa could be anywhere and nobody knew where to begin the search. Ghanazaqi sent all the djinns to look for the sanaa. Finally, he got word from a djinn that the last sanaa had been spotted. Now, Ghanazaqi had to plan out its retrieval carefully. He knew that he could not interfere in human affairs by passing on the information to any one side. So, he waited for an opportune moment to set his plans into action.

Chapter 11

Symphony of the Frogs

Much like the earth welcomes rain to smoothen its parched cracks, time-worn humans seek the rejuvenation of their wrinkled souls.

Rain-bearing clouds were approaching Hatasa. The sky longed to meet the earth, and he thus extended his moist fingers towards her. And when she experienced his touch, after countless agonising days of being parched, she quivered in ecstasy, unable to stop the petrichor from finding release.

Peacocks raised their beautiful plumage to acknowledge the cosmic lovers. It rained gently but it rained for long. It was not an angry, punishing deluge, but a smooth, free-flowing release of the pent-up emotions of long-separated lovers—these emotions say, 'Do not stop. Let it flow.'

With the rains came the frogs, which were a symbol of fertility and plenty. They appeared on ponds and lily pads, unabashedly croaking to woo their lovers. The not-so-coy females of the species responded with enthusiasm to the amorous calls, not so much due to passion but annoyance at their noisy suitors. Nevertheless, the frogs grew in their multitudes and spread all across the land.

Hittash loved the sight and sound of the rain until a frog took up the chorus. When he croaked, all the frogs across the royal palace croaked back in unison. It was a loud and ugly sound. The symphony of a hundred frogs singing together stunned the Hatasan courtiers. They had never experienced something like that before. Generally, when frogs croaked, the sounds were spaced out and even seemed relaxing, but this combined croaking was really strange and disturbing.

In an attempt to find out the master croaker, Hittash wandered the palace gardens. After two days of searching his extensive gardens, he came across the frog. It was an ordinary frog in a small, slushy pond at one corner of the garden. The frog let out a sharp croak and the others faithfully croaked back in unison.

As he approached the conductor of the croaky chorus, it slipped back into the water. Every day, Hittash would stealthily creep up and watch the frog climb a lily pad, like a king climbing up a throne. The frog would then let out a croak, leading hundreds of frogs to reply dutifully. After three days, he had the frog caught and showed it off to his courtiers. He called it the 'king of frogs'.

Hittash grew very fond of the frog and, for the first time in his life, indulged in a pet's care. He would bring the frog with himself to the court in the morning and, during noon, leave him in a small pond with lily pads guarded by royal guards. It was also the duty of the guards to catch insects, grasshoppers and worms for the frog to eat. He even arranged for frog playmates, which were changed every two days, to entertain the royal croaker.

The court astrologer decreed the frog as some kind of a king who was cursed and declared that the arrival of the frog king was a favourable sign that would bolster Hittash's rule. One lazy afternoon, as the frog was out on a pad, a crane swooped in, grabbed it in its mouth and gulped it down its leathery throat. The croaker croaked one last time and croaked out, followed by a tragic, synchronised reply of its pained subjects. Before the soldiers guarding the frog realised what had happened, the crane flew away from the royal garden. The furious soldiers gave chase with hopes of rescuing the royal amphibian from a gruesome death.

The crane, unaware of the frog's exalted status, settled down on a tree near a hut and savoured its meal, with the satisfaction of every tasty morsel writ large on its face. The hut belonged to a carpet dyer, who unwittingly threw water with leftover dye on the crane, colouring the bird red. The soldiers were just in time to watch the crane being dyed red. Before they could release a single arrow, the canny bird flew away.

Hittash ordered the red crane to be traced. He was informed that although the crane was distinctive with the red dye, it would not be easy to track the bird since it could fly hundreds of miles. So Hittash sent emissaries to other kingdoms with the message that if a red crane were to be found, it should be captured and sent back to Hatasa. Months later, there was word that the red crane had been found in the far-off kingdom of Musra. However, the ruler of Musra refused to capture and return the bird, given that cranes were considered holy in that kingdom. The red crane was sheltered in a massive cage, which had a garden and a small pond.

Someone had refused a favour to the King of Hatasa, and he did not know why anyone would incur the wrath of another king all for a crane. He had heard of the powerful kingdom of Musra and longed to visit it.

It was seven years since Hittash had assumed the role of king, and he was getting bored and stifled with the court affairs. There was no threat to the kingdom since both brothers had promised not to attack each other and instead resolve the claim to the joint kingdom by retrieving the last sanaa. He put his trusted ministers in charge and, along with an attendant, set off for Musra. He felt light and welcomed this journey as a holiday. Disguised as merchants, the two men took a large merchant ship to Musra. It was a long and comfortable journey. After three months of sailing, they reached Musra.

Hittash found Musra wondrous, with giant monuments, amazing food, and a wide variety of wildlife. It was a powerful kingdom with a large army. No wonder the Musrans did not worry about incurring the wrath of the Hatasans. One thing in particular that amazed Hittash was the Musran obsession with birds like cranes and ibis. They considered the birds holy, and thousands of birds were captured and sold as pets to make sacrifices.

Musra was ruled by a queen famous for her beauty. It was barely a month since she had ascended the throne after the untimely death of the king. The queen appeared in court wearing an ibis or a crane headdress. The ibis headdress denoted wisdom, implying the queen to be the ultimate keeper of wisdom. The queen herself was well versed with magic and was guided by a celebrated and feared mage called Dedi. The legend goes that when Dedi was young and wanted to make an impression on the former king—the present queen's father—he severed a bull's head and stuck it back together. This one feat alone so impressed the king that he appointed Dedi as the chief mage of Musra. The coming of the red crane was considered as a portent, and with great ceremony, the bird was presented to the queen. The crane was considered holy, and nobody except the queen was allowed to touch it. The red crane was kept in a large cage, which had a small garden that was entirely covered with a net. Upon learning the symbolism, Hittash became sure that she would not hand it over easily as it would symbolically denote giving away wisdom to another king. He decided to leave. It was not wise to wage war or incur enmity over a crane that was dyed red accidentally. He laughed out loud at the very idea. The day before he was to depart, there was a lunar eclipse, and the queen, accompanied by her mage Dedi, stood on a lofty temple platform to perform rituals to appease the moon god and coax him to return. As Hittash watched her, she took out a stone that looked like a big ruby. It was almost dancing as it reflected the light from the fire torches. Seven years ago, the ruby had been presented to the former king by the simorgh for his devotion towards the great eagle. Since the king had died abruptly, the ruby had unwittingly passed on to the queen, who was not aware of its importance.

Hittash's jaw dropped. He immediately knew that the stone was not a ruby—it was the fabled sanaa. Perhaps, the diminished simorgh did not have any further use of the sanaa and had passed it on to the then Musran king for safekeeping. Meanwhile, unaware of its importance, the Musran queen continued her rituals. This was the first eclipse during her reign as the queen, and in order to appease the moon god, she wanted to feed the red ruby to the red crane.

She coated the ruby with fish batter and fed it to the red crane. As the assembled Musrans looked to heaven, the moon slowly slipped out from the darkness. With the moon god pacified, the grateful queen released the bird as a token of gratitude. Hittash stood in a trance. He knew now that he had to get the bird for sure.

Dedi, the Musran mage, also had his eye on the ruby even though he did not know that it was not a ruby but a red pearl made by the djinns. The next day, Hittash, accompanied by his attendant, started moving in the general direction that the crane had flown towards and, after travelling for a day, came upon a large lake. On a tree near the lake sat the red crane, soaking up the sun. There was a movement on the tree trunk, and Hittash saw a snake crawl up the tree. The snake crept up stealthily on the unsuspecting bird and coiled around it. The red crane fell to the ground struggling and gasping for life in the throes of the snake's hold, and after a spirited struggle, succumbed to the steel-like coils. Hittash was about to rush to the scene when he stopped abruptly. He had just spotted Dedi walk up to the snake. To his shock, the snake released its prey and disappeared into Dedi's long sleeves. Dedi slit the bird's stomach and took out the pearl. He stared at it for a long time, mesmerised by its beauty, before placing the gem safely in a pouch and proceeding to bury the dead bird.

This is when Dedi spotted Hittash watching him. He immediately cast a spell on Hittash and his attendant. The curse hit the attendant, who turned into a panicked ibis, but Hittash was quicker to duck behind a rock before running away into the thick forested area nearby. The next day, Hittash wrote an anonymous note to the queen detailing Dedi's treachery along with the location of the murdered red crane's burial spot.

The queen summoned Dedi and asked, 'Did you commit blasphemy?'

Dedi denied it vehemently and replied, 'Yes! There is the body of the bird, and yes, the ruby is stolen, but where is the proof that I did it? I am being framed. Someone else committed the crime and I'm being punished for it. Give me a day's time and I will prove myself to not be guilty.'

The queen could tell by his body language that Dedi was guilty. Moreover, she had made enquiries and found out that he had been missing for a day after the ceremony, but she was curious to know what he might come up with, so she gave him a day's time to prove his innocence.

That night, Dedi sent his snake to kill the queen. When the snake reached her chamber, the queen was fast asleep, but her pet leopard sensed the reptile moving and attacked it. In the ensuing fight, the snake, although severely wounded, killed the leopard. Hearing the commotion, the queen woke up to see Dedi's snake bearing towards her. She turned to pick up a sword, but the snake was quicker, and it bit and killed her before succumbing to its wounds.

Dedi crowned himself the king. He adopted a cobra as his crest and wore a crown with a hooded cobra. In the middle of his crown, below the hooded cobra, he installed the sanaa.

After being self-crowned 'the absolute monarch', Dedi unleashed a reign of terror on his subjects. He wanted to find out the whereabouts of the stranger who had seen him and tipped off the queen. He made enquiries and found out where Hittash was. One night, while Hittash was fast asleep, he had him arrested. During the questioning, someone recognised him and informed Dedi of his real identity.

'Well! Well!' Dedi chuckled with delight. 'Look, who we have here! The King of Hatasa, Hittash. The son of the fabled Rhuzbeh the Fearless. What do I do with him?' he asked himself aloud. 'I know! I need a royal pet badly,' he added and cast a spell on Hittash, transforming him into an ibis as a cruel joke.

Hittash, as an ibis, was kept chained to the throne. 'You are not the legendary warrior your father was, and you are nothing without the mage Darya. You are fit only to be a pet bird that lives on scraps,' he laughingly declared.

Dedi liked to take his new pet ibis everywhere he went, keeping it on a leash like a dog. Once, while walking in the royal garden, Dedi heard a low growl of a leopard. He turned quickly in the direction of the sound but slipped on the wet grass and fell. Dedi recovered quickly and managed to kill the leopard with his magic. In the whole melee, he forgot about the ibis and let go of the leash. Taking advantage of the situation, the ibis flew away. Hittash was free, albeit in the body of an ibis. He needed his human form to be restored.

Meanwhile, Dedi decided to take advantage of the leaderless Hatasa and march to the kingdom to take over the throne. He prepared a massive army to invade Hatasa. When Axer heard that Hittash was missing and Dedi was bearing towards Hatasa, he instantly rode into the kingdom with his army. Soon after his arrival, Axer was crowned as the King of the joint kingdom of Zanda and Hatasa as he followed in the footsteps of his father. Dedi's initial plan was to invade Hatasa, but since Axer occupied Hatasa, he decided to invade the joint kingdom. He changed course and headed towards Zanda. His army was better suited to fight on the flat Zandian plains rather than the mountainous Hatasan region.

In the past, the two kingdoms had never been subjected to a foreign invasion. Dedi's army was truly formidable. Five hundred ships bearing fifty thousand soldiers landed on the Zandian shores. He had also brought with him five hundred armoured war elephants, four hundred armoured rhinos and a number of great horned buffaloes. His army further boasted ten thousand horses, chariots, siege machines and mages. His mages were mostly female, and also accompanying him were the elite force of warriors that wore crocodile helmets.

Axer rallied fifteen thousand Hatasans, which included chariot-mounted archers, horse- and ibex-mounted cavalry and foot soldiers. He hurried to Zanda, where he was joined by twenty thousand strong Zandian forces to meet the threat of the Musran invaders. He had combined the mages of Zanda and Hatasa to be able to fight any magic, and he carried gajmuk, which made him immune to any attacks through the use of magic.

Both armies faced each other on the plains of Zanda. Dedi was mounted on a war elephant in the middle and surrounded by his elite soldiers in crocodile helmets. His army had been arranged in well-planned rows—the frontline had armoured rhinos and buffaloes that acted as battering rams. As per his expectations, upon the rhinos and buffaloes charging, the enemy would scatter and break formations. The second row was mostly composed of archers and siege machines. The archers would pick off the soldiers that ran after breaking formation. The third row had infantry in the middle and cavalry on both flanks. And the last row had Dedi on an elephant, along with fifty such armoured animals to the right and left sides. He held his elite troops along with the mages in reserve.

The eagle came face-to-face with the cobra as the joint army of Zanda and Hatasa stood facing the formidable Musrans.

Axer, clad in golden armour, oversaw the battle formations personally.

He knew the enemy was stronger due to the sheer size of its army. He counted on speed and mobility rather than strength. The Zandians had assembled their forces in the traditional formation. Axer split his forces into three divisions. He personally commanded the vanguard in the middle, which comprised chariot-mounted archers along with his elite Zandian troops and mages.

On his right was the well-trained Zandian army with its fabled horsemen, followed by the foot soldiers.

The only weak point was the Hatasan ibex cavalry on Axer's left. The ibex-mounted warriors were a soft target as the ibexes were not suited to fight on plains. If ever the heavily armoured and mounted Musrans charged at the ibexes, it would be a massacre. Axer decided to use the ibex cavalry as bait, a role that they'd traditionally played to perfection.

Axer drew his zer sword and sounded his ivory horn. This was the most decisive battle ever faced by the joint kingdom. Losing this meant the end of their centuries-old civilisation, and even Rhuzbeh had never had to face such a threat in his lifetime.

Axer addressed his troops: 'Soldiers of the joint kingdom! Today, we do not fight as Zandians or Hatasans. Today, we fight together, rubbing shoulders as brothers and ready to fall for each other. Today, we do not fight for fame and glory. We fight to defend our homes! We fight the foreign invaders who seek to raze our homes, enslave our women and children and mount our heads on pikes outside our very homes! Today, we fight for ourselves and to defend everything that we hold dear! The enemy forgets that we are a breed of warriors that is stronger than the mountains of Musra.' The joint army roared in approval, and Axer continued, 'Let the enemy strike! Line upon line of the bestial hordes shall break like water on rocks! Our counterattack will be swift, and we shall scatter them like hay in the winds! The remnants would be fed to the Zandian wolves for their daring to lift their gaze to our lands and women. We will cover ourselves in the glory that will make even Rhuzbeh the Fearless feel proud. Soldiers of the joint kingdom, will you follow me to glory?'

The joint army roared back in approval.

Dedi was watching the activity in the enemy camp. His main advantage was his unstoppable mobile battering ram of rhinos and buffaloes. He planned to crush the vanguard and scatter battle formations. The buffaloes were Dedi's favourite. A rampaging buffalo was so powerful that it could take on a lion, and the buffaloes were also a great source of milk and meat during lean times.

Dedi made the first move. He wanted to smash Axer's centre, so he sent his mobile hammer of the armoured rhinos and buffaloes ahead. Three hundred rhinos and buffaloes, along with their riders, charged. The ground below trembled and the earth shook.

Axer did not make a move. He stood his ground. The soldiers were sweating out of nervous tension. And when the thundering animals were almost upon them, Axer gave his signal and the troops split at the last minute. The rhinos and buffaloes passed by harmlessly. Since the animals were heavy, they were not manoeuvrable, and as the rhinos and buffaloes passed them by, the archers picked off their riders easily. Without their riders, the animals charged straight into the wood.

Axer ordered his chariot-mounted Hatasan cavalry to kill or drive away the buffaloes. The buffaloes had a tendency to be loyal to their masters and might've wheeled around and attacked from the rear even without their riders. The centre closed ranks again. The mobility and speed of Axer's army surprised Dedi. With the danger of rhinos and buffaloes neutralised, the joint army heaved a sigh of relief.

Axer made his move. He ordered his ibex cavalry on the left to charge. Predictably, Dedi ordered the heavy cavalry on his right to meet the charge head-on. The Musran heavy cavalry charged, and midway through, the ibexes turned tail and bolted. The Musran cavalry, sensing victory, charged after them. As they crossed Axer's lines, his centre turned around, and the archers attacked the riders. Suddenly the ibexes wheeled around and charged head-on. Consequently, the Musran cavalry was trapped between ibexes and the Zandian centre.

Dedi had anticipated this move. He knew the tactics of the Zandians and rushed his crack troops—the crocodile-helmeted warriors—to the centre, along with his cavalry. This forced the Zandian centre to abandon the flank and reassemble back at the centre. The centre was already stretched as the chariot mounted archers were mopping up the buffaloes and rhinos. The remainder of the Musran cavalry turned on the ibex mounted Hatasans and mowed them down.

As the Zandian centre was engaged fighting the elite Musran forces, Axer sent the Hatasan chariots to the aid of the ibex-mounted cavalry. They eventually beat back the Musrans, but it was too late for the ibex-mounted cavalry, which was completely decimated. The day was almost over, and both sides had suffered heavy losses.

The next day, Dedi sent his elephants to the Zandian right flank. He wanted to break through the flanks and surround the centre from behind. Axer knew it was impossible to hold the elephants. The great lumbering beasts charged, and the horses panicked and turned tail.

Dedi was turning out to be a master tactician. The tide was turning against Axer, and so he decided to play his ace card. He called on Butosh, the singer, who had allied with him upon realising that Hittash was indisposed.

Butosh sang and Ungaal appeared. The Musrans had never seen anything like it before. Ungaal made fearful hissing and roaring sounds. The elephants panicked and, out of fear, rampaged through their own army. Ungaal picked up the riders mounted on the elephants and smashed them to the ground.

It looked like all was lost for the Musrans as they watched Ungaal single-handedly decimate their numbers. Dedi scanned across the lines until he spotted Butosh, who was singing and directing Ungaal. Having learnt from his past experiences, Axer had placed elite soldiers and mages around Butosh to protect him.

Nevertheless, Dedi directed his snake to slide through the ring of warriors and the creature instantly killed Butosh.

Axer was livid. He charged head-on towards Dedi along with his vanguard, intent on slaying him. Dedi deliberately allowed him to do so. He knew that with the jann armour and gajmuk, Axer was immune to magic. No spell or earthly weapon could hurt him. Dedi had a different plan. He ordered his army to part like waves, little by little. He wanted Axer to believe that he was winning, and when he was close enough, he ordered his elite troops to seal the gap between Axer and his soldiers. The crocodile-helmeted warriors formed a wall and closed his retreat. Axer was cut off from his troops. Unaware of this, he charged at Dedi. As he drew closer, he noticed a mage from the Musran side brandishing the flute of Tummaru.

Dedi had planned it all well. In the last battle, the djinn shepherd who was killed by the jann Awa had dropped the flat flute of Tummaru on the battlefield. The Zandians presumed that the flute was damaged in the battle. A Zandian soldier, who saw no point in returning the flute as by doing so he would just be doing his duty and might not be rewarded, picked up the flute. He kept the flute with himself, waiting for the right person who might pay him a fortune for it. When Dedi invaded Zanda, he sold it to him for five hundred gold coins.

Dedi had anticipated Ungaal's participation in the battle and kept the flute as a cautionary measure.

When Ungaal finally made an appearance, Dedi killed Butosh and had his mage blow the flute of Tummaru ordering Ungaal to strike Axer.

As Axer looked up in shock, Ungaal swept in, picked him off the ground, flew up high and bit his face mid-air. His gajmuk dropped to the ground. The Ungaal brought Axer's dead body back to the shepherd. The shepherd, in turn, handed the dead Axer to Dedi, who stripped him of his armour and zer sword.

With the death of Axer, a great cry rent the air and the soldiers stopped fighting. The king of the joint kingdom was no more. His subjects, who defended his name and drank to his health in every inn, mourned his loss:

The cream of the Zandians
Who forgave even his vilest enemies
The scion of the mighty
Unaffected by a golden armour
The bearer of gajmuk
Never touched by treachery
The wielder of the zer sword
Swung only for honour
Two brothers sacrificed
Yet he forgave the murderous father
A hundred maidens sold in his name
Yet we mourn and beat our breasts
Lying still on the battlefield
Slain by a mighty mythical beast
Rent your clothes and tear your hair
For the beloved king is no more
Axer, Axer, noble Axer

The Zandians asked Dedi for a seven-day mourning period, after which they would decide to defend or hand over the joint kingdom. Dedi agreed. The funeral lasted for seven days and the whole of Zanda, Hatasa, and the other kingdoms in all four directions mourned Axer for he was a great king, noble and just.

After seven days of mourning, Dedi marched his army to the plains. The Musrans were here for the handover ceremony. They expected an unconditional surrender but were greeted by a shocking sight. The joint army in full battle formation led by Hittash awaited them. When Ungaal had lifted Axer up in the air, he had dropped the gajmuk. A Hatasan general had picked it up and handed it over to Hitti.

Hittash, in the form of the ibis, had entered Hitti's tent and placed his head on her lap, the way he had done since he was a boy. Hitti knew it was her son. She had heard how Dedi had bragged about turning her son into an ibis and paraded him around like a pet. Upon receiving the gajmuk from the soldier, she had used it to reverse the spell.

The mother and son kept his return secret, and on the last day of mourning, Hittash called on all the commanders, who rallied them behind him.

Dedi was not prepared for war, although he wore Axer's jann armour, making him invulnerable to attacks on his torso. Before anyone could react, Hittash ordered all his archers to attack the shepherd who had summoned Ungaal. The Musrans were not expecting an attack, so the shepherd was standing unprotected. A hundred arrows rained on the undefended shepherd, who died instantly. Hittash led a cavalry charge to the dead shepherd and crushed the wooden flute of Tummaru under the hooves of his horse, negating the threat of Ungaal forever.

Hittash turned back, regrouped and attacked the surprised Musrans. Dedi himself heroically led back the attack, his golden armour shining; he counterattacked with the elephants and his elite forces, reversing the damage. Although Hittash had to order his forces to retreat, the Musran losses were heavy. They had lost a significant chunk of cavalry and foot soldiers. The day ended with the Musrans licking their wounds. Despite these heavy losses though, Dedi was not worried. As long as he had the elephants, he was unbeatable.

The next day, when Dedi led his army to the front, he was shocked—the joint army was gone. The camp was empty. They had left behind the chariots and heavy machinery. There was chaos everywhere. Things had been flung around recklessly and not even packed. All the pots and pans were left scattered. The camp tents were still pegged on. Had the army just fled and ran? Or was it a tactical retreat? He was not sure. They spent a day consulting about their future course of action. Should they pursue the fleeing army, or should they head straight to Zanda and capture it? They decided to pursue the fleeing army and kill them while they were still weak. After seven days of pursuit, they came across a heavily wooded area.

The Musrans decided to march the elephants ahead as they would trample the vegetation making it easy for the foot soldiers to follow. As the elephants marched ahead, they saw a band of Zandian soldiers eating. The Musrans decided to take them by surprise, and led by the elephants, they charged at the camp. The Zandians appeared to have been caught unawares. They raised the alarm and tried to run. The Musran elephants charged after the hapless soldiers. Just when all seemed lost for the Zandians, the elephants started falling into the ditch that was covered in bamboo and leaves—it had been a trap, a very clever trap.

The ditch was wide, almost fifty feet. The first portion of the ditch was covered by wooden planks that could support the weight, followed by bamboo sticks, which collapsed under the weight of the elephants. When the bamboo sticks collapsed, the planks gave in as well. Anticipating an easy kill, the Musrans had charged the elephants into the camouflaged ditch without looking at the ground. The remaining elephants now ground to a halt. The band of Zandian soldiers were the bait, and the elephants had been sent after them thinking that they were easy meat. Half the elephants were in the ditch and the other half at the edge. Behind the elephants, the Musran soldiers and cavalry ground to a halt.

Suddenly, Zandian and Hatasan horsemen charged in from the right and left, cutting off the crocodile-helmeted soldiers and the cavalry from the elephants. In this gap, they poured incendiary liquid, set the place on fire and melted away to the right and left.

The woods were thick and caught fire easily. The elephants were caught between the fire and the ditch. As the fire raged, the elephants panicked and ran into the ditches. The Musran elephants had been neutralised.

The Musran army now split into two and chased the horsemen, only to run into a hail of arrows from well-concealed archers. The Musran cavalry on horseback was exposed and picked off easily by the archers. They dropped like flies on the forest floor. With the elephants gone and the numbers evened out, Dedi realised his mistake and marched his army to the flat plains and waited for Hittash. This style of warfare suited the Musrans. Dedi's crocodile-helmeted soldiers were still intact, and he fancied his chances good.

Hittash knew he had to take Dedi head-on. After the initial victories, his army was buoyed and both the armies' numbers were evened out. It would be an equal battle!

Dedi gave the signal and both armies charged at each other; it was a gruesome battle right from the start. Slowly, the tide of the battle began to turn—Dedi was winning. The elite Musran warriors were beating the Zandians. Finally, Hittash decided to charge at Dedi and kill him. As he stepped forward, his opponent said, 'Ah! My pet bird misses his master.' Dedi then cast a spell on Hittash but with no luck as the latter carried the gajmuk on him.

A shocked Dedi spurred his horse and fearlessly charged towards Hittash. Both warriors were well-matched but Dedi was strong and accomplished, and he wore the jann armour that protected him against Hittash's weapons. His zer sword was cutting into Hittash's manticore skin armour. It looked like Hittash was losing the battle. Dedi rode towards his opponent and, while passing by him, swung his zer sword into Hittash's sword, slicing it into two. Dedi then turned his horse and rode towards Hittash again, this time landing a mighty blow to his head with the hilt of his sword. Hittash reeled and fell down.

The charge carried Dedi forward. He turned back to finish Hittash, but to his dismay, Hittash had been snatched up by Hitti on a magic carpet and whisked away. Dedi was cheated from his kill and screamed out of fury. The carpet, bearing Hittash, flew away as Dedi watched helplessly. Suddenly the carpet turned, and Hittash stood up on the carpet. He had a bow in his hand. It was the same bow that belonged to the Descendant of Edal.

Hittash had been accused of killing the descendant and stealing his bow, but since the charges could not be proved, he had been let off. The Bow of Edal was made of simorgh bones, and the arrow had an ash-silver tip that could pierce through any armour. Hitti had been upset that her husband

Rhuzbeh had given away the jann armour to Axer. If ever Axer and Hittash clashed, her son would be killed, she had worried. Hitti had wanted the Bow of Edal for her son. She had had the Descendent of Edal, along with his bow, abducted. She had further offered him enormous gold and even the throne of the eastern lands. But the Descendant, being a proud man, had refused. He had snatched a guard's sword and attacked her, but Hitti's guards had quickly parried the blow, and in the ensuing tussle, the Descendant of Edal had been killed.

It had been an accident. She had not meant to kill him. But the situation had spiralled out of her hands quickly. She had secretly buried his body and hidden the bow. Her trusted soldiers had been sworn to secrecy on pain of death. When the time arrived, she dug up the bow and brought it to Hittash.

Meanwhile, the battle was at a decisive stage. Hittash, armed with the Bow of Edal, was bearing down on Dedi, who was on horseback and brandishing a long spear. Hittash had one chance. If he missed it, he would be dead. As they were bearing on each other, a Musran archer shot an arrow at Hitti's head, killing her instantly.

Hittash also lost balance and fell from the carpet. He narrowly missed being trampled by Dedi's horse. Little did he realise that Dedi was focused on the bow and managed to intercept the bow with his spear and yanked it away from Hittash's hands. The bow, along with the arrow, was flung away with violence. Hittash was left unarmed. He tried to make a run for it and managed to jump onto a horse already laden with a soldier. The heroic Hatasan soldier had risked his life to come to the rescue of his king. The horse galloped away, with Dedi and the Musrans in hot pursuit. But the horse bearing Hittash was slowed down by the twin burden. Dedi and the Musrans were catching up fast. Hittash made one final attempt to kill Dedi. He asked the rider to slow down the horse. When Dedi was within striking distance, he picked a spear from the Hatasan soldier, turned and, in a supreme display of athleticism, stood erect with one leg on the saddle, the other leg bent backwards, and feet latched on to the collar bone of the rider for grip.

Hittash knew that no armour could protect Dedi if he threw a spear at his face. Dedi was within touching distance of Hittash's horse. He was flabbergasted when he saw Hittash standing erect on the horse facing backwards, his spear aimed at Dedi's face. Both horses were galloping at a steady speed and were very close to each other. Hittash aimed his spear at Dedi's face and let fly his weapon, but unfortunately, the horse stumbled on a hole in the ground and lost its balance. The spear missed its mark, and the horse and the riders tumbled down. Hittash had the wind knocked out of his lungs because of the fall. Dedi jumped down from his horse, grabbed Hittash's hair and with the other hand, he swung the zer sword and sliced apart Hittash's head clean from the shoulders. The Musran soldiers cheered as Dedi turned and displayed the severed head of Hittash—Rhuzbeh's descendants were wiped out. There would be no son to carry the name of Rhuzbeh. The joint kingdom of Zanda and Hatasa belonged to Dedi and the Musrans.

Dedi, in a gesture of victory, raised both hands in the air. In his right hand, he held the severed head of Hittash, and in his left, he held the zer sword. At that moment, he saw a flying carpet approach. It grew bigger and bigger until he could clearly see Rhuzbeh standing on the carpet. Rhuzbeh held the Bow of Edal, and he let fly the arrow with the ash-silver tip. The arrow pierced the armour clean and passed to the other side. Dedi dropped dead. His soldiers panicked and ran.

Rhuzbeh jumped down from the carpet and chopped Dedi's head from his body. Dedi's glassy eyes, grey and black, stared back at Rhuzbeh. He threw Dedi's head down and picked up Hittash's head. He held it in his lap, cradling and rocking it back and forth. He wailed and moaned. He heaped mud and dust on his head and flailed around. So uncontrollable was his grief that the whole battlefield heard it. The carrion birds stopped feeding on dead soldiers and flew away.

With the death of Dedi, his soldiers surrendered. The cobra was snatched up in the eagle's talons. When he recovered, Rhuzbeh removed his pierced armour from Dedi's headless body and retrieved the zer sword and the ivory horn as well. He also picked up Dedi's crown with the sanaa on it. Dedi's body was handed to his soldiers, who sailed back to Musra with it.

Rhuzbeh held a seven-day mourning period for his family. The only surviving member was Hittash's wife, Zera, who was inconsolable with grief.

Rhuzbeh was back on the throne of Zanda. Kings from far-off visited Rhuzbeh to pay their respects to the king and to offer condolences. Among the visitors were Amirast, Ghanazaqi and Irash.

'So, the king of Zanda returns!' remarked Ghanazaqi.

'Alas! A little late. Had I returned earlier, my sons would have been alive. The crown that I wear is heavy. There is no fate worse than to see your grown children die before you. The House of Rhuzbeh is barren; no seeds sprout and no flowers blossom. I long to lie in the comfort of my wives' bosoms; my hands ache to ruffle the hair of my sons. Neither food nor wine comforts me.'

Ghanazaqi placed a comforting hand on Rhuzbeh's shoulder and tried to console him. 'Where have you been all these years?' asked Amirast gently, trying to distract Rhuzbeh.

'After I killed my son Tiran, I did not want to fight anymore,' said Rhuzbeh. 'I had a long conversation with Ghanazaqi and decided to let go,' he continued. 'I gave up everything that I wanted to control. Earlier, I was punch-drunk on power. I had thought I could steer people's fate like a reed boat on a river. I had raped and murdered. Now, I was so sick of myself that I decided to leave Zanda. If I stuck around, I was afraid that the evil would creep back inside me. I had a loyal soldier dress up in the manticore skin and presented in my stead. I wanted him to merely step out of the tent and wave at the soldiers and step back in. The mere sight would have galvanised the sagging morale of my troops. I was confident that Axer would win the war in a couple of days. After that, my absence would have made no difference. What I did not take into account was a direct attack behind the lines. Unfortunately the poor wretch had to step out and meet the charge and was killed by Metishin. Is Metishin alive?' Rhuzbeh asked.

'No,' replied Ghanazaqi, 'Metishin is dead. He was beheaded by Axer. Darya is dead as well. She was killed by Ungaal.' Ghanazaqi narrated the whole tale to Rhuzbeh.

Rhuzbeh put his head into his hands when he heard of his losses.

'Ghanazaqi, did you know that Metishin was planning to kill me?' asked Rhuzbeh.

Ghanazaqi looked away and said, 'I had an inkling but I was not sure.'

'But what about the sanaa? Had I been killed, who would have brought back the sanaa?' asked Rhuzbeh.

'I learnt from you. No matter how much you try and manipulate, if something is not destined to be, it would slip out from your hands. The tighter you grip the sand, the more it slips out through your fingers. If you are destined to return the sanaa, then you will,' replied Ghanazaqi.

'Where did you go away for seven years?' Amirast asked.

'Far away,' said Rhuzbeh with a glazed look in his eyes. 'I shall tell you all about it some other time.'

Rhuzbeh returned to his palace. His subjects rejoiced; their king had returned from the dead.

But Rhuzbeh knew that he had lost everything.

He had tried his best to shield his son Axer; he had killed for him, literally. Was it a mistake to leave Axer to his destiny? Should he not have left at all? He felt angry and disappointed with himself. He should have been by Axer's side, helping him, shielding him and slaying his enemies. Rhuzbeh broke down and started wailing. At the time of leaving, he had known in his heart of hearts that if he ever went away, he would lose his son and his loved ones. But then he had reasoned that one day, he himself would die; then what would happen to his loved ones? Holding on was unhealthy and had made Rhuzbeh do abominable things, he had felt. Besides, an oak couldn't flourish under a shade, he had concluded. He now let out a cry. He had had no choice, he had to let go.

What pained him the most was that he could not even see the dead bodies of his beloved ones. He could not hold Ceba, the love of his life. He never got a chance to say goodbye to her and his son Axer. The very thought of the latter was gut-wrenching. It was as if someone had punched him hard in the stomach.

He tried to recreate the situation for closure. He imagined it thus:

Axer was dead on the battlefield
Bit by the mighty beast, Ungaal
Rhuzbeh killed Ungaal and ordered it be skinned
Ungaal's fur dumped at Zanda for all to trample over

Ungaal's flesh fed to crows and hyenas
Rhuzbeh did not allow anyone to touch Axer's body
He did not burn or bury it
He held his son against his chest
He memorised every feature
He dressed his son in the golden armour
And took him to Zanda and Hatasa
And to the north, to Wastra, to Sedra and to Musra even
Every man, woman and child saw Axer, his beloved son
'The memory of my son shall not be erased'
Finally, he laid him to rest in a casket of cedar
He made a shrine encrusted with lapis lazuli for all to visit
'Dear Axer—your name will be remembered forever'

Rhuzbeh did build an ornate blue shrine and buried the remains of all his family members. And in a special corner, he placed the remains of Axer in a cedar casket and built an enclosure encrusted with lapis lazuli.

Rhuzbeh then proceeded to Alainis to meet the djinns.

'It is time to return what rightfully belongs to you,' he said and opened a pouch to produce the last of three legendary stones—the third sanaa. He handed over the sanaa to Amirast and said, 'The House of Rhuzbeh, in whose blood the gus ambergris flows, has upheld the covenant. May the rise of Afra-Zun strengthen the relationship between djinns and men.'

The last of the three sanaa was in djinn hands. Amirast and Ghanazaqi were overwhelmed; the greatest of djinn treasures was in their hands. They thanked Rhuzbeh profusely and bid him goodbye.

Amirast turned to Ghanazaqi and asked, 'Did you know that Rhuzbeh was alive?'

'Yes,' replied Ghanazaqi. 'I knew that Rhuzbeh was alive. I wanted to respect his wishes. If he wanted to go away, I needed to let him. We cannot alter destiny.'

'Well said! We cannot alter destiny, but we can give it a push in the right direction,' said Amirast. 'By the way, who was the djinn? The frog or the crane?' he asked.

'Neither,' replied Ghanazaqi. 'I waited until the right moment. The frog king appearing was indeed a stroke of fortune. I did not want any djinn to assume the form of crane because Dedi was a skilled sorcerer, and he would have seen through the transformation. I made a shiq possess a crane and had it eat the frog. I then made the crane fly to Musra and had it submit to be captured. The shiq left the crane's body as soon as it was captured. Meanwhile, as the crane started to fly to Musra, I made a jann take human form and inform Hittash, so he lost no time in setting out for Musra.'

Amirast embraced Ghanazaqi and said, 'Ghanazaqi, you are indeed the wisest and greatest of djinns! You have managed to get back the sanaa without bloodshed or interference in human affairs directly. Your name shall be etched in the annals of djinn history in golden letters!'

The entire court stood and bowed before Ghanazaqi.

It was time to raise the city of Afra-Zun from dust. Amirast had repaired the moat and buried the three sanaa in the three corners of the moat. They ceremoniously opened the gate of the moat, and water rushed in. The assembled multitudes of djinns gasped as they saw the moat being filled with water. They waited with bated breath the whole day and nothing happened. The djinns were crestfallen and left. The next day when the djinns visited the site again, they let out great shouts of joy—for the city of Afra-Zun had risen from the ruins!

The magnificent buildings, sprawling gardens and musical fountains were back, and so were the songbirds of Afra-Zun. The djinns streamed back into the great city, which was now free from the curse of Zoa and restored their glory. The djinns let out great cheers, and there was much revelry and celebration. Amirast settled all hues of djinns in their quarters. There was a grand ceremony in which Amirast took control of Afra-Zun. He had done what his predecessors couldn't. He would go down as one of the greatest jann kings to have ever ruled, perhaps surpassing even his own illustrious ancestor, King Ammuna.

Amirast called on Ghanazaqi and Irash and thanked them both. He magnanimously crowned Ghanazaqi as the King of Afra-Zun and awarded him the title of the Resurrector of Afra-Zun.

Ghanazaqi would be more acceptable in a multicultural society, and Amirast would always be partial to the janns. Regardless, his heart belonged to the hallowed halls of Alainis, his beloved city. Ghanazaqi gracefully accepted and in turn appointed Irash as the Hakif of Afra-Zun to rule on behalf of Ghanazaqi.

Peace descended on all djinn kingdoms. Ghanazaqi wanted to spend some time with Irash to guide him in administrative duties before he left for Tamiir. Irash said, 'Dadash, I cannot believe it. I, Irash, am the Hakif of the legendary city of Afra-Zun.'

'I can't believe it either,' said Ghanazaqi laughingly. 'So, what is the first order that you will pass?' he asked.

'My first order is to ban all hornhoney bees,' he said, and both of them rolled in laughter.

It was time for Ghanazaqi to leave for Tamiir. He left with a smile on his face, knowing well that Irash would administer Afra-Zun with capability, simplicity and honesty, ushering in another golden era of the djinns. And he was right.

Even today, Afra-Zun stands tall as a testimony of friendship and cooperation between humans and djinns.

Acknowledgements

I would like to acknowledge the writer Haruki Murakami, who appeared in my dream and asked me to write a book. I do, however, confess that I had not seen his photo or even read a single book of his until then. I did finally read his first book—two years after writing the one presently in your hand.

I extend sincere thanks to my friends, who stood by me and believed in my abilities, as well as my family, who take far too much pride in my humble achievements.

Om